Best Wishes —
Hope you enjoy
Darrell Egbert

The Ravensbruck Legacy

An Historic Novel By
Darrell Egbert

Other Novels by
Darrell Egbert

Zachary's Gold

The Indenture of Edward St Ives

The Secret of Recapture Creek

The Third Gambit

Publisher's Place
St. George, Utah

ISBN 0-9754460-4-5
v.1

Published by Publisher's Place
St. George, Utah
www.publishersplace.com

Cover designed by Wallace Brazzeal

Printing in the United States of America
10 9 8 7 6 5 4 3 2 1

FORWARD

This book is based on the recollections of several veterans of Third Army who served with Lieutenant General George Patton. Dates, places, and major incidents were taken from the history of Third Army; from the written memoirs of participating American generals; from the writings of reputable German historians, including Albert Speer and Clemens M. Hutter; and from personal interviews with German civilians soon after the War ended. Additional content is based on conversations with a friend, Jean Burgoyne, a former member of a French Maqui cell that operated in Paris during the German occupation, and her husband, who served with the Free French under Charles deGaull.

Special thanks is given to long-time friend, former S/Sgt Robert Forsgren, AUS, of Bountiful, Utah, who served with Patton's Field Headquarters from Normandy to Bad Tolz, for his insight and advice.

The Ravensbruck Legacy

CHAPTER 1

The porter passed three men in the passageway of the sleeper car. They appeared to be on their way to the diner for an early cup of coffee before arriving in Frankfurt. As the porter disappeared through the vestibule, two of them stopped and double-checked a number written on a piece of paper. They turned around and walked back three doors. Then without hesitating, they burst into the compartment in front of them. The third stood gazing out the darkened window at the mirrored violence erupting like a ghostly shadow behind him.

The male occupant was unceremoniously jerked from his berth and mercilessly clubbed into unconsciousness by one of the two intruders. Neither man spoke, while a woman in the lower bunk looked on in horror and disbelief.

He was revived and forced to sit on the floor at the foot of the woman's bed. When he was fully cognizant of what was going on, the taller of the two men said: "We've been waiting a long time for this. I'll just bet you thought you were going to get away with it, right? I figure we have about thirty minutes before the *bahnhoff*. And I swear they're going to be the longest thirty minutes of your life if you don't tell us where it is."

Later, the woman would repeat the conversation to the *politzi*, whose report was liberally sprinkled with four letter words in both English and German.

"I don't know what you're talking about," he said.

"Of course not. We did not think you would." With that he hit him across the face again with his heavy Luger.

"We are going to pistol whip you each time we ask a question and we are not satisfied with your answer. Then, we are going to put a knife in your ribs and throw you off this train. Now, where is *Ravensbruck*? If you do not tell us right now, we will carry out our threat, and you know we will. Then after we are through with you, we are going to rape your pal here and throw her off behind you. If you want to live, you will tell us what we want to know, and then you had better tell us where we can find old Red."

Hours before, the Streamliner bound for Frankfurt had pulled out of the *Banhoff* at Salzburg, Austria. On board were Carl and Cynthia Jorgensen, booked into a first-class *wagon lits* for the overnight run. They had eaten an early dinner and were planning to retire after the train cleared the station. They were looking forward to an uninterrupted trip and to a quiet stay in Frankfurt, after a rather hectic sight-seeing trip in and around Hitler's *Obersalzberg*. Carl was looking forward to a side excursion, north across the Rhine to the site of one of his old campaigns, while Cynthia planned to spend time at one of the new shopping malls in Frankfurt. Ten days before, they had caught a local at Munich, stopping at several small towns in route to Bavaria and Austria. In Bavaria, they stayed several days at the hotel on the shore of the *Eibsee*, in the shadow of the picturesque *Zugspitz*. Carl rented a Volkswagen and embarked on two overnight drives to explore several towns he had passed through during the War. He told Cynthia he had made friends with several people in the area, and he was anxious to return for a visit. She stayed behind, hiking, and visiting the nearby town of Garmisch.

"This is Cynthia Jorgensen speaking." I had called her back at this number in Germany after receiving notification from my service that somebody wanted to talk to me; it was an emergency. "Captain, we've never met. I'm the wife of Sergeant Carl Jorgenson."

"How did you get my number?" I asked her.

"Carl gave it to me. He told me to call if something ever happened to him. Thanks to you, it has happened. What's left of him is lying in a morgue in Frankfurt."

"What are the two of you doing there?"

"You know damn good and well what we're doing here. You sent him looking for it again, didn't you? Those childish games the two of you have been playing, along with your other army buddy, have gotten him killed. And by the way, they made me give them your number or they would have killed me, too. They're coming for you. And for your information, Carl told me all about it. He told me the whole story. The whole bunch of you are crazy."

"Tell me one thing," I coaxed, "did any of them speak with a German accent. I need to know, did they…?"

"They know who you are," she interrupted. "I told them everything I know about you. I suggest you change your number, and then get out of town. They're after you, and I'm glad. It serves you right. I hope they get you."

I could hear her sobbing hysterically on the other end of the line. I hoped she was angry enough to stop crying and tell me more about what had happened. But it became worse, until finally she could no longer talk at all and hung up, cursing me and the army.

As hard as I tried, I couldn't get her to say anything more. I wanted to know about the accent thing, but she wouldn't say another word.

Her home phone was disconnected when I called two weeks later, and I was never able to contact her again.

In Germany, I talked to the investigating police. It was really a waste of time. They had nothing more to say than what was in their comprehensive report, from which I was able to take notes. However, the only thing of interest to me was her description of his attackers. She told them one was older than the other two, and that only one of them spoke to Carl. She told them he could have had a German accent, a small one maybe, but discernable. More than that she couldn't remember. Things happened too fast, she said.

It came to me that maybe I ought to write my own version of why Carl lost his life, and why I was sitting in a German police station staring at a rather dirty green wall, scared to death. Who I intend to give it to, though, is another matter. Suffice to say, if you're reading this, things might have turned out well for me, and maybe I did live happily ever after. But it's my story, which includes some strange people from some strange places; some of it is quite unbelievable, because history has been slow to record the facts.

CHAPTER 2

I had forgotten how far it is across West Texas. It's a bummer by car and much worse by bus. Greyhound has cut back on their schedules. They don't run at near capacity anymore, the way they did during the War. Now, many of their former passengers are flying because it has become more convenient. And let's face it, there's a different class of people riding buses nowadays. They're more interested in the price of their tickets than they are in convenience. Unlike most of them, I could have flown. Money is no object with me. Why then do I insist on torturing myself with endless hours of boredom, staring out a window at a never-changing landscape? Good question. But, if I answered you truthfully, I'm not too sure my explanation would make much sense. Let's just say I have a fear of air-ports–not airplanes, particularly–just airports.

"Crossroads up ahead, buddy," the driver turned his head slightly and called out. "San Angelo is straight ahead, about fifteen minutes." I had taken the empty seat next to the door. I wanted to be able to hear him when we reached my destination.

"Let me ask again, are you sure you want to get off here? Unless you have somebody meeting you, you're going to have a long walk. The closest farm is six miles down this county road up ahead, and it's another ten back to town. You know your business, but it's getting dark, and it's going to be awfully lonesome out there. And if you don't mind my repeating myself, you're no cowboy and that ground is going to be mighty hard sleeping. Why don't you ride on in and come back in the morning?"

We had discussed this when I got on at San Antonio. He knew what time we were going to arrive here. And he was curious as to what I could possibly be doing at such a remote crossroads this time of night. Now, he was reluctant to let me off; he felt responsible for me.

To tell you the truth, I don't know exactly what I am doing here. I'm playing it by ear, I guess. In fact, the last five years of my life have been played out pretty much this way. I mean, I haven't always been too sure what I was doing. All I know with any degree of certainty is that somebody is trying to kill me, and I have no idea who it is. I know why, all right, of course I do; I just don't know who. I've spent a lot of time these past few years trying to solve this riddle and trying to stay alive. It might explain some of my peculiar behavior–such as why I don't enjoy hanging around airports.

The first two miles was a bitch-kitty. I even fell down once on the edge of the graveled road. But after the moon came up, walking became a lot easier. The road was straight. Now, I could see the wooden fence posts like a kind of tunnel stretching for yards ahead of me and vanishing in the dark.

The long walk was giving me time to think. But then really that's all I have been doing for the past five years; ever since I left the army, this thing has been on my mind. I can't seem to get it and the army out of my head for very long at a time. It just keeps creeping back in and for good reason. As I said, somebody is looking for me, and they want me awfully bad. Now, the long walk is reminding me again of time spent in the infantry, of forced marches, bivouacs, and hard ground waiting when we pitched shelter-half's.

Strange how little things set your mind off. Some are pleasant; some are frightening; and some are just downright distasteful. You take the time I worked for a guy who was in the fur business. He had me digging ditches to bury the wire for his fox pens. They had to be buried deep and on a slant, or the fox would dig under them and escape.

Fox are something like skunks when they want to be, and the hot sun and their offensive scent made me ill. There was this popular song at the time. It just happened to be playing on a portable radio one afternoon, when the sun and the smell ganged up on me and I got sick to my stomach. Now, when I hear this particular song something clicks inside my head. I think I can smell the fox, and I want to throw up all over again. Oh, and another thing, I worked the summer before I went in the army as a roughneck on an oil rig near Big Spring, Texas. The hard work and the smell of the crude reminded me of the fox. I heard tell that's the way combat is with some people. Certain sounds and smells remind them of battle experiences, and it makes them sick in the same way.

I used to hate tramping at night through unfamiliar country. The endless moving forward hour after endless hour was something I came to detest as much as I did the fox. I stopped short of getting sick, though. But I should tell you: it's not something I ever want to do again.

It took me less than three hours to reach the farmhouse the driver was talking about. Not bad for an old-out-of shape soldier. But then I wasn't carrying a rifle with a full field pack and ammunition either.

It was late when I walked the last hundred yards or so up a rock-lined gravel drive to the house. I think I can see cotton or Milo growing on both sides; at least I think it is, because that's what I've been looking at all afternoon. There are no lights showing, and I hoped they had no big dog lying about the porch waiting to earn his keep.

I can see the house is unpretentious. That's a euphemism for a large run-down shack. In the part of the South where I'm from, good people who are just struggling to get along usually inhabit these places. We call them *croppers* if we're not feeling overly generous and our prejudices are showing, which is a good deal of the time. They usually sit back off the roads, unpainted, weathered, showing their age. I'm unable to see, but I'll bet the roof has an overlay of rusting metal sheeting protecting the tarpaper underneath; they usually do. The front steps leading to this particular porch have also seen better days. They're worn like the rest of the house, with cracks and loose boards waiting to trip up anybody foolish enough to give them a try in the dark. There is also a screen door serving no useful purpose. If it's supposed to keep out flies, it's doing a poor job. I can see by the moonlight that it's torn loose from the molding at the lower right-hand corner, leaving a hole about a foot in diameter.

No sooner did my foot touch the first step than the creaking woke a small dog. That might account for the hole in the screen not being repaired; it probably serves as his private exit to the outside. His sudden loud yapping must have scared the daylights out of those inside. But there wasn't anything I could do about it now.

Showing up at this time of night unannounced can be a dangerous proposition anyplace in the country. But in West Texas, it might be doubly so. I'll make you an even money bet there's not one of these isolated farmhouses that doesn't harbor at least one rifle or shot gun. As it turned out, this farm was to be no exception. It was even more dangerous than most, because the rifle in this house was being wielded by a woman.

The dog had abruptly awakened her. And she had managed to negotiate the stairs and to open the door before I had a chance to check the place out, feel my way up the steps to the porch, and knock.

She presented in front of a kerosene lantern, which she had placed on an end table. She was not dressed in a negligee, exactly; it was more like a thin nightshirt made of some kind of thin white cotton muslin. I wouldn't have been surprised had it been made of sewn-together flour sacks.

She never spoke, as she stood there silhouetted in the lantern's glow. I wondered if she realized she had nothing on under her nightgown. But I don't suppose she cared all that much. She had other more important things on her mind–namely me.

She was waiting for me to say something. I hesitated, although I had memorized my arrival speech back a couple of miles. I was tongue-tied looking at her. She reminded me of a character in a children's show, the kind of *light-movie* produced in your neighborhood when you were a kid. You know what I mean. We used to take silhouettes of people cut from magazines and pin them to a sheet. Somebody would stand behind the sheet with a flashlight in the dark and make the silhouettes appear to come to life, while others of the cast supplied the voices.

She appeared to me to be one of those beautiful silhouette models cut from a magazine. And with the backlighting in my favor, I could tell she had a near perfect figure.

The thought run through my mind, as I stood gazing at her: *what a* lucky *guy my friend Eric is. Who cares what kind of dump you live in if you have a wife who looks this good?*

She was not the least bit frightened of me. I guess it was because of the lever-action saddle-rifle cradled in the crook of her arm. She stood there for the longest time, waiting for me to say something. But in reality, it was only a few seconds. Finally, she broke the silence by saying simply: "Well?"

When I had gathered my wits about me, I stammered: "Is this the Schneider residence?" I didn't know what else to say.

She looked at me with a smile in the dim light and said: "Residence? Where you from, mister? Yeah, I'm Lucille Schneider."

"Can I speak to Eric please? I'm an old friend of his."

She took two steps back and un-cradled the Winchester, pointing it at the floor, the smile gone now, completely erased from her face. "Show me some identification. What's your name, and how do you know my husband?"

"I was his platoon leader in Europe. My name is Michael Adair. Captain Michael Adair. Maybe he has referred to me as *Red Adair* in his letters? It's my nick-name." I was talking now as fast as I could, trying to explain who I was, as I saw the tip of the rifle barrel rise to about the forty-five degree position. I hurriedly bent over, pushing my wallet through the hole in the screen. "Take a look at my AGO card with my picture. It's cancelled, because I'm no longer in the army…the picture was taken some years ago." I stammered some more, my eyes focused on the gun barrel.

"What do you want, Captain?"

"I would like to speak with Eric." No sooner had I said it than I realized it was a dumb thing to say. Obviously, if he were here, he would be the one holding the rifle. She would still be in bed or at least in a bathrobe and not confronting me with a gun and an expression on her face labeling me a threat to her home and honor.

"No, I've never heard your name, Captain. But then we never corresponded much during the War. I expect if you were such good friends, you would have known that. Didn't he tell you we were planning on a divorce? He wrote me a

Dear John, just before the War ended, to tell me he wasn't coming home.

"Don't look so shocked," she went on, "you must have known, and you must have been there when he was shot." With that she opened the door, and without saying another word, she invited me in.

I wasted no time pulling out an antique looking chair from under a round oak table and sitting down. I was starting to feel faint. She sat down across from me, carefully laying the rifle down on the table, barrel pointing toward the wall.

"I never heard anything about a divorce," I said. "But then they broke up my unit a few weeks after the War ended, and I never saw him again." In spite of the late hour, I had a dozen questions I wanted to ask her. I was eager to find out what had happened to him. The fact he had been killed after he left me came as a complete surprise. And like she just said, I must have looked shocked.

"Look," she said, "I don't want to appear cold. But he dumped me. Why I don't know. Now, I don't care; it was a long time ago. But I suspect you came a long way for nothing. We can talk in the morning and if you want me to, I'll listen. But it's late; I have to get up early for work. Is the sofa okay?"

She crossed over the room to a bureau, opened a drawer, and handed me a blanket and pillow, and a clean white pillowcase. The thought occurred to me that the pillowcase might be hand-made from the same shear material as her nightgown. She made it a point to take her rifle, leaving the lantern burning on the table as she turned and climbed the stairs.

You might think my near state of shock has something to do with Eric's death. I guess it does in a way, but not like you think. I'm going to miss him, that's for sure. But the Dear John thing is what bothers me the most, and the precise time he chose to write it. It's a clear indicator he had other things on his mind with no intentions of coming home, and that's what has me upset. That's the thing that tells me bundles about what I didn't want to hear. It makes me more apprehensive, and even more scared than I've been in a long time. That's the thing that puts me in fear of my life, almost as much as does the Jorgenson murder of a few weeks back. And then there's this incident that happened to me on a fishing trip to Southern Louisiana soon after I came home. Then I left school scared to death, and I haven't stayed in one place for very long since. But that was a long time ago, and to tell you the truth I had almost forgotten about it. Forgotten about it, that is, until tonight. Now it has all come flooding back like a very bad dream.

I couldn't get to sleep. In spite of the unaccustomed exercise, I was unable to relax. I was in trouble. I stared at the blackness of the strange room and contemplated my tormentors for the millionth time since *it* happened. I want to throw in the towel, admit defeat, and plead for some kind of mercy. I would too if I could. But where and how to do it is beyond me.

For the longest time, I've been deluding myself with another thought that keeps returning, a kind of rationalization I've been using to keep from coming completely unhinged. I think I might be suffering from an overly active mind, one that has been in high gear for a lot of years. I've been working overtime, convincing myself I've been worrying unnecessarily. I've forced myself to believe they might have given up and left me alone. What success I've had in this endeavor is gone now. Now, the whole nightmare has come rolling back over me, just as it used to do at three every morning. I realize, once again, it's as real as it ever was. And now this overly-active mind theory, this defense mechanism to protect me from losing my sanity, has all gone out the window. Suffice to say, this Dear John, and the news of Eric's death coming on the heels of the Jorgensen disaster a few weeks ago, has me really shook-up. And that's why I know now I'll never be able to let my guard down and why I can't get to sleep.

We were driving into town the next morning. She was running late and never had the time to even fix a cup of coffee. She had invited me back the next night, with a promise to talk to me and to answer any of my questions. However, I was anxious about one thing in particular, and I didn't care to wait all day to find out. Before we left, I asked her if she had received any of my letters or letters from any of Eric's friends from the army. She said she had, but confessed she was so angry at the time and never bothered to open any of them. I asked her if I could read them now. She didn't want to take the time, but she went upstairs and came back in a few minutes with a dozen or so tied with a string, along with Eric's duffle bag. She couldn't imagine what I wanted with them; but I was free to keep them and the bag if I wanted. I put the letters in my jacket pocket. With the duffle in the back seat, we climbed into her automobile and headed down the road.

"Let me off, will you, before we get too far into town?"

"What in the world for?"

"Look, Lucille…"

"Call me Lucy, please."

"Can you take a long lunch?"

"I suppose so, why?

"I can't tell you right now but I have my reasons.

"Where do you want me to meet you?" I asked, with a sense of urgency in my voice. "It should be someplace out of the way, someplace where we won't be recognized."

I knew she had misunderstood by the way she quickly glanced over at me with a hurt expression on her face. "Are you ashamed to be seen with me?"

"No, it's nothing like that." I said. "Quite the contrary, I think you're one of the more desirable women I've ever met. I do want to be seen with you and I want to come back this evening; but there are certain things going on in my life I can't tell you about–at least not now."

"Why are you being so mysterious. First, you show up in the middle of the night, acting like you're paying a social call on a man who has been dead for five years. Then, you ask about some old letters as though they were the most important things in your life. And now you're reluctant to be seen with me. Besides all of this, you're acting kind of strange, to say the least." This last statement was made with a smile on her face. In fact it was the second thing I had noticed about her–she smiled easily.

She let me off, and I walked a couple of blocks into what appeared to be the downtown area. She had volunteered to later drop the heavy duffle bag off for me at the bus station. I accepted.

I located a corner telephone booth and was surprised to see the Yellow Pages were intact. I suppose it is one of the advantages of having an RFD address, people seem to be more considerate of each other. And another thing: people don't usually lock their doors at night. What's the use? Why do you need a lock when you have the best of security systems–a barking dog and a repeating rifle?

I found what I was looking for, the name and address of the local undertaking parlor. There was only one. It struck me they didn't have much competition, and it also occurred to me there was not much competition in the taxi business either. In fact, the one on the opposite corner looked as though it might be the only one in town.

I got in and gave the driver the street and number. He looked at me kind of funny; as it turned out the address was within walking distance. I didn't know this, nor would I have cared very much if I had. The last thing I wanted was to be noticed. I didn't want to look conspicuous. I didn't want to be remembered as a stranger wandering around asking for directions to a mortuary.

I gave the cabbie a twenty and asked him to forget he had seen me. After he pulled away, I realized I might have made a mistake. What if somebody else had given him a few hundred to remember any strangers passing out large tips to remain incognito? But on second thought, I figured I had better get a better grip or I was going to soon end up on a couch diagnosed with extreme paranoia.

I walked up a long cement walkway that divided a huge expanse of lawn. Down here all lawns seem to be extra large. I guess it's because they're planted with Bermuda grass that doesn't require too much tending and very little water to survive.

At the end of the walkway was a long semi-circular driveway with a building-matching Austin stone *porte-cochere*. I suppose it was intended to lend a little more dignity to the proceedings, rather than to protect anybody from the elements. Then again, if you alight from an expensive Cadillac limousine, you might ought do it under a *porte-cochere* regardless of the condition you're in.

Through a double-door was a large reception room with an over-done, in-vogue high-low nap. The high was thick enough to resemble an off-fairway rough that might have housed a family of ground squirrels. The low was as low as a manicured green, having some kind of repeating floral pattern on which you could play hopscotch for a quarter mile–if you hadn't brought your putter. When I looked up from trying to figure the flowers, I could see a number of clearly marked offices. I chose one marked *Director*.

I halfway expected to see a woman sitting at a desk with a typewriter. I knew she was going to ask me some questions I intended to ignore. I was hoping I could keep my explanations for why I was there to a minimum. I wanted to see the headman, the guy who did the *work*. I was reluctant to talk at length to any insulation between him and me.

I was not disappointed. I mean, she was there as I expected. And I found myself evading the questions she was asking, but having a hard time concentrating on what I was saying. She was good looking. She was outfitted in a white starched shirt-thing with a paisley scarf around her neck, and I guess a fitted skirt that I couldn't see for the desk. Her long thick hair was done up in a bun with some kind of plastic thingy holding it all together. She looked nothing like a school *marm*, but I got the impression she was trying to look as though she was and was having a hard time doing it. She was one of those women who no matter what they do they can't hide who they are–she was one beautiful, very sexy woman. I couldn't understand what she was doing working in a place like this. Nothing seemed to fit. But I hadn't the time to dwell on it further.

After some preliminary sparring, I was forced to tell her that my business was more or less a personal matter between me and the individual who did *it*.

My request was out of the ordinary, and I was met with some resistance. In any other line of work, she might have given me more of a hard time than she did. But raised voices were never heard of in here, and I was thankful for that.

It took me another ten minutes or so before I finally hooked up with the guy I was looking for.

I wasted no time in getting to the point. I was uncomfortable being this close to where it all took place. Yes, I'm deathly afraid of dying, no pun intended. I've seen plenty who did die. And I've seen plenty who were buried. But I've only seen a couple accompanied by a funeral director, and all the rest of the civilized trappings. Those others I saw were simply lowered into the ground by their buddies, who then stood around for a few minutes looking kind of goofy, not knowing what to say. They planted his rifle in the ground, bayonet first, with his helmet hanging from the stock. Not very formal, but it did do away with the ceremony so dear to the hearts of civilians. Later on, he would be *dug up* by strangers and reburied by relatives. But I've never been a party to any of that macabre ritual.

"My name is Alfred Worthington. I believe I'm the person you're looking for." He was tall, heavy-set; he looked nothing like your stereotypical mortician. I mean, he looked nothing like I thought a mortician should look. He had on a business suit with fashionable wide lapels that gave way to a belted back and button-down scalloped pockets, the only indicators it might have been tailor-made in Dallas rather than in New York.

"I hope so, Mr. Worthington. I'm here on a very sensitive matter, which must be kept in the strictest confidence. I prefer that only the two of us be privy to our conversation." He looked at me for a second before nodding his head in the affirmative.

"Allow me to introduce myself. My name is Abbott. Major James Abbott."

I told him a big lie. I didn't want to use my real name, so I gave him the first one entering my head. The name Abbott was the first on an old cadet roll-call roster, followed by Abernathy. I guess I had heard it so often it was imprinted on my brain, and it was waiting back there for just such an occasion to pop out. So, I became Abbott on the spot, promoting myself in the bargain. Before I sat down in the chair offered me, across from his desk, I flashed my army identification card, making sure my thumb covered my name and the word *Inactive* perforated across one corner.

"I'm with *Graves Registration.* I'm here from the Pentagon on a matter, as I said, having a certain degree of sensitivity." He appeared to accept me as one of the *broth-*

erhood. Not a card-carrying member, maybe, but a first cousin, someone working in the *business*.

"How can I help you, Major," he said.

"May I ask how long you've worked here?" I tried to ask in a way that wouldn't offend him.

"I'm the owner, and we have been providing a service to the community for twenty years." I took that to mean he had been doing his thing for at least five, the requisite number.

"Would you mind checking your records and telling me if you officiated in the service of an army technical sergeant by the name of Eric Schneider."

"It's not necessary," was his quick reply. "I've known his wife and brother for years. He was a hero brought home right after the War. Most of the town turned out for his funeral.

"What do you want to know and why?" He asked, without hesitating, but with a quizzical expression on his face.

"There's some confusion as to exactly how he died," I said. "The *Awards* people have brought it to our attention that our records might be in error. There's no question he was entitled to the *Purple Heart,* of course, but they're not sure about the *Bronze Star*. This citation for gallantry in action was apparently overlooked at the time of his demise.

"A recent review indicates a mistake might have been made. I'm here to investigate, and then to make my recommendations to the board, who will approve of any final posthumous decoration. I need to know how he died, and given the circumstances, if there was anything out of the ordinary about his body."

Worthington looked at me with the oddest expression on his face. He made me feel more ill at ease than his secretary had when I came in. Then when he spoke, I began to feel as I did last night when Lucy told me Eric had never intended to come home.

"I don't understand the army's position here, Major. Your records must really be in disarray. For starters: he didn't die in action–he was murdered."

He started to tell me in clinical detail why that was. But I only halfway heard him.... He continued: "He never had any gunshot or shrapnel wounds. He had been bayoneted twice. Death was almost instantaneous. But the big thing is, and I never included this in my payment statement, because I thought the army knew: he had been brutally tortured by a determined enemy. I had known him, but now he was unrecognizable. It was almost as though somebody had been trying to extract information of some sort from him. I took pictures for my record of services performed. I can get them for you if you like."

I heard myself reply something to the effect that it wouldn't be necessary. I had heard more than I wanted to hear. And it had confirmed my worst suspicions. I almost told him he was correct that somebody had wanted information, all right. And if I was right in my suspicions, his injuries were not suffered *in the line of duty.*

"I want your promise," the undertaker said, "I want you to promise me–if it's not against your regulations–I want you to promise me that this information will not go into your report. Lucille and her brother are friends of mine. I see no good reason to dredge this up. I've kept it secret all these years, and I hope you will do the same. Nothing is to be gained by changing the record if the circumstances of his death are not already in there–and apparently they're not. Eric Schneider died in action a hero, as far as I'm concerned."

"I agree completely," I said. "My report will simply recommend that the official record not be changed. I'll say my investigation indicates the criteria for the *gallantry above the call of duty* has not been met in his case. That should close it out." This last part of the charade was quite convincing, I thought. But apparently it wasn't; something had alerted him; something had jogged his memory. Something was wrong; I could see it written on his face.

I stood up, wanting to leave. But then I sat back down again, abruptly, when he said: "There's something very fishy about your visit, Major, or whatever your rank is or was and you know it. There was a guy in here about two years ago. He offered me a thousand dollars to report back to him if anybody ever came in asking the same questions you have just asked me. Rest assured I have no intentions of getting mixed up in whatever it is that's going on here. Your secret is safe with me. But please–do not contact me ever again!"

I never said another word to him. I didn't need to. I stood up, and he never offered me his hand. I never even said goodbye or thanked him. I simply walked out as fast as I could, past his secretary in the outer office, who continued to give me the fish eye. I did check to see if she was wearing a fitted skirt and whether she had on heels. She did. And I was more than ever convinced she was in the wrong racket. She was. But it would take a long time before I found out why.

I walked over to the same taxi corner. My friend of an hour ago was still there. I gave him the name of the place Lucy told me about earlier, the place she recommended for lunch.

It turned out to be a kind of roadhouse in the country, about five miles on the opposite side of town. I gave him another twenty, and then asked him for some information. I wanted to know if he knew of any new residents who had moved in during the last four or five years. He said he did, and I quickly wrote down the family names of six people in my pocket notebook and what they were doing for a living.

"What's your name" I asked him.

"Frank Fogarty," he replied, looking up at me through his rear view mirror.

"Frank, how would you like to earn the biggest tip of your career?"

"Career?" he said smiling. "Is it legal? Never mind, I don't care. I don't want to know. Just tell me what you want me to do."

I peeled off a hundred-dollar bill from my roll and handed it to him over his shoulder.

"All right," I said, "you work for me for the rest of the day, okay?"

"Okay," he said, with emphasis and a broader smile.

"I want you to take this list of names you just gave me and check them out. This is the county seat, isn't it? Go over to the courthouse and find out as much as you can about these people. I specifically want to know who's carrying the mortgages on their homes or businesses if they have any. I want to know where they came from if you can find out. What I really want to know is if any of them are immigrants or do they have relatives in Europe, stuff like that. And Frank…?"

"Yes?"

"Keep it quiet. Don't make a big thing of it. And above all, keep it to yourself. Don't worry if you don't find much of anything. At any rate, come back here promptly at three and pick me up." He nodded his head as he pulled into the gravel parking lot and let me out.

I went inside the joint, past a window lit with neon *Pearl, Falstaff,* and *Lone Star* signs and took a seat. I wondered what would happen to the barkeep's psyche if anybody ever ordered a *Heineken*.

There were two hangers-on, shooting a game near the other end of the bar. The bartender handed me a Coke and charged me lunch prices, after I told him I would be around awhile and that I was expecting a lady to join me.

I took the bottle over to a booth, away from the clacking of the pool balls, and sat down. I opened the first of the letters and began reading. I read them all through once, and then again before I decided there was nothing new in any of them. I bundled them back up, intending to give them back to Lucy. I had no reason to keep them.

According to our agreement, there was to be a fake return address on the envelopes for the benefit of any mailman who might be on the take. The three of us agreed years ago to never use the telephone unless there was a dire emergency. And since I was moving around a lot, we used an answering service, which I checked periodically. Eric never had a phone, and I purposely never knew Carl's number. We were to keep in touch by mail through Eric, since he had the most permanent address, and his farm was the least likely to be bulldozed away in some urban renewal scheme. However, Eric was not supposed to know either of our addresses. He was to correspond with each of us through a professional mail forwarding business. That's why Lucy had this bundle of letters. And that's why I came to visit Eric, to see why our communication system had broken down.

Lucy came in an hour later, unseen by the bartender. The temporary lunch waitress took our order. Neither of us wanted to bother with a menu; after all, hamburgers with fries are just that hamburgers with fries. Some places like this do a good lunch business in hamburgers, though, because they're somewhat better, something like bowling alleys in this respect.

"Do you know the waitress?" I asked her.

"No, nor the bartender, either. You said you wanted a place where I was unknown. This is it, but I can't vouch for the food."

"Good," I said.

"Look, Lucy, I like you very much. However, I can't

stay at your place tonight."

I thought as much," she said, with a frown instead of the usual smile. "And you're not coming back again, are you. It's just as well I found out about you now as later. You're not married, and you never have been, have you? You have no roots, and you never will. You're a lot like your buddy Eric in this respect."

"It's not that at all–you misunderstand, believe me.

"Lucy, I have to tell you something. I'm going to take off in a couple of hours, and you believe you're never going to see me again. You think I'm a bum on some trip down memory lane to see his old War buddy. Not so. You and I are closer than you ever imagined. I'm not going to walk out the door and out of your life forever. You and I are joined together closer than we would be with any marriage contract. I couldn't leave you, even if I wanted to."

She was really confused now, and I couldn't blame her. But I was not wanting to explain further. I thought I had said too much already. If she really knew the score, it might put her life in unnecessary danger without accomplishing a thing. I wanted to change the subject before I got in any deeper and couldn't get out. I had enough problems as it was; I didn't need any more.

"Do you mind if I ask you why you never re-married?"

"What does that have to do with anything?" she replied, with a look of frustration bordering on exasperation. She wanted information, and she was getting tired of playing games. She was starting to suspect I was involved in something serious, and she wanted to know what it was. If I wasn't going to take her into my confidence completely, then she wanted me to leave.

"A beautiful woman like you, living out in the boondocks alone doesn't make any sense. You think I'm mysterious. You're more complicated than I am. What's going on? Do you want to tell me?"

"Nothing very out of the ordinary, I'm afraid," was her answer.

"Look around you. Have you seen any good husband material? You haven't been around long, but take it from me there isn't any. Those with real ambition have taken off; those with some substance are married; the rest want my land. They don't want to work it; they want to sell it."

"Why don't you sell it then, and move to one of the larger cities? You could find a serious partner in a minute if you wanted to. This life you lead must be as lonely as mine."

"I could, and believe me I've thought about it."

"What's stopping you then?" I said, with kind of an edge to my voice. This line of questioning was not just to pass the time. I wanted to know how attached to the land she really was. To tell you the truth, her farm, and her home, such as they are, will not fit into my long-range plans. And as I said, she and I are joined at the hip.

"Maybe I'll sell it someday. But right now it's next to worthless for farming. I have a sharecropper who works it, but my share hardly pays the taxes. We farm cotton and some Milo, but the price is way down on both. The textile industry is starting to move out of the country. In a few more years if things continue the way they are, and if the government doesn't step in and do something, there won't be any textile industry left. And no more textiles means no more cotton market. The only thing making the land out here of any value at all is oil."

"Do you have oil on your land?" I asked, surprised. This turn of events was going to throw my rather shaky plans into a cocked hat, quickly. I'm calling them my plans, but actually I'm playing it by ear again, making them up as I go along.

"No," she said, "not oil with derricks and producers and money and the rest of the trappings you associate with oil.

What I'm talking about is gambling, scams masquerading as long-term investments. I'm talking about oil leases."

"Tell me some more," I said, "I thought I knew something about the oil business, but I'm not altogether sure I understand."

"Well, there's a lot of flimflam connected with oil. There is a whole segment of the business making a good living with smoke and mirrors. They show up at your door wanting to lease the mineral rights to your property for, say, three years. They'll tell you they're going to sell leases to the locals and speculators. You of course are going to get a percentage. Then the salespeople tell the innocents they're going to need more geologic survey work to determine just what the probability is of bringing in a well and, if they're smart, they'll get on board now before they start to drill. They tell them there is oil shale in the area. This is probably true, and hard to disprove, because much of the state sits on shale. What they don't mention is that you need more than shale to bring in a producer. You need a *cap rock*. You need a particular folding of the geologic stratification to dam up the oil seeping from the shale; this forms a lake of oil hundreds of feet below the surface. But the odds of the shale and the cap existing together under property like mine are few and far between. Still, it makes for a good story, and they don't call oil *black gold* for nothing. It stimulates certain people's imaginations like you wouldn't believe. And then their greed sets them up to lose their money."

"Do they ever drill to find out?" I asked her.

"Not very often. It's too expensive. And the odds of finding anything are too long. They sell their leases and pocket their money, and after three years, when the life of the lease runs out, it reverts back to the owner. But while it's under lease, the owner doesn't have clear title and it can't be sold."

"You mean they never intended to do anything with it

when they sold the lease?"

"You got it. That's where the scam comes in. It gives a whole new meaning to the word speculation."

"But what about your percentage of the lease sales?"

"That's more or less of a joke, too, but not to hear the oil companies tell it. I call it *creative accounting*. After all the deductions for all their expenses they say they've incurred, there's not much left for me."

"Lucy, is your land under lease?"

"Yes, that's what I've been trying to say, I guess. That's why I couldn't sell, even if I wanted, to.

"For how long?"

"Why do you ask? Is this some kind of proposal?" She looked at me with that smile on her face, but I could tell she was more than half serious.

I changed the subject: "Tell me something, how did you meet Eric. He came from Fredericksburg or Seguine, one of those predominantly German cities down by San Antonio. It's a long way there, believe me. What was he doing way out here?"

"He was stationed here as an aviation cadet at our air base. Something happened, and he was eliminated from the program. Because he spoke German fluently, with hardly an accent, they put him in a special unit. But then you would know more about that than I do.

"I met him at a dance. We hit it off. We thought we had fallen in love; before he was transferred, we were married. He wanted me to follow him. But I couldn't leave the land, so I stayed behind. He came back a couple of times. But each time, we realized we were becoming more and more distant. When he went overseas, it was the end of our marriage for all intents and purposes. I guess ours was not unlike a lot of other wartime marriages.

"Now, I've answered your questions. How about telling me what it is with you? And how come you say we have this close association? Do you owe Eric some money? Is that what this is all about? Are we joined together because you want to pay the debt on the installment plan?" This time her smile merged into a laugh.

There are times when you reach a crossroad. Decisions and even statements you make at this crucial time lock you into situations that can forever change your life. Right now, I'm feeling as though I've come to a crossroads. And I'm not sure how I got here. What I'm trying to say is: I want this woman for my wife. I guess I did the instant I saw her. But, I realize how preposterous the idea is, what with me on the run and all. And I can't keep coming back here, going through the usual mating ritual. There just isn't time, nor will circumstances permit. I don't want to be seen around here, and I don't quite know how to explain it to Lucy. I guess what I really want is to talk to her about it. I want to have some kind of an understanding. I want her to consider me first, before she makes a hasty decision and gets tied up with somebody else. I guess what I want is an option for an understanding to have a future engagement, when we know each other better, if that makes any sense. But regardless of how I put it, I know it isn't going to come out right. And the last thing I want right now is to appear ridiculous and off the wall.

"Lucy, would you be willing to join me, say in a large city somewhere, if I asked you? Would you be willing to haul off and bring your dog and let go of your life here? Bear in mind, you would never want for anything." It sounded worse than I thought it would. But there it was. That's exactly what I wanted.

"Then when this lease arrangement of yours runs-out, you could sell your farm. The price you get is not of any real consequence; or you could give it to a relative and let them sell it. Would you be willing to marry me at some future date, when things are more settled with me? I know this is crazy, but I don't have much time to monkey around with formalities. I know this is real sudden. However, I have one thing going for me, which should make it sound a lot less preposterous. I'm rich. I mean, your house and land are small potatoes in comparison. At the risk of mixing metaphors, I want to re-introduce you to some real tall cotton, but not right now. If you can wait for, maybe, another year, and things work out for me, I can guarantee to end your life of loneliness. I guess I'm saying I would make a pretty good husband. I haven't been single all these years because I wanted to be. It's because I have had no other choice.

"Think it over. I don't want to hear your answer now. Even if you say no, there'll be no hard feelings; I'll understand. But whatever your decision is, it will not end our relationship. Rest assured, no matter what you decide, you can't get rid of me. Not now, maybe not ever."

I walked her to the car through the outside double doors. The pool game was still going on, joined now by another welfare recipient. We paused for a minute in the vacant vestibule before stepping onto the steps leading down to the graveled parking lot. As she preceded me through thc first door, I touched her by the shoulder and pulled her back.

"The next time we meet," I said, "I hope to be in a position to tell you everything, and to do things in a more civilized fashion. I want you to know I'm serious, and that I'm not just some screwball off the street who wants your property."

I was feeling better about it, I mean about the approach I had taken. If I had given her some kind of a line or tried to make some kind of an advance toward her, she would've been put on guard. Likely as not, she would've categorized me as a loser with all the rest of them.

She didn't seem put off by anything I said. Quite the

contrary, she appeared to be in favor of my proposal without saying so, in spite of how crazy it must have sounded.

As she prepared to drive away, I leaned in and kissed her goodbye. This time I removed her hand from the steering wheel and gave her a thousand dollars.

She looked at me surprised. But before she could say anything or hand it back, I walked away. I stopped and turned around. I was unable to hear what she was saying, but at this point it didn't matter. She never dropped the money on the ground, as I halfway expected she would. I waved goodbye, yelling out: "I told you we were partners; this money belongs to you. And get your steps fixed."

Instead of waving and driving away, she pulled over and parked.

"Come here," she said through the rolled-down window.

"Come here and get in. I have no intention of taking this money unless you tell me where it came from."

I opened the door and sat down in the passenger seat. I had to tell her something or she was going to be rid of me; I could see it in her eyes. On the spur of he moment, I decided to tell her where it did come from. Not the whole story, mind you, but just enough to let me off the hook.

"You stole that money, didn't you? And Eric helped you, didn't he?" She wasted no time laying into me. "That's why you came here isn't it? When your letters were not answered, you came to see why not. How much of your loot did Eric have anyway? And is that why he never intended to come home?"

"Hey, first things first. It's a long story, and you have to get back to work."

"No, I don't. I took the afternoon off.

"Listen, there were a lot of things that happened early on," she volunteered. "I mean there were a lot of things that bothered me about him. For starters: I was never sure he was killed in action. Don't ask me why, but I always suspected he wrote me that Dear John after the War."

"What makes you think he wrote it after the War, Lucy?" I asked. "Answer this one question, and then I'll tell you everything you want to know." I wasn't going to, of course, but I had to say something.

"Okay. Well, to begin with, the dates of some of the things never jived. For instance: he said he wasn't coming home to be a farmer, because he had re-enlisted to make a career of the army. This couldn't have happened. Like most everybody else, he was *drafted* into the *Army of the United States;* he didn't enlist in the *Regular Service*. The army offered an *Active Duty Reserve* option to certain people, but it was after the War ended. How could he have known about this program before the army did?

"Then, too, the envelope was postmarked after Germany surrendered, but the letter was dated weeks before. And there were several other things as well, which made no sense. Is that enough to satisfy your curiosity?"

"Yes," I answered. "But can we talk about these so called other things? It's very important I know whatever it is you know; it really is."

"All right, but go ahead and tell me whether the two of you stole some money. And whom did you steal it from?"

"Yes, we stole it, if you want to call it stealing. We got it from Hitler's *Waffen SS,* who got much of it from the poor hapless Jews they murdered." I paused to see how she was going to take what I had just told her.

She turned partway around in the seat and asked me, "Is that it? Is that all you're going to say. Are you going to keep the details from me?"

"To tell you the truth," I said, "I wasn't planning on telling you anything at all. It's for your own safety."

"Nonsense," she countered. "More mystery–each time you pretend to answer a question, you open yourself up for a dozen more.

"Are you going to start anywhere near the beginning? Do you intend to keep me confused, hoping I'll shut up and let you slip on out of here?"

"Okay, then, this is all I *am* going to say, for right now at least.

"Three of us, myself, a sergeant named Carl Jorgensen, and Eric took a sack of their diamonds from a potassium mine near the town of Merkers, Germany.

"I was in command of a squad of specialists, attached to General Patton's field headquarters. All of us spoke at least one European language; that was our particular specialty. Eric, of course, spoke German. Carl spoke Norwegian, but could converse in passable German. I come from Louisiana, Southern Louisiana, down around Houma. French was my first language, and I spoke it exclusively until I started public school. And even then, our teacher lapsed into French when she had forgotten an English word. Others of my unit spoke other European languages.

"Our job with Patton was to roam ahead of his advancing forces. We talked to anybody who would talk to us; usually it was in French, German, Polish, or Norwegian. We would report back by radio, telling headquarters anything we had learned of importance, and then we would go on ahead to another assignment. That's what we were doing when we found the mine."

"Where did the Norwegian come in?" she interrupted to ask me.

"Good question. We ran into all kinds of Scandinavians–mostly Norwegians and Danish. Like the Poles, Dutch, and Belgians, it seemed half the population was slave laborers. They were everywhere we went, willing to talk to any American who could understand them."

"I didn't know you were *Cajun*," she said, giving forth with that broad smile of hers, wanting to slow me down.

"Yeah, I'll answer to *Cajun*, but I don't particularly care for *Coon Ass*."

"Don't worry, I'll not call you that if you don't call me *Tex*."

She had a sense of humor. I liked that. In fact, there wasn't anything I had discovered so far I didn't like.

"All right, then, I've changed my mind. I'll tell you as much as I can in two hours. And that'll have to do for now."

"What's so all-fired important you have to rush off?"

"Ask me when I've told you my story."

"Okay, you had better get started then."

CHAPTER 3
GERMANY. THE RHINE RIVER, 1945

I had good reason to remember the crossing date. General Patton wrote about it, as did Generals Bradley, Eisenhower, and the Nineteenth Division commanding officer, Major General Herbert L. Earnest and his superior, Corps Commander Manson Eddy.

The bridge across the Rhine at Remagen had been shelled and bombed extensively. It was not considered safe for transport of heavy tanks; indeed, two days after it was captured, it collapsed of its own accord and fell in the river.

Eisenhower had tasked the British commander, Bernard Montgomery, who was downstream of the bridge, and at his own request, with the assault against the Germans on the other side. Patton, on the other hand, had his own plans. He was intent on beating his archrival across. He had no intention of sitting idly by watching the show, while Montgomery "piddled around and hogged all the glory."

My first squad and I were no longer on foot. We had been traveling in a Carryall and two Jeeps ahead of the lead elements of Patton's Third Army. I had recently been relieved of my second and third squads, because we were moving too fast and a platoon had become too unwieldy.

My diary informs me we arrived at the crossing point at a town about ten miles from the industrial center of Koblenz on the afternoon of 20 March. General Patton was supposed to arrive the next day.

Sure enough, as advertised, Patton drove up accompanied by his senior aide, several of his field headquarters staff, and more tanks.

I was standing at the water's edge when his Jeep pulled-up. Patton saw me and walked over: "*Comment ca va*?" Adair, he asked.

I replied: "*Ca va bien, mon general.*"

Patton was one of those West Point graduates who loved to speak French. That may be one of the reasons he remembered me. I have known a few other Academy officers. Some were like Patton; however, there were others who could care less about the language. I always figured the ones who sought me out to keep in practice were the ones who had done well in the mandatory course.

After the informal greeting, he continued in French, asking me whether I had anything of interest to report. I told him no. I said in French: "I'm stymied by the river, and I'm waiting for the general to float me across so I can get back to work." He laughed, and then gave out in English with some uncomplimentary words about Montgomery, and how his malingering had slowed us all up and stopped his advance.

And then he said he was expecting a battalion of his combat engineers: "They're supposed to arrive in a couple of hours to build a pontoon bridge. They're down below inflating rafts and loading bridging material right now. As soon as they're finished, they're going to truck it up here, and then they'll start floating it across. We should be able to cross by tomorrow." He chuckled, telling his aide that Montgomery was not going to make it until the 24th, two days late.

His aide, the one to whom he had been directing most of his remarks, appeared to be confused about how the bridge was going to be constructed.

The general anticipated his questions by telling us all that the actual work would start from the other side. "There's a reason," he said, "if we start from this bank and a float gets away or a powered launch malfunctions, the swift current will take it into our new bridge and maybe tear it apart. Anyway, they know what they're doing. We'll give them the time they need, and then we'll all drive across without getting our feet wet."

He turned to me again: "Adair, how come I haven't promoted you yet?"

"I guess you've been too busy, General," I replied, smiling.

"Well I'm not too busy right now, Captain."

I glanced at his aide, who was already fishing around in a box he carried, looking for a set of captain's bars. It was rumored the General had a cigar box half-full of insignia of all ranks. He liberally removed rank from non-performers and promoted others at will. Today was my lucky day; tomorrow, I just might be a lieutenant again.

He beckoned to me to come up the few yards to his Jeep. He handed me the new insignia. I came to attention, saluted, and said: "*Je vous remarcie beaucoup.*"

"*De rien. Je vous en prie,*" he replied.

He offered me a few words of congratulations in French about the good job I had been doing. He said something else in French that I missed. Then in English for all to hear, he loudly spit out some expletives about Germans in general and Montgomery in particular.

Weeks before, my squad had advised Patton through the officer in charge of counter-intelligence that the general's plan to put soldiers across the river was not necessary. Patton had assumed opposition was going to be too heavy to attempt a river crossing by the book. Never one to admit something couldn't be done, and always the innovator, he had formulated a daring plan. He had been in the process of requisitioning all the L-5's in Third Army. What he intended to do was fly infantryman across one at a time in the small two-seated airplanes, with each aircraft making several flights an hour. He anticipated putting enough troops across to secure the area some ten miles south of Mainz, the obliterated industrial city of the Ruhr. His howitzers and dug-in tanks would shell the area several miles along a front, beginning at the water's edge, and some ten miles to the rear. In this way his light airplanes could land and take off with minimum casualties. Air Corps fighters, armed with rockets, would fly top-cover to stop a *panzer* counter attack.

I had advised him there was opposition. But it wasn't that heavy, thus making his aerial operation unnecessary. And thus making the pontoon river crossing more efficient and practical.

I watched him as he turned around and walked back to the edge of the water, all the while talking to this colonel, his senior aide. At one time, I knew his name, but I've forgotten it now. Anyway, I heard him tell Patton. "This river doesn't look too formidable, General." I could tell he was joking. But Patton missed the point, replying in his own inimitable expletive-sprinkled vernacular: "You're right. If that paper-hanging *sonofabitch* thinks he's going to hide behind this piddlin' drink of water, he's badly mistaken." All this time, his *performance* and remarks were being directed toward a group who had joined us near the water. Random shells were falling around us from a German unit that had moved in across the river. Patton, who knew he was being watched by fifty or so of his men, showed absolutely no fear of the shells. He stayed longer than his staff would have liked, and then drove off to check on his engineers.

As soon as the bridge was finished and the first of his units were over, he returned. He walked out on the new pontoon bridge and stared at the river a few feet below for what seemed the longest time. Then he started to walk across. When he got to the middle, he turned away from his aide and unbuttoned his cavalry trousers. He removed his *appendage,* while turning his head toward the group following him in Jeeps, as if he was waiting for some kind of recognition. Then he turned back toward the river and started to pee. The crowd began to cheer and applaud. Patton, ever the showman, turned his head halfway around again with a broad smile on his face. Occupied by his business, he peed for the longest time into the German *Ganges*; the vaunted Rhine River, the pride of the German nation. Finished, he buttoned up his pants while the cameras clicked away for the benefit of posterity. Then bowing to the photographers, he walked on across, climbed into his Jeep, and drove away to the laughter of his cheering section.

Within a few days, the bridge was completely finished. But, I might add, it was not accomplished without his combat engineers taking casualties. But it *was* finished. And then the remainder of Third Army crossed over this span and one other below and advanced toward the cities of Gotha and Leipzig.

I was with Patton's G-2 Section, but attached to the Nineteenth Infantry Division for rations. Within three days, they had secured the area around the small village of Merkers.

A captain in counter-intelligence, at their command post in the nearby village of Keiselbach, had asked me to keep my eyes and ears open. He said they had heard unsubstantiated rumors from displaced persons about a potassium mine in the Merkers area. He told me: "None of them have been confirmed, but there are too many, all alike, to ignore.

Hundreds of millions of dollars of stolen loot has supposedly been hidden in this mine by Hitler's elite troops, the Waffen SS, using slave laborers to do the work." According to him, they had moved the entire German money reserve from Berlin to this mysterious mine in the area where we were working.

I told him I would, and then put it out of my mind. There had been all kinds of rumors floating around about secret German stashes, and how the SS was going to use them in their plans to re-group in the mountains around Bavaria for a last ditch stand. General Patton had no choice but to believe them, and months earlier, he had been pushing toward Bavaria to cut them off. However, his plans had to be changed when he was ordered to divert north to relieve Bastone at the *Battle of the Bulge.* He figured if the SS could settle into what he referred to as *redoubt fortifications*, we would lose a lot of people trying to roust them out. But that was then, and this is now. Now, he had abandoned the idea as just another of Hitler's too little, too late, pipe dreams.

About two weeks later, my men and I stopped at a hastily erected checkpoint on the road outside Merkers. Two soldiers had stopped two young French women walking from Merkers to Keiselbach. One of them was very pregnant. She looked as though shc was about to deliver at any moment. Neither of the soldiers spoke French or German, so when I told them the score, they were happy to turn them over to me.

We put the mother to be in the front seat, while her sister, whose name was Françoise, rode in the back with me; Carl transferred to our second Jeep.

When we started back to Merkers, both women objected, loudly. When I told them I would take them to one of our doctors, they were elated. They had been on their way to a German midwife in Keiselbach, whom they had heard about; but they were not sure she was still there. Now, confident of qualified medical assistance, they were most interested in conversing with me in my *peculiar* brand of French.

I took a chance: "Have either of you heard of a potassium mine around here where the SS has hidden a lot of treasure? We know it exists, we just don't know where."

"Yes," Françoise, the younger of the two, replied. "If you keep your promise, I will come back with you and show you where it is." I could not be sure then, but I am now, that her sister Murielle gave Françoise a look of real disdain, as if a glance was meant to tell her to *keep her mouth shut among these strangers.*

I took them to a mobile hospital unit just setting up about five miles west of Merkers. I was hoping the doctor in charge would cooperate in this instance and consent to treat a civilian. I was fully prepared to lean on him with whatever assets I had at my disposal, but it turned out to be unnecessary. He had no choice: either he admitted her or some of his people were going to have to birth her sitting in my Jeep.

We wasted no time after the medics took over. With her sister Murielle out of the picture, Françoise was eager to take us to the mine. Furthermore, as it turned out, she had valuable information, which I was able to pass up the chain of command to General Patton.

The mine was located on the outskirts of Merkers, on the road to Keiselbach. When we arrived, the bunch of us stopped at the mine entrance and ate a package of field rations. She told us the mine had several entrances. They were all located in different towns close by. She named them for me, and I wrote them down. But I've forgotten them now, and I've lost my old notebook. However, I remembered she said this one was the main entrance. She said the tunnel in front of us led to a shaft a mile or so back in the mine.

When I asked her how she knew so much about it, she told me

her pregnant sister knew an *SS* officer who helped move the treasure from the *Reichsbank* in Berlin to this mine. She also said there were other mines in the area, which she said she would show us later.

"Françoise, was this Waffen SS guy the boyfriend of your sister?"

"Yes, he was."

"Where is he now?"

"He was transferred to the Russian front, up by Berlin, a few weeks ago, along with his unit. His name is Kurt Steinmann, in case you want to know." She talked as though she had no great love for the SS. However, I realized Murielle was still very much in love with him; that's why she preferred her sister keep quiet about things involving the Waffen SS.

I gave her another ration; she hadn't seen much food in days.

"Is there anybody they left behind?" I asked her. The last thing I wanted was to run into some of Kurt's friends who might have been left as guards.

"No, there are no soldiers. They ran away two days ago. There are some civilians though. Two I know of are officers of the *Reichsbank*, and another one is a curator for some valuable paintings. And there is one technician who runs the elevator. There is no one who is going to give you any trouble if we went in right now."

"If it's so easy to access, how come the locals haven't carted it all away?"

"Because," she said, "they don't know what I just told you. They think the SS left some people behind as guards. And they do not know how to operate the elevator. Anyway, Murielle told me there is a vault with a time lock and everything."

"Are there any lights inside?" I ask her.

"There are, but only a few are turned on. They have limited diesel oil to run the generator units. But I understand, from what my sister has told me, they do work. They do keep some of them going, because it is necessary to keep the air conditioners working. I understand a constant cool temperature is necessary to preserve the paintings."

"Let me ask you: how come the Germans never moved the treasure when they knew we were coming?"

"They tried. They even had some of it loaded on a train headed towards Bavaria. But they found the bridge bombed out about twenty miles from here and they had to come back."

"*Cheri*, did this Steinmann talk about other caches of loot down in Bavaria?" I didn't mean anything by this term of endearment; it was just what we called Cajun girls from Lafayette to Bayou Barateria. That is, we did if they were pretty, and Françoise was pretty, in spite of being a little on the lean side.

"He did not say so in so many words, because it was highly classified. But he was gone much of the time, and she did say he had been working in the area around Bavaria."

Françoise didn't know much more than what she had just told me. She suggested I talk directly to her sister, whom she was sure would tell me anything she knew. Françoise felt her German officer had abandoned her sister. But as it turned out, this was not exactly the case. And as I was later to find out, Murielle was anything but eager to divulge the slightest bit of information regarding Kurt Steinmann, who was soon to become a *public enemy* in his own country.

The four of us drove back into the mine to the elevator she was talking about. We found it to be operational. The day before, slave laborers, supervised by bank officials, had unloaded millions of dollars worth of German currency. And just hours before, they had been in the process of cart-ing it below. The elevator operator explained to Eric how they anticipated our arrival, and fearing us, had fled, leaving him with a ton of money. It was lying in the tunnel next to the lift, where he had just finished taking it below.

I couldn't help but notice the state-of-the-art timbering in the tunnel. I had majored in geology at LSU, before the War caught up with me. I say state of the art; it was to the extent they had adopted the American *square set* method first used at the Comstock Mine in Virginia City. The Germans were noted innovators in most of the sciences of the time, but they had to take a back seat to American know-how when it came to hard rock mining.

At the operator's suggestion, we parked our trailer and drove the Jeep on-board the huge freight elevator. Then we started the descent of two thousand feet or more into the mine proper. The rickety ride in the dark was somewhat unnerving; however, the operator assured Eric and Carl that it was perfectly safe and capable of carrying a far heavier load than was on-board now.

Eric was translating his remarks for me. I asked him to ask the operator why he was being so accommodating. He said the guy was interested in a tip, not money but food. He had been working all day and he was hungry. Then, too, he was most relieved when he realized we were not going to shoot him. He saw us as his new friends, and he was most eager to keep us this way.

We unloaded the Jeep from the elevator, and with Françoise sitting on my lap in the front seat, the gang of us drove down the tunnel to the vault.

The door looked like a bank vault. I knew nothing about vault doors, but this one looked formidable. However, it did appear to be overdone, as though it was mostly for show. It was not mounted in steel but in a wall of masonry and bricks, which appeared as though it could be circumvented in a few minutes with a good pick and a strong back.

The operator didn't have the safe combination, and the only Reichsbank officer who did was one of those who had run off, fearing what might happen to him. I asked the operator what was behind the door. He told me there were hundreds of millions in gold, silver, platinum, coin, and more currency. I knew it had been looted from Jews and from several banks in Europe and Russia, without him having to tell me.

Then, he escorted us down a smaller tunnel to a storage area. Lining the walls for hundreds of feet were crated paintings from the Berlin museum, as well as other museums from all over Europe. The names of the painters were stenciled on each crate. Some of them were not in crates, but were standing against the wall with canvas coverings. There were dozens of French, Dutch, Flemish, Italian, and a few Russian paintings. I jotted down some of the names, in order to brief General Patton and my superiors in the intelligence unit I worked for.

We stayed below for the better part of an hour. All this time, we were talking to the operator about what was behind the door. He said it had taken days to transport the loot from the top down to the vault. He explained how much of it belonged to the Waffen SS, as well as the *Schutstaffein SS.* I was to learn that this latter unit was responsible for running the concentration camps.

He said that, some of the bags and boxes he handled were stenciled with the name of *Melmer*. Later, I was told by one of the bank officials, a guy by the name of Albert Thoms, who had also run off but who had returned, that Melmer was the name of an SS captain by the name of Bruno Melmer. It turned out the Melmer account was actually credited to a fictitious officer by the name of *Hilliger*. The next day, Thoms told me Hilliger was a code name for Heinrich Himmler, head of the Gestapo, the Schutstaffein, and the Waffen SS.

The other two officers of the Reichsbank could be made available to answer any more of my questions, according to the operator. They were knowledgeable of the contents, but didn't have the combination to the vault, he said.

"Where are these people now?" Eric asked him.

"They were here earlier, but they left by another entrance when they saw you coming. I am sure they will come back if you promise not to shoot them or put them in jail."

I told him and Eric translated: "You get in touch with these people and have them standing by in the morning. I want them to be here and available every day to answer any questions. And you, and all the others, who have had anything to do with this treasure, should be here as well. You tell them I am taking possession of this mine, and everything in it, in the name of the American Army. You work for us now and not the bank of Germany."

He was not the least bit surprised. He told Eric they were hoping we would get here first, and relieve them of the treasure before the Russians did. He said they knew the Russians would be incensed by the outrage since some of the loot was Russian. This was especially true of their masterpieces. They fully expected the Russians to shoot them on the spot as criminals. Somehow, I wasn't surprised.

I went back to Keiselbach and briefed my superior, Lt. Col. Russell, and the officer I had spoken to who was with counter-intelligence. They, in turn, contacted Gen. Earnest, the Nineteenth commander, who passed it on to Gen. Manson Eddy. Eddy wasted no time in calling General Patton to tell him the treasure had been located.

Patton was reluctant to advise Eisenhower, until he heard it was me who had first seen the vault and the hoard of currency stacked in the tunnel. Eddy told him what the elevator operator had told me, but it was the truckloads of currency that convinced him. Patton had recently been worked over by the press on this subject and he was gun shy. He wanted to be absolutely sure before he said anything to Eisenhower about something as sensational as this. I can't say as I blamed him. He told Eddy to keep it quiet, and to blow the vault and then to get back to him.

In the meantime, Earnest took action to move several units of infantry to the mine entrance, supported by tanks and anti-aircraft guns. When I told him where the other entrances were, he deployed combat units to guard them as well.

My men and I were on site to translate and answer any questions when Generals Eddy and Earnest, accompanied by Col. Russell, arrived with some combat engineers. They estimated it would take only a half stick of dynamite to blow the vault wall.

The group of us wasted no time entering what came to be known as Room Eight.

There were lights in the room, which one of the bank officials turned on for us, but there was no ventilation. The room was huge. Stacked in neat rows, about three feet high the length of the room, were bags of gold and silver bars. As the group of us wandered between the bags and boxes of loot, we noticed several of them were unsealed. It was explained why: these bags had been opened for inventory and had not been resealed.

General Earnest was quick to see the obvious: unsealed bags, particularly of such things as valuable coins and diamonds, could be easily pilfered. He directed me to stay on site to prevent this from happening. Although infantry cordoned off the entrances, it still didn't guarantee the security of the cache from everybody, including the elevator operator or the officials of the bank, now that accountability was no longer their business.

In the meantime, Patton had asked Eisenhower to get

his finance people involved. He wanted to be about the War; he didn't want the responsibility for the treasure.

Eisenhower appointed a Colonel Bernstein, head of the European Finance Department of the Army to take charge.

The next day, Eisenhower, Bradley, and Patton flew over from Patton's headquarters at Hersfeld. Bernstein, and a brigadier by the name of Weyland from the Air Corps, had arrived earlier and were on site to greet them.

When Patton saw me at the elevator shaft with Carl and Eric, he returned my salute, and then told me to stay close to answer any questions he might want translated with the bank officials.

We accompanied them down the shaft. As I said, the trip down was long and unnerving, helped a little bit by a flashlight Bernstein had thought to bring along.

As it turned out, I would get to know Bernstein well. I would come to recognize his many attributes as an administrator, but not as a soldier. He had been commissioned a colonel directly from civilian life, and he was void of any knowledge of even the basic fundamentals of soldiering.

The rickety elevator had been operating only a few minutes when Patton thought he should break the silence with some conversation. I guess he figured it would relieve the tension, which was being felt by everybody. He said: "Ike, do you believe this rig is supported by only one small cable?" Then he directed his next *faux pas* at Bradley. "Brad, wouldn't promotions in the United States Army be considerably stimulated if that cable busted?"

Eisenhower, who was standing next to me, was fidgeting, and he didn't think Patton was being very funny. He turned to him saying, "Okay, George, no more cracks until we're above ground again."

A few minutes later, Patton again interrupted the silence by introducing me to the other three generals as the officer who discovered the treasure.

Then Bradley said to Patton: "George, have you any idea how rich you and the captain here would be if this were the old free-booting days?" He went on for the next few minutes explaining the military and historical traditions of dividing conquered spoils. That evening at dinner, Eisenhower asked Patton what he would really do if he turned most of the loot over to him, as they would have in ancient times when every soldier had a vested interest in the captured spoils. Eisenhower had heard Patton's discourses on how he believed in reincarnation, and how he believed he had served at various times in the Roman Legions.

Patton was reported to have told him: "The first thing I would do is melt down the gold. And then I would strike medallions and give one to every sonofabitch in Third Army. The alternative would be to bury it, then when times got tough, like they used to be, I would dig it up and buy some modern tanks with it."

Eisenhower turned to Bradley and said: "See I told you, he has an answer for everything."

Before they left, Patton called me aside. "Leave your men here, but accompany me topside. I want to talk to you before I go."

An hour later, he found the time and the occasion to pass on what he had on his mind. He chose to speak in French, in case he was overheard. "Get below. Stay close to that stuff. I mean camp next to it for a couple of days. I don't know this Bernstein from Adam's house cat. What I do know is, I am responsible for it all and I don't like it. They are my troops who are guarding this place, and we don't know how much is even in there. If the word gets around some of it is missing, the press is going to fry my butt. Things are in a state of flux right now. I'll send down your trailers, and see you are relieved in a couple of days. Until Bernstein gets things organized and decides where he's going to put it, keep everybody the hell away from the vault, except him and your bosses. I'll clear it with them and advise Bernstein."

I never bothered to tell him that I had already been ordered to do that exact same thing.

The trailers carried our rations and sleeping bags. We were pleasantly surprised to find Patton had added some good wine, cheese, and bratwurst. And that's how come Carl and Eric and I, along with three others from my first squad, ended up babysitting the treasure.

The first night underground, Eric and Carl stayed with me by the vault. The other guys were posted down the tunnel, where they could stop anybody coming down the elevator or from coming through the tunnel by way of the other entrances. They had erected a barricade with the other Jeep and trailer and a heavy Browning automatic rifle.

We had left the light on in Room Eight, behind the blown-out wall. There was plenty of light coming from the hole in the vault to see what we were doing. We found some wood and lit a fire to heat some coffee and cook the *bratwurst.* We sat around talking, discussing what Bradley had said about the spoils of war belonging to the conquering troops. We had also discussed what Patton had said about spoils being the legacy of the Roman Legionnaire, and countless other professional soldiers in former times. It had always been understood by their progenitors that the reason they were fighting was to inherit most of the treasure they captured from the enemy. This was part of the contract a Legionnaire made with the emperor and the Roman Senate when he volunteered and put his life on the line.

"Captain, did you see all the money stacked in the tunnel. Do you suppose it's going to be worth anything when this is all over?" Carl was making conversation to pass the time. It was early and not yet time to hit the sack.

"Are you planning on swiping some?" I said. "If you

are, you're going to have to carry a Jeep full to buy a cup of coffee."

"Do you think it's going to be *that* worthless?"

"I think it's going to be about like German money was after the First War or Confederate money was after you carpet-bagging Yankees got through with us a few years back." My chiding remark was leveled at Carl, who was from Minnesota.

"You know, as much as they hate giving it back, any one of those generals would court-martial our collective butts if we were to pocket as much as one mark of that worthless money." I told them.

"Captain, who's going to get back all the gold?" Carl asked.

"Yeah, and who's going to get back all the teeth?" Eric asked me, rhetorically, with disgust in his voice. "Did you see those open sacks in the back against the wall." We had heard about a crematorium the Russians had run into soon after they entered Poland.

"Those gold teeth and those separate bags of gold fillings and inlays belonged to those poor bastards they burnt up. Are they going to give them back to them? And what about all those personal items like those sacks full of gold cigarette cases, lighters, jewelry, and other things. And what about the sack of diamonds? Where do you think the diamonds came from, the ones stenciled Melmer?" Carl asked me.

"I never saw any diamonds," I said.

Carl replied: "There was an open sack of them. Where do you think they came from? And there was a sack of what looked like American gold coins. I have never seen anything like them. They were stamped twenty dollars on the face. Why do you suppose the Germans would be hording coins only worth twenty dollars? Do you suppose, Captain, they're collectors' items and worth a lot more?"

Eric ignored the subject of gold coins and gave Carl his opinion about where the diamonds came from. "They were looted from Jewish jewelry. The jewelry must have been taken from their homes or confiscated from their personal belongings before they murdered them."

They were both getting worked up talking about it. And to see the physical evidence in sacks a few yards away didn't help much.

"Which one of you saw a bag of Melmer diamonds?"

"We both did. It said 10 kg. on the bag. How much is a kg. anyway, Captain?" Carl asked.

"It's a kilogram, and it's equivalent to a little more than two pounds. That means the sack weighs 22 pounds," I answered.

"How much do you think a pound of diamonds is worth?" Carl asked me.

"I have no idea. I guess it depends on their size and quality. How big are they, anyway?"

"I don't know. Did you see them close-up, Eric?" Carl asked him.

"Yes, I shined my flashlight inside, and I can tell you they're huge. They're twice as large as any engagement ring I ever saw."

"How big is that?" Carl wanted to know.

"I guess the biggest was on Mary Kitchen's finger. Her husband owned some oil wells over Huston way. I heard it was more than two carats. These are bigger, some of them could be as large as five, maybe six carats. I mean they're gigantic."

"Can we go take a look, just for something to do?" Carl asked me.

I should have shut the conversation down right then but I didn't. I was as eager to see them as they were. And furthermore, I knew I was going to help *liberate* them. They were our legacy, just as the general had said. They were ours; the American people owed us them. The system had changed, and not for the better–now, all you got for fighting for your country was a small monthly salary; it was hardly enough to buy more than some tobacco and a few beers. We rationalized we were the rightful owners, since they were never going to find their way back to the Jewish people. And the idea of them unlawfully enriching some wealthy German woman's finger or a *do-dad* around her neck, after what had happened, almost made us sick.

I knew what we were about to do was against the law. But then against whose law–military law? It must have been new military law, because it certainly wasn't against old law–General Bradley had said as much.

But, whatever, I knew taking them was wrong and I didn't care. Anyway, like the millions of times I had committed a sin–I knew I was going to do it before I ever did. There was some wrestling went on with my conscience at the outset. But I knew my conscience was outmatched and that eventually I was going to win. It was something akin to the thoughts coming over me awhile ago, when Françoise was sitting on my lap.

"How much did that Kitchen broad's ring cost?" Carl asked Eric.

"I can't remember, exactly. But something like two thousand rings a bell. And that was ten years ago."

"Wholly, Jeez!" Carl retorted.

"How many double handfuls do you think is there," Carl asked him.

Eric answered: "There has to be at least five, six, or maybe more. So conservatively, what do you think a double handful is worth, Captain?"

"I have no idea," I said. "Your guess is as good as mine. It's like those promotional contests you used to see. They would put a large bottle full of beans in a store window for a month. And every five bucks you spent you got a chance at a guess. The winner won fifty bucks. But remember, during the Depression, a man worked a lot of hours for fifty dollars."

"Captain, do you know anything about diamonds?" Carl asked me.

"I know a little about how they're formed, but not too much about how they're marketed. I do know they hold their value. But the big diamond merchants control the price, so they don't fluctuate very much. Their price usually rises with the rate of inflation."

"How much more is say a three carat than a two?" Eric wanted to know.

"Well, it's a lot more than you might expect. They're priced by the carat, which rises almost geometrically. However, three-carat diamonds are a rarity."

"What does that mean exactly?" he wanted to know.

I answered him by saying: "Well, say a one carat is 300 dollars, then a two would be nine multiplied by two or 1,800 bucks. Then a three would be over 2,400. But a four would be astronomical, maybe as much as 26,000 dollars. You can see as the progression moves upward, the value of a carat goes up rapidly.

"I'm going to take a wild guess, though, and say at about 20,000 a stone, a level double handful of clear cut diamonds is conservatively worth over three million dollars. If there's six doubles, then the bag is worth about eighteen million. But then we have to divide that by three. And don't forget the fence that would want a double share; so we have five into that gives us roughly three million each, give or take.

"I read the other day in the *Stars and Stripes* where they're planning to build a lot of homes for returning veterans in the San Fernando Valley, *where everybody is never going to more roam and make the San Fernando Valley their home.* The paper said they should run around 10,000 each. To put it into perspective, your share would be worth about 300 of those new homes."

We all had a chuckle, and one of us commented about how crowded it was going to be if everybody who was humming that tune was moving to the San Fernando Valley when the War was over. And how we didn't expect houses or diamonds to stay at that price for long.

"What are the guys down the tunnel going to get if we own all that real estate?" Carl wondered out loud.

"To tell you the truth, they're replacements, and I never thought about them. And anyway, one or more of them might squeal and get us all a stint in Leavenworth," Eric said, and we both nodded in agreement.

One of the problems in the combat infantry is the business of friendships. In the beginning, in training, individuals began liking each other. Later on, they became closer than family. When some of them were killed, the rest of us were never able to forget. We didn't want to add to their number; none of us could mentally stand the strain. It was about the time of the battle of the *Falaise Pocket,* when we decided we didn't want any more friends. That's when we started treating replacements badly. They were not part of our primary group. We didn't want to get close to them; it hurt too much when they died. I rarely spoke to mine; I relied on the ranking sergeant to deal with them. Not once did I ask where they were from–I was cold and distant, and they resented me.

Our platoon was never to be the family it was when we first started out. At the *Mosell River Crossing* and the Bulge and in between, we had taken twenty-five percent casualties, of whom some had been replacements. The four down the tunnel had joined us after the Bulge. They never knew what it was like to be seriously shelled. They had never even fired their rifles. They were not veterans; they were little more than civilians, and that's how we thought of them.

It wasn't their fault; it was just the way things were. The way we figured it, they were not entitled to a share.

CHAPTER 4
SAN ANGELO, TEXAS, 1950

Fogerty pulled into the graveled drive alongside Lucy's car. I motioned him to join us.

"Did you find out anything?" I asked.

He looked at Lucy and then back at me.

"It's okay, you can talk. You can tell her." I said, after introducing her.

Lucy saw the look on Fogarty's face and excused herself to go to the bathroom inside. When she closed the car door, he started to tell me what he had been doing. But before he started, he let me know, if he was going to be of any help, he wanted to deal with me only. No third parties, he said. I agreed.

"Well, the Miller family has changed their name from Muller. They came from the Frankfurt area. And his brother was in the German Army."

"What branch?" I asked him.

"He told some friends of mine a couple of years ago how some of his family were killed in the War, and that his brother emigrated to South America. Also, I found out he paid cash for his home and his auto repair business. I have no idea where he got the money."

"Did he ever talk to you about your meeting any suspicious fares? I mean, people like me asking a lot of seemingly meaningless questions, drawing attention to themselves?"

"No, I've never talked to him."

"Could he have asked you this question through another person? Has anybody asked you any questions like this? Does any of this conversation ring a bell?"

"No," he said, again. And then he stopped and got an odd expression on his face before continuing. "Come to think of it, there was a guy around here a year or so ago. But I had the idea he was a private detective looking into some phony business deal or maybe a marital problem. I thought at the time, the questions he asked me were off the wall and really peculiar. Another thing, he was staying with the Miller family. He might have been a relative or something. He stayed around the area acting like he was visiting his family. I later found out he had been in our army. Whether he was a citizen or not, I don't know. A lot of our troops were not citizens, but then you knew that."

Fogerty was doing his best not to patronize me; but then again he might have been making conversation just to earn his money. But it would turn out that what he just told me would be worth all the money I had paid him.

"What did hc want to know?"

"Among other things, he was interested in whether I had picked up a fare at the airport and driven them out to one of the farms on the other side of town...."

Before he could fully explain, Lucy approached the car and sat down in the front seat again.

"Did you boys have a nice little chat about me?" she asked.

Fogerty looked surprised at her innocuous statement. I could see his curiosity was about to get the better of him. He wanted to ask me in the worst way what was going on.

But he was bright enough to know I hadn't given him all that money for just a couple of hours of easy work. He knew he was being paid to keep his mouth shut and to mind his own business.

And he also understood there might be more coming, maybe lots more, if he played his cards right. He was correct; there would be. Before he left, I took him around the side of his cab and told him I wanted to hire him permanently.

"What do I have to do?" He asked me.

"Keep your eye on her," I said.

"For any particular reason? I mean, what am I watching her for?"

"Check on her once in a while and make sure she's all right. If you see any newcomers in town, check them out and let me know the score. Here's a number you can call. I'll give them your name. Tell them who you are and they'll call me. I'll get back to you at your home or at your cabstand as soon as I can. If she needs anything, you take care of it. But don't let on we had this chat. Here is an additional few hundred. I'll slip you some more when I see you again, but it will appear to be a tip. I don't want any mail coming from me to you, okay?"

"Okay," he said. But just before he left, he acted like he had something he wanted to say.

"Mr. Adair, there is something, maybe.... Never mind, it isn't important. I'll tell you some other time."

Looking back on it now, I wish he had told me. Later was almost too late. But he wasn't sure what was going on, so he decided to mind his own business and keep his mouth shut. That's what I liked about him. That's why I trusted him to do what I told him.

"I suspect you paid Fogarty to look out for me. But it's not necessary, you know. I can take care of myself."

"I gave him a number where he could reach my service

in an emergency."

"Why don't you give it to me and cut out the middle man?" she asked.

"I have my reasons, the main one being I don't want to involve you any more than I have." She seemed satisfied with this explanation, and we dropped the subject. Still, she looked at me as though she thought it was rather odd. But then, I couldn't fault her for thinking that most of my behavior since she met me was odd.

We sat in the car and talked for another hour or so and then went inside to go to the bathroom and ended up staying still another hour. I had given up on catching the last bus at four, and had sent Fogerty away with instructions and more words of caution to keep things to himself. I repeated before he left about how Lucy might need his services, without defining exactly what those services might be. He was not of much further help; he couldn't remember the name of the farm in which his fare had been interested. But he told me this outside the car, where she couldn't hear him. I figured he didn't want her thinking it might be her farm and getting her all upset.

Before he left, I ask him to drop around to the bus station and tag Eric's bag for San Antonio, and to tell them to hold it for me until tomorrow.

After supper at her place, we sat at the table and talked. She came right out and asked me what I was afraid of. I guess my behavior and the look on my face most of the time had given me away.

"The way you hand money around indicates to me you have dipped into that sack of diamonds you swiped. You did say you were rich; are you still rich?

"I'm curious, how did you get them out of the mine, and how did you get them back to the States. A sack that large wouldn't fit into your pocket. Besides being a thief, you're some kind of an accomplished smuggler, aren't you?"

Coming from her, with that perpetual smile on her face, I took no offense. But it was another clear indicator of how the general public might disapprove of what we did. To most everybody, we would be judged as thieves rather than as liberators. Still, there were millions who would have seen it our way and given us the benefit of any doubt. But obviously Lucy was not one of them–not yet anyway.

"I had to get them out. I mean, neither Carl nor Eric could have sent them home by mail. And before they left Europe, the two of them would have been searched several times. The army would have gone over them and their belongings with a fine-tooth comb, before they were allowed to board a troopship. They were mainly looking for souvenirs. Everybody wanted a Luger or a Walther. And some of the troops had them. But I never knew an enlisted man who managed to make it into civilian life with one.

"Officers were not searched. And as far as the mails were concerned, they simply signed a piece of paper swearing they were not sending out any contraband souvenirs.

"You know those bronzed baby shoes you sometimes see hanging from automobile mirrors?" I asked her. "Well, I hit on the idea of having my old combat boots bronzed as souvenirs of my trip across Europe. I found a guy in Frankfurt who did the job. He didn't bronze them exactly. I mean he didn't dip them in bronze the way they usually do; he washed them good, and then he painted them with a light coat of liquid bronze. The way he did it, it hardly added to the weight…."

"I get it," she interrupted, "you stuffed your shoes with diamonds and newspapers and sent them home in the mail. Nobody was going to question an old pair of boots. They figured you were going to give them to your grandkids or somebody; old worn out shoes were not exactly pistols, now were they?

"And people at the military post office had no idea how

much a real bronzed boot would weigh, did they? A twenty-pound bronzed shoe would not have been suspicious." She looked at me as though I was a little boy who had just gotten caught with his hand in the cookie jar.

She started to laugh at the expression on my face. It was infectious, and I joined her. We both laughed like couples often do who genuinely like each other.

"So tell me," she said, bringing me back sharply to reality. "Who's after you, and what are they going to do if they catch you? Why can't you just give them back the jewels? Hey, I said jewels, but I really meant diamonds. Oh, oh, by the look on your face just now, it might be more then diamonds–what?" She strung the last word out, and then said with an all-knowing look on her face. "Did you guys walk off with more than diamonds? How about the Kaiser's crown jewels?

"Before you answer, let me ask you again. If you're able to get *shed* of what's left, will they leave you alone? Is it the military people who are after you or the government–who?"

"I don't really know," I answered. "I mean, I don't have a clue. There was an incident that happened a few years back while I was on a fishing trip by myself. Somebody tried to kill me. There was no mistaking it for an accident; somebody was really after me. I won't go into the details now. Another time maybe.

"When I came home, I enrolled at LSU to finish up my degree. I wanted to do the expected thing, to blend in with everybody else. I wasn't exactly looking forward to working for an oil company. I had other things on my mind. I just wanted to appear normal and wait out the next few years until we made the split. So I figured I would go back to school and finish a degree in geology, and then stay on and study more physics, something I was always interested in. It was the natural thing to do for a graduate in geology in those days. Then my first semester back, this incident happened. It really shook me up, and I have been on the run ever since.

"For a long time, I thought Carl might have been behind it. And then my focus shifted to Eric. I never had any intentions of cheating either of them out of anything. But looking back on it now, I can see why Carl might have thought so. We had an agreement to stay in touch but to do nothing for five years, something like bank robbers do who make off with a big haul. We didn't want to draw attention to ourselves. I got rid of a couple of the larger diamonds at eighty percent of their value. I had to; I had to have money to live on after I quit school. I couldn't settle down with a real job and pay Social Security. It wouldn't have worked. I had to keep moving. But even at eighty percent, they were so valuable that I ended up with a fortune. My problem, believe it or not, was to locate the others and make the split. I tried to contact them via our mail scheme, but you never forwarded my letters. And you never had a telephone. Now, I realize I would've only been able to find Carl. But I was unable to get back to him. I tried, but apparently he had moved a couple of times and I lost track. It's easy to see why, when his letters were not answered, it would have seemed to him as though I had reneged on our agreement. I can see why he might have been really upset, and he would have figured I cheated him." This was only part of the story. But I hesitated to tell her any more.

"What made you think you could get the diamonds out of the mine without being discovered? And why didn't you go for some of the gold ingots?"

"The gold was too closely guarded. I might have been able to get some out under the Jeep before Colonel Bernstein set up his security program. But we didn't try. Actually, we planned on getting assigned as monitors on one of his teams removing the gold. We were naturals for the job, since we had already been tentatively assigned to accompany him on his sorties into the heartland looking for more stashes. We really anticipated getting our hands on a large quantity, when they carried the ingots by Jeep trailers between Room Eight and the trucks at one of the entranceways. But we didn't anticipate the thoroughness of Bernstein's checking and control system. As it turned out, there was just no way to pull it off.

"When we first started talking about the diamonds, we didn't think we could get away with taking any of them. It was just talk, something to pass the time. But we changed our minds when we went inside the vault and saw all those suitcases full of jewelry. And Eric and Carl, of course, easily located the Melmer sack. We also saw an inventory list made by this guy named Thoms, who I later found out was in charge of the bank's precious metals department. The diamonds and the jewelry were not on his list, probably because there was not much by way of metal involved.

"It dawned on the three of us at the same time: there had been no accounting made of the jewelry or the diamonds. Unless one of the generals had remembered seeing the open Melmer bag, we knew we were home free. None of the Germans were going to say anything. If the diamonds were not on some inventory list, and they were reported as missing, the Germans would have been more suspect then we were.

"We knew the generals saw some of the jewelry, but not all of it. Thoms only opened a couple of the suitcases to show them, and there were half a hundred or more stacked in the back. You see, the Germans kept precise records of the precious metals. But what we didn't know at the time, they had also inventoried the suitcases full of jewelry and the diamonds. They just didn't carry the jewels and the diamonds on the same list with the gold. I have always thought Thoms believed we took the diamonds. However, he was afraid of telling anybody because he might have been accused himself. It was his word against ours, and I was a friend of Patton's, while he was an enemy with the taint of the criminal about him. Later, he couldn't say anything because they would have wanted to know how come he didn't say something the first day when he discovered they were missing.

"And another thing, as long as I'm telling you everything: We did make off with a double-handful of American coins. I carried them out in the pockets of my field jacket. It was cold outside and hot below in the shaft and tunnel. That's the way it is with deep rock mines. It can be freezing outside in winter and hot as blazes at the bottom of a deep shaft. Nobody thought anything of my not wearing my jacket, which allowed me to fill the pockets. As for the diamonds, they were easy. We simply tied the sack to the undercarriage of our Jeep and drove off.

"I gave the coins to the other two, but it wasn't really any part of what the diamonds were worth. They might have been under the impression that I thought the coins were supposed to compensate for the diamonds. If so, then they had a right to believe they were cheated.

"As I said, we assumed there was no record of the diamonds or the coins."

"Why was that?" she asked.

I answered her: " Thoms was on site the day after we got there. It was his inventory list we saw the first night, which caused us to believe they hadn't had time to count and record anything but the gold, silver, and the paintings; no one was really monitoring the jewelry, coins, or the diamonds or so we thought.

"It was the impetus we needed. If they were not recorded, they were not going to be missed in all the confusion.

"Lucy, when you told me yesterday about Eric, it was the first I heard he hadn't survived more than a few weeks after the War. It came as quite a shock, not only because he was a good friend, but now it means somebody whom I don't know is after me. And that somebody may very well have killed both Carl and Eric."

It was still early, about an hour before bedtime. Lucy and I spent it speculating about who it was who was searching for me. We made a list, obviously leaving off Carl and Eric. I told her about Carl's widow and what she told me on the phone. I even told Lucy about the statement she made, which at the time struck me as being curious. I mean the one about *the childish games you and your other Army buddy have been playing have gotten him killed.*

"She did say *buddy* in the singular. And if Carl had really told her everything, as she said he did, then his widow knew there was only the three of us conspirators. It meant, according to Carl, the others in the squad were not involved. In fact, it was confirmation they never knew there were any diamonds missing, let alone that we took them. And she wouldn't have known that Eric was dead."

This might not be exactly the truth. I wanted to change the subject. Lucy was just too sharp. I suspected she was capable of deducing the truth of something rather quickly from just a small amount of information. I wanted to talk about something else, but she wanted to continue.

Our list included the FBI and the Army Counter Intelligence Command, and even the Army Criminal Investigation people. We even considered undercover operatives in the Office of Strategic Services, the OSS. They were known to be operating in the area. In fact, I understood they were the first to pick up on rumors of the mine and to pass it on to the CIC.

The German Reichsbank surely had an interest, since they considered the missing property belonged to them; it's a definite possibility. They might have suspected us all along. We had to consider they might have hired private investigators to watch us and then to finally do away with

Carl and Eric after they tortured them.

We even talked about members of the Waffen SS, and others still loyal to the memory of Adolph Hitler. Those people could surely lay claim to the loot. And it wasn't hard to make a case favoring them; after all, they were career assassins. And then there were those in the know from within the ranks of the Army Finance and Accounting Department who might have suspected us. In short: there were a lot of people who knew there was a shortage of Merkers treasure, and they knew we had been the closest to it at one time. And knowing how much was missing, they might have chosen to cut themselves in. It might not even be a stretch for somebody to have told the rest of our squad members, during the course of their investigations. If those guys knew, then you better believe they were mad at us. They would have considered us to be cheats for not including them. Surely, they would have been angry enough to do something drastic if they reasoned they had been cheated out of what they considered their part of an *inheritance.*

And there was another suspect, somebody who was more than just a person of interest. Fogarty had told us about a member of the Muller family and how one of them had gone to Brazil after the War. I didn't explain the ramifications of his statement to Lucy, because it might have caused her needless worry. I didn't explain about the people who went to Brazil being mostly *outcasts*, the *persona non grata* in Germany after the War. And most of those people came from the ranks of the dreaded Waffen SS.

It is not common knowledge, but most people in this country don't know that members of the three branches of the SS are fugitives wanted for murder. Their own people want them for war crimes and crimes against humanity. Many of them joined the French Foreign Legion, and many others immigrated to Argentina and Brazil.

Maybe it was my paranoia acting up again. But I always

believed if the SS was involved, they might have moved a mole here, somebody to watch for me to eventually show up. And that somebody would be keeping his eyes on Lucy. If they couldn't find me, why not stake out the only lead they had–Lucy? And maybe that mole was a Muller; I don't know.

We talked for another couple of hours, longer than we intended. We talked about all my suspected enemies–all but one and I didn't want to talk about him. Was it possible the man in the casket was not Eric? Then who was in the casket the undertaker had seen? Who was wearing Eric's dog tags? Who then had killed this stranger? If it was not Eric, who was it? And if it wasn't Eric, then Eric must have known who it was–Eric must have been the one who killed him, or he was in some way involved. Was it the same three guys on the train, the ones who killed Carl? Had they also killed the stranger? Was Eric one of them? Had they killed Eric, too? Carl's widow told the cops one of their attackers spoke with some kind of an accent; I had read it in her report. Eric spoke with a trace of an accent. Could it really have been him."

In fact, if by some bizarre turn of events Eric killed the stranger and then Carl, it's not likely he is even interested in diamonds or jewelry. Because there's more involved besides the paltry millions in diamonds we took from the Merkers mine. There are such large amounts involved that even the best of friends might fall out and start hunting one another. And right now, I'm skirting the subject, afraid to tell her any more than I have.

Finally, she went to the same bureau as last night to get my bedclothes and pillow. She saw the expression on my face, and sat down beside me on the sofa.

"Look Mike," she said, "I know what you're thinking about us. Okay, I suppose I have no objections to your proposal. But there is more to it than that. And I don't want you to get the wrong idea. It reminds me of something our pastor said on the subject."

She went on to tell me what he had told his congregation. He was preaching on the subject of *Marriage and Family Relations*. "The trouble with young people today," he said, "they want to jump into bed with one another with only the slightest provocation. And, thereby, lies a big problem, which often leads to a break-up. If a marriage is to have a chance of beating the high odds of divorce, then something has to happen: They must first become acquainted; then they must become friends; and they then must marry before becoming intimate. If any one of the steps is left out, they're in danger of ending up as statistics."

That's what she said her pastor said, anyway, and she said it made good sense to her. She went on: "In fact, when I heard him say it, I thought of Eric and me. That's exactly what we did; we skipped the middle part. We never became friends; we became lovers first, before we ever really became acquainted, and we paid the price. Let's not you and I make the same mistake. You stay on the couch, yah' hear?"

What was there to argue about? I lost before I had ever gotten started.

I lay on the sofa thinking about what I had already told her. As I said, we sat in her car for another hour talking after Fogerty left. Then we went inside and ended up staying longer, still talking, endlessly talking. And me continually wondering how much more I should tell her about this strange tale of mine. And all the time wondering how much she was going to believe, and wondering whether she might conclude I had some kind of ulterior motive in contacting her in the first place. I wouldn't have been surprised if this had been her reaction after I told her what else happened after Merkers.

And it has just occurred to me. What about her brother?

Worthington, the undertaker, told me she had a brother. How close is he to Muller. And who is Muller anyway, besides a figment of my active imagination.

As it turned out, when Lucy inherited the farm, her brother acquired no legal interest; apparently her father figured her brother would have forced her to sell if he was included in some kind of trust. She told me this didn't set well with him, which might be expected. Did her brother fall in with Muller then? But why would Muller tell him anything in the first place? Muller doesn't need him, or does he? Why does her brother hang around the area when there's no future for him here; he's not that close to his sister. Is he waiting, hoping they'll drill for oil and maybe she'll cut him in?

I haven't asked Lucy much about him on purpose. I don't want to infer her brother is hooked up with murderers. Still, I can't rule him out; everybody is suspect when you're dealing with figures as large as those I'm talking about. Anyway, the list goes on and on, seemingly with no end in sight. And the more I think about it the more confused I get.

CHAPTER 5...MERKERS, GERMANY, 1945

I liked Françoise; I liked her a lot. Strictly speaking, I should have stayed away from her because *indigenous personnel* were off-limits. But I didn't care. Anyway, the way I chose to interpret the order she was not indigenous because she wasn't German. And it was my job to fraternize with anybody who could supply me with intelligence of interest to Patton's headquarters. If I saw fit to fraternize with a displaced person by the name of Françoise Jardine, then it was in the line of duty and my own business.

I call her displaced, because at first glance she appeared to be one of the vast numbers of Hitler's conscripted who were uprooted and transported to Germany. But in reality, she was far from one of them; she might even be classified as a Nazi sympathizer. You might say she was, once you got to know her and to understand why she was in Germany. But like I say, I didn't care.

The thing that struck me as being rather odd, though, was where she and her sister were quartered. Then, too, maybe it wasn't all that strange when you consider she had a sponsor. If her new nephew's father was an officer in the Waffen SS, then you might expect she would be living in some place besides a barracks without heat or running water. I quickly discovered there were plenty of those, after driving around Merkers *looking things over.*

I tried to stay away from her, but it was difficult. As I told you earlier, I knew I was going to succumb to temptation a few minutes after she sat on my lap in the Jeep. I knew the next time I saw her I would only appear to be engaged in army business. But I wasn't going to let my two sergeant friends and her sister suspect my real intentions.

Our medics kept Murielle for a few days before turning her loose. Since she couldn't walk the mile or so to her quarters, carrying her new baby, I volunteered to give her a ride home. It's not that I am such a nice guy; I wanted to see Françoise again and to learn where the two of them were living.

As we pulled up to her apartment, I saw our other Jeep parked out front. I had no way of knowing whether it was Carl or Eric who was inside. Murielle shrugged her shoulders, meaning she had no idea either. I looked at Murielle and she looked at me, but neither of us spoke.

I carried the baby. As we started climbing the stairs to the second floor, Françoise standing at the top of the landing met us. I wasn't invited in. I figured only one of them was there; otherwise, she would have invited me to at least bring the baby upstairs. I took this as a bad omen for me. I never considered that one or both of my men had the same idea I had. I couldn't fault either of them; but I must say I didn't like it. I handed the baby back to Murielle, telling Françoise I would return to talk to her in a couple of hours.

I started my conversation as though she was being formally interrogated. And maybe she was; if I gave myself the benefit of the doubt. But I knew what I really had in mind. What I didn't know was where it was all going to lead. I told myself my interest in her was the same as Carl's or Eric's, because none of the three of us had been close to a pretty woman since we left England. But my attraction to her was more–much more–and it worried me.

"Françoise, how did Murielle meet Kurt Steinmann?" I had come back later, giving whoever was with her time to find something else to do. Among other things, I wanted to talk to her about Steinmann and what exactly he had been doing in Bavaria.

She had shown me the other mines near Merkers, as she promised. Unfortunately, I had to take Carl and Eric with me on our excursion and Françoise had spent most of the time in the back seat with Eric. I had yet to spend any personal time with her.

There were three mines we visited that day. Two of them were small and appeared to be empty. We found some new Wermacht uniforms and several crates of shells in the third, but no treasure.

In answer to my question about where Murielle met Steinmann, she said: "They met in Paris, shortly after the surrender."

"What was he doing in Paris?" I asked. She had an odd expression on her face as though she might be ashamed to tell me.

"You have to understand what things were like for us a few years ago when Hitler marched into France. But first you have to understand, the War you have been fighting is really an outgrowth of World War One. It supposedly ended in 1918, but it did not. There was just a lull of a few years before it started up all over again.

"Marshall Petain, the hero of Verdun in the first one, became incensed with Winston Churchill for not supporting him against the invading Germans in this War. Petain wanted air support against the overwhelming army of German tanks descending on Paris. But Churchill knew if the RAF was drawn into combat so far from their home bases, they would be all but annihilated, because they would have been sitting ducks, low on fuel, trying to get home after only a few minutes over the interior of France. Petain, on the other hand, saw it as just one more refusal to come to his aid. Britain had refused to help him at Verdun in the First War. And still being angry, he surrendered the French Army and Navy and allied with Germany against Britain."

I interrupted her to ask a question: "Yes, but we Americans stepped in and saved France in those dark days of the First War. As I recall, Britain had her hands full on the Somme and was unable to help Petain. Why was Petain so angry, then?"

"I suppose what you say is true," she said, "but the fact still remains, he had not gotten over his feelings of betrayal by the British. And now here it was being repeated all over again.

"After Petain surrendered, he established a provisional government at a city called Vichy in the south of France. He appointed an administrator, who was a German collaborator, by the name of Pierre Laval as our new leader. This did not sit well with a minority of our population, who branded them both traitors to France."

"How did you feel about what he did?" I asked her. I was interested in whether she, too, was a German collaborator or whether she had ended up in Germany because her sister had gone with Steinmann, and she didn't want to stay behind in occupied France.

"I was no different than the majority. Those who joined the exiled General Charles deGaulle in England were few and far between. Likewise, it was a small number of people who stayed behind and resisted the Germans. As I said, the vast majority of the French supported Petain.

"France was tired of war, and we did not want another long protracted conflict with Germany. We could not afford to lose another generation of our young men.

"I was quite young myself, in those days," she went on to say, "and I was interested in other things besides politics. But the older members of my family were glued to the radio nightly, listening to the news. They were very apprehensive at the rapid rise of Adolph Hitler. At first, they were afraid of him and of the *nationalistic spirit*, which he had revived throughout Germany. But as they watched Germany transition from a nation mired in debt and unemployment to one with a stable currency and economy, they changed their minds about him, as did most of the others we knew.

"We were all impressed with his new German government, and we wearied of the seeming inability of our democracy to solve our problems. We longed to have a dictator of our own; we wanted similar changes in France. Also, there was another large segment of our population who believed communism was the wave of the future. Petain saw an alliance with Germany as the best way to stop this creeping Russian political influence. So you can see, we were a fractionated people; indeed, it was said by some authorities that a civil war would have broken out in France a few months after her surrender if it had not been for the German occupation…."

I broke in to say: "I have been with a few of the forward elements entering your towns, and the people turned out to welcome us with open arms. How do you reconcile this with your statement that the vast majority of people supported Adolph Hitler?"

"Have you seen the picture of Hitler taken standing alongside Petain, immediately after the occupation?" she said, a little miffed that I would question her. "But as soon as the fortunes of the Fuhrer began to change, so did our people. By the advent of the Invasion, there was hardly a Frenchman who was not pro-Allies and against the occupiers. We could see the *handwriting on the wall* and wanted no more of Hitler. Almost the same thing happened with Mussolini in Italy."

"Françoise, I can see a need for the Gestapo, and of course, the regular army, the Wermacht, as occupiers. But I'm not sure I understand why the SS was in Paris." I did, but I wanted her to talk more about Steinmann and less about recent history. As I saw it, he was the key to more treasure in Bavaria. And I didn't want her to stray too far from the subject. What she had been telling me was interesting, but I was running out of time. And as I said, I came to see her for personal reasons as well. And I didn't want to spend the rest of the afternoon talking about politics and the War.

She had apparently not made her point yet and wanted to continue on. I didn't stop her. "When I told you we French allied with Hitler, I meant that literally. From the outset we fell in with the goals of National Socialism. And of course, one of those was the eradication of world Jewry. This had been a more or less hidden agenda in France. But once the Germans descended on us with their message of hatred for the Jews, we fell right in step with them; we hated Jews, too, because it was German and the thing to do.

"I never personally hated Jews," she said. "In fact, I could not see how they were going to pollute the Aryan blood line. I did not even know what that was, but I was soon to find out from Kurt.

"Where did he meet your sister?" I asked

"I don't remember," she said. "It might have been in the *Bois* or on the *Champs*, I don't know. We used to go walking on Sunday, and there were many German soldiers who were always trying to pick her up. I was, of course, sent along as the *duenea,* and they weren't interested in me."

"Not then, maybe. But I expect they are now." That was the boldest I had been to date. I could tell she was still innocent by the way she looked at me. I almost thought she blushed.

"Kurt spent a lot of time at our house; Murielle and my father liked him. The three of them spent endless hours talking about how a greater Germany was going to make a better world. Kurt practically worshipped Adolph Hitler. And he was not a bit bashful about extolling the virtues of the Fuhrer to anybody ready to listen. In fact, that was his job when he first arrived–I mean, indoctrinating various worker groups and students of all grades at our schools. You understand, of course, that in the beginning the Waffen SS was charged with the task of furthering Nazi doctrine by propaganda if possible–but by force if that became necessary. It was the force I objected to. However, in the case of my sister and family, force was not necessary. Then, too, food was hard to come by and Kurt always showed up with groceries and a huge salami or bratwurst. And he always seemed to have a couple of bottles of fine wine with him. I figured he was not only an officer, but one who associated with those in high places. He seemed to be able to get anything or do just about anything he wanted to do."

"I know, but what was he really doing in Paris. I mean he was not there to teach political science to students, was he?" I asked her, appearing naïve.

"Oh, no!" she said, the smile gone now, replaced by a frown. "His task was much grimmer than that, I am afraid. And here you should pay close attention to what I am going to tell you. I know this to be a fact; but I have never told anyone what he told Murielle."

"What did he tell her?" She had my undivided attention now; the gold in Bavaria could wait.

"There are American airmen in *Buchanwald*!"

"What's Buchanwald?" I asked.

"It is an SS *death camp* like *Dachau* to the south of us, only much worse, according to Kurt."

"You mean like those in Poland? Like the one at Auschwitz the Russians have reported finding?"

"Yes. Let me start at the beginning; you are getting confused."

At almost the exact same time she was telling me this story, Patton was personally entering the camp at Buchanwald. A few days earlier, an element of his Third Army had discovered Ordruf, one of the notorious satellites to that place. Patton was notified of the horror, his men had encountered and he didn't believe them. It was like the last War, he said. Germany had committed atrocities, but nothing to live up to the Hearst newspapers' accounts. This, he said, was the same thing as in 1918. For the longest time, Patton had been in denial about reports coming from the Russians about Auschwitz. Such a thing as death camps was too horrible to contemplate and, therefore, it must all be just a rumor, an exaggeration. But when his officers insisted he come and see for himself, he did just that. But first, he invited Bradley and Eisenhower to accompany him.

When my radio dispatch reached his ears that American officers were prisoners there or had been, Patton was beside himself. His anger had been mixed with shock and a deep sadness. But now he became furious and he wanted action. Better than that, he wanted revenge.

Patton had just been shown hundreds of bodies stacked like cordwood waiting to be cremated. Thousands more, who were nothing but skin and bones, were lying side by side waiting to die. He was inspecting a warehouse full of naked bodies when he got the word from me through General Earnest that American airmen had been imprisoned in that hellhole. He never questioned what I told him. He was prepared to believe almost anything of the Germans now. He could take no more. He walked out of sight of the others and became physically ill, and then he asked Eisenhower if he could be excused. He said he wanted to get on with the War.

Eisenhower flew into a rage at this news and what he was looking at. He ordered General Earnest to round up all the residents of the towns of Buchanwald and Ordruf and to parade them through the camp. He had a battery of journalists and photographers on hand, taking pictures of the townspeople standing next to piles of corpses. He made sure there was no one who could later say it never happened or that it had been staged or that they never saw anything. He told one group of journalists it was for the benefit of German grandchildren, and to show the American fighting man what he had been fighting for, in case he was still in doubt.

Word had gotten to Eisenhower months before that some of his soldiers were reported as saying they didn't personally have anything against the Germans. He turned to Bradley, saying: "Well I guess this will take care of that problem."

Immediately, he began to dole out rations to those who were the worst off. Then he issued a formal statement: "I have seen one of the death camps for myself, and it's much worse than the world has been led to believe."

General Eisenhower issued an order to his senior aide to find out from his medical people what the minimum number of calories was to sustain life. Then he ordered all German prisoners to be fed just that amount and no more.

Our forces had cordoned off an area upstream of the Remagen bridge for a hurry-up confinement area for prisoners. It had none of the facilities of a Geneva Convention camp. It was a makeshift, crowded, muddy, vermin ridden hole. Unfortunately, most of their veterans returning from combat were in poor health, and thousands died within a few weeks as a result of the imposed living conditions and General Eisenhower's diet restrictions.

According to Françoise, Steinmann knew about our aircrews at Buchanwald. In fact, it was the real reason he was stationed in Paris. The *French Resistance* had set up a network to find and extricate downed flyers from France back to England. The Gestapo knew about it, but so far had little luck in bringing much of it to a halt. Finally, it became Steinmann's job to set up a counter-intelligence group to penetrate the Resistance and to capture American and British flyers.

Françoise told me he jumped into this new job with gusto. Here was finally something he could get his hands on–something that would make a real contribution. He told Murielle and her father at dinner one night that he was elated with his new assignment. Furthermore, he said, it was guaranteed to keep him in the Paris area near Murielle for some time to come. Françoise remembered that particular night as one of the happiest for her family. But the idea of capturing young Allied flyers and sending them to a probable death was repugnant to her, especially when Kurt explained in such livid detail how it was all going to work.

Kurt told them the old prison near Fresnes, on the outskirts of Paris, was to be used as temporary housing for these prisoners of war. There, the Gestapo would extract all the information he wanted about the *Underground* and the *Maqui*, by legitimate methods if possible, but by torture if it wasn't. Once in the hands of the Waffen SS, the Germans no longer considered them to be under the protection of the Geneva Convention.

Steinmann explained that when they were through with them at Fresnes, if they were still alive, they would be shipped to one of the death camps. There they would be systematically worked to death for the good of the *Fatherland.* But she said it was obvious there wasn't going to be any distinction made between them and Jewish prisoners, because they couldn't afford to have any survivors who had witnessed the atrocities committed at Fresnes.

She said the three of them sat and discussed the horrors of Kurt's new plan as though they were talking about cattle.

It was at this point she started becoming disillusioned with the *New Reich*. And she realized then her family were traitors to France.

The following day we continued our discussion. I told her there must have been a mistake, because Patton's troops found no Americans at Buchenwald.

It was then Françoise told me a curious story. Murielle said Kurt told them a *Luftwaffe* officer had earlier made a routine courtesy call at Buchenwald. He said one of the American prisoners, who spoke German, and at the risk of his life, stepped forward and blurted out that he and some sixty-five aircrew members were being held there. The Luftwaffe flyer said nothing; what could he say under the circumstances? But Kurt expected there might be trouble. It was obvious the Luftwaffe wanted to transport them to one of their *Stalags*; the reason being that if the word got out, the Americans and British might also ignore the Geneva Convention's rules and take reprisal on thousands of German fliers in English and American prisons. They could not afford to start a war within a war. She then went on to tell me how the Luftwaffe came back in force with trucks and troops and made the SS give them up. She said, according to Kurt, this had occurred two months earlier.

Steinmann had advised the camp commander to shoot the Americans when he suspected the Luftwaffe officer might return. The commandant considered doing so, but he was afraid the War was going to end in an unconditional surrender. He was afraid they would hang him for such an offense. Kurt told Murielle they were all going to be hung, anyway, if they ever fell into Allied hands. He told her that he had personally shot several flyers he caught trying to escape at Fresnes; it was an object lesson to the others. That was another reason he wanted to shoot them all, because their comrades could identify him later.

Françoise wanted to talk some more. She wanted to

continue to tell me about Buchanwald. It was as though she needed to let loose for the first time, to release all her pent-up emotions. She knew so much and had said so little that she felt guilty, as though she had played a role in it all. Where Murielle had been in love with Kurt and approved of everything he'd done, Françoise was more or less an innocent bystander. She wasn't, of course, but there was nothing she could have done to change a thing. Objection to Kurt and his business would have alienated Murielle, and might even have brought the wrath of the Gestapo down on her head. So, in the end, she said nothing and acted as though she approved, which she didn't.

We had been talking about Kurt and Murielle and how they first met, and how she ended up leaving France to come to Germany. "He was a few years older than Murielle–about your age now." With that comment, she smiled, and I confess I started to feel warm all over. I liked her. She was young and pretty, and she was smart, sharp, and well informed.

When I first met Françoise, I couldn't help but wonder whether the circumstances of her daily life might have jeopardized her innocence. But now sitting across from her, listening, I put those thoughts out of my mind, simply because she had had Murielle and Steinmann to look after her. And of course, Steinmann now thought of himself as a member of the family and he treated her as though she was his younger sister. Any soldier caught in a compromising situation with a young French girl, who was under the protection of a *rising* SS officer, was axiomatically headed for the Russian Front. I suspected it would have been a brave *Aryan lothario*, indeed, who paid her any more attention than to say *guten morgen.*

A funny thing happened to me while listening to her story. My mind began to wander; my sinful thoughts had vanished. And I found myself entertaining others that were not only downright honorable, but might well have been born in heaven.

I always thought marriage was a desirable institution. I also thought it was better to first seek out and find a way to support a family before getting seriously involved with a woman. I had observed that activity outside this pattern often led to difficulty in later life. As far as I was concerned, it increased the already high odds of divorce or of somebody getting themselves hurt.

To date, I hadn't progressed very far down this *royal road to romance*. When the War came along, I became more of a *will of the wisp* than I had been before. And up to a few days ago, I had no idea what I was going to do with the rest of my life. Now, everything had fallen into place. I can do anything I want. I can go anyplace and stay as long as I want; and of course, I'm now in a position to marry anytime I please and to support a wife in grand style. In short: I had taken a quantum leap forward, bypassing a very important step, which was whittling out a career for myself. The diamonds had made me independent. And from the moment we decided to take them, I had all but forgotten about the thing weighing most heavily on my mind since I started school several years ago–the problem of my career or lack of one.

"What was Kurt's unit doing here is what you really want to know," she said. "Well, when Hitler saw how the new Vichy government welcomed him, he wasted no time in instituting his *final solution to the Jewish problem* in France. And do you know what happened? No! Well, I will tell you–and this is something no Frenchmen should ever forget–we helped Kurt and his SS round up other Frenchmen who just happened to be Jews. And in spite of our national motto, '*Liberte, Equalite, Fraternite*,' we helped them carry our neighbors off to slave labor camps, where they were worked and starved to death just like Jews from other enslaved countries."

I had been kind of daydreaming as she talked. All of a sudden a crazy thought brought me back from a place warm and comfortable where I had been languishing; in fact, it came sailing through my brain like an express train. You know the kind of thing you keep a secret because it's just too preposterous to discuss with anybody, not that you would want to. Well, this one flashed through in an instant; and thankfully, it never rattled around much at all before it flew out the other side. But unfortunately it wasn't gone forever; it would return again and again–*how was I going to feel about having Kurt Steinmann, a monster of the first water, for a brother-in-law.*

It took Bernstein and two of his officers a week to arrange for the storage of the treasure in a bank vault in Frankfurt. And then it took another three days to move it. In the meantime, Bernstein had contacted Manson Eddy and asked his permission to organize a company strength task force for the purpose of ferreting out more hiding places. Based on what Françoise told me, and corroborating statements from displaced persons, there were more. And perhaps they contained other millions in gold waiting to be discovered.

Eddy liked the scheme, as did Patton. But Eisenhower was reluctant to approve of the idea at first. Then he hesitated to agree to the size of the search expedition Bernstein had in mind. Actually, Eisenhower, and to some extent Bradley, believed all Germany's confiscated loot was stored in the Merkers mine. After seeing it for themselves, they didn't understand how the country could still possess any more gold. Eisenhower's intelligence people agreed, and so did the bank officials at the mine. They told him the Merkers treasure was all Germany had left. In fact, they had been trying to figure out a way to get some of it distributed or Germany wasn't going to be able to pay her troops. Also, a supposedly neutral Sweden had threatened months before to curtail the shipping of any more machine tools, unless Germany took care of the millions she owed in unpaid bills.

I remember Bradley telling the bank guy not to worry too much about paying the troops, because they weren't going to be in business much longer. And then he added something to the effect that as soon as Patton left Merkers, the last thing on the Wermacht's mind was going to be their paychecks.

According to my own analysis of Eisenhower's intelligence reports, the Waffen SS had given up on the Wermacht being able to stop the Allied and Russian advances. That's why they were hoarding the country's remaining assets, along with their own stolen loot. They saw their only hope for survival as being a mass retreat to the Bavarian Alps. There, they hoped to fight on indefinitely, forcing an eventual negotiated peace.

They wanted desperately to avoid unconditional surrender, likely to result in them being tried as war criminals and hanged. It was a wild dream of Hitler's, planned out by the remnants of his most fanatical supporters, who had pledged to die for him. But Patton's advance caught them before they could put their wild scheme into action, and he stopped them cold. That's why there had to be more treasure, squirreled up somewhere closer to Bavaria, unknown to all but a few SS officers. Colonel Bernstein agreed with me.

In the end, Eisenhower acquiesced. But he approved of a much smaller organization than Bernstein wanted. He authorized him to proceed with only two Jeeps and two Carryalls, along with my squad and one more. We were ordered to stay behind our lines and to quietly proceed in our hunt without alerting the population. The last thing the

general wanted was rioting by millions of starving home-
less looking for Nazi gold.

CHAPTER 6...SAN ANGELO, TEXAS, 1950

We had been sitting in this joint outside of town most of the afternoon while Lucy listened to me talk. Of course I left out the personal stuff involving Françoise.

It was one of those places you find all over the Southwest where they have a string band and crowds pour in after dark. The music is *Texmex,* although Mexicans are seldom in attendance. And any one of them foolish enough to venture in for any reason might find himself virtually in enemy territory. These places, and I suspect this one is no different from all the others I have known, is rough and downright dangerous if you're a stranger and insist on having a few beers and then start shooting your mouth off. And for a southerner like myself, from another part of the South, well, I might just as well have been a Yankee or a Mexican.

Lucy had asked me about the Waffen SS. And I confess I knew very little about them at the time I met Françoise other than that we had the utmost respect for them as soldiers, but not as human beings. When we were in their area of operations, our intelligence briefer was the first to let us know. Always, we were warned of the stiff resistance we could expect from the Wermacht when the SS was behind them. That's one of the reasons they put them there in the first place. Regardless of how badly things were going for the regular army, they were afraid to retreat. The SS were far more ruthless with retreating Wermacht troops than we ever were.

The poor reputation of the SS in this country started at the Bulge, where they took several hundreds of our soldiers prisoner and then summarily shot them. Of course, if you talked to Russian soldiers from the Eastern Front, they would have told you this was a common occurrence. I mean, we are just now coming to understand the extent of the atrocities they committed among prisoners, and among the Russian population as a whole.

"Who were these people anyway that you should be so darned scared of them?" She wanted to know.

I knew she was like most Americans. That is, she had heard about the SS but had not paid much attention to what she had heard. Others, particularly Americans of German extraction, were in a *mind-set*, which came to be called *psychological denial*. That is, the stories about their atrocities among the Russian population were like the death camps; they were just too hideous for comprehension. No human being was capable of treating other human beings the way they treated civilians on the Eastern Front. It just was not believable, so it was mostly denied.

I felt that way in the beginning. But then I was to change my mind as the War came to a close, and the truth slowly began to emerge.

To me the SS is little more than recent history now. But I still have a need to justify my taking of the diamonds from Merkers. A long time ago I settled with my conscience, but I'm a long way from convincing Lucy that it wasn't a crime. And if I can't do that, then there's going to be a hole develop in my plans rather rapidly. Maybe if I could convey exactly how we felt about the SS while sitting in the Merkers tunnel that night, she might understand.

There we were with unknown millions of Reichsbank and stolen Waffen SS loot right in front of us. No, it was more than stolen; it was taken by force by the most ruthless hoard of soldiers since the ancient Khans. And we were afraid our army was going to give it back, not to the rightful owners, who were mostly dead, but to a fund to restore the society of a people who were responsible for siring these very monsters in the first place.

If I could answer her question as to who these men were, if I could show her in some small way what they were, then maybe she would see it as we had. There's one thing for sure; I have no intention of giving any part of it back–I have made up my mind to that. I want Lucy, but I want the diamonds, too. They say money is not everything in life. But I figure it's mostly poor people who go around saying it. I have been poor, and I have been rich. But between the two, I decided long ago that rich was much better than poor. However, like George Patton, I would have split up the gold between the combat veterans of Third Army, that is, if I could've stolen it and gotten away with it. But I still would've kept the sack of diamonds for the three of us. Under my plan, there would have been no need for any *International Tripartite Commission* to decide who owned the treasure which, incidentally, as of this date, has proven virtually impossible to determine.

CHAPTER 7… CAMERON, LOUISIANA, 1946

I like to fish. In fact, as far as I'm concerned, bass fishing with a popping bug and a fly rod among the burns of the bayous is a serious substitute for heaven. The burns, as we call them, are high grass, reeds, and cattails in the swamps that have caught fire, usually from lightening strikes. They burn for several acres before they die out, leaving a good sized lake of fresh water where the large mouth *lunkers* proliferate.

I started going there with *mon oncle Renee* when I was a boy, and I never tired of it. He lived up near Lake Charles. We used to drive down to this favorite fishing spot of his at least once a week when I stayed with him and my aunt over the summers. And I used to manage to go back a couple of times a year, after I grew up and started college. During the War, I couldn't wait to get home to go fishing again.

I thought about staying in the army after the War. In fact, George Patton encouraged me to do so. He had been appointed military governor of part of Germany, and he was putting together a staff of people he liked who could speak another language besides English.

Maybe I would have–I mean maybe I would have stayed in if I hadn't been heir to a third of a fortune in diamonds that you know about. And then there's this Ravensbruck thing, which you know nothing about.

I had started back to school to get the few credits needed for a degree, but mostly to have something to do while trying to keep out of sight. Working in Patton's headquarters would have made me too visible, while this Commission took an inventory of the Merkers mine and then decided to pronounce it all present or accounted for. They never really would have, you know. But they had to go through the motions. Then, also, they had to divide it up in an *equitable* fashion–we three being the only Americans who ever got so much as a *phennig* of it, no thanks to them.

Albert Thoms and Werner Veick, the Reichsbank officers who were the original custodians, were still very visible and still unknowns. And I had no way of knowing if or when either one of them was going to change his mind and tattle on us to the authorities. I just knew I didn't care to be around if one of them ever did; I didn't cotton to the idea of sitting around in some office where I could be plucked out of my chair and tossed into the military prison at Leavenworth.

These thoughts about fishing were running through my mind early one Saturday morning soon after I returned to school. I had called and reserved a boat and motor from this *Coonie,* a friend of my uncle's I had known for years.

I parked my car and quickly disappeared among the ferns and other semi-tropical vegetation. In front of me loomed a large homemade, home-lettered sign. It was secured by four guy-wires holding it to the roof of a bait shack at the end of a path overgrown with Spanish moss, hanging down almost head high. It announced the proprietor's name as Jean Brulet. And that he sold or rented just about anything you were in the market for fish-wise, including bait, motors, and boats.

His shack had one of those old-fashioned round Coca-Cola signs with a pretty girl telling you it was *refreshing*, nailed to the side. And next to it was a rusting Lucky Strike sign, soon to be a pre-war collector's item, with a pack of *satisfaction* on a green background with a red oval.

Inside could be found everything from soup to nuts, including a large bowl of fresh boiled shrimp and one of hard-boiled eggs. He kept them in a cooler, where he would bring them out if you were hungry and had six-bits. The opposite counter was lined with punchboards, beef jerky, pickled eggs, an assortment of razors, combs, ball caps, and you name it. Under his glass countertop, which he kept locked, was fishing tackle of a hundred varieties.

I walked in, and we exchanged the usual Cajun greetings. He welcomed me back in French, telling me he had been thinking about me and wondering if I was ever coming to see him again. French, incidentally, is about all that is spoken in these parts. Tourists, unless they are known and have ties to someone in the area, are not usually welcomed. They are not exactly prohibited from coming down from Lake Charles and over from Baton Rouge spoiling the fishing, but they are not welcome either.

Papa Brulet was of the old school of *coon-ass,* a synonym for the stereotypical *redneck* found in some other parts of the South. He was *Old World*, having never been much farther than New Orleans. And then he never stayed there very long, once he got there.

He was turned out in mufti: felt hat, bib overalls with front pocket bulging a can of Prince Albert, and a red bandanna encircling his neck, which he was fond of removing every once in a while to wipe the sweat from his corpulent features. I had noticed before how he did this, more from nervous habit than from necessity. I guess it gave his hands something to do. He would untie the loose slipknot with one hand; then with a swipe across his face, he would rewrap it around his neck. When I was a boy, I was fascinated with his dexterity.

I wondered if he still had this same nervous tic, as I turned off the highway and onto a dirt road leading to his parking lot and the swamps. He did. But now it was even more pronounced. I mean, it was noticeable as though something was really bothering him. He kept glancing out the window at his dock, while he fiddled with his neckerchief. The thought occurred to me that maybe he had other customers who were using his boat ramp or were loading up a rental.

But there was nobody outside. And there were no other cars in his small parking lot, either, which made me wonder even more why he was doing that neckerchief thing of his. Also, he did not offer me a cup of *burnt bean* coffee, a trademark of the bayous, and a custom among the descendants of the Acadian French. I thought this might be a little odd, too. But then I figured, in spite of what he said, he might have forgotten who I was. He knew I was native because I spoke to him in French. But I figured he might be getting old and had forgotten me after a four-year absence.

The eastern sky was just turning pink as I maneuvered my aluminum rental through the narrow, twisting, channel to the burn. As I said, I had phoned old man Brulet and reserved the motor and the boat days before, although I didn't think he had enough business this late in the season to warrant my doing so.

I started out, motoring at less than walking pace through the narrow bayou to the local burn. The grass and reeds were even more pronounced since last I was there, probably because of reduced traffic resulting from the War. In some places, I still had to use the paddle to negotiate the sharp turns. Nothing had changed. My job, when I came with my uncle, was to sit in the bow and push off with an oar when we hung up in the turns.

I remembered two places where there were nests of *cottonmouths*. I had good reason to remember both of them. Once, I almost stuck my hand in the open mouth of one in the near dark of the early morning. It was coiled to strike, and I used my hand instead of a paddle to push off a nearly submerged log. I fell back in the boat as though I had been propelled from a howitzer, and I hurt myself, much to the laughter of another coon-ass, my Uncle Renee. I wondered if they were still there–the snakes I mean.

He used this occasion as a teaching moment: "Every Cajun boy should be familiar with the moccasin snake if he was going to survive in the swamps," he said. I remember the lesson and the occasion well. I had picked myself up from the bottom of the boat, even as my uncle retrieved the paddle from the bottom of our skiff. I thought he was going to club the coiled snake that must have been most confused at what was transpiring around him. But Uncle never hit him, which he could have easily done. No, he watched the snake watch the raised paddle just within reach of his coiled length. As the snake measured the distance by instinct, Uncle reached around to the side of him and snatched him off the log. He threw him over in the reeds with one easy motion, all the time lecturing me on how it was to be accomplished without getting bitten. Snake bit this far from a hospital was to find yourself in a world of hurt. He explained that all the Boy Scout techniques of cutting the fang wound and then sucking out the blood was useless. Blood, he explained, circulated once through the body every two or three minutes. The dose of poison reached the heart in half that time. If you survived the initial shock, you could be in danger of losing the limb without immediate hospital attention. And the closest hospital was fifty miles away. So, in short, you had better put yourself in the hands of a higher power if you were ever moccasin bit. And it helped immensely, he explained, if you were of the persuasion that believed in something besides the Boy Scout manual.

You might wonder how anybody could enjoy themselves alone out here in this wilderness at this time of the morning, thinking about such a macabre and off-the-wall subject. But I was home, home among the Spanish moss, the reeds, the snakes, and the occasional alligator. This was the place; this was what I most often thought about over the past few years. When others were thinking about bright lights, malted milks, and the girl next door, this was my favorite memory of home.

I was about halfway to the lake when I heard the distant sound of another outboard. Where it came from, I had no idea. It wasn't at the boat landing, which made me wonder for a second if it had, for some unexplained reason, been hiding in the tall grass of a feeder to the main bayou.

My first strike was a two-pound mullet. They hit hard, harder even than bass. But they're considered to be a trash fish, heavy scales, and full of bones. Whether they're good to eat or not, I don't know; I never ate one. Anyway, I was looking for bass. Usually, I catch and release them, but this time I was hungry for good fresh fish.

Another thing about the bayou country: you can easily find a Cajun girl who is most interested in cooking blackened bass, with real butter and poured over wine, for some young fisherman who has the makings on a stringer of an interesting *tete a tete*. There were several I knew, who were waiting back at LSU for just such an invitation. That might have been on my mind when I hooked the big mullet and then through it back, wishing it had been a bass.

It was times like this when my mind often wandered to the subject of girls. It didn't usually stay long on girls in general, but usually homed in on one in particular–Françoise. It had been several months since I had last seen her. She was still living with Murielle, who was waiting for her Kurt Steinmann to come home. Murielle had not come to terms with what she had been told: Steinmann was not coming home. Not in the foreseeable future, anyway. If he had not been killed or captured, he would have been arrested when our forces caught up to him.

Once the darlings of the nation, now the German in the street eschewed everything SS. By some convoluted reasoning, they sought to purge themselves of their guilt by blaming it all on Hitler and his fanatical Waffen SS. Somehow, no matter how many atrocities draftees in the regular army committed, they had been held blameless. They had all been *forced* to fight, don't you know. And they were all just doing their duty. *But the brave SS units*, as Eisenhower once called them, were something else again. They were not only guilty–they had been thc willing instruments Hitler used to bring on the chaos in the first place, according to the new German mind-set. And, they were no longer held up to the youth as objects of hero worship, either, to admire and emulate

I had approached the opening to the burn and motored across the small lake to the far side. All along the *shoreline* was fall-down, rotting trees, home to the big bass. The water was fairly shallow, covered by lily pads and overhang. What appeared to be land was not land at all. If you stepped out of your boat you would sink to at least your waist in water, and perhaps another six inches or so into a silt-covered bottom. The water was dark, like most swamp water in these parts. It was that way, not because it was dirty, but because there was no sunlight radiating off thc bottom and the water itself was filled with humus.

The first time I saw the people in the motorboat was when they entered the burn. I could see they had rented the boat from Papa Brulet. But when did they do this? I had no idea, and it sent a chill up my spine. And where were they hiding when I came down the narrow channel?

There were two of them with fishing poles. But it was soon evident that they were not much interested in fishing; you could tell, because they had casting rods instead of fly rods. Not many people want the expense of coming to this place to fish off the bottom with the heavier rod. Not this time of day anyway. You could do that better most anyplace in the state with no trouble at all.

I watched them take position about fifty yards or so to my right. They broke out a cup of coffee, threaded some worms on hooks, and dropped their lines over the side as though they were fishing for brim, a flat fish we call *Sac-a-Lai.*

That was the first thing that gave them away. They were not from around here. I knew they weren't. But to make sure, I hailed them in French, asking them where the best bass fishing was. They gave me a funny look and a shrug of the shoulder. I suspected they couldn't understand me, and as it turned out I was right.

The way this lake is best fished is by standing up in the boat and casting a small feathered *bug* close by the logs and lily pads, which run out about fifteen feet from the burn line. The bass often rise from under the pads and snatch this small wooden lure as it hits the top of a pad or lands close by in the water. Some people prefer a *dead horse floater*, a kind of heavier top water lure, sold by Brulet. These are good, also, but with light tackle they're too heavy for very much fun. But whatever lure you fancied, few ever fished among the logs and lily pads with worms. It just wasn't done by anybody I ever knew; it was too easy to snag your hook. And then most of the time you lost your fish among these same snags.

I folded my bug in toward the pads, whipping the line back and forth every few minutes. This is one advantage in fishing alone; you're not in danger of hooking somebody next to you with a bass hook. As the feathered bug touched the water, I gently pulled it back toward the boat with erratic little jerks, causing it to make a kind of popping sound. After a few of these, if there was no strike, I would lift the lure from the water. Then with wrist motion, not unlike with a dry fly, I would whip it forward toward the *bank* again. Then I would reach down and paddle a few yards and try it again in a new area to my left.

The two in the boat to my right watched me for a few minutes and then lifted their anchor and moved a few feet toward me, keeping the same distance between us.

This was not only peculiar behavior, but it was considered to be downright rude. The sun was well up by now, and I could see these guys were not from here. Their complexions were white as though they had not been out in the tanning sun all year long, the color of your average fisherman in these parts.

I never expected what happened next: without any apparent reason, they started their motor and headed straight for me. I waved them off, but it was evident they had no intention of going around to take position on my other side or motoring over to the far side of the small lake. Before I could do anything, they rammed me. I realize now their object was to knock me in the lake, where they intended to do their thing.

I had just picked up the paddle to oar a few more yards to my right, to offset the breeze, which was now moving me in toward the shoreline. When they plowed into me, my first instinct was survival. I confess, before my stint in combat, I would have done nothing at all, except hang on and act outraged. But now I swung the paddle at the *jabroni* in the bow, as I fell backward in the boat. The sharp edge caught him across the ear, knocking him in the water. He grabbed what was left of his nearly severed ear, letting out a piercing howl. It must have hurt terribly, but I didn't care.

My senses had shifted into survival mode and I was acting on instinct, reflexes, and training.

I started the motor and advanced the throttle. I headed toward the burn opening as fast as the five horses attached to the stern would allow. I entered the narrow channel too fast and plowed into the reeds on the far side. My goal was to navigate the narrow bayou faster than they could, abandon the boat as close to my car as I could, and get away from there as fast as I could.

But I lost valuable time backing out of the reeds. As I prepared to head for the boat dock, I saw the one in the stern struggling to pull the one with the cropped ear out of the water and back into the boat. I was scarcely more than fifty yards down the channel when I heard their motor start up behind me. I could also tell it was more than a small trolling motor. It sounded as though it was made to cross large lakes at high speed. I suspected they were going to do the same thing I did. They were going to plow deep into the reeds trying to negotiate the turn. Hopefully, they wouldn't be able to back out. And hopefully, one of them was going to have to get out to pull the boat free. And more hope–I wanted their prop to jam and allow me to get away while they spent time cleaning the fouled propeller.

But none of this happened. This was to be my unlucky day in several ways. I heard their motor start. They were coming, and I was going as fast as I could.

There is an optimum speed for these narrow reed channels. If you go too fast, you end up in the reeds just as I had. It happened to me again on the very next turn and again before the winding bayou fetched the dock. This time, though, I fouled the propeller and killed the motor. I had to lever it up forty-five degrees and then lean over the stern to clear it with my hands.

I was not afraid of being shot. This was not on their agenda. I knew what they were after, and I knew they wanted me alive. I was scared now, very scared–scared almost into a state of panic. I had to keep talking to myself, telling myself to slow down.

One of the quickest ways to lose your life in an emergency is to panic. I had been taught this by old soldiers and had passed it on to replacements as the senior voice of experience. Still, it was easy to talk about but hard to do. Not only do you lose valuable time when you panic, but you start making silly mistakes. That's what I was doing now. I seemed almost helpless to stop it from happening.

I had been listening to their larger motor become louder and louder as I struggled to free my propeller. At one point, I knew I was going to be overtaken, even if my motor started on the first try. If it hesitated more than a couple of turns of the flywheel before starting, I knew it was all going to happen right here, right now. And after they found out what they wanted to know, they were going to weight me down with my own anchor and leave me on the black bottom.

I had all but given up when I began settling down. When I realized this might well be my last day anywhere, for some reason I calmed down and began to think. *I can't outrun them; we have another mile to go*...Then I hit on an idea. *I would let them catch me.* The only out I had was to get caught–but I was going to choose the spot.

I was fast approaching the sharp turn where the second nest of moccasins used to congregate. I could plainly see the logs where one of them had been waiting for a fat frog when I interrupted his vigil years ago. I hastily scanned the log, as the enemy boat drew nearer and nearer. But there was no snake this morning. I gunned my engine and made for the other nest. If there were none there, which was highly probable, I intended to reach in where I knew they had been and feel around for one. If the snakes had moved to another residence, my only alternative would be to pull up a broken limb and throw it in their boat, yelling *Cottonmouth! Cottonmouth!* I had seen this done a couple of times as a dumb practical joke, indulged in by characters having consumed too much Falstaff, and it never failed to empty a boat–rapidly. Even if you know it's a stick, if it's the same color as a snake, your brain can't cope with the shock when you hear those words. No matter what you do, your brain will not over-ride your instincts. You become scared out of your wits. You shift into panic mode and you bail out, feeling very foolish afterward. But, nevertheless, you find yourself in the water, while your boat churns away out of reach.

I would like to tell you this nest was still doing its duty, I mean checking and balancing the frog population, and that it was chock-full of nasty little critters with white mouths, resembling a large cotton bole or a newly washed golf ball. But even as I reached in, I felt nothing but old rotting tree limbs. I knew if I was to survive without a real live snake, *plan B* was going to have to work. I stopped my boat and reached into the old nest and went through the motions of feeling around. I came up with a reasonable facsimile of a snake; it was a limb, tapered, crooked, dark and slippery with moss. I pulled it up from the water, dripping, feigning a struggle to hold on. If it slipped from my grasp, I would be undone, a victim of my own genius. I raised it over my head, exaggerating the strength of the writhing *snake*. All the time I was acting terrified; screeching the magic words that was hopefully going to bring about the desired results.

The tapered limb landed in the middle of the adjacent boat. The guy with the ugly ear ducked, and it landed next to the guy with his hand on the throttle. He saw the crooked branch as a flash in the sun, a kind of glimpse, as he let out a scream and rolled over into the murky water. The boat crowded by me in the narrow channel; raging, with open throttle. I had just enough time to swing again with the heavy, sharp oar at the guy having only one good ear. This time the other one was completely severed. I could see it dangling, as the former owner flew, catapulted into the reeds at high speed.

Just before I started my motor to pull away, I yelled out again: "Hey *Patch*, look out! Alligator! Alligator!" Then I slapped the water twice with my paddle and repeated these other magic words. The water was apparently deeper than I thought, because the two of them were clinging to the reeds and a few cattails, screaming unintelligibly for dear life. I took no further notice of this crazy scene of two grown men climbing over each other, floundering in the reeds, trying to escape an imaginary alligator.

I thought about burning down Brulet's business. But instead, I busted his motor and punched a hole in his boat, by way of showing my contempt for what he did. And I never took the time that night for any co-ed cooked gourmand bass dinner, even though I could have filled out my stringer from a fish market. I hurriedly packed my car and drove out of town, swearing never to be so predictable again, or ever to locate in one place very long.

CHAPTER 8...SAN ANGELO, 1950

The night was sultry, typically West Texas in the early fall just before the *blue northers'* set in. The pull down shades in her upper bedroom were rolled up, and just a hint of moving air was testing the chintz, single panels, suspended from five-and-dime brass rods. The trimmed kerosene lantern had been set back from the curtains in the unlikely event of a gust from a freshening breeze.

There was a harvest moon. But it would go virtually unnoticed here, since cash from the cotton crop would not likely be sufficient to warrant any celebration.

What exactly awakened her, she was unable to say, when she later told me the story.

It seems her little dog was the first to detect something unusual happening outside. He started to growl, quietly, climbing upon the bed beside her. She reached over and stroked his coat, thinking an animal outside had awakened him and that he would go back to sleep. But he didn't. In fact, he grew more restless, if anything. She said she knew the dog and could tell by the way he was acting how far away it was. Then she realized this *whatever* was not an animal and that it was close by. She supposed it was some kids in a car parked down the road.

The dog settled down momentarily; she went back to sleep, only to awaken with a start. She glanced at the illuminated dial on the bedstand clock. She had only been asleep an hour. It seemed much longer. She must have been dreaming the dog was barking

She reached down at her side from force of habit, and he wasn't there. She sat bold upright now. The dog never went outside in the middle of the night. In fact, he seldom left her bedside at night without a compelling reason. What was going on? She stepped toward the open window and looked out, banging her head on the screen. She had done this before without thinking, when she was scared for some reason or other. She reached first for her robe and then her *pacifier*–her Winchester, wrapped in an oiled rag under the foot of the bed.

A man in her bed would be welcomed at a time like this, if for no other reason than his presence. And maybe all she needed was assurance, somebody to lean on, somebody to tell her to go back to sleep. But the cold steel of the rifle barrel was more than assurance. She could feel it against her bare leg, and it gave her a sense of power. When it was in her hands, it was as though she was no longer submissive prey at the mercy of unknown elements that might threaten her. It was times like this that she felt energized and the equal of any man. *Is this the same power a man feels with an increased level of adrenaline? Is this the way he feels when he hears the clang of the bell for the first round or the whistle for the kick-off, or the charge into no-mans-land? Is he scared, but confident of victory, because of his strength and superiority, maybe in proportion to his natural level of testosterone? Do I have an elevated level of testosterone that makes me feel this way? Does it make me want to attack instead of cower or run away? If I do, I'm glad I do; I like it.*

She had cut a small hole in the right pocket of her

bathrobe, solely for the purpose of carrying the short-barreled rifle. She found the deep pocket almost covered the lever and stock, while the folds of her robe hid the barrel. The wide sleeve of her robe concealed the top part of the stock when her finger was on the trigger guard. She often carried the rifle this way when she went outside at night. Not that there was any real danger lurking about, but it just gave her this feeling of power she enjoyed so much. She would have been surprised if a professional had described it as a libido thing–one having psychosexual overtones. But then again, maybe not.

She removed the rifle from her robe and actuated the lever action, placing a shell in the breach. She closed it and double-checked the safety before replacing it in her pocket. Most firearms load in the safe position. But most people double-check to make sure the safety is on. They know it is, but they always check just the same. She was no different. Now with her hand on the stock inside her pocket, she was ready to look for her dog. She still looked the part of a defenseless woman living alone, but the hormones driving her mind and body were anything but female at this moment. She was armed and dangerous and she liked the feeling. It was different and unique, and she liked it.

She felt her way down the darkened stairs, softly calling for her dog. But he never came; apparently he had gone outside through his hole in the screen door. She had the advantage over any intruder. She was like a blind person who has lived in a house for years, one who knows every sharp corner and the exact placement of every stumbling block in every room. But outside it was different. Outside, under the full moon, she would lose her advantage.

She moved to the screen door and peered outside, hoping to see the dog in the yard. It was then she saw the hint of a shadow moving at the edge of the cotton. The moonlight, reflecting off the few boles left on the waist high plants, reminded her of Christmas tree ornaments on a dry tree still standing after New Year's had come and gone. She couldn't be sure, but was there a car parked on the side of the road midway up the next rise? She saw the shadow again. But instead of panic, she felt a kind of adrenalin rush from the gained advantage in position, as though she had seen an opponent's hole card in a game of stud. She could see him standing there now in the moonlight. She could shoot him anytime she pleased. She hesitated for an instant, wondering if he had her dog. Then it came to her that he was not coming toward the house, nor did he intend to. He was standing there as if he was some kind of guard–a posted sentry–which might mean there was somebody else lurking about.

She latched the screen, and then slowly closed and locked the wooden door. *If I had my dog, as far as I'm concerned, they would be free to fool around out there all night long.* She was in her fortress, her castle, and she was armed. She moved silently through the house to the kitchen. *My plan is to exit the back door and then crawl to my garage, where I can observe anybody coming alongside the house. I'll be able to see the sentry and his accomplice. And I'll be able to shoot them both and be done with them. And then I'll be at liberty to search for my dog; my dog is the important thing.*

These thoughts were racing through her mind as she slowly entered her kitchen. A shaft of moonlight was entering through the side window above the sink. And then she saw it, just below the towel and the dishes on the counter set out to dry a few hours ago; the drawer where she kept her larger knives was open. Somebody who knew it was going to make a squeaking sound when it was closed left it that way. But maybe her cabinet was not unique; maybe most old wooden cabinet drawers in this part of the country did the same thing. Somebody locally would have known this. She froze at the thought. But still no panic, which surprised her. She was still in the attack mode, and would stay that way as long as her dog was in danger.

She had discontinued wondering *who* the intruder was and where he was from, and she was now giving the problem of *where* he was her full and undivided attention. Her mind was focused, her senses alert as they had never been before in her life. She felt good, like a drug addict with a fix. She felt a kind of elation and a desire for combat. Her hand felt the stock of the rifle, even as her index finger inched down the lever and found the guard encircling the trigger. Her thumb felt along the side of the *action,* searching for the safety. All she had to do now was tilt the tip of the barrel and pull the trigger.

Strange how your senses are energized at a time like this. She had never paid much attention to the intricate scrollwork on the side of the rifle before. But now she caught herself unconsciously tracing the pattern with her thumb. Crazy thoughts were dancing in and out of her mind, trying to disrupt her focus–*how does the scrollwork on my commemorative Winchester differ from the regular scroll on the standard rifle? And what sort of husband would have thought to give his wife an expensive rifle for a Christmas present? Maybe an un-romantic one who had considered giving her a box of tools instead. But my rifle turned out to be more personal than any lingerie or perfume ever could be, and it was more appreciated than any gift I ever received. Are these extraneous thoughts of mine nature's way of slowing things down? Is it the way things in the body are set up to control the flow of adrenaline? No doubt about it; too much, at a time like this, would make for a disaster. Marvelous how the body works to insure preservation. Just enough of the drug to make me think clearly, but not enough to confuse me with ideas about screaming or running about and giving my position away to my enemy, who might be waiting in the dark.*

She moved along the kitchen wall in front of her refrigerator. *Why isn't my dog barking? Somebody will pay dearly if they've harmed him, beginning with the shadow at the edge of the yard.*

All at once she could smell something, something foreign to her nostrils. She tested the air like a doe sensing danger raises her head and sniffs, nostrils flared and ears cocked high. *The smell is a composite of several smells. One is definitely onion; the other is garlic mixed with wine and tobacco. Who drinks wine and eats garlic around here?* And then it happened. She had inched another foot forward past the refrigerator when she was literally lifted off her feet. Her right arm inside her robe was pinned to her side by a steel-like band. Her left arm was dangling free but useless. She could feel the cold of a butcher knife pressing against her throat, even as her head was tilted back and upward in an uncomfortable position. She could feel a trickle of blood running down between her breasts as the sharp knife broke the skin. He did not utter a single word.

He carried her upright in one arm through her darkened living room and up the stairs.

She removed her finger from the trigger and thumbed the safety back *on*. Her mind was telling her finger to wait. If she made a mistake now she could very well shoot herself in the leg. She remembered, of all things, reading someplace where a high percentage of gunshot wounds in the old west were self-inflicted. Gunfighters shot themselves in the leg practicing or executing the fast draw. If her rifle went off now, it would put a hole through her leg, and she would probably bleed to death. But she had to keep her hand in her pocket on the trigger guard to keep the rifle from flopping around and being discovered. As long as she could keep her finger near the trigger with her palm holding the stock, she could remove the safety in an instant, and her assailant would be the one to meet his maker.

They entered her bedroom, which was somewhat brighter than the staircase due to the open window. He unceremoniously dumped her on her side on her bed. She landed on the rifle; it cut into her leg and made her cry out. He took no notice, but sat down beside her. She could see him now, a rather large man with a stocking cap pulled over his face. There were two generous holes and a slit for a mouth. *No way will I be able to identify him unless he talks. He's not going to just walk away. Whatever he wants, he is going to kill me when he gets it. But if this is so, why does he bother to hide his face?*

But then maybe it was not what she thought he was after; as she felt his hand move up her bare leg, she instinctively moved it away, sensing he was smiling under his cap. Still he said nothing. Then he removed a five-by-eight card from his shirt pocket and handed it to her. She couldn't see what was written on it–*more evidenc*e *he is local and I know his voice.*

He rose from the bed, as though her leg had been a fleeting thought that superceded for a moment his real purpose for being there. He stuck the knife into the wooden closet door and reached for the lantern. He turned up the wick with a practiced hand. Lifting the shade, he struck a light with a *Zippo*, and then replaced it.

I can shoot him now at any time, and then pick his buddy off from the window. When it comes right down to it, though, it's not all that easy to shoot somebody close up. What does he really want? That's it–money–he thinks I have oil or cotton money squirreled up somewhere. He has access to my bank records. He knows I've nothing saved, and he thinks I keep it in my mattress. But if he thinks that, he's not really from around here.

She hadn't long to wait. As she strained to see what was written on the card, he moved the lantern closer to the end of the table so she could see. It read: "I am going to ask you three questions, and if you do not answer, I am going to rape you and then burn your house down on top of you. How do I get in touch with Red Adair? Where is Ravensbruck? And where are the letters from Eric's army buddies?"

She motioned to her bureau drawer, telling him there was a bundle of letters, the ones I had given back to her, in the corner. He walked over and took them out, putting them in two separate pockets of his trousers. Then he walked back over to the bed and pointed to the names Ravensbruck and Adair on the card.

She tried to explain that she had never heard of Ravensbruck. She told him that the two of us, Eric and I, never mentioned or wrote her about any such place. And she didn't know how to contact me directly. She told him she reached me through a third party, and that she would give him a name and an address if he would leave her alone. He appeared to be dissatisfied with her answer, although she was at a loss to understand why.

He motioned that he was going to spill the lantern on the floor and barricade her in the room. Then she said he did a curious thing. She said he turned the lantern down and motioned for her to undress as he undid his belt and prepared to violate her. She waited no longer. Her finger found the trigger again. Her thumb found the safety and she applied pressure. The rifle bucked in her hand. He was plummeted back against the dresser, falling face forward in the middle of the table. The lantern went crashing to the floor, and the room erupted in flames. She grabbed the bedspread, threw it over her head, and bolted through the flames to the door. She never had a chance to see whose face was under the cap.

The dry wooden house went up like the tinderbox it was. She ran down the stairs and out on the porch. The man she had seen earlier was running toward the house now with a pistol in his hand. She loaded another round in the breach and fired. He dropped and never moved. She had hit him squarely in the chest.

She found keys to the car, but no identity cards in his pocket. She kept the keys and several hundred-dollar bills and some change she found in his wallet.

She ran around the back to the tool shed looking for a shovel. Her immediate thought was to bury him and then leave as quickly as possible, never to return. Her only regret was her dog. She called him again and again, hoping the light of the fire would cause him to come to her from wherever he was hiding. She waited, calling, but he never came.

The door hasp to the shed was secured by a wooden peg, which she lifted and entered. There was her dog; busily gnawing on a large bone that earlier must have contained a generous helping of fresh beef. The dog was oblivious to her or to the fire or anything but the bone. *No wonder he never barked or came when he was called.* She locked him back up for safekeeping, satisfied the flames wouldn't reach him. Then she went about her grizzly work, like some Halloween ghoul silhouetted by the light of the burning house.

She rang the doorbell three times at Worthington's palatial home. There was no answer, so she went around to the second-story bedroom window and called for him. His wife got out of bed and answered: "Who's there, and what do you want?"

"It's Lucy Schneider, and I want to talk to your husband."

And then the inevitable question: "Is it important?"

Of course it is, you idiot, why do you think I'm here in the middle of the night, to talk about dead people? But on second thought, maybe that's not completely wrong. "Yes, it is.... No, it can't wait till morning.... Right now, if you don't mind,"

A moment later she opened the door and invited her in, telling Lucy her husband would be down in a minute. She never offered her any coffee or a cold drink; a breach of etiquette that told Lucy his wife was miffed by her abruptness. But Lucy didn't care what she thought. They had never been friends, and they were not likely to ever become such.

"What's this all about, then?" he asked, as he took a seat immediately across from her chair. The undertaker deliberately avoided sitting across from the coffee table in order to be closer. He suspected what she had to say need not fall on the ears of any of his family, and he was right.

"We're in trouble," she said, just above a whisper.

"We," he said, "how do you figure *we*?"

"I think I just killed Eric Schneider and shot another friend of yours by the name of Kurt Steinmann."

He took a deep breath and turned almost as white as one of his clients. "What in the world are you talking about?"

"Listen to me, you old fool, and listen closely. Unless you want to be in a federal prison by morning, you'll quit being coy with me. I know everything about you."

The undertaker looked at her with an all-knowing look on his face and then he said: "Joyce? You mean my secretary–it figures...anything she's told you is a lie. Be careful what you believe about me...."

She cut him off in mid-sentence, all business: "Get that stupid look off your face and get rid of that smarmy tone in your voice. Joyce is a dear friend of mine. She was a friend when none of the others of you sanctimonious hypocrites would be my friend. What else she might be is none of your business, either. And if you try and make it so, you better believe I'll call your wife down here and tell her exactly, and in the greatest detail, what Joyce means to you and not to me."

"Lucy, believe me I have no inkling of what's going on. If this has something to do with that army major that popped in a few months ago, I'm going to tell you what I told him: I don't know anything and I don't want to know. And I resent your inferring that Eric was alive up until a few hours ago. My professional reputation is at stake here."

Worthington stopped talking, setting back in the sofa-chair, thinking over what Lucy had said about him and her friend Joyce Wagner. He looked at Lucy, and contemplated the shambles his life was about to become if she breathed a word of this to his wife. It mattered not if Lucy had any proof; he realized for the umpteenth time, he and Joyce had been skating on thin ice for a long time. Anything Lucy had to say, his wife would believe, and it would result in him breaking through and drowning in icy water.

"What do you want from me? What do you want me to do?"

"That's better," she said, with an air of triumph. "Now pay attention!"

"Hello, Fogerty, Lucy Schneider here, get hold of Mike Adair, and tell him if his offer still stands to meet me at noon the day after tomorrow on the first bridge of the *Riverwalk* in San Antonio. Got it? No questions remember? And Fogerty, you'll find a hundred-dollar bill tucked under your name in the phone book by your cabstand. Yeah, and I'll see you. Good luck to you, too." With that she put the money in the telephone book and left.

She went by Joyce Wagner's apartment. She asked Joyce if she could take a shower and borrow some clothes. She explained to her what had happened. But Joyce didn't seem particularly upset. She was not as surprised as she should have been. In fact, Lucy suspected Joyce of knowing more about what was going on than Lucy did. Joyce didn't seem outraged or curious or anything of the sort, which left Lucy even more confused. Maybe Worthington was innocent, as he said. Maybe Joyce was the only one knee-deep in my business. Now she suspected Joyce might have been one of the principle players from the beginning.

There was no time for explanations. She knew if Joyce was being paid to report to some sinister group when I showed up at the mortuary, then she was not going to say anything now. And if Lucy had misjudged her, then she knew no amount of questioning was going to tell Lucy a thing she didn't already know.

She dressed hurriedly and then poured some water for her dog into a throwaway plastic bowl. Then she helped herself to one of Joyce's Cokes in her refrigerator. She kissed her on the cheek and left. Joyce stood at the head of the stairs and watched her leave, crying.

CHAPTER 9…SAN ANTONIO, TEXAS, 1950

Young men, new in the service, have a need to extol the virtues of their hometowns. I guess it's because they're homesick, and talking about it makes them feel better. I don't know for sure about this, I just know they do. One of the landmarks worth talking about is the Riverwalk in San Antonio. But this was not always the case. During the War years, no self-respecting Texan would mention the walk by the river, even if he was goaded into doing so. Then, it was a sorry blight on the community: bottles, cans, and debris strewn about, a hangout for drunks, thieves, lower classes, and unsavory elements to be found in any large city.

Bob Wills, the country and western star, used to sing about his San Antonio Rose–*deep within my heart lies a melody, a song of old San Antone'…Enchantment strange as the moon up above.* And then years later, the good citizens went to work on his enchanted *moonlit path by the Alamo,* eventually making it a showplace for tourists as well as the natives. Now, it's the place to go, sidewalk cafes, hidden gardens, terraced restaurants with up-scale dining, a few luxury hotels catering to those of the money class. And it's still being developed.

This is where Lucy told Fogerty she would meet me, on

the bridge across from the Alamo. It was a place of some prominence, somewhere I had never been before. I parked my car and took a cab. She was prompt. The driver knew where to let me off. I kissed her, and the two off us walked down the promenade alongside the river for half a block or so. It was a pleasant fall day. We both wanted to walk for several more blocks, but not wanting to take the time now; we had too much to talk about.

The river was wider than I expected. It was very slow moving and coming within inches of the bank, resembling a swimming pool. We stopped at one of the sidewalk cafes just yards from the water. It was shaded with a large overhang, rivaling the best in ambiance of those on the Paris West Bank.

A waiter, whom I first suspected of affecting the manner of a European wine steward, complete with key to the *cellar* hanging from his neck, approached us with his list of libations. I looked it over, and then showing off a little myself, ordered a medium-priced Medoc from the St. Julian vineyards. His ears pricked up, and he began taking more than casual notice of us when I spoke to him in French. I was as surprised as he was when he replied in a Paris vernacular.

I tasted the wine, and he poured. I've never gotten used to this ritual. I suppose it's all right for the French in France. But most Americans are uncomfortable ordering wine, and then acting as though they know the difference between a *Gargonne* and a *Chaud Soliel* table offering. We roll it around on our tongues, because we have seen other people do the same thing. Are we supposed to bc determining if the vintage suits our palate or if there are pieces of cork floating about and some have gotten stuck in our teeth? And what does *Joe-Blow Six Pack* know about vintages anyway?

When the waiters ceased their hovering, retiring out of

earshot, we started talking. That's when she told me the story I've just told you. We lingered after lunch, confused, watching the passing parade. She knew what was on my mind: "Lucy, why did you tell me about your friendship with Joyce?"

"Because you were going to hear about it from somebody besides me. I didn't want that. I wanted to tell you it was no big deal. It's not what you might think or what Worthington thinks. We were two lonely people, just friends and that's all. In fact, I think now she cultivated my friendship for another reason entirely. I think she and Worthington might be part of an organization that killed Eric and your other friend."

"But you told Worthington you thought you had killed Eric. You thought he was the intruder bent on raping and torturing you. What makes you think so? You know this sounds really far fetched…?"

"I know. I'm confused. But there was a moment when I would have sworn he was Eric. And then when I found my dog…. You know, Eric gave me the dog when he was a pup for my birthday. He fell in love with him and would never have harmed him. Anybody as violent as the people you've been telling me about would have killed the dog to be rid of him. I can't reconcile the intruder's other actions with those of somebody who planned to carry around a bone just to occupy a dog. First off, who knew I had a dog? But then I guess Joyce did, and maybe some of the others in town. She had been to my house several times over the years."

"Let's come back to that in a minute," I said. "Why did you go to see Worthington in the first place?"

"Well, he's the county coroner. He'll be called to examine the remains they'll find among the ashes of the house. I want him to report them as being me at the inquest. Easy enough for him to do. I want to disappear. Whoever sent the two I shot will likely send others. I don't want to live forever under this shadow, waiting for the other shoe, so I want to disappear. And I want to leave Joyce and the rest of them behind me, too."

"Does this mean me, as well."

"No, not you. But the others–yes.

"I had a long time to think, driving down here. Now I believe Joyce befriended me because Worthington put her up to it. And now I know some of the story about what the three of you did in Germany, I can see the picture more clearly. Now, I can see why she sought me out soon after she came to town. And now I don't feel the same at all about her. I feel used, and a little chagrined that I didn't see through her much earlier."

"Do you think there was anybody else in town who might be on the take from whoever wants to find me?"

"I don't know, but I wouldn't be surprised."

"What did you do with their car? Was it rented?"

"Yes, I dropped it off in front of the local Hertz with a note and some money. The rental agreement was in the glove compartment. They both probably gave fake addresses that won't be of any help, I don't think. They're square with Hertz. Nobody's going to miss them or be looking for them."

"How can you be so sure?" I asked.

"Because I have it figured the people who want you will conclude the obvious: the two got what they wanted from me, and then took off on their own, sort of freelance, looking for you. What else are they going to think when they fail to show up? And then when they read my obituary and the articles that are sure to be in the newspaper… and neither Joyce nor Worthington is going to say anything I don't want them to say. They've nothing to gain and everything to lose if I were to talk to his wife later on. And another thing: whoever they are will assume I knew about this mysterious Ravensbruck or Ravensberg thing, and that I told those two all about it…geez, I can hardly spell it"

"You never heard the word before I mentioned it?"

"Never."

"Then I'm satisfied Joyce, and maybe Worthington also, were using you as a contact to eventually get to me."

"What is it? Where is this place? What's it all about, anyway?" she asked me, her voice rising, but not really expecting an answer.

"One more question about you and Joyce, and then I want to forget about it forever." She nodded her head, and started to cry.

"Was Fogerty aware of your friendship with Joyce?"

"I think so. Why? Did he promise to tell you some big gossip secret if you gave him some more money?" she asked, wiping her eyes.

"No, nothing like that. It's just that I think he was about to tell me something once. It was something he thought I might consider important. I guess he thought your friendship with Joyce was something I should know about.

"Can you think of anything distinguishing about either of those two guys," I said, wanting to change the subject. "Try hard. Was there anything about them out of the ordinary?"

"Yes, I do remember something. The one who grabbed me reeked of garlic and wine. And his clothes smelled of a different odor of tobacco."

"Okay," I said, "now we're getting somewhere. Many Europeans smoke a cheap Arabic tobacco because Turkish blends cost too much. Also, some of them just like it; it's more pungent, more acrid. But one thing about it, as you say, it's different. As bad as our cigarettes are, those are twice as bad, and the odor permeates their breath and clothes for twice as long. And once you get a whiff of it, you never forget. I've never known an American who used it; I never knew one to acquire the taste–never. So that rules out Eric. I think we can forget about him. But then who contacted Worthington the undertaker a couple of years after the War–and why? Is there some kind of payoff to keep Worthington and Joyce quiet about who is buried in Eric's grave, or were the two of them being paid to wait for me or Carl to show up at your place? Could it be that simple?

"Tell me something. Do you remember how tall either of them were?"

"Not too tall–about your height, I guess. Why? Oh, there is something else," she said, after a long pause. "The one I buried carried a cane and walked with a severe limp. And something else, his ears: he looked like somebody had stuck his head in a lawn mower."

CHAPTER 10...SAN ANTONIO, 1950

We rented a room in one of the hotels mid-way down the walk. I was planning on staying for only a day or so, but ended up changing my mind. I told myself I needed to help her find an apartment. We never looked for an apartment. We toured around the countryside, even swimming with some kids in the river at San Marcus. We thought about going over to Seguine and visiting Eric's mother, but gave it up. We were getting to know each other, something she said we had to do before we even thought of marriage.

We looked forward to nightfall on the river and a new restaurant every night. And then the after-dinner conversation. And sooner or later it came back to the same thing: who were those two back in San Angelo?

"Why do you think the one you buried was Kurt Steinmann?" I asked again. "You know, Lucy, I've told you Steinmann was SS, and that they were a special breed. Maybe the world will never see the likes of them again.

"In the early days of the *New Reich*, after Hitler came to power, there was a rush to enlist. They were Hitler's *special troops*, and he had to keep their membership low, building up slowly and quietly to offset the regular army. The old guard in Germany, the industrialists, intellectuals, and the

Prussian officer elite, who were worried about Hitler, supported the army. They figured he could not do much to change the old ways, as long as they controlled the armed forces of the country. That's why Hitler made sure this new army of his was the best trained and best equipped in all of Europe. Sooner than later it became the equal of the regular army, and then it far surpassed them. At that point, he didn't need the support of the *feldmarshals*. Then he began changing things on a large scale. And the people liked the changes; and they liked him even more. Then it went further, much further. They began to venerate, if not worship him.

"The point is he had his choice of the *crème* of Germany's youth. They were going to be an elite army made up of a master race. In the beginning, when all they were supposed to be were ceremonial guards, they had to pass a rigorous mental and physical examination. There was also a height requirement. You had to be at least six feet two inches tall. You say the guy you buried was about five nine or ten.

"Steinmann was the equivalent of a colonel, and from what Françoise told me, he would have had to have been one of Hitler's early members. Later in the War, when manpower was becoming scarcer, they had to settle for shorter volunteers–some as short as six feet. No, we can forget the guys back at your place; they were not tall enough. I don't think we'll ever find out who either one of them was. My thinking tells me they were professionals, hired to find me and torture me until I told them about Ravensbruck. That doesn't mean they weren't SS-sponsored; they well might have been. But you have to understand the SS didn't enjoy freedom of movement around the world. They had been convicted as war criminals at Nuremberg, and several nations, including Israel, had their best operatives looking for them. When the SS wanted something, they hired it done–directing the operation from Brazil or Argentina."

I never told her they were the two guys from Cameron bayou. But that doesn't mean they're not buddies of Kurt Steinmann's. I thought if I told her that story it would upset her all the more. What I wanted was for her to settle down. Maybe she gets a job and stays put until I can get my business concluded.

The last night we were together, she asked me yet another question. Why this particular one, I don't know. "Mike, why did Hitler invade Russia, and squander his armed forces. I thought he was allied with Stalin?"

"He was," I said, "but he never trusted Stalin. His intelligence people convinced him Stalin was only being his friend in order to give the Soviets time to build up their army. Stalin had the largest and best-equipped army in Europe. It might not have been as up-to-date as some, but it was huge, and Hitler knew it. He invaded Russia then, because he was afraid the longer he waited the more powerful the Soviets would become. He was afraid England and Russia would attack him first. He figured if he did nothing, and Stalin had time to modernize his equipment, then Germany was doomed for sure. He couldn't wait and gamble on a war on two fronts, but that's exactly what happened. You see, he thought Churchill and Stalin were conspiring to destroy Germany.

"Hitler couldn't understand why they were so jealous of him; after all, what he was doing to make Germany prosperous and the envy of all the world could easily be accomplished in the rest of Europe. In point of fact, he said he wanted to help them build a Utopia just like his. That is, he did until they ganged up on him, which they did, according to him.

"And that's where the Waffen SS played a major role," I said. "They were the most intelligent men in all of Europe. They were recruited from every nation, even from those nations that were occupied, including France. Their officers came from the ranks, in most instances, and they trained with their men. They fought at the front. Even their senior officers led from the front and not from the rear. This resulted in an *esprit* unsurpassed by any army before or since. This, plus their rigorous conditioning and indoctrination as to why they were fighting, made them the most feared adversaries on any battlefield. They were more feared than the Knights Templar of the Crusades.

"I don't mean to bore you, Lucy, but this is the kind of people the two of us are up against. This is a capsulated view of our enemy, who was indirectly responsible for the lives of 26,000,000 Russians, and directly responsible for murdering 6,000,000 Jews and gypsies. Last of all: they are monsters, and we mustn't forget it."

"Yeah, but that's my point," she said. "Why a personal war with them? Why can't you just give them back the diamonds? Why must we live like multimillionaires? Why can't we just be plain everyday people?"

"Lucy, it's not about diamonds. It has nothing to do with diamonds–nothing at all. It has everything to do with gold. Gold, Lucy! I have, or did have, 700 of their large gold bars. By my calculations that's almost 14,000,000 dollars of 1945 Waffen SS money–not Reichsbank money–Waffen SS money. But due to circumstances I couldn't control, I lost most of it. But I do have more than two and a half million in gold bullion left. But if the government ever removes the 35-dollar limit, as they're expected to do, that could balloon to an astronomical sum–maybe even to hundreds of dollars an ounce. And don't be confused; none of it came from the Merkers mine. It's a separate hoard.

"You can see it has little to do with diamonds and everything to do with gold. And there's something else we took, which is almost of equal value to them…."

"What in the world could that be? And even if it is, why

not give it back along with the gold?"

"You don't understand. It's nothing tangible–nothing having any intrinsic value, nothing marketable that I know of...."

"Indeed. Something as valuable to them as that much gold...."

I interrupted again, getting myself in deeper and deeper, wishing I had never said anything, knowing I shouldn't try to explain it.

Then I blurted out something. I was trying my best to get her to stop questioning me without scaring her to death, but I was not succeeding. I said: "Lucy, this thing I'm talking about is so sinister I don't want to talk about it now–maybe not ever."

CHAPTER 11…NEW YORK, 1950

That story I told Lucy implied the Waffen SS was after us. Actually, I'm not as sure now as I used to be. But I just don't know. But after the incident at the burns and now this one involving Lucy, I really don't think they're members of the old SS. At least those two were not. That is, I'm reasonably sure they're not. But as I say, I've no reason to suspect anybody in particular.

That's why I'm here in New York. I come here once in a while to check on a couple of investigators who work for me. You see, several governments got together some years back and formed this International Tripartite Commission I have mentioned. It has been given the task of accounting for the Merkers treasure; then they're supposed to be giving it back to the rightful owners, whoever they might be. But this outfit is a joke, a laughingstock. They've been working now for almost five years, and have made absolutely no progress. That's not quite true either. They've made some: they're close to drawing up a paper about how they're going to proceed–one they can all agree on. How do I know this? you ask. Well, I've a friend who works for them, a good friend who owes me a bunch of favors. And as long as I don't get too pushy and ask him specific questions, he's willing to keep me pretty well informed about what's been going on. Whether he knows what I did during the War, I don't know. But I'm pretty sure he knows about most of it, the real important things, that is, because he was there.

His name is Ralph Wahl. He comes from Salt Lake City, where they speak German at home.

Ralph was an undercover OSS agent who spent the War working under deep cover in and around Hitler's Obersalzberg. He reported to an OSS supervisor who worked closely with our counter-intelligence group. That's how I came to meet him. The three of us, myself and two of my sergeants, helped him out of the area. We did in fact save his life. However, that's another story, which I'll tell you about later. But that's where the favors come in, and suffice it to say, he has never forgotten.

He was in the inner circle of the OSS before he hooked up with these commission people I'm talking about. That's how come he knows about most of what we swiped. Then, too, I had to talk to somebody after Carl was killed, so I went to him for advice several times. Actually, it was not advice I was after. I just wanted to feel him out as to what the Commission was doing, so our lunches were billed as social affairs rather than what they really were.

We walked around the subject of treasure a couple of times during the next few months. Each time I saw him, he opened up a little more to me. This last time he advised me in the third person, in so many words, to keep a low profile and to keep my mouth shut. He said anybody who stole any of that loot was going to be *putting his tit in a wringer* if he came forward now and confessed. Even if he gave it back, it wouldn't change anything. The reason was, he said, because they figure there's no way anybody was going to give it all back. The Commission's brain trust has conclud-ed the *thieves* might want to return some of it as a way of getting them off their backs. Then the perpetrators would continue to live comfortably off the rest. But there's no way the Commission is going to believe it's all coming back intact, just as if nothing had happened.

First off, this Commission doesn't understand how anybody could do such a dumb stunt. I mean, they figure it was really off-the-wall for anybody to believe they could just walk off with millions without getting caught. And secondly, it would be double-dumb if they tried to give it back now. The Commission never considered that keeping it might be more of a chore than it was worth. This would never occur to them, Ralph said.

I lost no time contacting him again when I arrived in the city. He was kind enough to have lunch after I told him I was only going to be in town a few days. He said he was glad I called, because he had something important to tell me.

He told me there were some new things afoot. He said the Commission had assumed certain additional police powers. Whether they're constitutional, however, has been mostly ignored. At any rate, they have officially added two new branches to what they're calling their *Operations Division.* People in these new branches have been given the responsibility for tracking down anyone who might be a player in a scheme to keep part of the treasure. These tracking guys are professionals, recruited from the ranks of wartime counter intelligence organizations. He said they were little more than ruthless soldiers of fortune. They're kind of *salaried bounty hunters*, is the way he describes them.

I asked him how all this differed from what they had been doing for the past five years. He tells me that heretofore, these so-called trackers or enforcers or whatever have been freelance. Now they're part of the organization. Now they have *official status* and the support of all government intelligence and police agencies, including Interpol. It's going to make a lot of difference, he tells me.

While he was talking, he was looking straight into my eyes. I knew what it all meant, and I was becoming even more afraid than I had been.

He went on to tell me these teams had been furnished dossiers on more than a dozen people. They contain not only fingerprints and photographs, but everything the army knows about them, including family and friends, and friends of family, acquaintances, etc. Some of them are accused fugitives, while others have been designated persons of interest. And this is the big thing–the real big thing–he said; these trackers are going to be given huge bonuses if and when they catch somebody on their list. And they'll be given another bonus if they take them alive and then make them reveal where they've hidden the stolen loot.

This was illegal as all get out. Everybody knows it, he told me, but nobody cares. There are big payoffs anticipated, so nobody cares.

Then he told me something I knew nothing about. He said there were some ex-British soldiers on this list also. He said the Commission believed they had gotten wind of the Merkers treasure through their own sources and had made a try to find it before we did. He said the two Germans, Veick and Thoms, who showed up on site the day after we got there, told them this. He said the Germans don't suspect them of pilfering any gold, but they could have gotten off with a lot of Reichmarks, which were stacked near the elevator in the tunnel.

Something occurred to me as I was listening to him. I thought those marks were going to be almost worthless, but not so. Backed by American gold, they haven't lost much of their value–at least not as much as I believed they would.

Ralph went on to tell me how Germany stood to be the

big winners from the Commission's reorganization. Germany was in shambles after the War and had no money to rebuild. They wanted their allotment of the Marshall Plan money, but then they wanted most of the treasure returned also. They argued that only a small part of it had been taken from conquered countries, including Jews who died in concentration camps. Things had settled down a little, and Germany was feeling her oats again. They were starting to assert themselves. They were telling the other nations the money belonged to the Reichsbank and should be used to help re-start German industry. But according to Ralph, the Commission felt Germany didn't need any further help; she was already on her way to becoming the leading industrialist nation in Europe.

Ralph waited for me to finish my beer and then stood up to leave. I said nothing, and neither did he. I knew it was coming though, and he didn't disappoint me. He said, as he left a tip on the table and prepared to walk out: "Red, take care of yourself. Keep your dumb ass out of drafts. You're on their list. In fact, you and your entire squad head it up."

Before I left to go back to New Orleans, and incidentally, that's where I stay most of the time, I checked in with these two private detectives I was telling you about. They're professionals at finding lost persons. That means they're *skip tracers*, as well as specialists at finding out the intimate details of people's lives.

If you're wondering why I stay in New Orleans, as opposed to any other big city, it's because there I blend in–my accent and speech patterns don't draw attention to me. I rent a hotel room and act as though I'm down and out, maybe on the verge of welfare. Then in a couple of weeks I change rooms and hang out at some other seedy place: different bars, different restaurants, different people–that sort of thing. A lonely life to say the least, but I prefer it this way.

I hire these two detectives more or less permanently. They have been working for me overseas and have just returned with their report. I think I'll give them a break, that is, I'll give them something different to do; I think they might be getting stale. I'm thinking about having them find out what they can about Worthington and Joyce Wagner. I halfway expect Joyce and maybe Worthington of taking money from the Commission or somebody else–and I want all the details. If my guys turn up anything, I might go back to San Angelo and put some pressure on them both. I might even hire it done. I'm not above sweating the two of them a little; I have to get a horse up on somebody before I end up like Carl and Eric.

CHAPTER, 12...BAD HERSFELD, GERMANY, 1945

Just days after the Merkers mine treasure was officially placed in his care and keeping, Colonel Bernstein, as I've told you, was given orders to organize two squads of counter-intelligence people into two teams. Their purpose was to ferret out any remaining SS gold that might still be hidden away. That's how I came to work for him. I was still in Merkers trying to get better acquainted with Françoise, while the Colonel was in Frankfort working with two of his other officers and some Germans to transfer the treasure to the bank there. Before I hardly had a chance to meet him, I was given a set of orders for the three of us, Carl, Eric, and myself, to report to Patton's headquarters on the double. We left immediately and hastily drove the sixty or seventy miles to a former German army post at Hersfeld.

I reported to one of his staff officers, who informed me the General was waiting. I walked into his office after being announced by one of his sergeants. I walked up to his desk and saluted. Before I could say anything, he told me I took my sweet time getting there. He knew how far it was, and he knew I knew he knew. That's why I took his remark as a compliment.

There was a civilian in his office who looked to me as

though he might be a displaced slave laborer. To say he was run down and seedy would be a gross understatement. His clothes were threadbare and his shoes were almost completely worn out. He hadn't shaved or had a haircut in weeks, maybe months. I was astonished, to say the least. I had no idea the general would get that close to a foreigner without his security people hovering close by.

"Adair, this is Doctor Dockstetter. We call him Oddly or Oddy or just plain Doc Oddlie or whatever comes to mind. His first name is Odilio.... I've a hard time remembering exactly how to say it."

The man sitting across from me stood up and placed a coffee cup on an end table by the sofa chair. "I have heard a lot about you, Captain. I have heard they call you 'Red.' Do they call you that for a reason; is it because of the color of your hair?" He spoke with a thick German accent.

I shook his filthy hand, noting how the dirt was ingrained in the pores and had not been cosmetically applied as some part of a disguise. If he was an actor, he was a good one; that's the first impression I had of him.

Patton interrupted us before I could say or do much more than reluctantly shake this disgusting hand of his visitor. However, I did notice his knuckles were gnarly, raw, and badly in need of treatment. They were chapped with ground in dirt, and I knew they smarted. I knew, because that's the way my own hands looked and felt during marble season when I was a boy.

"Adair, Oddlie here is not what he appears to be. He's with OSS. He's sometimes in contact with one of his operatives on the Obersalzberg–more than that he doesn't want me to discuss, not even with you.

"I want the two of you to have lunch in my private dining room in a few minutes." The general motioned with his hand to a side door. "I want the Doc here to fill you in on some details; and then I want you and your two sidekicks to high-tail it down there and meet this guy of his. Oddlie here is aware of something very important to me that's coming off soon. And his friend is going to play an important role in helping him bring it about.

"This brave American friend of Oddlie's lives next door to several battalions of SS troopers, some of whom spend a lot of time looking for transient radio signals. He has only a few minutes every few weeks to make *key* contact. He can receive, but he's reluctant to send words and never his voice–not enough time. They would home in on him in a minute, and then shoot him ten minutes later. When he sends a short series of letters, it means he wants to talk." With that last remark, he stood up; as I saluted, he shook my hand and for the second time in a couple of weeks he told me I was doing a good job. He wished me luck and then sat back down, my cue to turn around and leave by the side door with Oddlie at my heels.

Patton's dining room at Hersfeld was a converted bedroom in his quarters. The chow was regular field rations prepared in the mess hall. He hardly ever ate lunch in his dining room, unless he had guests, preferring a tray at his desk or K rations alongside the road when he was with his troops. He would often leave in the morning with one of his aides and a driver, and come back in the late evening.

Senior generals in the U.S. Army have a live-in noncommissioned aide. He is a combat infantryman in the regular service, who is usually a master sergeant. He functions as a bodyguard, as well as a valet, butler, and special confident to the general. Overseas, he is the first to greet him in the morning and the last to see him at night. He's not a servant in the strict sense, but is there to perform dozens of tasks not performed by the general's commissioned aides. He never associates with other enlisted staff members; he doesn't want to be thought of as being in a position to discuss the general's personal life.

The table was set with china and silverware appropriated from the Wermacht officer's mess. The former owners had abandoned it in haste, along with valuable personal belongings. The general took the dinner service for his own table and allowed his soldiers to keep whatever they wanted from the rest.

The food was brought in by one of the kitchen staff, supervised by the general's non-commissioned aide, and placed on the table in large ornate serving bowls. When we were alone, Oddlie began to speak:

"Captain, I do not suppose you have ever been to the Obersalzberg in Austria?"

"I was never in Europe before the War," I answered.

"Yes, well I was born here. Not far from there," he added as an afterthought.

"I think my man, the one the general was referring to, wants to leave. Among other things, we want you to bring him out with you. You see, the entire area is going to be struck by our bombers on the 25th of this month. We know Goering has his home there, and we know he is at home now. For how long we do not know. There is also a large SS contingency stationed there, and again we do not know for how long. This latter thing is of the utmost importance, because they are fanatics who will resist to the last man."

"Why don't we just by-pass them? What do we care about the place? As far as I can see, it has no military importance, so why place our people in jeopardy?"

"Good point, except for one thing."

"What's that?"

"We don't know for sure of the whereabouts of two other SS divisions. We know they were on the outskirts of Berlin three weeks ago, and now they are missing. We think Hitler has ordered them to the Obersalzberg, but we are not sure. We think he, along with Himmler and Bormann and some lesser lights, are planning to break out of Berlin and take refuge in those mountains any day now. We originally thought Hitler would head for Bavaria, but now we have changed our minds. We think he might end up on the Obersalzberg in that last-ditch effort we have all heard about. If this is the case, then the missing SS units are there now."

"I thought we all gave up on that idea weeks ago? The last time I looked, the Wermacht was surrendering in droves. What's changed Eisenhower's thinking? I know Patton hasn't changed his mind."

"General Patton has given up on the idea, as you say. But Eisenhower has not–not completely. Patton thinks this so-called national redoubt business is all inside Eisenhower's head. We were discussing it when you arrived a few minutes ago. But the point is moot, because of right now, he has ordered Patton to attack. His ultimate objective is Austria and the Obersalzberg."

"So what? I don't get it. Why don't we just bomb them out? We have plenty of airplanes and plenty of bombs. What's the problem?" Oddlie just looked at me with a kind of all-knowing smile, knowing he had an ace in the hole.

"There's a lot more to it, isn't there?" I remarked, wondering what any of this had to do with me.

"Captain, I have been directed to let you in on a closely guarded secret. Outside of a few high ranking Waffen SS officers, nobody knows about it except me, Eisenhower, Bradley, Patton, and now you.

"This is the secret: the Melmer treasure at Merkers is only part of the SS loot. Much of it right now is secured inside a granite vault, inside the Obersalzberg mountain. And we are afraid Goering is there to supervise the movement of some of it to Argentina. The rest, we think, will be dumped in the local lake and hidden until later. If we are wrong about Goering, and Hitler has no plans to move part of the gold, then Goering has no business being there at this critical time.

"Goering has seen his stock steadily fall with the Fuhrer over the past few years. He was once a hero, having distinguished himself in aerial combat in the First War. More recently, he took over the reigns of German industry and guided the country to a successful wartime footing. But since then, he has been resting on his laurels. Now it is easy for Hitler to believe what Bormann has been telling him all along: Goering is a loser, a corpulent, drug-addicted degenerate, which amounts to being a borderline traitor. Hitler has started to listen to Bormann, plus he can see with his own eyes. If Hitler decides to dump all of the gold into the lake for safekeeping, until it can be recovered and transported to Argentina, then he has no need of Goering. If this happens, we think he is going to have Goering shot for leaving Berlin without his permission.

"Let me fill you in on what we know for sure," Oddlie continued. "Recall Thoms, and the other bank official by the name of Veick, telling you and your Col. Russell at Merkers that the gold in the mine was all the reserves Germany had. Well, we find now they were either lying to you or simply did not know the score.

"Three weeks ago, we discovered there was actually a lot more in the Reichsbank in Berlin. Hitler had made the decision to transport the rest of it to the *Oberbayern* in Southern Bavaria. At the time, the plan was for the surviving Waffen SS, Hitler, and his entourage to retreat to that part of the Alps, where we expected they would reform and regroup. It was a natural fortification. We first thought they would take the remaining treasure to the top of the Zugspitz at Garmisch, via a narrow-gage tourist train that winds back and forth inside the mountain. The alternative would be to dump it in the Eibsee, the alpine lake at the foot of the Zugspitz.

"Days later, as things progressed, we received reports through our OSS sources that they had changed their minds. Now we believe they have transported more than nine tons of it out of Berlin in the dead of night. But they did not go to the Zugspitz or the Eibsee; they went to another lake called the *Wachensee*."

I began to fidget. I still wasn't sure what all this had to do with me.

"I am not finished with the story yet," he continued, watching me closely. "They only went through the motions of dumping the treasure in the Wachensee, but what they actually did was truck it to a vault deep in the Obersalzberg. This also coincides with intelligence reports coming into Eisenhower's headquarters concerning the movement of those Waffen SS divisions. We are almost sure they have moved from Berlin to reinforce the units on the Obersalzberg. And it begs the question: What did they move them for? Why are they there?

"You and Patton may be right in your summation of the German's intentions concerning the redoubt. I think you are, because time is running out for Hitler. He has to make his move soon if he is going to. But Eisenhower cannot take the chance and just walk away, as you suggest. He has to assume Hitler is going to join his SS units there to fight on. Then there is the gold; it might be the real reason for moving the SS. And I suspect it is. I suspect it is the main reason Eisenhower is attacking the Obersalzberg. If Eisenhower loses track of it, and it eventually ends up in SS hands in South America, he will never hear the end of it."

Conversation halted for a moment while I pondered what he just told me. Then I said: "There's another person who knows about this gold. This agent of yours, the one whom the general wants me to meet, knows about it. And if I'm not mistaken, he somehow got word to you that it has arrived. And now he doesn't know what to do about it, right?"

"Right."

"Why does the general want me to go there? What can I do he can't, your agent I mean?"

"He needs help. He can't shoot the SS commander, and you can."

"Why not?" I asked. I guess I had a quizzical expression on my face.

"We are civilians and not supposed to, according to the Geneva Convention. Not unless we are placed in fear of our lives. It has something to do with an assassination clause. I do not know any more about it than that…."

"Can't he find an *excuse* to be in fear of his life? I mean…."

"It has been known to happen," Oddlie countered. "This much I do know though–this is not the time for it to happen again. Not right now, anyway. After this is all over in a few weeks, they are going to start some high-level inquiries about who on which side honored the Geneva Convention. Now do you see?"

"Why do you want him shot?"

"Because we suspect he is going to pick out a dozen slave laborers from the area. He will use them to load some trucks and haul the gold to the nearby *Konigssee*. Then he is going to kill them, and probably tie their bodies to gold ingots and throw them in the lake, which, incidentally, is over a hundred kilometers deep. That, as you know, is over 300 feet down–somewhat deeper than other alpine lakes in the region. Their skeletons will be used as future markers–if you can stomach that?"

"How much gold?" I questioned him.

"At least 700 new bars, plus whatever was already there," he replied. "I'm not sure of the exact tally. I don't seem to be able to pin it down.

"Let me put you a little further into the picture: There were over two thousand SS troops stationed there before last week. They started moving them in when they realized

Hitler's *Berghof*, and the surrounding area, was vulnerable to our bombers. These troops are mostly anti-aircraft artillery gunners and support personnel. But in point of fact, as a target it had no military purpose whatsoever. It still does not, but what it does have now is the largest accumulation of gold outside the Merkers storehouse, and of course Fort Knox. If this were not the case, then the anti-aircraft battalions would have been transferred to the Berlin front, where they are badly needed. No, Patton thinks they are keeping them there to protect the gold, which will be used to finance a future Waffen SS.

"There were a couple of SS battalions stationed there shortly after the War started to go badly for the Germans. And since then there has been a slow, secret build-up, in the event they ever had to use the area as part of Hitler's redoubt plan. That is the movement Patton was attempting to avert when Third Army was diverted to Bastogne and the Battle of the Bulge several months ago.

"About the time they started bolstering their air defenses, Martin Bormann started building a fortress in earnest. Now there are three miles of tunnels and over 12,000 square feet of luxurious living quarters inside the mountain. There are ten air defense batteries, having 54 .88 millimeter cannons, which can be depressed and used against infantry or tanks. That is why Eisenhower's staff, and others, believe they are going to make their last-ditch stand in Hitler's adopted home and not in Bavaria.

"This is what we want you to do, Red. We want you and your men to go there. There is a five-ton truck parked out front. There are some duffle bags in the back, which contain everything you will need to dress-up to look like me. Don't worry that nothing fits properly, except the shoes. We have gone to great lengths to get the proper fitting shoes, even though they look well worn. I don't have to tell you to leave behind all rings, cigarette lighters etc., anything that will identify you as an American and for which you cannot explain. Remember that many escaping prisoners never heeded this advice. They wore things like issued underwear, socks, etc. And they got caught. Oh, and I don't have to tell you to keep your uniforms hidden; you are going to need them later.

"This is classified, so keep it to yourself. Your men need not know: Patton received orders three days ago. He is moving his staff tomorrow. He has not laid on the usual *wirbein grosser* associated with his other moves, because this operation is not his idea. And frankly, he is taking much longer to get things underway. I say longer, I mean longer for him anyway."

"So, do I understand then his main body is still headed for Berlin? He doesn't need an entire army in Austria. I thought his primary objective was Berlin?" I questioned.

"So did everybody else, including the general. As of a week before last, Patton thought he was jumping off from Leipzig, and then heading north to take Berlin ahead of the Russians. But then, so did Simpson of First Army on his left flank, and so did Montgomery to the left of Simpson. Now, Eisenhower and Bradley do not think the taking of Berlin is a worthwhile endeavor. They did a month ago, and that was the plan then. But they have since changed their minds. They even went so far as to notify Stalin of the change. And that has the British hopping mad. They figure Eisenhower is way out of line. They see him as overstepping his mandate as supreme commander.

"I want you to know, but I also want you to keep this to yourself: as of last week there was dissention at the highest levels. Churchill wants Montgomery to be the first to Berlin, ahead of the Russians. He sees some political mileage to be gained. He also thinks it will be a needed boost to the morale of the British people something to do with their long haul back from the brink. But it is not going to happen the way any of them want it to. Bradley told Eisenhower we could expect to lose at least 100,000 men needlessly if we attacked across the low flat lands between Leipzig and Berlin. And maybe even more if Montgomery and Simpson have their way. Then, too, they all seem to have forgotten the agreement Roosevelt and Churchill made with Stalin…."

"What was that?" I interrupted to ask.

"They agreed before in principle, and confirmed the plan at their meeting at Yalta, to divide Germany into sectors controlled by each of the contending Allied countries. Yalta was not intended to determine military objectives; the Allies could proceed beyond the Elbe River if it was expedient. But what was really the sense in doing so?

"So why struggle on to Berlin, only to turn around and give it all back to the Russians, since it will eventually become their territory?" Oddlie said, rhetorically. "That is essentially what Bradley asked Eisenhower. And Ike agreed with him. But that made Patton furious. He thinks Bradley and Eisenhower still have the crazy notion in their heads that Hitler is going to abandon Berlin at some point and then make for Bavaria or Austria. Patton thinks that is why Eisenhower changed his mind at the last minute about going on to Berlin. Patton thought he, Patton, was taking Leipzig as just another city on the road to Berlin. Now he realizes it is a pivot point to turn all of Third Army to the south into Austria.

"I think Churchill has appealed to Roosevelt to pressure Eisenhower to change his mind. He and Montgomery are angry because the new plan will minimize the effort put forth by the British Army so far. As of right now, they have no further role to play in the European war. But neither Roosevelt nor Army Chief of Staff Marshall will go along with Montgomery. They say Eisenhower is the supreme commander, and they intend to let him command. Frankly,

I think they are a little fed up with Montgomery. They have lost confidence in him, and have gained confidence in Eisenhower as a tactician. Marshall and Roosevelt are still smarting from Montgomery's botched Market Garden and Falaise Pocket operations. Then, too, when Montgomery wanted to take undue credit with the British press for the outcome of the Bulge, Churchill had to quiet him down. Now, his going over the head of Eisenhower to Churchill has them all a little miffed again. But Eisenhower has told Churchill that if he sees an opportunity to take Berlin cheaply, he will do it. But right now he wants Austria; he has no intention of sending Patton or Montgomery to Berlin."

"Do you know what the new master plan is then?" I asked him. *I marveled that he knew so much. But then that's his business: advising generals of situations so they can better plan operations. I guess if he didn't know what was going on, he wouldn't be of much use to them. But he's telling me all of this for a reason, and I'm not sure I like it.*

"Yes, I do," was his reply. "Patton has already begun an attack south from Leipzig instead of continuing north to Berlin. He will stop at the Czech border. He will regroup, and then push on to Pilzen, and then on south. And if all goes according to plan, he will stop at Linz in Austria.

"But here is the problem: nobody can be sure he will stop at Linz and await further orders. They think he might push into Salzburg and then take Berchtesgaden. But General Patch's Seventh Army has been ordered to take Berchtesgaden and then secure the nearby Obersalzburg. When he finishes with Munich, Patch is going to swing wide to attack SS units at the Brenner Pass on his way to Salzburg. But in order to do so, he is going to run smack into Patton's Third Army because of a terrain problem.

"Now, Patton has a hunch that before they let this happen, Eisenhower will take Salzburg from Third Army's zone of operations and give it to Seventh. Patton says that is exactly what he would do if he were Eisenhower."

Oddlie paused to let me think a minute. Then he continued: "In an area of about seventy-five miles around Salzburg, there is going to be five armies converging on each other. This includes Mark Clark's Fifth coming through the Brenner Pass from Italy. And then there is the French on the right of Patch, both of them advancing toward Austria from Munich. On top of all this, Simpson is coming to join the circus from the east. And last but not least, we have Patton in the north chomping at the bit to drive a wedge down the middle from Linz. All this activity is apparently to stop something Patton no longer considers an issue. Still it will trap a lot of Germans, and it will go a long way to stop the War.

"Patton will eventually move from Linz to Bad Tolz in Germany," Oddlie went on to tell me. "He is slated to become the military governor of the entire area. His forward headquarters will be at Bad Tolz, about thirty-five miles or so south of Munich.

"You know what has occurred to me?" I asked him.

"What?"

"If Patch sends a pincer toward Salzburg and Berchtesgaden, he and Patton, coming down from Linz, are going to collide head on. It looks to me as though all that's going to happen is one big rush-hour traffic jam. Geez–they're all going to be bumper-to-bumper."

"I know it. That is what I have been talking about." I guess I hadn't been paying too close attention, because he looked at me as though I was a student and he was my teacher.

"What the Joint Chiefs have planned, though," he went on to say, "is for Patch to send O'Daniel's Third Infantry Division into Berchtesgaden before Patton reaches Linz. That is one solution anyway."

"That's going to make Patton even angrier than he is," I said. "He's going to miss out on Berlin; now he'll also miss taking Hitler's favorite domicile where all the gold is stored."

"I know that too," Oddlie answered me. "You see, Patton is planning on just such an eventuality–that is where you come in. He wants you there before O'Daniel's troops arrive, and before the SS can ditch the gold. That means you have to be in Salzburg by the 23rd of April, so that you can make it to Hitler's compound before the night of the 24th. The SS is moving it to the lake on that night. Patton wants you to secure the gold hoard and move it out before anybody knows it is there. He wants to take credit for recovering the gold. It is a poor substitute for Berlin, but right now it is all he has left.

"He wants you to eventually bring the gold to Tolz after the cease-fire. Your Colonel Bernstein will be waiting to take it off your hands. But it will be done with much fanfare and press coverage.

"General Patton is really upset, as I said. He has no real interest in attacking a few SS battalions around Linz. And frankly, he says, there is no glory in prospecting for gold. What he wanted in the worst way was to push on to Berlin. He wanted to confront the remaining German armies and to whip them before the Russians took over. What he really wanted was to be the first into Berlin, as did Montgomery. He wanted to use commandos to take Hitler's bunker; he wanted to take him alive. He actually wanted his picture taken with him. Do you believe it?"

"I believe it," I said. "But I probably would be more apt to believe it if you told me he wanted a picture of him stringing the Fuhrer up to a lamp post."

Oddlie started to laugh and then said: "I agree, he might have done it, too, if he could have found a lamp post still standing.

"He always said he was going to do it," Oddlie continued. "When Patton found out Hitler had not yet moved to the Obersalzberg, he told General Weyland, of the Tactical Air Command, to wipe it out. This was with Eisenhower's approval, of course. Patton told Bradley he Patton thought the Germans might turn Hitler's compound into some sort of shrine after the War. He told Bradley if they wanted to level the place, they had better do it now rather than later, when all the politicians got involved. Bradley agreed. Now, as I said, it is going to happen on the 25th. You want to have come and gone; you do not want to be anywhere near the place on that date. Weyland has been waiting for this, and I assure you he is going to leave nothing but a pile of rubble at Hitler's doorstep.

"Leave your Jeep here," Oddlie said. "Take the five ton truck; it is full of jerry cans of gasoline, hundreds of pounds of food supplies for trading purposes, and three bicycles. Trust me on this: you have everything you will need. Drive it to the edge of our lines and then go into Salzburg on the bicycles. Hide the truck until you have secured the gold and are ready to come back out, then transfer it from the German trucks to your heavier truck. You should have no problems. You look like factory workers, and you talk like them. Furthermore, your credentials are impeccable. They are even printed with German ink on regulation forms. How we did it is our business, if you do not mind. To allay any fears you might have, let me tell you I have been there twice before and have had no problems.

"Your cover story is you are volunteer laborers, and that your supervisors expect Munich to fall within days. You were told you are needed more in Berchtesgaden. You have been given to understand you are to build defensive installations on Hitler's mountain. You personally cannot go home, because the Vichy government has been overthrown. And right now you are *persona non grata* in France. And your two sergeants, whose story is they are from Norway, cannot go back for the same reason. You have also been told the Allies will not be able to breach the defenses in the Austrian Alps, and that the War will end in a few months with a negotiated surrender. One of the agreements will be that those who volunteered from German occupied countries to work for Germany will be allowed to go home with full amnesty. You cannot go back now, because you are going to be faced with long prison terms or worse if you do.

"I have put plenty of Reichmarks in your dufflebags to see you through. In case they lose all their value in the next few weeks, I have given you several hundred more in greenbacks and some silver dollars. I would have given you more silver, but you can only carry so much on your bicycles. If you have to explain where you got the American money, your story is that you took it off dead Americans. They will believe anything when they see your *authentic* credentials.

"As I have said, we think Goering might be on the final outs with Hitler. Goering has been talking to Himmler; he wants Himmler's support. Goering thinks if Hitler insists on staying in his underground Berlin bunker, he is doomed. And Goering wants to take over now and make peace with either Patton or Patch's advancing armies. Himmler told Bormann, and Bormann the ever-faithful lap dog, went straight to his boss with the tale. As a result, we think the SS commandant has been given orders by Bormann to shoot Goering. Hitler swears he is not going to be taken alive by the Russians, who are still several miles from the Reich Chancellery. You knew he had a bunker under the ruins, did you not?

"We do not think the SS will shoot Goering unless they get a direct order from the Fuhrer. More than likely they will arrest him and hold him, awaiting further instructions from Hitler."

Oddlie paused for a minute, waiting to see if I might have a question. When I said nothing, he pushed on with his discourse, repeating what he'd already told me: "Goering knows the SS is going to give the gold the *deep six*, and according to our reliable informant in Berlin, this is going to happen on the 24th. Goering figures if he cannot get away with some of it, then he intends to buy his freedom by telling us where they dumped it. That is, he will if he can make contact with some of our officers before he gets himself shot by some of our soldiers. How is that for some kind of grasping-at-straws plan? Bormann knows about it, and has told the SS commander to make doubly sure it never happens. This SS commander will personally take charge of the lake-dumping detail, as a last request from his Fuhrer. Adolph wants the whole thing kept secret. When things cool off, as they are bound to do, the gold will be retrieved and spirited off to South America. As I have said, they intend to use it to support the remaining loyal SS who escaped from the Russian front. And for those who survive Patch and Weyland and what the two generals have planned for them at the Obersalzberg.

"You understand, of course, that much of what I have told you depends on whether Hitler stays in Berlin. And right now it looks to me as though that is what he intends to do."

"You say they plan to hide part of their loot in the lake–that is, the part Goering doesn't get away with?" When Oddlie was hesitant to answer, I asked him: "You want me to stop the dumping, and then make off with the load back through our lines; is that about it?"

"No, the general has a lot of confidence in you, but he doesn't expect the impossible. No, what he wants is for you to stop the dumping, all right. But then he wants you to hide it until his troops arrive. I do not think he intends to stop at Linz and wait for Patch or the French to take

Berchtesgaden. If he does, it will be one of the few times he ever stopped an advance to wait for somebody else to get the credit.

LeClerc is on Patch's right and may be given the honor of being the first into Berchtesgaden. Your general does not like the Frenchman very much. Patton is still smarting from Eisenhower's order to let LeClerc be the first into Paris. The way Patton sees it, he, Patton, did all the work and, according to him, this phony Frenchmen got all the credit. At first, Patton did not want to take Paris; he wanted to bypass it and get on with the War. But when Eisenhower became convinced the Germans planned to burn it down, Patton wanted Third Army to lead the way and not LeClerc with deGaulle in tow. Now come the French again. And you better bet on Patton forgetting how his orders will read. Patton thinks he can have tanks there by 5 May, at the latest. But whoever gets there first, the thing to remember is: do not let the gold fall into anybody's hands except members of Third Army. I repeat: Patton wants credit for capturing the gold. And you and I work for him. But once more: whatever you decide to do, you should do it before the 25th. After that, there will be nothing left of the place.

"Remember now, we expect a very few SS will be at the lake, no more than three or four officers. After the gold is in the lake and they have done away with the slave laborers, they plan to follow their troops southwest toward *Kitzbuhel*. They will carry packs containing civilian clothes and provisions. From there they have elaborate plans to enter Italy and then make it on to Argentina.

"One more thing: many armies have been overcome and beaten soundly by the SS because they underestimated them. But your job is to secure the gold until Patton's forces arrive–under no circumstances seek out combat with these people–that is, after you have ambushed those at the lake. Then you secure the gold. Patton is delaying the bombing until the 25th just for you. He cannot wait any longer."

"I thought I was to get hold of it and then bring it to Tolz?"

"He wants you to eventually bring it to Tolz. But if Patton decides to obey his orders and stay in Linz, he wants you to hide it or bury it someplace or sit on it until that traffic mess clears up. Whatever, never let it get out of your hands. And if worst comes to worst, he says, shoot the Frenchman if he gets in the act and tries to take it away from you.

"One other thing, Red. I am privy to information you should know about. Patton likes you. If you pull this off, you are going to give him some good press, especially if we find and arrest Goering. He is going to invite you to become a member of the regular service if you want to be. And as I understand it, that is no mean thing. It is almost the same as graduating from West Point. Louisiana State and a reserve commission is one thing, but in the army, the name of the game is a regular commission."

We chatted for another fifteen minutes or so, until we finished lunch. I stuffed myself and so did he. Neither of us expected to eat another hot meal for some time to come. I suppose Patton knew this, and that's why he invited us to stay. One thing about Patton, he is a stickler for detail. He seldom overlooks anything–even something as small as a hot meal for two people he knew wouldn't see a mess hall or a restaurant for weeks.

"One last thing," Oddlie interjected. "I have supplied you with the latest walkie-talkie radios, but they still have limited range. However, my agent in Berchtesgaden has this short wave that is more sophisticated. Do not use it until you are ready to leave the area; then let me know the status of the gold. If you need more people to help you after you have cleared out of Berchtesgaden, let me know that as well. I will get in touch with Bernstein, and he will send the remainder of your squad, post haste. I will monitor our frequency every night at 2200 hours for one-half hour. And all night on the 24th."

"Oddlie, I have another question."

"What?"

"I'm curious. In what subject did you take your degrees?"

"Mathematics. I was a professor at Gottingen University, until I was dismissed because my mother was Jewish. I think she might be in Dachau right now, and I intend to appropriate your Jeep if you will give me the key. As soon as I hear from you on the radio, I am gone. So do not delay."

"Oddlie."

"Yes?"

"*Mentholatum* is the best thing for chapped hands. It smarts worse than *Vaseline,* but it acts quicker, too."

He smiled as I handed him the ignition rotor; the Jeep didn't have a key. Sometimes we remove the rotor to keep our own people from *borrowing* it. I didn't bother to shake his hand again.

CHAPTER 13...MUNICH GERMANY, 1933

Frau Wahlmuller had just finished her morning room inspection when a street fight broke out below her window in the *Kaiserhof* hotel. Another truckload of thugs, dressed in *SA* Brownshirt uniforms, had just appeared on the scene and had joined several of the brothers, who had been engaged in a shouting match with a group of Social Democrats. This *SD* party was the enemy of Adolph Hitler, the soon-to-be German Reich Chancellor, and his friend and fellow henchman, Ernst Rohm, head of the SA Brownshirt brigades. As it would turn out, Hitler and his top aides would soon come to fear the presence of Rohm and his SA stormtroopers as a threat to the new Nazi Party.

In the beginning, the SA provided protection for Hitler during his many street speeches and public rallies in Germany. But it was not long before they developed into a brawling force known for spreading havoc and descent from one end of the country to the other. Anyone who was not in favor of Adolph Hitler was the enemy of the SA bullies, and was put in fear of his or her life. It was from the ranks of the SA that Hitler's personal security force, the SS, arose. Then, when Hitler was elected to the Chancellery, following *The Night of the Long Knives,* when most of the

SA leadership was assassinated, he had Ernst Rohm executed on a trumped-up charge.

The street fight ended, as most of them did, with the police making a futile effort to subdue the Brownshirts. But more often than not of late, the Brownshirts, which outnumbered them, were chasing off the police. Then, too, the police, for the most part, were in sympathy with Hitler and his stated goals for Germany. And more and more they would show up to a street fight and then stand idly by doing absolutely nothing. This was one of those times.

The fight in front of the Kaiserhof now turned into a full-blown riot; windows were being broken and property was being damaged up and down the *Strasse.* Before the participants became either too tired to carry on or were injured and unable to do so, they had spilled into the hotel where Frau Wahlmuller was the concierge and housekeeper.

When things quieted down, she and her husband, Rudolph emerged from behind a locked door to their living quarters. The two of them walked over to a sofa in the lobby and sat down. Frau Wahlmuller spoke with a voice of despair, as she viewed the wreckage: "Rudi, I want to leave this place, I want to go home. I want to take Rolph and go home before the schools here turn him into a Nazi. We could get a job with your sister at the *Imperial.*"

Home was Salzburg, Austria. They were Austrian citizens who had a work permit to live in Germany for an indeterminate period. Rudi also owned a share of the family hotel. But he wasn't sure it would support both his family and that of his sister.

"You know, Gretchen," he said, "Austria is not going to be all that different. Herr Hitler will be a shoo-in to be elected Chancellor. And one of his priorities is to annex Austria. In a few years Austria will be Germany, mark my word. Then what?"

"Maybe we should consider leaving Europe altogether?"

"Where do you think we ought to go?" he asked, sarcastically, with a note of frustration at her seeming lack of understanding of the red tape associated with immigration departments. "Not nearly so easy as you think it is."

"Maybe not so difficult either. Remember those Mormon missionaries with their flannel board and silhouettes and their simplistic explanation of where we all came from and where we are going. Well, it made a lot of sense to me. But it was easy enough to see that if we believed them and consented to be baptized the way they wanted, we were going to be in real trouble. The new Reich, the one Hitler speaks of, is not going to be so tolerant of new religions. He says he is Catholic, but he talks and acts more as though he is an atheist. With all our troubles, I thought joining the Mormon church, regardless of whether it is true or not, would have placed just one more burden on us. There must be a lot of other people in Germany who feel the same way.

"But on the other hand–and this is the point I want to make they said converts could petition the government for a visa. One of the missionaries said the German immigration people are interested in helping all undesirable factions, such as Jews, Freemasons, Gypsies, and Mormons to leave Germany. How long the government will cooperate in this is unknown, he said. The missionary also said we could get on this special list if we had any kind of support in America. He said if we did not, we could list the church as our sponsor. Then he said it would be fairly easy to immigrate. He said America went by a quota system, and Germany has seldom filled her quota. But first off, we have to become members to get on this special list.

"You know, they were reluctant to expound on that part of their discussion for fear people would join just to go to America."

"Do you want to join?" Rudi asked her.

"Yes, I believe I do."

"To get out of Germany, or because you believe it is true?"

"Both, I guess. But maybe this unrest, with a promise of more to come, is the thing making me stop and think lately. And just now was the clincher. I believe it is true, and I want to leave."

"What about our families in Austria?" He asked.

"I did not say it was going to be easy. We are going to have to make some sacrifices to gain a better life for ourselves. And you know the Germans have not been all that kind to us. We speak with an accent. I had one last week actually accuse me of being a Jew."

A neatly dressed official stepped from a government automobile and walked up the sidewalk past a neatly trimmed lawn. He noted the address of the house in front of him and with a practiced eye, concluded the residents were industrious but not prosperous.

He was carrying a briefcase, walking with the confidence of a young man with a purpose and a well paying job. It was something to be proud of and thankful for during these Depression days.

The year was 1938, and good jobs were hard to come by, although Salt Lake City was not as bad off as some other places in the country.

As he rang the doorbell, he reached inside his suit coat for his wallet. At the exact time the door opened, he flashed his FBI badge and announced himself.

"Mrs. Wahl, could I come in for a moment and talk to you."

She didn't hesitate to open the screen door. She was used to authorities in Germany demanding to enter and not asking. She asked him to sit down, pointing to a comfortable chair opposite a worn sofa.

"I know you're curious as to what this is about," he said in stilted German with an accent she couldn't place. "Let me bring myself up-to-date: First of all, you're Austrian immigrants with a work permit. You have applied for citizenship, but your case is pending due to the European unrest. But, we here in America consider it to be an oversight, which will soon be rectified. We consider you and your family to be loyal citizens."

Mrs. Wahl nodded her head in the affirmative, saying: "Ya, ya."

"You came through Ellis Island some five years ago. The agents there shortened your name to Wahl, but your marriage license and the birth certificates of your husband and son is Wahlmuller." He looked up, waiting for a nod of her head. "You were not sure where you were going to live, so you told the people at Ellis you had joined the LDS church. They suggested you come here. The church suggested you locate in this part of town. And then they helped your husband get employment, right?"

"Right," she said, with another nod of her head.

"You have a son who went back to Austria on a church proselytizing mission. In fact, he is working right now in your hometown of Salzburg...am I right, again?

"And another fact, which has come to our attention, and which brings me here–as an Austrian citizen, he is in danger of being drafted into the German Army."

Gretchen Wahl sat back on the pillowed sofa and expelled a long sigh. *Rolph has never written to tell me anything about it, although it makes perfect sense. I wonder why it never occurred to me before.*

"We understand your son's name is Rolph or Ralph?'

"Yes, Ralph," she said, the unfamiliar name not coming to her easily. His name was Rolph, and she had a hard time with Ralph. Then, too, the name Ralph Wahl was completely alien to her.

"You knew, of course, that he was going to be released by church authorities from his mission ahead of time. Were you going to tell me about it?" he asked her, patronizingly.

"I was not sure you would be interested. Why are you, anyway?"

"We are extremely interested. Not because we want to pry into church affairs, but because we want him to work for us. Let me tell you that he is in danger of never walking correctly again. Our sources tell us this is the opinion of the best orthopedic surgeons in Germany, which means the world."

She let out another deep sigh. She had been informed that Rolph had been skiing on one of his days off, and had seriously broken his leg. German surgeons had pinned it, but it was going to be short. And at this point, they didn't know how stable it was going to be. Time would tell, but they were obviously being less than optimistic.

"Our sources further tell us he will be given an army physical when he is eventually released from the hospital. Don't be upset; we have also been told he will not pass. He will be given a medical deferment, which will relieve him of any obligation to serve or to work in a war factory. That is what makes him so valuable to us. Before the physical, we want him to make an application to join the SS. On the surface it will seem preposterous. But it will show them he is a loyal German, who does not want to come back here. They will believe him when he says he has been indoctrinated with the new German goals, and that he believes the new Germany is the wave of the future. He need not denounce any of his religious beliefs; they simply will not bring them up.

"What we want is for him to seek employment in one of the hotels on the Obersalzberg. We want him to report the comings and goings of Hitler, Goering, and Bormann, who have homes there."

"You want him to assassinate them, do you not? I will not permit it, you know."

"No, nothing of the sort. But if we ever go to war with them, we just might want to bomb the place. If we do it when one or more of those worthies are in attendance, so much the better.

"Incidentally, have you any old photographs or has Ralph sent you any new ones. What we are looking for are military installations, gun emplacements, or recent construction. Do you have any pictures that might show any of those things in the background? We're asking all tourists and recently returned missionaries the same questions."

She stood up and went to the bedroom off the small living room where they had been chatting. She came back with an album full of family photos, some of them of the town of Berchtesgaden, some taken on the mountainside, and some of Hitler's compound.

"This is what we are after. Do you know the dates of these?" he asked her, smiling as he thumbed through them.

"I would like to borrow these if I may. I will bring them back.

"Also, I want to tell you that all letters between the two of you are going to be censored by the German postal service and monitored by the Gestapo. Free speech is out, but then this is not news to you.

"And another thing: when you write, convey the impression you do not like it here. Tell Ralph you are proud of him for staying and doing his part as a loyal German. If they suspect he is German in name only, they will arrest him and put him in a concentration camp. Tell him you are proud he tried to enlist in the SS. Tell him you believe Hitler is doing a remarkable job. And that you wished you had stayed in Austria to reap the new benefits you understand are making Germany the better place to live. Spread it on, but not too thick. Do you understand what I am getting at?

"We want him to become acquainted with some of the SS enlisted men, whenever he goes to work at a hotel there. They are not likely to treat him as a run-of-the-mill civilian. They might even be more prone to accept him when they discover he tried to enlist in their organization; he might even be able to make close friends with some of them."

Arguably the most beautiful and picturesque place in the world is the Obersalzberg mountainside below the *Hoher Goll* massif in the Austrian Alps. It's simply breathtaking beyond words. When Hitler first saw it in 1923, after his release from Landsberg prison, he proclaimed it "splendid," "wonderful," and "indescribable."

He had been sentenced to five years for his role in a bloody coup attempt. There, he dictated his famous *Mein Kampf,* meaning *my struggle,* to his secretary Rudolph Hess. After serving only nine months, he was released and took temporary leave from public life at a friend's chalet on the Obersalzberg. He would return again and again to Berchtesgaden, following stressful journeys to party events and during planning periods for major political campaigns.

When in Berchtesgaden, Hitler, living under the alias of Herr Wolf, made frequent walking trips to the mountainside, where he first rented a room in a *pension* and then rented, and later purchased, a small chalet of his own. Later, he enlarged it some four times, providing himself with a second seat of government, which was used for this purpose until the end of the War.

This new home, paid for by the sale of this new book of his, in an absolutely dream location, was known as the *Haus Wachenfeld.* He would later rename it the *Berghof,* meaning *the estate on the mountain*. It was less then ostentatious, the exception being a large retracting 24-by 16-foot window, which looked out on the breathtaking view of the panorama between the *Hochkalter* mountain and Salzburg.

As the new Chancellor, he would avail himself for pictures and a chat to the ever growing number of tourists. But as the War descended on Germany, he had less and less time for them. And then, finally, a long fence cordoned off what became known as the *Fuhrer Area.*

Downhill, less than a football field from the Berghof, was a tavern. By 1933, it had evolved into a hotel called the *Zum Turken.* After he took over the government, it was declared to be too close to the Berghof. It was subsequently appropriated and turned into a barracks for his new SS security and Secret Service detachments.

An obscure but loyal party member by the name of Walter Reinicke had owned it. Regardless, an ordinance was passed, which declared his hotel to be too close to the Berghof for *respectability.* When Reinicke objected and refused to sell, he was arrested on a trumped-up charge; his property was confiscated, with Reinicke receiving only a small pittance. He and his wife, daughter, and three teenaged sons were summarily put into the streets, where friends and former neighbors took them in and gave him employment. They stayed in the area, refusing to leave.

The SS commander, whose idea it had been to take the property, with the concurrence of the Fuhrer, deemed them harmless and allowed them to stay. Everyone thought he did this to assuage his conscience. But, whatever, Reinicke vowed vengeance on the Fuhrer and the commander; of course, he kept this oath to himself.

CHAPTER 14...BAD HERSFELD, April, 1945

I found my two sergeants in the mess hall drinking coffee, waiting for me to come from Patton's office. We were ready to leave after taking a few minutes to inventory the truck. From above my head, I could see the General standing at a window looking into the square. When he saw I was about to depart, he gave me the thumbs up and backed away out of view. He no doubt would have come down to see us off, but he didn't want to draw undue attention to us.

I was quite surprised at what I found, but then Oddlie is a professional. I guess you can say he is, since he has survived behind enemy lines for some two years.

The bicycles are not those new balloon-tired rigs, the ones slow and hard to pump. Those he has chosen are of the European racing variety. They cruise along at a smooth fifteen miles an hour with hardly any effort. They are old and beat up, as might be expected; however, the working mechanism is in first-class condition. They even have spare tires, the narrow kind, tied in a figure eight and looped over the seat post. In addition to the duffle bags, containing our *new* clothes, are three backpacks. The packs are neither American nor of German army issue, which would have given us away. They look as though they might have been purchased by mountaineers from an outfitting shop at the foot of the *Jungfrau* or somewhere. There are even home-made sleeping bags and a change of clothing, made by a garment maker in Munich. Oddlie has left nothing to chance. Oh, and also in the duffle bags are the walkie-talkies he spoke of.

Carl and Eric are bewildered at what's going on. But neither of them says anything. They just know something big is about to happen, and they know I will brief them when I'm ready.

The three of us pile in the front seat and set off toward Munich. Some of this city has been taken, while some parts are still holding out. Oddlie says our forces are being aided by deserting Wermacht soldiers. He says, some of the German veterans have threatened the *burgermeister* if he carries out his plans to make a stand. They have had enough of war, and they don't want to stand-by and watch their city shelled any more than it has been. The fact is, General Doolittle's Eighth Air Force bombers have caused wide-spread destruction. There are a few buildings untouched; most of them, however, have been destroyed or left partially intact, about the same as other major cities in Germany. But continued heavy shelling may completely destroy anything of value left standing.

We drove for a few miles on a country road, and then connected to one of the many *autobahns* crisscrossing the nation. We had the highway practically to ourselves, except for *Red Ball Express* trucks high-balling passed us every few minutes. The Red Balls are coming from coastal cities. They began carrying fuel, ammunition, and food directly to the forward troops almost as soon as we had a beachhead. They are being driven by colored infantrymen, who have played a major role in our success in keeping the Germans off balance. Incidentally, after getting some bad press at a couple of engagements in Italy, the coloreds have distinguished themselves. They were the first into Orfurt. Can you picture those poor dying prisoners looking up at these colored infantryman busting down the gates of Buchanwald and taking over? Some of these people had never seen a colored man before. Black must have been the most beautiful color they had ever seen.

Finally, when I knew they could stand the suspense no longer, I told Carl and Eric what we were going to do. I started by telling them I had volunteered us for a hazardous mission. I saw the look of apprehension on their faces. After all, they had come this far, and the last thing they wanted was to be killed in the last few weeks of the War. And for nothing, as they saw it. What at this late date could be worth volunteering for? Combat was all but over. And you didn't have to be a general to realize it.

I reviewed the Merkers' gold operation in which we had recently been involved. I told them the diamonds would probably last us the rest of our lives if we didn't live too extravagantly. Since we took them, I had gained a better insight into their worth. My new estimate was considerably less than the *wag*–the wild-assed-guess–the one I made at the mine. Then, too, as I had told them previously, it would have to be split three ways–actually four or five, when you included the fence. Still, there would be plenty left; but I wanted more. I had the bit in my teeth; I was off and running and I wanted more. I couldn't speak for them, but I was sure they felt the same way.

There was no rehash of why we hadn't tried for some of the gold. We knew that swiping as much as a single bar would have gotten us caught. However, making off with some of it had been uppermost in our minds at the time we helped Colonel Bernstein's detail transport it to the waiting trucks outside the mine. The workers moving the loot had been picked at random, on purpose, from the ranks of an infantry outfit guarding the entrance to the main tunnel.

Unfortunately for us, Bernstein had a foolproof system to prevent pilferage. He had two officers inventorying every bag as it was loaded in a Jeep trailer. The senior man in charge of each three-man transportation detail signed for the load. When they arrived at the entrance, where they were unloaded, another inventory took place. Each bag, containing two bars each, had been sealed with an American finance officer's seal. There was no way of getting into the bags, nor was there any way of *losing* a few off the trailer in transit. Bernstein was way ahead of us, and we knew it. He was a professional at handling money, if nothing else. He even went so far as to post an armed sentry at each of the few *addits* connecting to the main tunnel.

I had given Carl and Eric the gold coins the night we took the diamonds. The first chance they got, they sewed them into the lining of their field jackets.

We had no idea how rare they were. Within days of Roosevelt's election in 1933, the government started taking them out of circulation. It was part of the president's Depression recovery program. There was a fine of ten-thousand dollars to be levied on anyone not authorized to hold gold after a certain date. They would later, as I said, become very valuable; but as of now, we had no way of knowing what they were worth.

"Are you guys interested in acquiring some ingots–I mean, are you interested in a lot of gold? Are you interested in taking a shot at maybe a truckload, without Colonel Bernstein looking over our shoulders?"

They both looked at me. Eric, who was driving, looked over at me for longer than I felt comfortable. Carl nudged him, and he re-acquired the road without crossing too far over the line separating the two lanes.

"I would expect it will entail some hazards. But I trust, Captain, the hazards will be commensurate with the rewards, so to speak." Carl, waxing mock-eloquent for our amusement, had a big grin on his face as he contemplated another stash of SS gold. After all, that was our new job–finding and liberating Nazi gold. In our view, the operative word was *liberating.* We had pretty well convinced ourselves that the system wasn't going to return the gold to the Jews it was taken from or to their close relatives, either.

The first couple of hours were spent discussing my new friend Oddlie and what he had told me. I wonder if Odilio is really his name. It could be, I guess. It's German. And his academic *bona fides* could be for real, as well. They probably are, since the OSS is noted for recruiting intellectuals of one stripe or another. Their ranks include professors, writers, musicians, and even a few artists; they are the kinds of people Colonel William Donovan, their founder, figures have more imagination and intelligence than your average. I guess they have to have something going for them, something a little different from the rest of us, in order to operate and to survive. Whoever chose the ones I knew personally did a good job. I never knew one who was a lemon or a bad apple.

There's going to be one major deviation from the way Oddlie briefed me. After some thought, I decided to change things. The idea of the three of us pedaling into Salzburg, which was where we were to meet Oddlie's pal, seemed a little much to me. We would be just a little too conspicuous, and to what purpose?

My idea is to have Carl stay with the truck while we cycle into the city. I want him to stay hidden in one of the hundreds of copses of trees close to the highway. When he sees some of the lead elements of Seventh Army or the French moving forward, he's to fall in some distance behind one of their convoys. Once within walkie-talkie range, he will breakaway from the column and keep the two of us informed of his new location. According to my timetable, we should have secured the gold and be waiting to make the transfer by the time he is in position. You understand, we can't be driving around in German trucks in the midst of American tanks, not if we want them to continue resembling trucks and not a wheelbarrow full of bobby pins.

I plan on transferring the loot to our larger, heavier vehicle and then taking off for someplace. This *someplace* thing has not been worked out quite yet. But first things first. First, we have to get the gold without getting ourselves killed by the SS, who, as I have said, are not exactly a bunch of pushovers. They are not exactly babes in the woods. And they must have plans of their own to avoid an ambush at the lake. Frankly, when the euphoria of becoming very, very rich wore off, I became very worried. This worry thing set in when we were about 150 miles from Munich.

We were almost talked out after a few hours. To make conversation, Eric asked me why Patton was circling around and coming back down to Linz. I replied by asking him how he knew, since it was supposed to be classified. They both looked at me as though I was some kind of recruit, but neither said anything. They knew all the details ten minutes after they sat down in the mess hall. They knew Seventh Army was about to take Munich. Why then did General Patch not push on to Bavaria and Austria? Why involve Patton? Why did they need him to come all the way down from Leipzig to Lintz?

I answered as best I could, without having been invited to attend any of Eisenhower's staff meetings.

"You both know General Patton is far and away the best field general in the U.S. Army. And when historians finish tallying up all his accomplishments, I think they're going to agree he's been the most successful general in the history of warfare. But where he's the best at what he does, he's no politician. From here on out, his statesmanship, and his ability as an administrator, will be the yardstick by which he'll be measured. Then, too, he has made some off-the-cuff remarks that hasn't set well with his superiors and the Congress–he told the press somewhere along the line that he thought we should press on to Moscow while we still had the chance. Needless to say, he knows more about communists than your average congressmen, and he doesn't like communism. And if Third Army ever meets the Russians, there might be trouble. And of course, the negative press will make him look foolish if they can. That's one of the reasons he's not going on to join up with the Russians.

"But there are other more important reasons. The Allies had agreed we should stop at the Elbe River and wait for the Russians to take Berlin. But they didn't reckon with George Patton. He has other ideas, or so they now think. They're afraid he'll ignore orders and press on to Berlin if they give him a chance to go north from Leipzig to the Elbe. They can't visualize him waiting for any Russians. He doesn't care; it's not his way. He knows nothing will happen to him if he does. He has the overwhelming support of his soldiers and the American people. Generals Bradley and Eisenhower are afraid this might happen. At any rate, they feel they can't take the chance, so they're sending him to Austria. Then, too, Eisenhower has more than a passing interest in this place called the Obersalzberg, where we're headed."

We made contact with a brigade from Seventh Army northeast of Munich. We bummed enough gas to replenish our fuel tanks; then we received a briefing as though we were on a routine scouting patrol for General Patton. No mention was made of any specifics. All we were supposed to be interested in was where the German lines were, and if they expected any opposition. This long talk we had with their intelligence people led us to believe we were going to have a nice uneventful cycling trip through the beautiful German countryside. We could, however, expect to encounter enemy patrols about fifty miles this side of Salzburg.

The Germans had set up artillery positions, and two divisions of panzers, backed by a division of Waffen SS, a few miles on either side of the autobahn leading to Salzburg. They were located around the northern end of lake *Chimsee*. It was obvious to us they were there to slow down General O'Daniel's Third Infantry Division, which was part of Seventh Army that would be racing for Berchtesgaden in a matter of days. What the French were going to be doing on O'Daniel's right flank, they didn't know.

There was a reason for the German holdout, which occurred to me half way through the briefing. The Waffen SS had been told to delay our forces until after the 24th of April. The reason had nothing to do with the War; it was over. I knew why; it was obvious to me why. It was obvious to me and to the generals, and to Oddlie, if not to anyone else, including the briefer, who kept repeating, rhetorically: "Why do they fight on? They're finished. Why don't they surrender? We don't know why."

Well, I know why. The gold is why. The future of this elite group of dedicated SS warriors is at stake. And Eisenhower and Patton are bound and determined to deny them the means to survive, even if it's in name only. Without the gold, the Waffen SS will simply become a page in the history books.

We left the autobahn outside of Munich about 25 miles, and took to parallel country roads. You have to see these roads to appreciate the scenery. Untouched by war, there is seemingly an endless parade of small gingerbread villages and hamlets, lined up like dominoes, all of them unique, yet almost indistinguishable from each other. Each one is clean and manicured, as are the fields reaching to the roads. They resemble a golf course at an expensive country club. Even in the midst of war, they are manicured; we have Hitler to thank for this. One of the good things he did was to decree that each man takes care of his own property. As for those passing by, woe to the litterbug who thinks he can get away with something. I wondered who maintained the grass and pastures bordering the autobahn and these village roads. There are no workmen out and about. We were soon to learn why.

When we got within artillery range of the units at the Chimsee, we hid the truck in the trees and Eric and I took to our bicycles. We had several days to get to Salzburg, plenty of time.

The closer we peddled toward Salzburg, the more we were seeing the influence of Mozart. Now the quaint hotels and businesses, those with broad sides presenting to the passer-by, are painted with breathtakingly beautiful murals depicting the muses. There are endless clouds, cherubim, and angels entangled in golden gossamer, resembling paintings on the ceiling of the Sistine Chapel. No military scenery is to be seen here in these backwaters of the Reich. At times, the reference to Mozart and his music, and to his home in Salzburg some 60 miles further on, is less subtle. Occasionally, we see a giant grand piano or a violin with bow, treated with the same theme of celestial beings playing ethereal music on a canvas of wet stucco.

Eric was the first to comment concerning this paradox. Here are people capable of painting barns with Madonna and child *en repose*; and at the same time, they are responsible for the hellish scene at Buchanwald. It's remembrance of things Buchenwald that jerks us up by our boot straps when the surroundings tend to lull us into some esoteric reverie. I couldn't help but remember again the comment of Eisenhower's about how our troops really never had anything against the Germans. *They were just doing what Hitler made them do. It was all a rough game, but a game seemingly without hatred or rancor.* It was, that is, before they saw or heard about the Buchenwald concentration camp. Then Muthausen and Dachau, and the others that added frosting to a ghoulish devil's cake. And it instilled a latent zest for combat in many a borderline malingerer.

Fortunately, the War was winding down for the Germans. Fortunately, indeed, because Seventh Army supported overhead by squadrons of marauding aircraft spoiling for a fight, was shifting into an even higher gear. The Germans were completely worn out, while our troops were just getting their second wind.

We peddled along the back roads for a reason. These fighters are patrolling uninterrupted along the autobahn, and we are well inside their fire zone. They are hunters, hunting for anything German that moves. Occasionally, we watch as one peels off and comes down across the treetops. We can see clearly the anti-tank rockets slung under his wings. And occasionally, a *gaggle* in a *rat race* would *buzz* the countryside, looking for anything moving that is a challenging target. We watched three just this morning in trail. We decided they might be having a shooting contest where bets were on about who could knock over a haystack. The one who uncovered an artillery position won the bet. It was common practice in France to conceal anti-aircraft artillery inside fake haystacks. These young pilots had no doubt seen gun-camera movies of the sides of haystacks coming down, and the gunners running pell-mell across pastures, seeking cover where none existed, as high velocity machine guns and cannon shells sought out and destroyed their target in a flash. At any rate, it's a scene to warm the cockles of any fighter pilot worthy of the name.

But for Eric and me, it's anything but a game. Because, dressed as we are and on bicycles, we are the prey. They are hawks and we are rabbits. When surprised, we could easily have been the subject of some would-be ace's description of how he chased two Germans. Then, demonstrating with his hands, he would show his friends at the bar that night how he strafed alongside the road–knowing our first instincts would be to take cover in the ditch in front of his guns.

Needless to say, our own aircraft were our worst enemy. We had planned on encountering enemy artillery. But there was none to be found.

There are sounds of exploding shells way off in the distance. But it's only background noise–a kind of periodic crescendo to some staged Wagnerian opera, where reluctantly we are the principal players.

It was late afternoon. Neither of us was tired, but we were afraid. We wanted to draw the curtain on this drama until after the sun went down and we knew the hawks had retired for the night. But then the hellish-looking Northrup *Black Widows* came out with their radar. And low-flying Martin *Mauraders,* with their stubby wings and powerful engines, could be heard on the way to their targets. But so far, we had not been attacked. We figured they were after bigger fish, maybe a weary locomotive or a convoy struggling to make the dolomites and perceived safety.

You might well ask why the Germans put up little or no fighter opposition. If you're curious, I should tell you it was all planned this way. Well into the air war, air staff reasoned the best way to eliminate German fighter superiority was to destroy the factories themselves. Then somebody got the idea that all machinery ran on ball bearings, so the main ball bearing factories at Schweinfurt were hit, with a staggering loss to our bomber groups. Then, when we lost even more aircraft due to their fighters and heavy concentration of anti-aircraft at Schweinfurt, another *somebody* came up with another solution. Instead of hitting the fighter factories, where they simply disbursed operations in some cases, and the ball bearing factories, where we realized they might have squirreled away enough for a dozen future wars, we changed tactics. Both strategic and tactical air power then went after oil refineries and transportation almost exclusively. That changed the complexion of the War overnight. Soon, most of their aircraft sat helplessly on the ground waiting for fuel that never came. And their trains were ideal targets made for low-flying fighters and medium bombers. They would skim along near the ground, while pouring cannon and rocket fire into the steam engines. A burst, and then a pull up to avoid fragments of steel from the exploding boilers. The only danger for them was staying too long on the target. Soon we dominated the air space, first over France and then over Germany.

General James Doolittle approved another tactic helping write *fini* to the Luftwaffe. Soon after he took command of Eighth Air Force in England, he authorized his fighters to leave off the escort of bombers and to roam out ahead of the bomber fleets. Our fighters caught the Germans, in many cases, trying to take off to engage our bombers. They destroyed hundreds, and then stayed on to strafe the remainder on the ground. Entire airdromes with their complement of aircraft were destroyed. Within a few months the sky was full of low-flying adventuresome boys, some no more than 21 years old, shooting up the German countryside unopposed. Now, there was no time for a siren warning to take cover. The fighters were on the hapless Germans immediately, and life became even more unbearable. By day, we devastated their larger cities with high-explosive bombs. And by night, they were rained on by the British dropping small white-phosphorous missiles; the ensuing firestorms resembling Dante's *Inferno*. Then, just when the inhabitants thought they might have a brief respite, low-level fighters and fighter-bombers struck them. On top of it all were the ground forces. Attempting to keep up with Patton's Third Army, they never let the enemy catch his breath. It was Patton's policy never to allow them to rest and regroup. With no air support, the enemy moved from one disorganized retreat to the next, suffering a tremendous number of casualties, prisoners, and loss of badly needed equipment and material, until mercifully for him, it finally came to an end.

I estimated we were about 50 miles from Salzburg when we saw the first real signs of war. A panzer, with tread blown off and ravaged by fire, was skewed cross-wise in the road. The crew must have been incinerated immediately after encountering one of our fighters. As we cycled around it, we could plainly see the hole the armor-piercing rocket had made in the turret.

We had seen war before, and I thought the two of us were steeled against such scenes. But out here in this beautiful pristine Hanzel-and-Gretel-like garden, the hulk that was once a tank seemed so incongruent and out of place. It seemed bizarre and gut-wrenching, knowing what had happened to the crew inside.

The next village was the first, but it was not to be the last, where we noticed plain cloth at the windows instead of the usual curtains.

Throughout Germany, Belgium, and Holland, homes were decorated with hand-made lace curtains bordering the windows. It was as though some intramural contest was afoot to see which housewife could make the best and most unique lace curtains. The houses were constructed near the roads or the sidewalks in most cases. In Holland and Belgium, large bay windows beckoned the passer-by to observe the interior of the home. Each one was spic and span, as though it had recently been spring-cleaned. It was obvious the residents were proud of their homes and wanted everyone to observe family life within. This was the subject of much conversation, especially among G.I.'s who came from the back woods and the large industrial cities of America. The contrast in life styles was sobering, and tended to favorably change the opinion of many an American and British soldier who was seeing the people in Hitler's Europe for the first time.

We had never been this close before to the Germans, and we were beginning to see them as fellow human beings who lived in families in homes, just as we did. Still, the specter of Buchanwald and the atrocities of the SS were not far from our minds. I kept wondering as we passed by a particularly cozy, family-oriented home if perhaps some SS *Sturmbannfhurer* might have lived there, and whether he might have had a hand in executing our prisoners and tens of thousands of innocent Russian civilians.

As I said, we had noticed a rather gray-looking cloth had replaced some of the front window curtains. Without thinking too much about it, we concluded they had taken down the curtains to preserve them from an advancing enemy. What better souvenir than hand-made German lace for one's wife or mother? This is what we concluded, as we moved along. Now, as we stopped for a rest and a drink of water at a town faucet, it became even more noticeable. In this particular village all the front window curtains had vanished, and in their place was dingy cloth, obscuring the interior. A pillowcase was hanging from a makeshift pole, suspended from one of the upstairs windows. Then it dawned on us–these were bedclothes. They were tattletale gray, because they had no bleach. And they were not there to hide what was going on inside or to replace the curtains, as we first thought; they were hanging there as tokens of surrender. They were showing the *white flag* of surrender. Throughout all the villages, we were now seeing signs of universal surrender.

They must have gotten word of our approaching armies, and they had seen the remnants of their own in disorganized retreat and they had quit.

I was to find out later that the national radio was railing against those who were giving up or talking about doing so. In fact, Hitler, a few days ago, had his favorite general, General Fegelein, who would have became his brother-in-law, shot for counseling surrender for the good of the country and then attempting to leave Berlin. Now, regardless of the consequences, the citizenry of Germany were surrendering en masse.

A few miles farther down the road, we encountered our first deserting Wermacht infantry. They had thrown down their weapons and were in route-step home, wherever that might be. This was of no concern of ours, except they were clogging the road. Now we were seeing dead Germans, littering the sides of the road, victims of our strafing fighters. More burned-out tanks, trucks, and abandoned field pieces are to be seen strewn everywhere. Where a tank or truck had blocked the road, the next one had pushed it off to make way for the column behind.

Everywhere was refugees. And now the hawks could be heard overhead if not seen through the canopy of trees. The buzz of long-range *Mustang* engines, and occasionally the unique sound of twin Allison's identified *Lockheed Lightning's*, the aircraft the Luftwaffe called the *fork tailed devils*.

We are due in Salzburg in 48 hours. We figure we have plenty of time, although our progress has slowed almost to a walk. At one point we took the wrong road, which further delayed us. Road signs had been taken down in a futile effort to slow the coming Allied advance.

At one place we encountered a crush of civilians struggling to go somewhere else. Eric asked one of them pushing a wheelbarrow laden with her worldly goods if she knew how far it was to Salzburg. She replied with a blank stare that it was another 35 kilometers.

At the rate we are progressing, we won't make it. We have to find a way to increase our speed.

We were briefed to go straight to a *Hotel Imperial,* someplace downtown. There we are to meet this American agent by the name of Ralph Wahl, who goes by his former name of Rolph Wahlmuller. We are to meet him in the basement at noon the day after tomorrow. I told Eric things were bound to change and there should be no problem. He asked me what we would do if we were further delayed and we missed him. I told him Wahlmuller had been instructed to stay put until we arrived. But I suspect he thinks I'm not all that sure of what I'm saying; I can tell by the expression on his face. We both know it will become a problem if he leaves without us, and we somehow fail to make contact. It could turn into an insurmountable problem and we both know it. What we intend to do about it, though, should be decided right now. But I'm reluctant to say anything, because I don't know what to say.

It was soon after we passed through the next town that we saw tank tracks leading from thc road across the green pastures into the trees beyond. We thought this would be a certain giveaway to our fighters. But then we saw more and still more. We decided it was an SS ploy to confuse them, since there couldn't be that many panzers hidden in the trees. And we were right.

It was about an hour later; the road was thicker with civilians and deserting Wermacht than at any other timc. Then we heard them before we saw them–a flight of P-47 *Jugs*, their barrel-shaped fuselages, stubby wings, and large round Pratt and Whitney engines, could be seen coming at us low across a field. We forgot our training not to take cover alongside the road. Lucky for us they were not after civilians; they began firing at a column of unseen SS panzers less than a hundred yards ahead of us.

When we scrambled for cover, we almost landed on a Wermacht soldier. We knew he was a deserter because he had thrown his rifle away, and he appeared to be as scared as we were. Eric made an attempt to talk to him: "Where are you coming from," Eric asked. The reply he got was downright surly, and Eric became angry. Before I could stop him, he reached out and slapped the soldier hard across the mouth. Then he said something known only to the two of them. But I took it to mean he should keep a civilized tongue in his head if he didn't want to be shot. The soldier was startled at the words as well as the blow. *What kind of laborer would have the audacity to speak to a German soldier, let alone strike one?*

"You are not conscripted labor," he blurted out, "Who are you? You better tell me or I will cry out, and there are SS not far from here. You are spies, are you not? You better tell me!"

With that, Eric hit him again with his fist, making his nose bleed. This took all the fight out of him, if indeed, he had any left. Eric called him a deserter, and instead of bristling, as would a member of the SS, he cowered like a whipped dog. Then Eric surprised me again.

"Here," he said, removing a large sausage from his coat pocket. He reached for a pocketknife and cut the guy off a large chunk and handed it to him.

He was obviously starving. He forgot us, his sore nose, the War, and everything around him as he devoured the meat. Eric watched until he had finished before speaking to him again. Then he apologized for not having any bread and wine to go along with it.

The soldier looked as though he was being kidded, which he was.

"Now," Eric said, "tell me where you came from."

The soldier answered by remarking that we were Americans. He said he knew this by Eric's accent and by his largess. Here was an enemy soldier who was being fed. Nobody but an American would part with precious food along this road.

"Why did you say there were SS nearby. You were lying. If they knew you were here, they would shoot you on sight."

The soldier never replied, but you could tell Eric was right by the expression on the soldier's face. Eric explained to me what they had been talking about, and then asked me if there was anything I wanted to know.

"Yes," I said, "ask him if there really is any SS in the area, and if so, where they are." Before Eric could say anything, the soldier pointed toward Salzburg. It was obvious he could speak some English. As it turned out, he could speak quite well. He was an officer, who had switched uniforms with a dead member of his recent command. He told us this, as he spoke further about the whereabouts of the SS.

He said a column of SS panzers had overtaken his disorganized band of deserters. The tanks stopped long enough for a pee call and to mockingly ask them where they were headed. Before anybody could say anything, one of the tank officers sarcastically told them they were going the wrong way. He said the War was up ahead, toward Munich. He said there was only beer, schnapps, and the ladies where they were headed. Nobody smiled. The SS were never funny. With that last remark, the officer drew his Walther P-38 and shot the soldier standing next to our new guest. Before a member of the second tank could charge his Mauser, the deserting officer dove in front of the lead tank and then behind a tree. The column gunned their idling engines. They then turned and were starting to pull into the opposite field and disappear into the forest beyond. He said he heard machine gun rattle as they made ready to leave, and he suspected his group had all been killed. He said he was just now getting ready to go back to see if anybody was still alive when the American fighters attacked.

"Ask him if he lives around here. Ask him if he knows of another road to Salzburg that might not be so crowded."

He said he was from a town a few more kilometers up ahead. He said there was a fork in the road. Not in the road exactly, but a kind of path leading from the *promenade*. He said we could make better time if we took it. He said it was unpaved and used mostly by townspeople who were traveling on foot and didn't want to risk getting run over.

Most, if not all, of the towns of any size in Germany and Austria have a promenade street. Usually, it's the second street over from the main drag. Vendors of all kinds have shops where they display their wares. Automobiles, for the most part, are *verboten*. This allows the townies to walk up and down on old bricks and worn cobble stones, conversing with their friends, and to just plain old-fashioned window shop, weather permitting.

I was most interested in this path and something else: I wanted to know how we could identify the exact location of the panzer unit that had deployed across the field. Our German said there was a hamlet up ahead with a large mural on the first building we came to. He said it was a portrait of a nature scene, with a lake and two deer. You couldn't miss it, he said. But he had no idea what I had in mind.

I planned to contact Oddlie or Carl or both, and to tell them where the SS unit was located.

The officer told us the Tiger tanks were planning to zero in on this road with their .88's, and that any of our advancing tanks and infantry would not have a chance. Now I had to raise somebody on our radio and let them know.

He told us he had been part of an anti-aircraft battery positioned just to the north of the Chimsee. His unit and one other had targeted the autobahn and this particular road. He said anything moving to this point would come under deadly fire from the panzer unit in the trees and his former unit's artillery. But he said there was not much danger from the artillery, because they had run out of ammunition. They had been waiting for re-supply for two weeks. When they gave up all hope of getting more, most of them left.

I knew I had no business doing this. I knew, but I also knew I wouldn't forgive myself if I didn't do something. So I took a chance. Not that much of a chance, really, since the SS were the only functioning military unit in the area. By now, I doubted there was any Wermacht artillery at the Chimsee. But our new friend thought there might be some. I doubted they were using the same crystals we used, even if they were there.

Since all our radios were electronically interconnected, and had been since the Louisiana Maneuvers before the War, thanks to George Patton, I knew any one of our radios picking me up could relay it on to Oddlie. He, of course, would pass it on to the right people who would, in turn, pass it on to Weyland's fighters and fighter-bombers. The reason I wanted to contact Oddlie and not Weyland directly was because neither Weyland nor Patch's headquarters would react to a strange call coming in without a code word of the day. Oddlie knew who would be calling him, and he had the right connections to get the desired action.

The three of us moved hurriedly down the road, passed the dead Germans and three burning panzers. We were looking out at the trees, where the rest of the panzers had marked up the adjoining pasture, when we heard a roar of diesels firing up. All of a sudden, the panzers moved out of the trees, across the field, and back to the road. The German officer volunteered his opinion: The panzers, he said, suspected the P-47's had been low on fuel and had made only one pass at them before breaking off the attack. But they and others would return. He said the panzer commander wanted to move a couple of miles down the road and into another copse while he still had the chance.

Whether the panzers expected to survive long, once they began firing at our people moving up this same road, was anybody's guess. Again, I was struck with the feeling they were fighting a delaying action. They were stalling for time. I figured they were going to expend as much ammunition against our people as they could. When Weyland's fighters started unleashing their rockets, they would move further into the trees on foot. They would return when the fighters left and begin to shell the road again. For how long they would continue to do this, I had no idea. But up the road, our German told me, another unit would start it all over again. The SS, it was now apparent, intended to defend Berchtesgaden while fighting a delaying action. At least they intended to apply stiff resistance at specific points for a specific time. That was my opinion and the German officer's as well.

I made a call, and picked up Carl after a few tries. I told him what was going to happen and where. I told him about the artillery at the Chimsee. I specifically warned him to tell the Air Corps not to attack the panzers now but to wait. I wanted them to wait until O'Daniel's units reached this point. And here the German earned his piece of sausage and another. He knew how far we were from the next town. He knew the name and a couple of more checkpoints that would help our people in identifying the panzers before they started shooting.

Carl passed on the information and then got back. He said Patch's headquarters, actually his corps commander, General Devers, had new orders for me. At first, Devers was confused as to who we were. Then he told Carl to have us stay put. He told him nothing was more important than for us to stay where we were and to spot for the Air Corps. He said he would have an infantry division, supported by tanks, at our present location in four or five days' time. Carl was smart enough to tell the General he didn't know who called him, and that he was not sure of his own position. I guess a court-martial was the last thing from his mind. I suppose he had a decision to make, Carl I mean; he had a choice of a medal or several million dollars in SS gold. It was no choice at all. He already had a handful of medals.

CHAPTER 15...AUSTRIA, April, 1945

We spent another two hours walking with the German officer. There were places where the debris and the crowds thinned to where it was practical to mount up and ride for short distances. But I didn't want to lose him. I wanted him to show me the path he had been talking about. And since he's in no shape to run alongside of us, even if he was inclined to do so, we walked with him. This gave us some time to talk.

We started our conversation by discussing the two opposing tanks, the Tiger and the Sherman. He told me the Sherman was not much of a tank at all. He said they expected more from us than the Sherman could deliver. He said it was little more than a toy when compared to the Tiger. The armor-piercing shells of the Tiger panzer went right through the Sherman, while the larger, more powerful shell of the Sherman bounced off the Tiger. Still, he said, the Tiger was not perfect. He said Adolph Hitler designed it. That is, he had made the important decisions as to its specifications and the tactical role it was to play. He told me Adolph's generals wanted secondary armament installed on the golf models. Hitler, on the other hand, wanted strictly a *blitzkrieg* weapon and would not back off on his demands.

Hitler saw the tank as a strike weapon supported by infantry, rather than the other way around. I asked him what he meant exactly. He said it had no machine guns, which meant the golf couldn't defend itself from entrenched infantry. He said this was the main cause for Germany's losses at the battle for Kursk on the Russian front. He said the Tigers rolled right over infantry, who then popped up and destroyed them with rifle grenades from the rear. There was very little armament in the rear. This, too, was Hitler's idea, he said. He explained why Kursk would go down in history as the greatest land battle ever fought. He said they lost, and consequently they lost the battle for Russia. He told me he had been there. He was an Oberst, a Colonel, who commanded a battalion.

I told him I thought Stalingrad was the turning point. He said it was important, but Germany really lost everything at Kursk. He reminded me that a victorious Germany, suffering minimal losses on the Russian front, would have been more than the Allies could have handled at Normandy. Then, too, he said, even with their losses in Russia, it would have been problematical if Patton could have moved very far inland if the German side had had air support. We both agreed that air power was going to determine who won any future wars. We also agreed there would never be another one. But then, we both could remember that's what both sides said after the first one. But if there ever is another, air power is going to be the deciding factor and not tanks, he said. This German is exceptionally well informed; he thinks the same as I do.

He showed us our new route to Salzburg. He called it the *German Alpine Road* or some such. We gave him the remainder of our sausage, the half he had not eaten plus another one I was carrying. Frankly, I'm tired of the stuff. It's good when fried and mixed with gravy. But by itself, it's too salty for my taste.

We parted friends. He told me his name was Lother Horner and that he came from a small town up ahead with a large harp on the first house. He said the town was called *Siegesdorf.* He told me his mother owned a small *Gasthaus*, but that it had been vacant for most of the War. It was much smaller than a hotel, having only four rooms and few of the amenities. However, it did have a kitchen and served restaurant meals to other than paying guests. It brought her some income, but he had to supplement it with his army pay. He gave me the address, which I wrote in my pocket notebook, while he watched and corrected my spelling. It was all for show, as I promised to come by and visit. He said to come anytime, even when I was out of the army if I wanted to. And to bring my wife and children. I thought the latter was a bit much, but I only smiled and thanked him. I never expected to, of course, but I promised. You know how that goes sometimes.

He told me one of his goals, when things settled down and came back to normal, was to add another four *zimmers* to his mother's place. Once he got started talking about what he was planning for the future, he didn't want to stop. He said he had plenty of room for the additions and off-street parking in the rear of the present building, but the problem was going to be accumulating the capital to make it happen. With eight rooms and a renovation, he figured the tourists were going to come. He said it was an easy day trip to the Obersalzberg. He had an advantage over closer accommodations, because he could afford to rent rooms cheaper. And then, too, his town was naturally old German and not so *ersatz* as those nearer Salzburg. He asked me what I thought of his plan. I told him it sounded good, but that I didn't think there was going to be much left for tourists to see at Hitler's compound. I refrained from telling him why.

This path he showed us turned out to be a field boundary marker that had been widened and packed by foot traffic over the centuries. It has some refugee traffic now, but not all that much, so it works pretty well for our bicycles. We started making good time, and I figured we are going to be very close to Salzburg by dark. I intend to sleep in a forest on the outskirts and then pump into the city early in the morning.

We found the hotel with about two hours to spare. We sat at a sidewalk café several doors down. They had no food, but they offered us a coffee. This was my introduction to Ersatz, a word I had heard Lothar Horner use. It means *replacement, substitute or fake,* or all of the above. Ersatz is made of acorns and whatever else is available; it consists of everything but real coffee beans. Cafes around there haven't sold real coffee in years. One taste and my mouth puckered up. But then it did the same thing when I tasted the real thing for the first time. Ersatz reminds me of Postum, and maybe it is. Postum has a limited appeal for those who want something hot, but for one reason or another they don't care to mess around with caffeine. I don't know if they even sell Ersatz anymore. Maybe they sell it under another name, but not outside Germany, I'm reasonably sure of that.

We wheeled our bikes to the back door of the Imperial and padlocked them. We opened this large, ornate oak-plank door that must have been hundreds of years old. We cautiously made our way into a musty inner chamber, down a creaking, haunted castle-like staircase to the basement floor. The place smelled of mouse urine and mold. All around were boxes stacked as high as my head. It resembled a warehouse. Between rows of boxes, we could see the loom of a naked bulb in the far corner. Someone was here–maybe it was Wahlmuller–or maybe it was one of his associates from the hotel where he worked. Maybe they had found him out and tortured him until he told them about us. Maybe they had come here to pick us up and interrogate us. Both of us were afraid, me more so than Eric. But then maybe my mind was more imaginative than his.

I nudged Eric, and he called out in German: "Is anybody here?" Then he called again, "Rolph, are you back there?"

There was a long pause of continuing silence. Then I felt the barrel of what must have been a Luger. A voice spoke in English: "Who are you people?"

Eric answered in German as though a sentry was challenging him: "We're friends." I almost expected the other voice to reply, advance friend, and be recognized.

Then I said without thinking: "Are you Rolph Wahlmuller?"

Dumb move. What if he's not?

"Who wants to know?"

I didn't know what to say, so I simply said: "Red Adair."

"Are you from Louisiana?"

"Close enough." Not very professional, but now I knew who he was and I wasn't in any mood for lengthy explanations.

We shook hands. This friend of Oddlies was taller than Eric or myself by several inches. He was blond with blue eyes. If Hitler had seen him, he no doubt would've recruited him for his *lebensborn* program. He definitely fit the profile, and he was the ideal age–somewhere in his middle twenties.

When Hitler concocted his master race scheme, championed by Heinrich Himmler, head of the Gestapo and the other two branches of the SS, his geneticists convinced him you could breed people the same as you could horses. I assume the genetic algebra worked the same way; it just had never been tried before. He earmarked the most genetically pure of the young volunteer German women as breeding stock; then he secreted them at mountain retreats and selected hotels, inviting his SS and Wermacht officers to do the stud honors, providing they could produce genealogies free of the taint of Jewish blood. In occupied Norway, Himmler encouraged temporary unions between *Viking* women and his *Aryan* soldiery. The *foals* were known as lebensborn–freely translated, it means *fountain* or *source of life*. They were to be the *fountainhead* of his master race, which was destined to rule the world for the next thousand years.

"Have you been broadcasting?" It was a stupid remark. I knew he hadn't, but I didn't know what else to say.

He smiled and said: "No, I do not keep a transmitter here."

"Where do you keep it?"

"All in good time," he replied. "These are cases of beer and schnapps. I use them as an excuse to come to town once or twice a week. They belong to the SS mess at the compound. They are brewed locally and delivered here. It is supposed to be good stuff, if you like it. I wouldn't know. One of my many nothing jobs is to see that they never run out at the bar in the mess.

"Help me load some cases of each, and we will be on our way. The truck is out back."

We placed several boxes in the bed of a curious looking utility vehicle. It has three wheels, the front being steered by a horizontal bar on the driver's side. I wouldn't call it a truck, exactly. I think I can remember seeing one before, but I'm not sure. I guessed it was low geared and slow. I can't see it being very safe at speeds above 25 miles an hour. I was right. It is underpowered with a two-cycle, four-cylinder engine. *Surely it's not what he plans to use tomorrow night.*

He looked at me and guessed what I was thinking. "No," he said, "this thing is almost overloaded right now.

We use it because we have it, and because it gets about 50 kilometers to one of your gallons.

"Enjoy the countryside, plenty of time to talk and ask questions when we get there."

"Just one," I said.

"Okay," he said.

"Incidentally," he said, "I have not spoken English in years. I never had anyone to talk to. Not healthy. The Gestapo is everywhere. Many aristocrats who used to visit here spoke it well. But they scrupulously avoided its usage for obvious reasons."

"I didn't know you were crippled. I wasn't aware you walked with a cane."

He laughed. "I had a mishap on one of the steeper runs of the *Jenner* years ago. But this old cane has kept me out of the army, and out of harm's way. I use it, but I don't have to; my leg healed years ago. Me and my cane are sort of a nondescript fixture around here. They are used to seeing me doing all kinds of things not involving heavy work. Nobody ever questions me any more. Not even the Gestapo watches me, although, they watch everybody else–and each other. You might say, I'm a professional goof-off. Nobody knows what I am supposed to be doing. I carry my cane and a clipboard around wherever I go. I goof-off counting things. I count everything. We Germans like people who count things. I think it has something to do with this penchant of ours, this national need for orderliness. Nobody bothers me as long as I appear to be busy, even if I do not accomplish much.

"I make sure everybody knows I broke my leg skiing. It would not do to have them think I was born this way."

The fact is if Rolph had been crippled by a birth defect instead of an athletic accident, he probably would have found himself in some kind of an institution, maybe an extermination camp. But as it was, the SS looked upon his injury as a kind of merit badge. I think it might have made him even more acceptable to them. Rolph knows this and has played up his old injury for all it's worth.

We purred along at the respectable speed of 25, about what I expected. This vehicle is built to get around in slow traffic with light loads, sort of a mechanized delivery cart. Trust the Germans. Our people would probably have used a heavy pick-up to do the same job, at three times the cost and three times the fuel.

All around us is the most spectacular scenery I've ever seen. I had heard about the Austrian Alps, but not in my wildest dreams did I imagine the outdoors could be so spectacularly beautiful. No wonder Adolph picked this place for his home. But what kept it from being overrun with like homebuilders? I'm curious, but I saved the question for later, and then forgot to ask.

Just when I thought things were as good as they could possibly get, another even more spectacular scene came into view. And when I remarked about this, Rolph laughed, saying: "You have not seen anything. We are not even to Berchtesgaden yet."

Another of the things I noticed, after I had been around him for a few minutes, he said he was not used to speaking English and he was right. He had lived in America for several years, before he came back to Austria. But he never lived there long enough to lose his accent. And what he did lose, he must have found again. He speaks with a thick tongue, more like an Austrian who never left the country in the first place. He gets things backward. He's always wanting to *throw mother from the train, a kiss.* And he seldom if ever uses contractions, which makes his speech patterns even more stilted.

He reminds me of an American woman I knew who married a Spaniard. She immigrated to Spain when she was young and lived there for some forty years, never speaking

English. When I spoke to her, she apologized, hesitatingly, with a kind of Spanish accent. Some kind of regression like that has probably taken place with Rolph.

The thought has occurred to me that Eric and I will have to include him in our plans for the next couple of weeks. We can't leave him on his own. Any infantry unit entering this area will have been in combat. When he tries to pawn himself off as an American, they will rough him up first and ask questions later. They won't see him as a slave laborer needing their protection. They are going to suspect he is just another German who speaks English and who's working for the SS. Worse yet, he has no identification; they might even think he is SS wearing civilian clothes and shoot him. At any rate, they are going to ask him a lot of trivia questions he can't answer–such as, who does Babe Ruth play for, and who is married to Harry James, things like that. He's certain to end up in a bad place for a long time, until they take the time to sort him out. None of this has escaped Oddlie, though. That's why we are here–to take care of him–and to take care of Patton's gold at the same time.

CHAPTER 16...SAN ANTONIO, 1950

I drove over from New Orleans to see Lucy. We met at our now favorite restaurant on the Riverwalk. I have a ring I purchased from a jeweler I know in the Quarter. I could've had one of my own diamonds set, but that would've really been too pretentious. The jeweler probably took me for a little, but that's one of the advantages of having some money–you don't sweat the small things. Anyway, I'm going to give it to her and see if we can settle on a date. I'm getting kind of antsy, and I hate to keep driving long distances to see her. Still, it gives me something to do and it does keep me moving around.

As I said, we met at this restaurant, where we have been talking for the past two hours. I don't know where she lives and she doesn't know anything about me. We keep in touch through Fogerty, whom I trust more than anyone I know, except maybe for Ralph Wahl.

The story I have been telling you, by way of explanation of why I'm in all this trouble, is the same story I have been telling her. She doesn't want to talk about our future particularly. She still thinks we ought to give it more time. When I realize she feels this way, I hold off on the ring thing. I feel my asking would only embarrass her. I think she figures if she accepts a ring it will formalize our engagement, and then I'm going to insist on sleeping with her. I'm not, but I've thought about it a lot. Maybe she's not too far off the mark.

She asks me more questions about the gold I have been talking about. The last time I saw her, I told her I was in possession of a fortune–some seven-hundred bars of fortune–at least that's what I started out with. Of course, that remark set off a barrage of questions, none of which were unexpected. When was the last time you were eating dinner with somebody, and out of a clear blue sky they told you they had this kind of money stashed away someplace? Would you have any questions?

She has known from early on that somebody is trying to find me to do me in if I don't tell them where it is. I'm not sure, but maybe that's the reason she doesn't want to get married. Maybe she doesn't want to have anything to do with the life I lead. Anyway, I've been telling her the story I've been telling you.

"Mike, do you know any more about what happened to Kurt Steinmann and those two French girls you told me about?"

"Yes I do, well maybe I do. No, I'm not absolutely sure, not about Steinmann anyway."

"Not much of an answer," she remarked.

"I suppose not, but the whole thing is pretty much a mess. And to tell you the truth, it hasn't gotten any clearer with the passing of time.

"I hired a couple of private detectives a while back, before I met you. They specialize in locating lost persons. They haven't come up with the whereabouts of Steinmann yet. However, the French women were pretty easy to find. They moved back to Paris." I didn't tell her much more than that, not anything personal, of course. Neither of them was married. When the detectives told me this, I went to see Françoise.

"Neither Murielle nor Françoise had seen Steinmann. He vanished. But whether he's hiding out in Argentina or Brazil is anybody's guess. I believe I have told you the SS are still wanted by several governments. I think, wherever he is, he's afraid to come home. Murielle still thought he was going to show-up one of these days. But wherever, I believe he's having a hard time of it. The SS didn't get any of the Merkers treasure, and as far as I know none of the Obersalzberg gold either. But I can't be absolutely sure of that. I'm reasonably sure, though, that Steinmann survived the raid on Hitler's place. In fact, I know he was at Berchtesgaden at the time. Later, if anybody made it to Argentina he would have. These people are survivors. They're tough as nails and conditioned to weather great hardships. I read something written by one of their generals to the effect that had the SS been at Stalingrad the Germans never would have surrendered." I told her all of this mostly to make conversation. Actually, I knew more about Steinmann than I let on.

I don't know why I went to see Françoise. I told myself I was there to see what Murielle really knew about the whereabouts of her lover. Maybe there was something she knew that she wouldn't tell my investigators. I thought maybe I could trade information with her, although I'm at a loss to say what it might be. Maybe I can fake it a little. I could tell her what most people know–many of the SS got away and are living in South America. If she thinks I have inside information along those lines, she might loosen up. Mainly, I guess I want to know if she thinks I have any of what she regards as Steinmann's gold.

I'm pretty sure she told him about me and my two sergeants. She might even have shown him copies of pictures of the three of us with Françoise, taken with one of those small Brownie cameras most of us carried around with us.

I know Murielle feels the Merkers gold belongs to him, and in some perverse way, she thinks some of it belongs to her and the child. That might not be the truth either. I just don't know. But that's what I was telling myself. In reality, I wanted to see Françoise again. I don't know why, but I did. No, that's not the truth either. I knew why I wanted to see her again. I can't explain it. But it's the same reason I later went to see Lucy, which I also can't explain.

Françoise had been married but was now divorced. She had no children, which would not have mattered to me if I was still in love with her. I once thought I was. And now I'm playing as though I still am. I did my best to convince myself things were the same as they were when I first met her. But they were not, and it took me about two weeks to realize they were never going to be.

She acted as though she had thought a lot of me in the old days, and that nothing had changed between us. There really had been nothing between us in the first place; I just wanted there to be. Maybe there had been between her and Eric, but not with us.

Françoise suspected I had some money. I didn't flash it around, but I know she did. But then I had no way of knowing if she thought I had any more than any other American. And this made a difference, because I would never have been sure where I began and the money left off.

At one point, I asked Françoise if Murielle ever heard from Steinmann after he left for the Eastern Front. She said she did. She said he had been in combat near Berlin and then was transferred rather quickly. From his description of his new station, it sounded to them both as though he might have been in the south of Germany. They thought he might have been in Austria. But neither of them could figure out what Steinmann was doing down there when the Russians were about to enter Berlin. They told me they thought they must be mistaken; maybe they were misinterpreting something he had been trying to say.

He did tell Murielle if everything worked out as he planned, they were going to be well off, and that they would eventually be able to be together and live happily ever after. He could have meant he had stolen some gold somewhere along the line, and they planned to live in Argentina. It might be his way of telling her without running afoul of the Gestapo, who still read the mail, even the mail of senior officers. Who knows?

CHAPTER 17...BERCHETESGADEN, APRIL 1945

I thought we were going straight from the Imperial to the compound on the Obersalzberg, but we never took the cutoff. We came south from Salzburg and then went directly to Berchtesgaden. I never said anything. I had the idea Rolph wanted to stop and stretch his legs. Three of us in his truck was very uncomfortable. Our going any further then Berchtesgaden was out of the question. My foot started going to sleep before we reached the outskirts of Salzburg, and I was glad to get out and walk around.

Wahlmuller had a friend he wanted to see; at least that's what he told us. We went behind this one house, done up like most of them we had been looking at for the past week or so–gingerbread trim, stucco artwork, and a rather unique rail leading to a basement apartment. Rolph walked down the steps and knocked on an ornate door, sporting a hand-carved hunting scene in bas-relief. An older man answered. They exchanged greetings and some words too fast for Eric, who looked at me and shrugged his shoulders. Rolph looked up and beckoned us to come down.

We were ushered into a small, quaint kitchen. And then into a kind of parlor, having a typical green-tinted ceramic wood-burning stove. The furniture was well worn, covered with some kind of intricate overlaid embroidery to hide the imperfections. There were the usual ancestors hanging from the walls, and a rather well-turned-out gun collection displayed in a standing glass case. The room seated the four of us nicely; however, any more would have spilled into the kitchen.

We were offered coffee. We hesitated, thinking we were going to get another cup of putrid-tasting Ersatz. We begged off, whereupon Rolph assured us we were being offered the real thing. It seems our host has a friend who is well connected to the black market, and this friend of his is none other than Rolph Wahlmuller. Then I recalled Rolph's comment about the number of odd jobs he had at the compound. One of them must be taking care of the food stores in the officer's mess, which should be infinitely better stocked than any black market.

Before we sat down, we were introduced to Rolph's friend, this older gentleman by the name of Walter Reinicke. In order to remember his name, I immediately attached a *memory peg.* I used the popular saxophone player and soloist in Glenn Miller's orchestra by the name of Tex Beneke. I often use memory pegs for names. In this case, Reinicke rhymed with Beneke, and Beneke played the saxophone and Reinicke had a large nose that reminded me of an upside-down saxophone and…well, you get the idea.

"Red, Herr Reinicke is a friend and a confederate of mine, not because I give him sausage and real coffee from time to time, but because he hates Hitler. I brought you here to meet him and to show you how our radio operates. We can receive coded messages, but we cannot transmit by voice–sometimes by key for very short periods but never by voice. The nearby radio station would immediately detect our position. And that brings me to my first point of interest. I guess it is as good a place as any to start…." He paused momentarily, thinking about something as if to change his mind. Then, apparently satisfied everything was all right, he pushed on.

"I started to tell you about the radio station," he began again. "One of the five operators is a good friend of mine. Unlike my friend Reinicke here, we are friends only because I treat him well. I give him an occasional bottle of schnapps and a case of *Tuborg* once in a while. And I often hang around when he is lonesome on the midnight shift. We play a game of chess or two and talk. His supervisor does not seem to care. Anyway, we have been doing this for over a year now. In return, he keeps me posted on things he hears that he considers to be unclassified, yet of a personal interest to me.

"In the beginning, it was just routine War news. Now, of late, it has been the status of the German forces. He knows this interests me, because he knows at some point I am going to have to leave this part of Austria. He realizes I can't stay here until the American army shows up and then just disappear. He wants me to think about going with the rest of them to Argentina. He tells me I am a true believer in the cause. And when the organization reverts to semi-civilian status, they will let me *enlist.* He thinks the doctors made a mistake with my leg. And then, too, he thinks I am disappointed about not being able to be one of them–a real credentialed member of the Waffen SS family. And now, he says, this is my chance to serve where I was unable to during the War. More than a few times, he has told me the Fuhrer would be proud of me. But more to the point: he thinks the Allies are going to shoot me if I stay, when they show up here in a few days. He thinks the townspeople might even beat them to it, since some people think I am already a member of his organization. He believes the town's citizens will not make any distinctions. If I'm left behind, this operator friend of mine worries I will have no place to go. He realizes stragglers will be branded criminals and imprisoned. Worse yet, they might be executed if they fall into the hands of the locals. He tells me his own countrymen now openly hate the SS. It's hidden, undercover for now, but it is hate nevertheless. And they will include me, because of my volunteer close association with them.

"There is no question about it," Rolph continued in English, "The SS are hated. Of course, nobody says anything or openly lets on, and they will not as long as they can retaliate. But for the past year now, they have not been welcome in the residents' homes. Nor will their former friends and acquaintances so much as say hello to them. Even their families have shunned them. Where once they were heroes, they are now pariahs. Once they were looked upon as Hitler's darlings; now most people believe they were just as much involved in starting the War as was Hitler."

We talked with Rolph and Reinicke for another half-hour. Occasionally Rolph would say something in German, which he would translate for my benefit. But for the most part, everything he said was in English because Reinicke couldn't speak more than a few words of the language. And this seemed to Rolph to be important. It struck me that he was intentionally keeping the *jist* of the conversation from the old man.

It was at this point that I asked Rolph or Ralph–I use his names interchangeably–if he had ever run into an oberststurmbannfuhrer or maybe a standartenfuhrer by the name of Kurt Steinmann. I couldn't help but notice the expression on his face when he heard me mention the name. I definitely believe I saw his jaw drop. But you can't be sure about things like that.

Ralph, with Reinicke's permission, ushered us to one of the back bedrooms. He shoved the bed aside, and then lifted up several pieces from the hardwood floor. Beneath the floor was a radio with a sending key, a small microphone, and earphones. Without turning it on, he showed Eric and me how it operated. I didn't hesitate, but handed over our walkie-talkies, asking him to keep them there. We could no longer pack them around, and we wouldn't be using them to contact Carl again until we came back from the lake.

I noticed a third small bedroom adjacent to the master; the door was slightly ajar. I sensed somebody was inside and could hear us. Then, as we exited the kitchen door, I heard a loud, deep, and uncontrolled, racking cough–something like whooping cough, or perhaps tuberculosis.

I turned around from the third step and looked at Walter Reinicke, who was about to close the door. I guess he thought he had to say something; there was no question that someone else was in the house, and that person had to have been listening to us.

Reinicke said to Eric, whom he knew spoke his language: "Take no mind of him. He is one of my three sons who came home sick. The third one is missing. We have not heard from him in months." When Eric looked at Reinicke as though he wanted more of an explanation, the old man unhesitatingly told us more about his sons. He knew we were no threat to their safety, and he didn't care how much we knew.

"The two who are here have had harrowing experiences. They're lucky to be alive," Eric translated: "They've been on the Eastern Front. One of them is shell-shocked and has been maimed by frostbite; he uses a cane and may never walk normally again. The other could die from a lung infection if he's not treated."

Eric explained that Reinicke can't get either of them help, because the German authorities will arrest the three of them if he does. And the Gestapo will shoot them without hesitation. Their only hope is to wait for our troops and then beg for some medicine. However, he is afraid our people might lock them up as prisoners. If they do, he's afraid the one with the cough will die quickly.

"Everything is in such turmoil and so uncertain," Eric continued, "if it weren't for Ralph here, Reinicke says, they would also be starving." Our host stopped talking, and Eric stopped translating. There was nothing left to say.

Reinicke looked at me, pleadingly, as if I could or would do something for them. In our debriefing of hundreds of deserters, we slowly came to the conclusion that the Wermacht also committed many atrocities. However, they were quick to blame it on the SS; but now it appears your average German soldier won't be held blameless. However, I have no intention of holding any of this against his sons. Walter Reinicke is our ally. He possess a radio, which is a capital offense. And he hates the SS and Hitler the same as we do. And that's enough for me.

Reinicke desperately wants me to intervene with some of our medics. But even if I could I wouldn't; as far as Eric and I are concerned, his sons are unrepentant deserters. They are sorry only because they've lost. Who knows what they would really be like if circumstances were any different or if things change later? As I said, I've no intentions of turning them in, but I'm not going to write him a letter to our medics either. He thinks I should–he thinks he's entitled to some compensation for helping Ralph all these years.

Then it struck me: Walter just might take it in his head to tell our people about us being here in exchange for medical help for his sons. But I can't see how he's going to hurt us after we're gone. And we will be before the first Americans arrive. That's another reason for getting out of here as quickly as possible. But how much does Reinicke know about the gold? And will he tell somebody later if he feels we've betrayed him by not helping his sons?

Oddlie told me Reinicke once owned the Turken and that it was taken away from him; Ralph confirms it. That's the main reason he was helping Ralph. Food is important;

but hatred because he had everything stolen from him is the real reason.

He told Ralph he expects to be back in business within weeks of the SS departure, unless they trash the place or burn it. Now, it has just occurred to me: how is he going to feel if the Turken is handed back to him in ruins? What will happen to the compound on the 25th? What are his feelings going to be when it's leveled in accordance with Patton and Weyland's plans?

CHAPTER 18...OBERSALZBERG, MARCH 1945

The high-pitched roar of a half-dozen diesel engines climbing in low gear past the Berghof, up past the Turken, awakened Rolph Wahlmuller. It was the 10th of March, just before midnight on a bright moonlit night, and tensions were running high. There were no headlights on the vehicles or spotlights turned on in the compound. The security people were standing by, but hadn't been ordered to stop and search the trucks. It was as though somebody was trying to sneak them in unnoticed under the cover of darkness, such as it was. What the convoy was carrying was a mystery, but it wouldn't remain so for long.

Whoever was leading knew the layout well. There was no starting and stopping, no shouting of orders, nothing to indicate the leader in the command car might be confused as to where he was going.

The door to Rolph's quarters was thrown open. The lights were turned on, and his sleep was interrupted by a duty *sturmann* shouting *rouse, rouse mitten ze*!

Rolph rolled over, wondering if members of the Wermacht were in the habit of shouting whenever they wanted something, or was it just the SS. What about the American army? Does every corporal in every army exercise his limited authority by shouting? He concluded they did. But if the convoy was trying to be extra quiet and not awaken the general population, why hadn't the sturmann been told. He decided, as he pulled on his boots and reached for his clipboard, that nobody knew they were coming. But Rolph knew; he had been expecting them for days.

One of Rolph's many jobs was inventorying and listing all supplies coming in from the outside. A convoy meant inventory and storage. As he left his cubicle in the basement of the Turken, he could see several blacked-out three-ton trucks parked near the *Hintereck*. Why? He knew why. Oddlie had told him, but the security people didn't know. They thought they were loaded with food supplies. But if they were, they were parked in the wrong place. The kitchens and the barracks were several hundred meters further up. However, if it was ammunition, which was their second guess, it was destined for an underground magazine in the shooting range. But if it was ammunition, the security chief thought he should have been told. Something was very much out of the ordinary here; the security officer was seriously considering arresting the officer in charge of the convoy as a suspected intruder.

Part of the massive building program of Martin Bormann's was the building of a sports field west of the Hintereck. Then, two years ago, when attack from the air became a serious consideration, Bormann again took it upon himself to have hundreds of meters of tunneling cut into the mountain. He carved out elaborate rooms and interconnected them with still more tunnels. Machine gun posts guarded the tunnel entrances, which were primarily to be used as bomb shelters in the event the unthinkable happened.

There had been previous excavation through solid granite underneath the sports field to build a small arms shooting range, a huge vault, and a bomb-proof ammunition magazine. But the real purpose for this extravagant underground layout, as envisioned by Bormann, was to ensure the Fuhrer wasn't disturbed when he was in residence. And then too, it made an excellent bomb shelter; but nobody talked of such things back before the War started.

Rolph, of course, was on hand to watch the construction as it proceeded toward completion. He was also there the day they brought up a huge steel door. He watched them install it in what would later become a secret vault in back of a wall in the shooting range. The target area itself was faced with dirt to a depth of several feet. If the vault was to be opened any shooting ceased and the area was vacated.

Kurt Steinmann was prepared for trouble from the security officer who was approaching him. Kurt quickly handed him a set of orders, which stated his cargo was classified and he didn't need to know. With a smirk, he told him it was none of his business, to dismiss his people and to go back to bed.

Rolph, with his cane and clipboard in plain view, was the next to approach the haughty oberststurmbannfuhrer. Steinmann, standing straight with a studied posture, slowly removed his gloves. He paid no attention to Rolph, his mind seemingly lost in thought. As he turned, he glanced at Rolph and then looked away again, prepared to dislike him without further due. Then out of the corner of his eye, he saw his cane. His exaggerated limp stood out in the bright moonlight. *My first appraisal may have been hasty. This tall man with the Nordic features and complexion similar to my own has obviously been in the SS. He has probably been invalided-out after being severely wounded, maybe on the Eastern Front. Why else would a civilian be allowed to serve close to an SS commandant and his permanent party?*

Kurt saw Rolph's position as an honor bestowed on

somebody having distinguished himself in combat. And there was something else about this blond Wagnerian with the serious limb impairment; Steinmann had seen him someplace before.

Minutes later the Commandant arrived in a staff car. Granted, it would have been easier and faster for him to walk the few hundred meters from his quarters. But that's not the way things were done. No lapsing into slovenly ways. The convoy officer might regard any procedural deviation on his part as defeatist. And there were no defeatists in the Waffen SS and never had been.

Steinmann turned his attention from Rolph to the officer alighting from the staff car. The two saluted with an exaggerated Heil Hitler, and then took the measure of each other like two dogs meeting on a street corner. Kurt pronounced him fit and capable. However, the Commandant was not so condescending; taking notice of Kurt's blond hair, he allowed that he might bear watching.

Hitler was known to be enamored of the stereotypical Aryan physiognomy, as represented by the relatively few Germans who resembled Kurt and Rolph. Their blond hair and blue eyes was not the look of your off-the-street German. Someday, maybe, but not now. In fact, neither Hitler, Bormann, Hess, Goering, Himmler, or Speer had blond hair or blue eyes. They were all dark complexioned. They could pass for Slavs if the light was right, or Jews in any light. This was significant; whether any of them liked it or not, the perception of having Aryan blood stood any officer in good stead. It pronounced him *prima facia* a leader of men, because after all, history's great leaders came from this preferred blood line.

But of more significance to the Commandant, who didn't put much stock in racial propaganda, was the probability that Kurt was sent here to report on the readiness of things. He had been waiting for weeks now to hear confirmation of the Fuhrer's rumored change in plans. *Here, at last, is the word; he is ready to join his troops here instead of in Bavaria. This cargo is probably ammunition, which could have been brought by anybody. But Steinmann brought it because he is known to be one of the Fuhrer's favorites; he is one of the few Hitler trusts to tell him the truth of how things are.*

And then there is Goering, sitting over in his house doing who knows what, defying Berlin's orders to come back, fearing he might be shot as a traitor–maybe Steinmann is here to report to Bormann on just what Goering is up to. That is it. Berlin wants to know about Goering; maybe they even want this emissary of Hitler's to shoot him; maybe they don't trust me to do it. As if I didn't have enough to think about.

But there were other problems potentially more hazardous to the Commandant's health than the nearby presence of the malingering Reichminister–four large mountains of gold bars glistened back at him from four truck beds. As the full extent of his new problem became apparent, he didn't know whether to rejoice or to sink into deep despair. He was stunned. On the one hand, it was the answer to their survival problems; on the other, he was destined to be shot if so much as one of the bars came up missing. Now, as he halfway gained his composure, the Commandant began mumbling quietly; just above a whisper, he asked if Kurt might have some instructions for him. Kurt told him he did, as he handed him an envelope with orders from Bormann.

The Commandant opened the vault as directed, while a dozen ammunition carts were rolled out and loaded. Rolph took up position inside the vault, and counted each ingot as it was placed in two stacks eight courses high and seven rows square. When the trucks were emptied, both Kurt and Rolph re-counted the stacks. Sure of the tally, Rolph handed the inventory sheet to Kurt. Kurt glanced at it, and then looked around to make sure no one was standing nearby in the semi-darkness. Then he spoke, telling Rolph his tally of the last stack was in error. He told Rolph, looking at him through dull, unemotional and unwavering eyes that he, Rolph, had somehow miscounted. He said Rolph should adjust his tally to show an even total of seven hundred and not seven hundred and eighty four. Then he said something very curious. He told him to sign off on the sheet, and things would be explained later. Rolph was aware the senior officer, who obviously was highly placed in the hierarchy, could shoot him on the spot for any number of reasons and no one would have blinked an eye.

Rolph signed the false invoice. He presented it to the Commandant for his signature. Now he was in trouble; whichever way it turned out, he knew he was going to be shot.

The following day, Rolph was planting flowers behind the Berghof. This was not busy work, nor under the circumstances was it seen to be out of the ordinary. Quite the contrary, they were still expecting the Fuhrer at any moment. And Steinmann had told the Commandant that fresh flowers lent an air of stability and permanency to the scene.

Steinmann chose this particular time to take a stroll and admire the scenery. To anybody who might be watching, it appeared to be a casual conversation between a long-time resident gardener and a new arrival who might be asking dozens of questions. In this case, Kurt asked him if he liked goldenrods. He told Rolph it was the Fuhrer's favorite flower; he said he should consider planting some. He said the Fuhrer would be pleased if he did. Then he told him the correct way to plant them was to dig a trench some two feet deep and about five feet long. If Rolph would leave the trench uncovered, Kurt said he would make certain special seeds of the flower would be forthcoming.

Later in the day, in the presence of two junior officers, Kurt struck up a conversation with Rolph. The officers were sitting on the veranda, chatting, gazing up at the eagle's nest on the *Kelstien*. Rolph was serving them some of his Danish beer, when Kurt remarked that he understood Rolph had been in residence almost since the inception of Bormann's huge construction undertakings. Kurt told him that's where he thought he had seen him. He said he would like to talk to him about the changes made, since he, Kurt, had been here several times many years before. He said Rolph might be the only one who had the answers to some of his questions. It was put in such a way as to convey an order. Rolph understood and was prepared to hold himself available at the officer's request the following day. It didn't seem inappropriate when Kurt, in full view, but out of earshot of other members of the mess, told Rolph to come to his office in two hours' time.

Following lunch, Rolph presented himself at attention just as though he was in the military service of the Fuhrer. Steinmann did not mince words, but handed him Murielle's address in Germany and her father's residence in Paris. He said the missing eighty-four gold bars were behind the Berghof. He said he was to take two-thirds of them to Switzerland. He was to get gold certificates of deposit and to give them to her. He was free to keep the remaining twenty-eight bars. He said to tell her the certificates were to be used for the education of his son, whom he had never seen. And to always maintain sufficient cash on hand, in the event he called for her to join him. He told Rolph if he cheated him in any way, he would be hunted down and shot. Rolph was startled to hear him say he intended to do away with Rolph's parents in the United States if his instructions were not carried out to the letter. He made Rolph promise to do his bidding, although Rolph was at a loss to understand why the promise was necessary. As for the place she was to join him, Rolph suspected Steinmann was talking about bringing Murielle to Argentina.

CHAPTER 19...OBERSALZBERG, APRIL 1945

We left Reinicke's place in Berchtesgaden, backtracking toward Salzburg and then turning right at the cutoff to the Obersalzberg. We chugged up the grade in Ralph's three-wheeler straight to the officer's mess. He told us not to worry; we were with him. He explained how he made this trip with two of Bormann's slave laborers at least twice a week. Strangely enough, we felt comfortable. I did anyway.

If the scenery had been spectacular before, now it was breath-taking. But we had no time for sightseeing or for discussing what was supposed to happen tomorrow. He told us we should probably have stayed in the basement of the Imperial tonight; but then he couldn't be sure of getting into the city and back in time tomorrow. This way, we had time to spare.

Eric and I carried the boxes of spirits inside, placing them in a room adjacent the bar. Ralph leaned heavily on his cane as he loudly gave us orders in German. When the truck was unloaded, the three of us parked it in a nearby garage and then walked back to the officers' mess. We goofed around with the boxes in the back room, while Ralph played with his clipboard, making as though he was conducting yet another inventory. When he was sure the coast was clear, we sat on a bench, and for the first time, we listened to what he thought was going to happen tomorrow night.

He said we were to stay here tonight, and through tomorrow afternoon. Then we would start loading the gold. We made a kind of children's playroom by moving the boxes around. It was large enough to sit in and lie down, but not large enough to stand up. He apologized for the accommodations. But as he said, it was only going to be for a short time. He said not to worry about food. He said he would make sure we had all we wanted. He said there was going to be a banquet tonight, first a ceremony, and then a banquet to honor the Fuhrer, who had now declared his intentions to stay in Berlin until his death.

Ralph said: "Hitler has sent the Commandant a radio message, saying: 'I cannot thereby lead if I sit somewhere on a mountain. I did not come to the World merely to defend only my Berghof.'"

But Ralph doesn't expect the doings to be a somber affair. The War is not ending for them with Hitler's death. They intend carrying on from South America. They are confident their Fuhrer wouldn't leave them alone at the mercy of his enemies. The Wermacht maybe, but not the SS. They are sure their leaders have made long-range plans, which includes the necessary financing.

About two hours after dark, we heard the makings of a good party. There was loud laughter and an occasional outburst of voices having a good time, in spite of what was facing them. We took bets on whether they were or not. If they were, they were unlike any group of soldiers we knew. But then, too, they were famous for being just that. They were seen as a breed apart, even by our own generals and fighting men.

At one point they began singing a rousing hymn, keeping time by stomping their feet. It was an SS battle song we had never heard before. It made us both break out in goose bumps. I have since learned it was the *Horst Wessel Lied*, composed in honor of the first SA soldier to die in furtherance of the cause of National Socialism. So stirring is it that to this day it's banned throughout Germany. To play it or to sing it is an offense punishable by a stiff fine. The younger generation knows little about it; and that's just the way their elders, and especially the veterans of the Wermacht, want it to be.

CHAPTER 20...KONIGSSEE, APRIL 1945

The Konigssee is about four miles from Berchtesgaden. It's similar to hundreds of other alpine lakes in Europe, as well as other glaciated lakes in the world. They all began with huge masses of ice forming on granite mountaintops. The ice gouged out *glacial cirques* of dirt and rock before pushing down the mountainsides. Over millions of years, it ground away, cutting U-shaped valleys, *striating*, polishing, and *slickensiding* canyon walls. On the sides, it excavated and then deposited *lateral moraines* and then *terminal moraines* as it slowly melted and receded. Huge *chunks* were *chipped* and broken off as the ice advanced. These huge *erratics* were dropped helter-skelter as it melted; and the deep bowls at the terminus eventually filled to form large lakes.

Not only is the Konigssee close by Hitler's lair, but it's the deepest of the European glacial lakes. Only a very serious diver would stand a chance at the bottom in the numbing cold. Viewed from the top of the Kelstien, it appears to be what it is: beautiful, but foreboding, unforgiving, and dangerous beneath the surface. So dangerous is it that authorities banned diving there and in other glacial lakes soon after the War. However, this was no guarantee some foolhardy souls have not sought fortunes in SS gold rumored to be lurking below. But regardless, no such danger will deter the SS when the time comes to retrieve their life's blood.

Before Hitler, the road to the Konigssee was unimproved. It had little traffic and only an occasional tourist. But included in the Bormann laid-on construction projects of the Thirties, the road to the lake was widened and surfaced. It made it so much more convenient for the Fuhrer if he evidenced a desire to visit. However, Hitler was not one for picnicking or boating or the like. Having done it once or twice, he gave it up, and the road continued to be infrequently used through the War years.

Ralph came for us late this afternoon. He explained the role we were to play in the gold-loading detail. Then, he told us he had taped two Lugers under the back seat of a small bus we would be using. He told us to feel them out and then re-tape them to our legs when we had the chance. He told us there would be ten of Bormann's laborers, who would help us load the gold into two trucks and then accompany us to the lake.

Following the loading, we boarded this small bus having a rear mounted, air cooled engine. The engine resembles those you see on most of their small autos, something like those you see on small airplanes.

Ralph supervised the bus loading under the watchful eyes of an SS officer. He makes sure that Eric and I are the first to board. Crouching low in the small entranceway, we step up and shuffle back to the rear seat. We sit down facing forward. The officer is outside as the other passengers fill the aisle. He can't see either of us. I take this opportunity to run my hand under the seat, expecting to feel the weapon. I can't feel anything. It's like an electric shock, this non-feel. I almost faint dead away. I stare at Eric in disbelief. He stares back. There's not one under his seat either.

We sit looking at each other, dumbfounded. I look at Eric who looks as though he wants to vomit.

I see now why Ralph didn't bring more laborers; the bus has only twelve seats. One of the three officers involved climbed aboard; he sat on a small pull-down facing us while Ralph took position behind the wheel. This officer was armed with a machine gun and a detached expression. He has a cold, lifeless stare, resembling a shark poised for the attack. This is my first up-close look at the SS. He has my attention. I'm intimidated, to say the least.

As expected, they are going to take every precaution to prevent anybody from escaping. The only exit is the entrance behind him, and he hasn't taken his eyes from us in the fading light. For some reason, I thought he was staring at Eric and me. It's as though he knows us or suspects we are not who we are supposed to be. The barrel of his weapon was pointed straight at me, and I know I'm going to be the first to be shot if any prisoner tries escaping. I hope no one has any such plan. Ralph says they don't. He says they were picked at random at the last minute to prevent just such an occurrence. He says they have seen each other before, but that it's not likely they know each other. He says they are not organized. He tells me when the time comes, they will all just break and run and hope they can make it to the trees. I hope he's right. If they rush the officer while we're still in the bus, it will result in a massacre. Ralph assures me that we are not to worry. He's told me this over and over again. He says they're smart enough not to pull such a stunt. Later maybe, but not on the bus. Somehow, nothing he has said is very reassuring or of much help now.

The Commandant and his deputy, as expected, are driving the two trucks. They also have machine guns similar to the British Sten and our Thompson. This term "machine gun," however, is a misnomer. We learned in infantry school about how Hitler insisted on an *assault rifle* for his troops that was accurate to two hundred yards. The model these officers are carrying is the one they came up with. Hitler didn't like it because it didn't meet his specifications. But both the army and the Waffen SS needed it desperately, and there was no time for a major redesign–so the armaments minister went ahead with its manufacture and distribution, risking court martial. Thinking he could fool Hitler, he called it a *machine pistol.* At a conference on the Eastern Front, several of Hitler's generals bragged about the weapon and then asked the Fuhrer when they could get some more. Hitler was furious, but there was nothing he could do. But from that time on it was known as the *MG 42 Assault Rifle*.

This third officer, according to Ralph, was supposed to guard the bus from the rear of the second truck. But at the last minute, he boards the bus instead–facing us in the lengthening shadows.

Darkness comes fast in the Alps. I guess this isn't news to anybody whose ever lived in the mountains. I come from bayou country, where dusk seems to go on forever, especially in the summer months. But in the mountains of Austria, I have been amazed at how rapidly darkness approaches; one minute it's light and the next you are stumbling about wondering what happened. In our case, I expected the sun to set rapidly behind a mountain on our right and put us in the dark before we reached the lake.

I think the SS officer in charge planned it this way. I wouldn't be a bit surprised. He obviously wants to arrive immediately after dark. This is certainly apropos. What they are about tonight is Devil's work. Mass killing of innocents is Devil's work. I think we all agree it needs take place in the dark, maybe the darker the better.

I can see it in their eyes, these prisoners. They are not exactly afraid, but tense, wary, and alert. They are wearing the same expressions I imagine gladiators wore who were picked for the arena. The officer, like Caesar, has the power of life or death over them. And like Caesar, he'll show them no mercy. And they know it's going to happen just as soon as the gold is loaded in the boats. They have been told we are headed for the lake and why we are going there.

They also know, that like the arena, death is not a forgone conclusion. It's going to be pitch black before the moon rises and once on the ground and spread out they will have an opportunity to break for the forest. Maybe all of them won't survive, but then each of them is an optimist–each of them is a positive thinker they have had to be in order to have stayed alive this long. They survived when hundreds succumbed to hardships and to the hazards involved with cutting a road to the top of the Kelstien. They have beaten the odds before, many times and, according to Ralph, those who don't believe in luck have come to think of themselves as blessed in some way.

Martin Bormann decided to build his Fuhrer a pompous *nest* on the very top of the Kelstien peak, as a surprise gift for his 49th birthday. Without prior approval, he squandered millions of marks and hundreds of lives in accomplishing what the world later saw as a manifestation of his dementia. All the more so when it was discovered Hitler hated heights. He never stayed overnight in his grandiose *tree house*, and it was seldom used as a gathering place for visiting dignitaries, as Bormann had intended. However, it did serve to impress prominent guests with the ingenuity and daring of German engineering. For this reason, Hitler thanked him. It stands today as another monument to some men's utter disregard for human life and for some men's disregard for the suffering of other men.

In order to accomplish this Herculean task by the appointed date, Bormann drove his slaves relentlessly, without regard for their health or safety. And in spite of the hell he put them through, some of them survived.

These men sitting beside me now are some of the remainders; they are survivors of Bormann's idiocy. They are tough; they are like gladiators. None of them will chicken out, panic, and get me shot. At least that's Ralph's opinion.

Ralph says the prisoners figure if they can get away tonight they are going to be free at last. One of them told him that he didn't believe the SS was going to let any of them go home to tell of the atrocities they had witnessed. He told him they consider themselves fortunate to be assigned to this detail; it gives them a last clear chance to escape. This prisoner believes the SS will leave in the morning. But before they go, he thinks they are going to machinegun everybody. They don't intend leaving anybody alive.

True, heretofore, there has been no firing squads or gassings; no violence of any kind has occurred on the Obersalzberg near the Berghof. This is in keeping with Hitler's wishes. This is his home. This is his haven, a place of peace, relaxation, and meditation. But behind all this tranquility, and not too far away, slave laborers have been systematically worked to death by their SS overseers. None were spared the rigors and hazards of the mountain road or working on the eagle's nest thousands of feet above the valley floor. Ralph says, at the lake, the prisoners will be looking forward to taking the ultimate revenge on their tormentors if the opportunity presents itself. My question is: How do they really feel toward Ralph? And who do they believe we are? And how are they going to treat us when the violence does break out? Will they see us as friends or foe; might they not believe we are SS plants to keep them in line; or will they not care who we are and just shoot us if they get their hands on one of the machine guns? One way or another, one side or the other is going to shoot us–and it isn't going to be too much longer before it happens.

I guess I knew it all along. But now as we come closer to the lake, it becomes more apparent that we are in this for keeps. We are among desperate men who realize the War will finally end in a few days. They have somehow survived. And I know they will take no unnecessary chances. They are going to kill us along with the officers if they get the chance. I see it as a very definite possibility.

To tell you the truth, up until now, Eric and I have been treating this assignment as some kind of youthful adventure. And like *sugar plum dreams*, it has been made more enjoyable by *visions of gold dancing in our heads.* And of course, we are going to make some kind of miraculous escape, the way they used to do it in the old Saturday matinee serials. Oddlie explained it all, making it sound so simple. Until now, I believed him. It has been a lark; it has never crossed our minds that somebody might actually shoot us. But now, as I look at this blond Adonis with the lightening bolts on his collar and the death's head embroidered on his sleeve and cap, I have to fight myself to retain my composure. I'm becoming scared. Before I was apprehensive; now I'm just plain scared. I want to get out of here. I want to get back to General Patton without delay. I want to tell him where the gold is located and be done with it. I want him to send professional deep-sea divers back if he really wants the gold as bad as Oddlie says he does. I just want to scram out of here and take Eric with me. We have the diamonds, the three of us do. Somebody else can have this gold. I don't care. I glanced at Eric, who gives me a look that says he feels the same way. The fun and games are over. We are not survivors the way they are. We aren't gladiators or anything of the kind.

Eric still looks sick. Now I feel as though I want to join him–I mean, join him throwing up on the floor.

We have been en route about ten minutes. Slowly, down past the Berghof and down to the crossroad, the overloaded trucks are creeping, carrying more than twice their designed capacity. The two officers driving are guarding against burning out clutches and overheating brakes.

To the right is Berchtesgaden and the road to Salzburg. We take the one to the left. It will make a sweeping turn and head due south. Then, according to Ralph, who gave us a thorough briefing among the boxes yesterday afternoon, it's about two more kilometers to the Konigssee.

Ralph was at the lake last week. They sent him to scout the area for the most practical place to load the boats. He told me he towed ten of them down from an upper boat rental, with another one having a large outboard motor. He said the boats were also large with a flat bottom and made of light aluminum. He was afraid ten might not be enough. I went over the figures with him, doing some calculations on the side of a box, and then assured him he was all right. The boats only require a few inches of freeboard, and they only plan on moving out in the lake a few hundred yards. But the important thing to remember, I told him, was the appearance that the project was workable. In case one of the officers takes it in his head to check Ralph's calculations, the plan must be realistic. Whether or not it will actually work, and the boats will actually float, is not the issue. Things are never going to get that far–at least we hope they are not.

He chose a shallow beach as the loading site. It looks back on a forest about fifty yards from the water. The beach, being formed of glacial till, is covered with odd-sized polished stones, making it difficult to walk along or too rough for lying about sunbathing.

The water is supposed to be the purest of any of the lakes. He says, you can drink from it just the way it is. It's supposed to be emerald green and more pure than tap water.

They apparently don't have to post swimming *verboten* signs, because it's too cold. Even during the hottest of summer days, it's much too uncomfortable on the surface; a few feet below, it's numbing to the senses.

He has put some thought into how we are going to load the boats without having to stand in the water very long. You can be sure the SS doesn't care whether we freeze our legs and feet, just as long as we are able to walk.

He has inter-connected the boats with their mooring chains and strung them together parallel with the shoreline. They will each be loaded with something near 2,000 pounds. When they are ready to go, the first one in line will be hooked to the motorboat. The plan is for the laborers to push each loaded boat into about two feet or so of water, and then the motorboat, with the help of the laborers, will slowly tow first one and then the other off the graveled bottom. Two of the officers are going to be in the motorboat. The one who accompanied us in the bus is staying with the prisoners. When they arrive at the drop-off point, they will punch a small hole in the bottom of each boat. Hooked together, they will all slowly sink at the same rate to the bottom. The gold should remain in each boat for easy retrieval.

Ralph fixed a three-hundred-meter line to a large erratic at the water's edge. Then, he oared out into the lake with the other end, which he fixed to a homemade reflecting marker buoy. He then took a compass bearing on a small flag attached to the buoy. He chiseled both the distance and the direction from the erratic into the stone. There'll be no problem finding the exact dumping spot tonight. And anybody coming back from Argentina can easily find the location, as long as he's able to interpret the figures carved in the rock. Of course, Ralph knows the code, as do the three officers. I don't much like the scheme. I think it will put Ralph's life in jeopardy, even more so than it has already.

Why would he be privy to the coordinates of the dumpsite, unless they plan to shoot him? Does the Commandant like him enough to have really made him one of them?

Obviously, the plan is for the officer to shoot them after the gold is loaded and the boats start moving into deep water. Incidentally, I keep saying them when I really mean us. We are them. We have been told what they have been told. And what happens to them will now happen to us. It wasn't planned this way. And it wasn't going to happen this way–that's before somebody confiscated the pistols under the seat–now Eric and I are about to join them in the coliseum. We are about to become part of the Sunday games. Without the pistols, we are defenseless–we are reduced to running through the trees with the rest of them–and so is Ralph.

There's no doubt Ralph attended last night's festivities. That means he's somewhere inside the SS. I should say was, because of what has happened. He could be in the organization as a kind of honorary member. But I think he purposely has misled me as to how valuable he is to them. I don't think his job is as innocuous as he's made it out to be. It's not likely he will tell us the truth. But, whatever, it's all off now. They know he put the Lugers under the seat. And of course it writes *fini* to any further association he has with them. He's going to be done away with the same as the rest of us, although he doesn't know it yet. If I can make eye contact with him in the mirror, I intend telling him about the non-Lugers, although, I don't know what good it will do.

To prevent a mutiny and a mass bug-out, resulting in the shooting of most of the labor force before the job is finished, the prisoners received a briefing before they boarded the bus. They were told if they did this one job they would be transported back to the compound. Then when the SS takes off in the morning, they will be allowed to go home. They were told the SS doesn't care if they know the gold is in the lake, since they have no idea where it's going to be dumped. The SS wants them to know that they don't enjoy killing people for no reason. And the way they have it worked out, there's no longer a reason. Everybody will return tonight and tomorrow everybody's going home. The War's over, and everybody should be happy. So, they can all relax and get on with the job. But according to the radio operator, Hitler's not interested in any fair play for prisoners. He's ordered the Commandant to execute all non-SS witnesses. He doesn't want to chance the gold later falling into unauthorized hands. But the fact the operator told Ralph, makes me wonder all the more if Ralph is one of them.

We've been told to keep our eyes straight to the front with our hands resting on our legs. I wait until I see the officer's eyes distracted and then look up to acquire the mirror. Ralph is glancing back at me, trying to get my attention. I check with our guard again, and then make an *everything has come unglued face*. A minute later, I imitate a pistol with my index finger, mimicking a gun barrel. Then I slowly move my head in the negative sign. Ralph catches on, and joins the two of us in being scared to death. He understands completely. He realizes we are up the creek. We have no defense. We're in a world of hurt. We're trapped like animals being led to the slaughter, and there's little or nothing we're going to be able to do about it now.

We are moving at a snail's pace behind the rear truck. All we can hear is the whine of the air-cooled engine behind us, working overtime. What Ralph has in mind if anything is unknown to the two of us? The prisoners plans are obvious. In spite of what happens, they're going to break and run the first chance they get. But if we're going to secure the gold and then do away with the SS, as we have been instructed to do, we must get hold of a weapon. This is the first order of business. But one follows the other. If we can get a gun, then we can escape unhurt and take the poor prisoners with us. To save all these lives is worth any reasonable gamble, as far as I'm concerned. I'm not going to have a chance to ask Eric how he feels about it. However, I think Ralph is game for most anything. But the two of us have no idea what Ralph intends to do.

A few minutes later, it is suddenly dark. The headlights are still off, and apparently they will remain so. There's not even a shadow of the truck in front of us. However, we must not be very close, because the officer is gesturing with his rifle barrel and yelling words I can't understand. But I take it; he wants Ralph to keep it closed up. At least that's what I think he wants. But he could be yelling just to have something to do, because he has no idea how far we are lagging behind, if we are.

But we are really moving slowly now. We make a turn off to the left on a diagonal. The road becomes unimproved, twisting, and rough. I assume we are getting close to the edge of the lake, but I have no way of knowing. The officer stands up, holding onto the support pole across from Ralph. He turns and looks out the windshield. He's checking to see how close we are to the back of the truck, and he wants to know how close we are to the water. It might be just curiosity, although, I hear him yell something to Ralph again. He turns around with his assault rifle slung over his shoulder with his finger on the trigger. I know the safety is off and the slightest misstep on our part will cause him to unleash a full magazine in one gigantic spray. We'll all be hit. It will be as though he has a garden hose he has decided to turn on us. The chance of not being hit by at least one bullet is about the same as not being hit by at least one drop of water.

Then all of a sudden Ralph completely ignores the officer. He shifts into a lower gear and guns the engine. The bus jumps as though it has been prodded from behind. It begins to accelerate. The SS officer doesn't panic. I watch spellbound, mesmerized, in a kind of trance, as he yells even louder in Ralph's ear. Ralph stares straight ahead paying no attention, all the time leaning forward in his seat as if to urge the underpowered bus to go faster. I feel the vehicle make a sharp turn to the left and back again. I suspect we just passed the two lumbering trucks, and still we are slowly accelerating. The officer swings the barrel of his weapon, catching Ralph in the back of the head. I know it must hurt, but still he keeps the gas pedal pressed to the floor. Within seconds, we crash into what I later determine is the large erratic with the chiseled location code. The boulder is misshapen and huge, at least twice the size of the bus, and buried deep in the ground like an iceberg.

The two of us are thrown from our seats, sprawling on the floor on top of each other. The German has been catapulted back against the windshield. And then, as if clutched by a giant hand, he's violently turned upside down in the doorwell.

Ralph opens the door. The officer rolls out, sprawling onto the rocks face down, unconscious. Ralph yells out something. It's meaningless to me but not to them. His voice is the sound of a clarion. It sounds like a chorus of all the angels in heaven to the poor sacrificial prisoners; it's something like Gabriel's horn on judgment day. They realize they have been resurrected. They shake off the shock of the sudden stop. Giving out with shouts of joy, they bolt for the door, falling over each other and us in a frenzy. They realize they have only seconds before the officers alight from the nearby trucks and turn their guns on the bus.

Ralph was the first out. He pulls the machine rifle from around the unconscious officer's neck, just as the truck lights go on. Ralph lets go a short burst, calculated to make the two officers stay in the trucks until the last of the prisoners reach the nearby pines. I get up from the floor with scraped and bruised hands and knees and a nasty bump on my head. I'm off the bus just in time to see the last of them running on the rocky beach, stumbling, falling, half crawling, disappearing from the headlights into the pines.

The truck lights are still pointed towards the bus. Eric and I are both headed for the trees behind the prisoners, when I see one of the officers charging towards Ralph. All of a sudden, a single high-powered rifle shot rings out and the Commandant falls forward face down in the gravel. The second officer quickly follows, as he is also ripped apart by what I later conclude is a hollow-nosed sporting shell. Somebody has been waiting in the trees close by. Using a flashlight taped to a barrel and a telescopic sight, he has killed them both, as though they were two helpless deer caught in his headlights along a forest road.

Ralph lets go with half a clip in the direction of the trees. He's shooting high so as not to hit anybody, but he wants whoever is there to stay back. It's an unbelievable scene. It's as though it has all been choreographed, as though it were a stage play. But I know it hasn't. I know it's all very real.

I hear a rustle in the trees; somebody clumsy and heavy falls next to me in the dark trying to get away from Ralph and his machine gun.

My first thought is Goering. It's Goering the hunter–Goering the outdoorsman–with some of his loyal lieutenants. I think this guy looks like Goering ought to look. And who else knew the gold was going to be unloaded tonight?

I jump up running, losing my footing a few yards down the side of the moraine. I fall, hitting my head against a large tree. I quickly jump up again, as a rifle bullet tears into another tree beside me. Lying in the mud in pain, I struggle to crawl into some underbrush, knowing that, whoever they are, they are looking for me. They intend to come back and hijack the gold. But they have to run off everybody before they can. And they can't take a chance they have been seen and identified. Clearly, they have become disorganized; they didn't count on this happening.

True, they intended to kill the officers and spook the others. Then they were going to have a clean hand to drive away in the trucks. But Ralph shooting off some limbs above their heads has changed everything.

Another burst from Ralph's assault rifle, and more slugs can be heard ripping into thick forestry. Another of the shooters runs past me, falling in the undergrowth. He's hesitant to turn on his flashlight for fear Ralph will see him and turn his weapon in his direction.

A crazy thought runs through my mind as I lie panting, mud covered, bruised, skinned, and nearly at my wits end. This gunfire is being directed at the assassins in a very professional manner. It's as though he, presuming it is Ralph, doesn't want to hit anybody; he just wants to scare the daylights out of them. Whoever is firing has been trained in its use. And I'm sure it's not Eric; it has to be Ralph–but how come…it makes no sense. I'm thinking about how the SS could have trained him as I faint dead away. The tree and the bus have finally taken their toll on my head, as though I had been injected with a delayed anesthetic. Whatever happened, happened all of a sudden; because the night became even blacker than it was.

It seemed as though it was an eternity, but it must have been only minutes, when I see a bright light shinning in my eyes. A voice I recognize as Ralph's, is yelling to Eric, "*Kommen sie*, he's over here."

But even as I gain consciousness, the thought still swirls around in my brain–a civilian like Ralph Wahl doesn't know how to use a sub-machine gun. And who were the people shooting the rifles? And why did I think Goering? Why not Walter Reinicke? But what makes me think it's either of them? Why not some perfect stranger from the town who knows what's going on? It could be anybody.

The first thing I do after they help me back to the lakeshore is to strip off my blue denim work shirt. Leaning over in the cold water, I cup my hands and drink deep of the most refreshing liquid I have ever tasted. I'm perspiring, suffering from some kind of shock. The tension of the last two hours is suddenly drained from me, leaving me with a tremendous thirst. Satisfied, I stand up and look around at the bodies a few yards away. I'm woozy on my feet, and kneel down again to soak my head. Both my friends are looking at me. I get the idea they are worried I have a concussion and maybe I do. But I'm at a loss to tell whether it's from the blow to my head in the bus or from the tree.

Eric is the first to ask me if I'm all right. He obviously wants my attention; he wants to discuss something important.

"Captain, can you come over here a minute." He and Ralph have procured flashlights from someplace. I recall being more interested in where they got them than anything he has to tell me. He wants to show me something. He wants to discuss the body of the officer who was guarding us in the bus.

"Come here and look at this guy." I didn't answer but dried my face and chest off as best I could with my hands, while shaking the loose mud from my shirt. I walk over to where he's standing, pointing. Ralph has taken up a position with the assault rifle behind the fender of one of the trucks, in case somebody decides to return. We know they will; we just don't know how far they're going to run in the dark before they come back for the gold. Nobody is going to give up that easily.

"What's up?" I hear myself say.

"This one's alive."

"How about the others."

"They've run off with the Valkyrie to join Odin in Valhalla." Eric's effort at gallows humor.

I go over to look at him. He's definitely alive, but appears to be paralyzed from the waist down. I ask him if he can move his feet; he just stares at me.

"How about your hands?" Still no answer.

"Look, Fritz," I said, "if you want our help, you'd better shape up." Eric translated.

He just stares with a haughty expression of the vanquished warrior who knows his time has come and whose first instinct is to show contempt for his enemy; after all, we both know his dignity is all he has left. He has no intention of asking for any favors; no quarter asked and none given-the code of the SS–that's what I have been given to understand anyway.

"Shoot me," he says in perfect English, with scarcely the trace of an accent. "I want you to shoot me, you swine."

"I'm not going to shoot you, my friend. Maybe one of the others will. Hey, Ralph, do you want to shoot this guy?"

"Not me!"

"Eric?" No answer.

"Well, there you have it then. I would give you a gun, but then you would shoot me.

"Look, let's be serious for a minute. Your back is probably broken. All I can do is make you comfortable. We will try and make you as warm as possible and hope your friends come for you in the morning. That's all we're going to do. I would take you back and dump you off at your infirmary, but we might kill you if your neck is broken. Then, too, I'm no doctor. I don't know; maybe the nerves in your back are just bruised. Maybe you are not permanently crippled."

"It does not matter. My people are going to shoot me in the morning," he said.

"What are you talking about?" I asked him. "I know

you people are crazy, but I thought the one thing you had going for you was loyalty, especially to your wounded."

"You don't understand," he said, now with a little less rancor in his voice.

"You mean, because you lost the gold?"

"That is part of it, but because of something else in the back of the first truck. There is a box that belongs to me. It has no real value to you, but it does to me. I have sworn to guard it with my life. Will you give it to me?"

"What's in it?"

"You do not want to know. But I give you my word; it has no military value to you. And you would not know what it was if you saw what was inside."

I ignored him and started to walk toward the truck. Ralph had been listening and left his post by the fender, yelling at me to stay back: "Leave it alone, do not go near the truck. And do not give it back to him. Leave it in the truck. Believe me, Captain, you do not want to become involved with him or his box. Let us leave. Let us get out of here–now!"

I was confused, as was Eric. Neither of us had any idea what he was yelling about, and we told him so; all the time the SS officer was watching, pleading for us to leave his box. He didn't care for his life; all he wanted was his box. Then when Ralph said something to him in German, he yelled back, telling him to shut up.

Eric was eager to be gone. He was around the other side of the bus checking the front wheel. Ralph was determined to take the box with us. He wanted it left on the truck. He didn't want me to listen to the begging of the officer. But he seemed equally determined to not let me see it or touch it.

"I beg of you, Captain. Listen to me–if you open that box or so much as touch it, you will rue this night all the rest of your life."

I guess I looked at Ralph with a quizzical expression. I

thought of asking him if he had taken leave of his senses, but I held my tongue.

"All right, then. Let's get going. Sorry, old boy. I tried," I said, as I started walking toward the trucks. "But I think you're both a little nuts." I said it as an afterthought, flippantly, and it made me ashamed. This man lying in the gravel was going to lose his life. I apologized, something that would never have crossed his mind to do. To him, an apology was a sign of weakness.

"Get in the trucks. I'll ride with Ralph."

"I'll drive," Ralph said. I shrugged my shoulders. My head ached too badly to argue any further about anything, but the guy on the ground must have hurt far worse than I did. But not a whimper, not even a sign he was in any kind of pain. I marveled again at these people. Where do they come from? What kind of training makes them this way? What is it that makes them this tough, this disciplined? But then as I climbed in the first truck and Ralph started the engine, I wondered if he really was hurting. If his back was broken, he shouldn't be able to feel anything, or so I had been led to believe.

Eric had been inspecting the bus. The front was bashed in, but the wheels turned and it steered. The engine was in the back so it wasn't a problem. He told me it would go, and then asked me if I wanted him to drive it away. I told him no, we were going to leave it–too much trouble. I told him to drive the other truck.

As we pulled away, I could hear the German screaming at me to shoot him or to unload this stupid box of his. I should have been more curious, but I had other things on my mind. I didn't care about any box. I had put it out of my mind, but only for a minute; later, when I was ready, I was going to satisfy my curiosity.

This box of his obviously contains long range plans for the SS recovery or names of important people–something like that. But if so, what has Ralph so energized? I had never seen him so serious or so anxious. He knew what was in it. But how did he know? And why did he care? But then, I suspected he might have something to do with them soon after I met him. He was somehow one of the brotherhood–and now this box. I realized it must have something major to do with this infamous cult organization; it must be as important to them as the gold.

For some curious reason, I cared about the officer as a human being. But there was nothing I could do for him. The last words I heard him screaming were not directed at me but at Ralph.

"Do not forget what I told you." He repeated it twice, once in German.

"Stop the truck," I said.

"Captain, you are not going to shoot him, are you?" Ralph asked, looking at me with a pained expression.

"Does it make any difference to you?" I'm thinking again what I had suspected all along–that he was in someway connected to the German. He never answered. He didn't have to. *At some point, I might have to shoot Ralph. I hope it never comes to that, but it might.*

The three of us got out, and I walked back a few yards. The German said nothing, he just looked up at me.

"You know, I have a baby son," he finally said in a low voice, pensively. I almost expected him to ask me if I wanted to see the picture he was carrying in his wallet. But he was not making an appeal for his life. He said it as though he knew I knew. I never replied; I let it pass.

"This is what I can do for you…it's up to you. You tell me what you want me to do," I said to him.

"We can put you in the bus. However, if we do, I can almost guarantee you'll never walk again. If we leave you here, you're going to go into shock, and maybe die from exposure before morning. That's a possibility, but not as sure as what else might happen to you. Those people are coming back. They can't stay away. They have to know if they've left anybody alive. And when they do, they're going to kill you.

"Now, here's what I propose: if we can find a way to cut two small trees, we might use the tunics of your buddies over there to make a field stretcher. We have no axe, so we'll have to find another way to break them off. Then, we can use their pistol belts to strap you on. We're going to have to put you on this stretcher thing face down or we're going to damage your spinal column even more–probably beyond repair. If this works out, we can lay you on top of one of the piles of gold. It'll be the most uncomfortable ride you ever took. But it's only going to be for a few miles–only as far as Berchtesgaden."

Ralph looked at me kind of funny: "What does Berchtesgaden have to do with anything? Who says we are going to take him there?" But I never paid any attention to him.

Eric had been listening. He was a good soldier. He never asked a lot of dumb questions. And he never made counterproposals unless he thought his ideas were better than mine. Usually they were not, so he kept his mouth shut for the most part. I wished I was the same way. I knew I had a future in the service with Patton as a sponsor if I could only be more like Eric.

"I'll get you a couple of saplings, Captain," is all he said. He had shouldered one of the machine guns, and now he took his flashlight and walked off into the trees.

There were two short bursts of machine gun fire. He walked back dragging two small saplings of just the right size.

He looked at me and laughed. "Back in Chicago this might give a whole new meaning to the term *chopper*."

"Ralph."

"Ya." He glanced over at me in the dark. We were almost to Berchetsgaden. He knew what I was after. He knew exactly what I wanted to hear. But I knew he didn't want to hear me ask it.

"Are you ready to tell me about this guy's box or whatever is in it?"

"No. But I am going to tell you something else. That officer knows you. And you know him." He looked over at me and then quickly back to the winding road."

"What makes you say a crazy thing like that?" I was astounded at what he just said. *Maybe it just popped out of his kidneys, because I had just saved this guy's life; maybe it was his way of kidding me.* "Are you the one who got hit in the head?"

"No," he said, "he knows you, really. He told me you are the boyfriend of his wife's sister. He has seen pictures of you, and he knows what you do."

"What! My girlfriend! If I have one, she has a sister all right, but she has no husband."

"Yes, she does, according to him she does, and he ought to know. Did you not ask me if I knew an oberststurmbannfuhrer by the name of Steinmann? Well, friend, that is exactly who is riding along in the back. Care to tell me about it?"

"No." I was in deep thought. I had nothing I wanted to share with him.

"This Steinmann is well placed, I understand. But then you knew he is one of Hitler's favorites...." Ralph paused for a minute, thinking, and then he started talking again. "How come you know him? Could it be he is working with us–you are in counter-intelligence? No, I do not believe it. No, not him! No, I know better. I really do. He genuinely is SS; I know this.... "

I interrupted: "I happen to know he is also. But I know

it from a whole different set of circumstances. But tell me why you're so sure he doesn't work for us. He doesn't; but why are you so sure–could it have something to do with that box or what's in it?" This remark got me nothing but silence.

We drove to the outskirts of Berchtesgaden before I spoke again: "Where are we going to get some supplies? I forgot all about them. I just assumed you were going back to the officer's mess with the bus, then you were going to load up and meet us at Reinicke's."

"Not to worry. Reinicke's garage is full. I have been laying them in for months, little by little. We will take what we need, and then you make your call to Oddlie. I suggest you also try to reach your man by walkie-talkie; tell him where to meet us; the closer the better. I am leery of going very far in these trucks. I figure our people are just over the horizon somewhere. The odds of running into a column of our tanks are much better than Tigers. The Tigers, however, will figure we are deserters, so it makes no difference–the one will blow us up as quickly as will the other."

We pulled into Reinicke's place and parked the trucks around back. The plan had always been to stop here and call Oddlie, who was supposed to be standing by all night. Likewise, Carl, if he was moving toward us, was awaiting our call. But now we had another problem besides what to do with my new friend Kurt. We had too much gold. The German trucks were not designed to carry five tons each, and that's what she weighed. They had bottomed their springs, and the tires were in danger of blowing out. Not even the five-ton truck being driven by Carl could handle it. We needed two of them. I figured our two German trucks, even limping down the road at a few miles an hour, were going to soon burn out their clutches. I didn't think they could go a hundred miles.

I plan to tell Oddlie to get me another two or three guys

with another five ton. I want him to send them as quickly as possible to an address I'm about to give him. Oh, and I want them to bring plenty of fuel, because our load of gold is heavy; it's twice as heavy as Oddlie's people estimated it would be.

The Germans had brought it from Berlin in four trucks and then were restricted to using two for the trip to the lake. Ralph told me Kurt had brought the Commandant orders from Berlin, authorizing only three officers besides the laborers to be at the lake. I hadn't quite figured out where that left Ralph. But after they discovered the Lugers, it didn't matter.

Reinicke came out to meet us. I expected him to be angry for bringing the trucks in his yard and drawing attention to him. But strangely enough he wasn't.

I took over the operation from Ralph, intending to run things from here on out. I asked him to assemble Reinicke and his sons in his kitchen for a short meeting. Ralph informed me they were not at home, which I thought was odd, as sick as they were supposed to be. Why would they be, though; it wasn't much past ten. They were grown men in a town full of lonesome women. Why would they be? I guess I would have to be pretty sick to be lying around at home under the circumstances. Still, it was curious, but I made no comment to Ralph.

The four of us gathered in Walter's kitchen after unloading Steinmann, who was still surly, as might be expected, but on the whole he was showing improvement. Still, he was who he was; and I bet if he lives, he will never change much. Yet Françoise told me on several occasions that, in spite of him being a monster, her words not mine, he had a soft spot. He worshipped Murielle and there's no accounting for that. Well, maybe there is–Hitler loved his dog–and you know the old saying: *anybody who loves dogs can't be all bad.* But in his case, we had all better find a new saying–that is, anybody who knows anything about Auschwitz and Buchenwald should anyway.

The first thing I did was present Walter Reinicke with a gold bar. I laid it on the table next to his salt and pepper shaker for effect. It looked humongous. I had no idea how much it was worth, so I pulled a whopping big number out of nowhere. Another one of those wags. Eric, who was a recipient of my last one in the mine, looked at me. I saw the expression on his face and amended my statement. I said that's what it should be worth on the black market. At any rate, whatever it was actually worth, Walter figured it was going to be more than enough to remodel and redecorate his recovered Zum Turken.

"Walter, in a few days you're going to regain ownership of your hotel. It belongs to you and not the Nazi government. In a couple of weeks, there will be no Nazi government.

"I have no idea what's in there now. But after tomorrow, whatever is will be yours by right of acquisition. You just get up there the day after the SS leaves. Lock it and board it up, and have one of your sons guard it until my people get here. You don't want the place looted."

I didn't know how much he was retaining of what Ralph was translating. He was not stupid and probably was way ahead of me. I bet he and his sons had discussed this very subject every day since they came home. But where they were going to get the money to remodel it was something else again.

Walter thanked me profusely, as might be expected. When he quieted down, I sprung it on him: "Walter, I want you to do something for me."

"Anything," was his expected reply.

"I have a seriously injured SS officer outside. No, he's not a deserter." I could see that look on his face as Ralph translated.

"I want you to take him to the compound–to the infirmary–and drop him off. Tell them he was injured in an automobile accident or something. Tell them anything. Anyway, the two of you get your stories straight. And I want you to do it right now, within the next few minutes. Then I want you to find your sons and get out of here. I mean get at least five miles away from the compound and from Berchtesgaden proper. Promise me you'll be gone before sun-up, and stay gone until the day after tomorrow."

He started nodding and smiling. I could tell he thought the request was crazy, but he didn't care; he figured he had gotten much the better of the bargain.

I have to tell you, I felt like some kind of con artist at work here. The three of us knew the 25th was just hours away. And like as not, a couple of hours after sunrise there wasn't going to be any Turken, Berghof, or anything else. And to my way of thinking, there might not be much left of Berchtesgaden either.

We removed one of Walter's interior doors and used it to transport Kurt. We tied him and the door to the top of Walter's small automobile, and then he drove off at about five miles an hour.

Kurt called me over just before they left: "Say hello to Murielle for me when you see her." He acted as though we were good friends, which really confused Reinicke. But he wasn't my friend. I had his coveted box and its contents, which supposedly euchred him out of a place in Valhalla or the SS hall of fame or whatever they were going to call it. And in a way, I was responsible for him being *up the well-known creek.* In short, you would have to look around to find somebody who had done more to screw up the life of another person than I had his. But maybe it was partial payment for just a few of the lives he had ruined–permanently. But where troubles were concerned, they were just starting for him. Whatever his fellow SS might do to him was small potatoes compared to what General Weyland was planning for all of them right this minute.

"Once more, Ralph, what's in the box? What big SS secret are you two sharing? Why didn't Steinmann want me to know anything about it? I've only a few seconds to transmit, and if it's anything important Patton needs to know, I need to get it to Oddlie quickly. And I'll be the judge of whether he needs to know." The two of us had gone back to the bedroom to pack up the radios. Eric was in the kitchen trying to scrounge up something to eat. We had already loaded the food, including several of those salty sausages I didn't care for, which managed to confuse Eric. Then we were going to take the radios and leave. The plan was to contact Oddlie when we found a power source away from Reinicke's place and then later when we got closer to Carl.

"Again your way off the base. There is nothing either of you need to know or would even begin to understand." Ralph, raising his voice, was obviously becoming perturbed.

"Humor me. All right? Forget curiosity. I'm becoming worried your big secret might have military ramifications you're not aware of. I'll make a bargain with you. If you tell me what's in the box, I'll leave you alone. I won't open it until you agree it's okay. What's with you anyway? Why are you so concerned? What have you to lose at this point? For that matter, what have I to lose that's so all-fired important?"

He replied: "You did not have anything to lose until you sent Steinmann off. Before he left, he told me to designate you the *Keeper.* The Commandant had been the *Guardian* and Steinmann was the Keeper. Now everything has changed for both of us."

The terms guardian and keeper sounded as though

Ralph might be involved with some kind of fraternity key or seal or something.

"Ralph, I heard of a college fraternity once, but maybe they all do, I don't know, who carried on secret rituals in secret rooms where they handled secret icons and such. These things were only available to initiated members. They were never discussed with outsiders. And they even went so far as to initiate the janitors of their *houses* who worked around those things. I'm just going by what I've heard on this. It does make a lot of sense, though. Tell me something: is this the sort of relationship you had with the SS, I mean being initiated like those janitors?"

Ralph glanced at me, clearly not wanting to discuss the subject further. But his look and his attitude gave him away.

Ralph is a good christian. Oddlie told me as much; he had served on a mission for the Mormon Church. And he considers himself a loyal American. Now he finds himself embroiled with one of the more notorious military brotherhoods known to history. His position is not compatible with his religion. Everything the SS stands for, the mysteries, the secret blood rituals, and many other things are counter to what he's been taught and believes. And I'm thinking he's been wrestling with his problem for some time. He's been able to live with it, but now that somebody else knows and understands his dilemma, he's not sure what he's going to do. He's determined, I think, to leave it alone; he's thinking it'll all go away. And the fewer people who know about it the better. I think he wants me to forget the subject–kind of like we all do when we've done things we're not too proud of. If we can forget them, they might just go away.

"Ralph, what's the difference between the keeper and the guardian?"

"Well, for one thing, the keeper has to be a military officer. He can be of company grade, but he must be commissioned. The guardian can be of any rank." I looked puzzled.

I know I did because I was. I didn't understand much more than before I asked.

He looked at me for the longest time, considering what he was going to say next and what he intended to do. Then he said: "What have you got to lose, you ask? What have you got to lose?" his voice dropping. "All right. All right, then, I'll tell you what you have to lose. Then when you know, because of your rank and new position, you will be obligated to become the keeper. And then, the thing you are going to lose, if you insist on probing further into this, is nothing less than your immortal soul."

CHAPTER 21...SAN ANTONIO, 1950

I had been talking to Lucy after dinner for the better part of two hours, telling her about how we acquired the gold and about Steinmann and all the rest of it. I didn't mean to go on like this, not at this time anyway. But it's part of the story. And it might help to explain the deaths of Eric and Carl, and why my life is so fouled up.

She earlier invited me to stay at her place again tonight, inasmuch as I didn't have a room. I came straight to our restaurant when I arrived in town.

I have told you I bought a ring, but was hesitant to give it to her. She was still trying to make up her mind what she wants to do with the rest of her life. The local paper carried a short article about her and the mysterious fire that consumed her house. Now, the property will automatically go to her brother. She doesn't care. She's almost glad it happened, ridding her of the responsibility. Now she tells me she might decide to stay in San Antonio. She has a job of sorts, however, it doesn't pay her enough to live on, and she doesn't like it all that much.

She owns half the Merkers diamonds, which I intend selling off one at a time. They're huge stones, fetching a pretty penny. I parcel out enough money to supplement her wages, which she's reluctant to take. To try and give her more would be out of the question. She doesn't want to know where it's coming from, because she still looks on the diamonds as being stolen. That's another reason for telling her this serialized story of mine; I need to convince her the loot from the Merkers mine belongs to somebody besides the Waffen SS who killed to get it.

There are a couple of waiters hovering over us waiting for me to pay the check and leave. It's getting late, and I think we might have worn out our welcome. Still, a healthy tip will put things to rights; it always does. And the one thing I have is money for large tips, small consolation, actually, when you consider I've traded this privilege for freedom and my *peace of mind*.

We never talked much on the way to her apartment. And we went straight to bed me on the sofa again.

She is still wary of me. She almost lost her life a few weeks ago because of me, and I suppose Eric can share some of the blame as well. I know she holds him partially responsible, but not much is needed to cause her more ill feelings toward him.

I know she likes me, and the chances of things blossoming into love and marriage are good; she has as much as told me so. But she is still traumatized by what happened that night at her farm. She wants me to give the rest of the diamonds back, but realizes I don't know who to give them to. But as they say around here, *I'm not about to*, even if I did.

I like the idea of having money. I like the idea of tipping big without having to think much about it. I told you before how I used to be poor, how I was at loose ends with my life until I joined the army. Then, I wasn't sure what I was going to do after I left. Now, that's all behind me. I'm going to continue to survive; like it or not, survival has become my career. You might even say it pays me well. But if I had to do it again, I might have left the diamonds alone and then taken General Patton up on his offer to stay in the service. But, mind you, I said I might have; I don't know. Anyway, the point is moot, I took the diamonds before I found out I could stay with a regular commission. Obviously, though, the army wouldn't pay me nearly so much. But I've learned there's something almost as important as money, peace of mind. But it's done–and like Omar's *moving pencil,* life moves on and I can't change a thing.

Speaking of the army: they do still want me. They want to put me in Leavenworth prison, is what they want. I'm sure of it, because of what happened after we left Berchtesgaden, which led up to this Ravensbruck thing.

I met Lucy after work. She was unable to get away for lunch; it's that kind of job. She had some shopping to do before she came home. In the meantime, I hung around reading and listening to the radio. After she changed clothes, we went back to that same restaurant on the Riverwalk. The waiters were happy to see us; I knew they would be. It's an excellent place to sit and talk. The nights are cool and the surroundings couldn't be more pleasant. I'm beginning to understand why she likes this town.

She didn't wait for me to continue with my story about what we did after we left Berchetesgaden. She started asking me specific questions right away.

"Mike, you keep talking about the 25th of April. I remember it was the date set to raid Hitler's place, but you've never told me what happened. What did happen, anyway?"

"Yes, well, when it was first being considered, they expected Hitler and his whole entourage to be there. Our intelligence had them leaving Berlin. But recall he changed his mind on the spur of the moment and stayed in his bunker. I guess when it came time to leave, he had a period of lucidity and realized that holding out in the mountains was a pipe dream. Goering was the only one at home; he was hiding out waiting to split for the Kitzbuhel."

"You talk as though you suspect Goering of being one of the shooters at the lake. Could it be he planned to hijack the gold and then use it to bargain for his life?"

"I thought so then, and in some ways I still do. In fact, I'm not sure his people are not some of those who are after me now. I can't rule them out. But to answer your first question: The SS gun batteries had for years been training to ward off a bombing from high altitude. But recently they had come to believe that a low-level attack was more practical. A quick look at the layout of the Obersalzberg will show you why. I always thought it was Weyland's Tactical Air Force that was going to be given this prestigious assignment. But in the end, politics prevailed...."

"Explain. I don't understand," she said, leaning toward me, interested.

"What happened was this: General Eisenhower took the mission away from Weyland and his fighter bombers stationed nearby and gave it to the RAF with their heavy Lancaster's based in England. If he had preferred heavy long-range bombers, then Doolittle was his man. But as it turned out, he did it strictly for political reasons. He gave it to the British instead of the American Eighth Air Force, with the stipulation that the RAF's Polish crews would lead the strike force.

"Hitler had devastated Warsaw with his *Stuka* dive bombers at the beginning of the War, so this raid on his cherished alpine domicile was symbolic; Polish crews would be given a last chance at settling the score. It's true, some Americans escorted them, but none of our bombers participated. British *pathfinder* mosquito aircraft were to mark the target, but fouled it up. They were off line, causing the lead Polish airmen to miss on their first approach. But once the Poles had a good look, they did a credible job, followed by several British groups participating.

"The Turken Hotel of Walter Reinicke's was left in ruins but salvageable. That's more than could be said for the Berghof. Anyway, before they left, the SS set fire to Hitler's place. I guess they didn't want scavengers messing around with the carcass. Later, it was bulldozed down when the remains were being treated as some kind of shrine, just as Patton said it would be. However, it's interesting to note that to this day wildflowers grow in profusion around the foundations where the Berghof used to stand. It tells me that not all the SS went to Argentina or even made an attempt. Still, there must be others who revere his memory, in spite of the millions of lives lost because of him."

CHAPTER 22...BERCHETSGADEN, APRIL 1945

The three of us in the heavily laden trucks are ambling along about ten miles from Berchetsgaden. We are heading north towards Munich. A few more miles from here, I intend to make a sweeping right turn and head back toward Lintz. At least that's what the others think I'm going to do.

We left Berchetsgaden with about as much food as we could carry; Reinicke kept the rest. We have more than he does, but he's satisfied because Ralph told him where he could get more, much more. Ralph told him to go straight to the officers' mess when he returns on the 26th. Ralph knows the departing SS can carry only a small part of what is stored there. Walter thanked him and left for the infirmary with Steinmann in good spirits. That is, Walter was, I can't speak for Steinmann. But I should think he would be; after all, he was alive. And both of his great toes showed a reaction to a pin being dragged across the bottom of his foot, so I suppose his spinal cord is intact, fortunately for him.

When I talked to Oddlie on the radio, I gave him the address of Lothar Horner's gasthaus in Siegesdorf, asking him to send me another truck and the rest of my first squad.

We're going to need help transferring the gold. But most of all, I suspect we might need help defending it.

My new instructions from Oddlie were to head for Lintz and George Patton's forces as soon as I made contact with Carl. Patton had been advised that O'Daniel's Third Infantry, part of Patch's Seventh Army, was about to start on their way to Salzburg from Munich. Patch expects Munich to be completely secured by the 30th. When Patton found out his friend O'Daniel and not LeClerc was to be first on the Obersalzberg, he gave up on the idea of moving one of his divisions in ahead of everyone else. He told Oddlie he would wait at Lintz for me. Patton said: "The big plumb making the headlines was going to be the gold, and not some undefended bombed out pile of rubble." Pure rationalization. But then again, he might be right.

Patton was my friend and, as it stood now, one of his trusted friends was going to let him down. I was going to cheat him out of his last big coup. Furthermore, If I hijacked the gold, he would be expected to keep it a secret for fear of being embarrassed by the usually hostile press. But eventually the story will leak out, these kinds of things always do. And then he'll be criticized just for knowing me. I don't like it, and it's going to make me feel bad. I know I'm going to be uncomfortable for a few days. I expect to be ashamed of myself, but I figure I'll get over it.

As we slowly motored along, a crazy thought crossed my mind: *I would be willing to give Patton some of it, enough to make him wealthy, certainly enough to assuage his conscience if he would take it. But he won't. I know he won't. But not necessarily because he has more honor than I do, which he does. But because he also has plenty of money. He's reputed to be the wealthiest general in the service, having inherited a large undisclosed sum from his family. Still, I have inherited a large undisclosed sum myself; you might say it, too, came from my family. And I might even be richer than the general. I'm sure I am, and that's important to me for some reason. But that's what comes of being dirt poor all your life. You establish a different set of values regarding money. He can have the honor–I want the money.*

It was just before sun-up when we heard them. We had stopped for the second time to refill our radiators in yet another small village. We were having difficulty keeping them from boiling over, what with our heavy loads and all.

A few minutes later we saw them, their dark forms plainly visible in the dawn of the early morning. What looked to be several squadrons of sleek American fighters were escorting several groups of ungainly looking British Lancasters. And they were all heading for the Obersalzberg. People began pouring from their homes in their night-clothes when they heard the rumble. One citizen even asked Eric if he knew where they were headed. Eric told me this guy knew all right; they all knew. They had been expecting this particular raid for years. They just didn't want to come to terms with the inevitable. The death knell was sounding for Hitler's beloved Berghof and all it stood for. It was the final blow to the Third Reich, which was supposed to have lasted a thousand years; it was supposed to have ushered in a new age of enlightenment, peace, and prosperity to rival *The Golden Age of Pericles*. But it did nothing of the sort. And now all they have to look forward to is chaos, uncertainty, and even imprisonment for their returning veterans. But worst of all, hunger and poverty will be their new bedfellows for many years to come, just the way it was following the First War. And they expect it to be the same again, only many times worse. They have George Patton to deal with this time. They have all heard of him. And everyone knows he is worse than their own Waffen SS. Everyone is talking about how he is the consummate warrior, a throwback to the Khans, a barbarian who will exact a terrible retribution on a defenseless enemy if left to his own devices. They're saying the American people are angry, and that they have no intentions of meddling in his affairs. Whatever he wants to do with Austria and Bavaria is all right with them. From one end to the other, they're discussing whether he'll be given free rein to do as he pleases–there's no doubt about it, they figure they're going to be in for hard times. However, as it would turn out, nothing was further from the truth. The best friend the Germans ever had was George Patton, who almost single-handedly saved those in his sector from starvation during the next winter.

A few minutes later, we heard the deep thrump, thrump of bursting 500 lb. bombs. I knew Hitler's digs were getting a terrible pasting. And I knew Berchetsgaden might be devastated as well. I looked at Ralph, who muttered something about hoping Reinicke and his sons had sense enough to heed my advice about getting clear of the place. If they hadn't, in all likelihood, we might never see them again. I didn't care all that much. To me, at the time, they were just another unfortunate German family who had brought the War upon themselves. But Ralph cared. Walter was his close friend and had been for many years.

The SS was not going to suffer much. Ralph told me they were well prepared for this raid so as to not be caught off guard. He said it was like lifeboat drill on a ship, only instead of once or twice during a voyage, they had simulated it hundreds of times through the years. Everybody knew exactly what he was supposed to do when the siren sounded. Non-essential personnel, those not manning anti-aircraft artillery, were to take cover in underground living quarters. And they would have had plenty of time to get there. The panzer units up ahead, the ones waiting in the forests for O'Daniel, would have warned them. Whether they would have been able to activate the fogging unit in time, though, was another matter.

Ralph told me about this fogging thing. He said they had an artificial fogger that could lay in a bank of fog sufficient to cover the valley and obscure the compound. He said this machine worked using dry ice. At first I thought he was kidding me. But he was serious. He told me in great detail about their genius, and how they had invented this huge fog-making contraption. But the effectiveness of the fog depended on the humidity at the time. Usually, it took some twenty minutes' notice to rev it up, according to him. *RAF crews would report weather over the area as being clear and the target unobstructed; so weather conditions must have been ideal for bombing but not suitable for the making of fog.*

I began wondering what might have happened to Kurt Steinmann. I never said anything to Ralph, but he guessed what was on my mind. If, indeed, I was concerned about my *friend,* as he put it, I shouldn't worry. He said they had a fully equipped underground hospital that occupied several large rooms cut from the granite mountain. But I was not worried about him lying about somewhere during the raid. I knew he was in their sheltered hospital. But what were they intending to do with him after it was over and they all took off?

The mention of Steinmann's name set Ralph's curiosity in gear again. He came right out and asked me for the third time if I had known Steinmann before, even though he knew I must have.

When the sound of explosions finally ceased, we watched the airplanes slowly turn in formation and head back in the direction of England. All of them did except for one trailing smoke from two engines. We watched it move out of formation, and with a fighter escort, it headed toward our lines and a probable crash landing. If they had crashed in one of the fields near us, the townspeople might have set upon them. This had happened to a number of our crews, before German military authorities could arrive on the scene and rescue them. Somehow, though, I doubt it would happen here. These people have only heard about the War on their radios; they have never experienced a bombing first-hand, and at this point, they're not interested in revenge; they're only interested in ending the War as soon as possible. Still, you can't be too sure. Most families in Germany have lost at least one member of their immediate family in a bombing raid or in combat. And many of them have lost several.

And it's true they have seen large numbers of American aircraft on their way to Salzburg, which was bombed a total of fifteen times. But never to the Obersalzberg. The reason being: the Allies were waiting to catch Hitler during one of the many times he was in residency. The notification never came from Ralph, something I considered curious at the time; and it did make me wonder about Ralph, as it must have Oddlie.

Later in the day, I espied a large mural of a harp on a building. It was the same as the one Lother Horner previously described to me. We stopped and verified the town as being Siegesdorf, his home. I looked up his address in my notebook. A few minutes later we were parked in front of his mother's inn, situated on a corner lot.

The sign on the building was made of polished brass, mounted on a tasteful oaken plaque. It read simply: *Gasthouse Horner*. The woodwork had recently been sanded and re-stained, making it appear as though it was a quality piece of furniture. The front of the building had been newly painted an off-white. Several beautifully carved geranium boxes, fastened below the windows of the two-story structure, had been refurbished and replaced by a carpenter who knew his trade. Scaffolding was standing along the southern side facing the other street; somebody, probably Lothar, had just begun another major clean up and repainting project. More geraniums were newly planted along the sidewalk in front and in small beds on both sides of steps leading to a bright red door, trimmed in brass. The color of the door blended perfectly with the color of the flowers. The whole effect was anything but offensive to the eye. As a matter of fact, it looked as though it had been planned to do just what it was doing; it was beckoning a stranger to look more closely if he was in the market for a reasonably priced clean room.

I could see Lother had hit the ground running, and he must have employed some help. He had accomplished wonders with the place in the limited time he had. He had explained to me how it had fallen on hard times during the War. However, as a result of his hard work, I could see it was recovering rapidly to its former state.

Eric went to the door and knocked. A woman answered and Eric asked her if she was open for business. They talked for a minute and then she invited him in. A few minutes later he emerged with Lothar, who was sporting a big grin. Somehow, I felt he was genuinely glad to see me. I really felt he was not putting on some kind of show, all the better to con me for food he suspected might be in the trucks. I confess I'm suspicious. I'm having a hard time grasping the idea that my former enemy could eventually become my friend. *I was not alone in this–it took years before citizens of our two countries were able to form genuine friendships, due in part to laws prohibiting fraternization.*

Lother had already told Eric they were open for guests. He said he had two rooms ready for occupancy. Two more would be ready when they were cleaned up tomorrow. I nodded, and the two of us walked around the side of the truck to talk.

"Lothar," I said, "is our presence here going to cause you trouble with your neighbors if they find out who we are?"

"I do not care if it does, although I do not see why it should. Anyway, they have more important things to think about. They are afraid. They are expecting your General Patton in a few days, and that is all they talk about. There are several dozen soldiers in town, just like me, who have left their units; they are even more afraid than the others. They think your general is going to put them in a concentration camp for safekeeping. They are talking about running off to Italy or up into the high Alps until things become more settled. There is no doubt they would if they had something to eat when they got there. They cannot take it with them because there is almost no food left. The SS went through here last month and confiscated everything."

"That's what I want to talk about, food I mean. I want to make you a deal...." I saw his perplexed look and realized my regular speech consisted mostly of slang, interspersed with profanity and army patois–a kind of army Creole he was having a hard time understanding.

"I mean, I want you to do some things for me. I'll pay you with food and silver American money–enough food to keep you and your mother supplied for several weeks–and enough money to finish your project here." I turned and looked toward his scaffolding as I said it. "I'm expecting some more of my people. When they get here, I'll give you a supply of military rations."

I had his undivided attention; he was listening closely. He knew what they were. It seems his unit once over-ran an American stronghold, and he became the benefactor of several trucks loaded with K rations. He especially liked the cigarettes, to say nothing of the canned meat and real coffee.

"Listen, let me start from the beginning. First, I want

you to show me where I can park these trucks. Then, I want to tell you I am carrying valuable cargo belonging to General Patton. But there are no military stores; there's no ammunition or weapons of any kind involved, so you can relax. And I want you to help me keep it secure until the people I told you about arrive in a few days."

I could see the wheels in his head beginning to turn. He knew the truck's cargo must be very important if it had brought us this far behind enemy lines and in civilian clothes. If we had been caught, we would have been immediately shot as spies. Nobody ventures into such dangerous waters as Eric and I have, not unless they're after something very valuable. But at the sound of *food* and *money*, Lothar went into survival mode, telling himself he could not afford to be curious. He agreed without further conversation.

At the time, I thought I was putting him at risk with the local authorities. But what I didn't know–he *was* the authority. As the ranking Wermacht officer in town, he had assumed the job of *Burgermeister*. Backed by other members of his army, he had all the support he needed to enact ordinances and to ensure the continuance of what he referred to as the *peaceful tranquility*. He likened himself to a town marshal in the movies.

I plan to give him the German trucks when we leave. But I have to be careful; I don't want him speculating on why I no longer need them. On the one hand, he knows they're a liability; on the other, he might conclude we're carrying such heavy loads we have to switch to something larger. He's most familiar with the German three-ton, so he might start thinking about how heavy our cargo really is. The last thing I want is for him to become curious and then conclude we might be carrying gold or some other precious metal. If he does, all bets are off; anything can happen then. Of course, the last thing I want is trouble, which might lead to an attack on us by the townspeople. Yet, if the cry of gold is ever raised, you can rest assured there'll be a stampede far exceeding the Klondike rush of '98.

"I want you to promise you'll keep our presence here quiet. And I want your word you'll not attempt to discover what it is I'm carrying. This is most important. Both our lives depend on it. If you do, there'll be bloodshed. And then George Patton will have our Gestapo transport your entire town to Russia." I had no idea what I was taking about. But no matter, he recognized some of the buzzwords; they matched some of those already indelibly implanted in his psyche. We were friends, but with that last remark, we became even more so.

That night we sat around Frau Horner's table and talked. She had cut into one of the large cured sausages and converted it into gravy. She also made some flour out of some of the wheat we gave her. The simple meal of meat-gravy and biscuits was one of the best I have ever eaten. And I know for a fact it was the first real meal they had had in weeks. Quality of food, I concluded, is dependent upon how hungry you are.

I was not sure exactly when Carl was arriving. But it would be after the first columns of O'Daniel's armor passed through town.

The next afternoon we heard sporadic cannon fire. Lothar told me it was .88 millimeter, probably from Tigers engaging our Sherman's. But, thankfully, we had air support for our tanks. Once the Germans opened up, they gave their positions away and waiting fighter-bombers descended on them almost immediately.

As the two of us had discussed, the Sherman was no match for the Tiger; but the Tiger was no match for our fighters and medium bombers. So the unfair fights started up, only to be ended in a flurry of gunfire. And then they started again, only to end the same way as Third Infantry, supported by the Air Corps, moved steadily toward Salzburg.

Oddlie told me, when I talked to him on the radio, that O'Daniel's timetable called for him to arrive at his final objective on the fifth of May. He also told me the now famous 102nd Airborne was following in reserve, as were the French under LeClerc. That means we'll not see Carl and my gang for another two days. What we are going to do in the meantime, is what we were talking about as we *scarfed* down Frau Horner's dinner.

Lother is going to a meeting tonight with his town council to discuss some matters of no interest to me. I figure it might be a good opportunity, though, to tell them what it is we're doing here. We have to be coming from somewhere for a reason. And we had to have a reason for staying when we got here. A social call between friends and relatives was just not very believable. And the last thing I wanted was to become the subject of general conversation among a highly volatile and potentially hostile citizenry.

Lothar suggests he tell them we're cousins from Salzburg, and that we're afraid of Patton, who is moving north from Lintz. We swiped the trucks and fuel, and we plan to stay until it's safe to go home. He also plans to tell them we're deserters, and that we were afraid of being placed in a concentration camp had we remained there. Since we're Lothar's relatives, we're going to help him with his remodeling projects to earn our keep until after the American army arrives and takes over. In short: we're afraid of Patton and hope it's not his soldiers who occupy Siegsdorf. At any rate, we don't want to be seen driving these stolen trucks. We want a place to hang out until things settle down.

It sounds good to me. Now, all we have to do is spread the word, which Lothar intends to do momentarily.

That night at sunset, I posted a guard on the trucks. I fully expect somebody will come snooping around looking for food. It might be more than one–and this same town council of Lothar's might even be involved in organizing it–unbeknownst to him, of course.

We took turns with four-hour shifts. Nothing happened, maybe tomorrow night. Maybe it'll take them a little longer to get organized, but I'm sure it's going to happen eventually. I never believed Lothar's story would be bought so easily. Still, if we're not who we say we are, then who are we?

The next morning, we started work on the new gasthaus. While Eric and Ralph painted, I talked to Lothar.

I asked him where he intended to put the additional rooms he told me about. With a stick, he laid out what he had in mind. It was a simple, straightforward add-on of two rooms on top of two more on the ground floor. There was to be an outside entrance with a hall leading through the kitchen to the restaurant.

I noticed Lothar was not approaching the project with much enthusiasm. When I asked him why, he said he didn't think this was the appropriate time to be thinking of such things. Anyway, he said he had no money. This is the kind of thing one thinks about and then it usually takes years before it ever happens, he said. I told him this might be the way things were done in his country, but not in mine. Still, where was the money coming from? It was one thing for me to finance the finishing up of the painting, and maybe popping for a mural on the sidewall if he could find one of the traveling mural painters, the kind who used to wander around before the War. But where was he going to get the money for a major remodeling of the building?

We went inside and sat down with a pencil and paper. It took him an hour to come up with a fair estimate of what had to be done and what it was going to cost. He kept saying he didn't know how much this or that was going to be, or whether he was going to be able to do this or that because of the situation–and so on.

When he realized I was not fooling around, and that I actually planned to give him some real money, he began concentrating on some realistic figures. He was afraid if his estimate was too high I might back out. He needn't have worried. I planned to give him at least one ingot just before we departed.

That afternoon we made a drawing and laid out the footings. Then he borrowed several shovels from his neighbors, and we all started digging. I hadn't used a shovel in years; I was enjoying the fresh air and the exercise. Eric was quite surprised to see me digging away. He was even more surprised to see I was more familiar with a shovel than he was. Digging fox pens and rough-necking on an oilrig called for my having a certain expertise on what I always looked upon as an *ignorant stick*.

Dinner was as satisfying as it had been the night before. It was the same thing, but I enjoyed it; I was having fun. The cool air and the pleasant surroundings were getting to me. To tell you the truth, there's nothing I would have liked better than to have stayed right there for the rest of the summer, doing just what I had been doing for the past three hours. I was getting into the spirit of the thing. I wanted to stay and see it finished. Eric felt the same way, and so did Ralph. One thing for sure, I told Frau Horner: "I'm coming back often and staying for a very long time." I had the money. I could come back any time I pleased, and stay as long as I liked. How prophetic these comments to her would turn out to be. Over the next six or seven years, I was to be her guest over and over again. But I wouldn't return for any walk down memory lane or for a vacation. But come back I did, for another altogether different reason than you can possibly imagine–and for lengthy stays each time.

The morning of the third day of May saw the first of the Sherman's crawling into town. And then for the next couple of hours they became a seemingly endless, deafening parade. There was no shouting or waving; neither side showed any emotion. For the most part, the German population stayed indoors. Nobody wanted to call attention to themselves. Nobody knew what was going to happen. They were confused, expecting the worst. They didn't really know whether they were going to be rounded up, shot, or fed. They knew nothing at all, and they were afraid to ask. Then, too, who were they going to ask?

The division rumbled through without stopping. They were here, and then all of a sudden quiet reigned. They were gone. All the time the sky overhead was full of menacing low-flying airplanes waiting for word of trouble. The town would have been reduced to rubble at the slightest hint of resistance. I knew it, and so did they. If Lothar and his mother were examples, then everybody in town realized what was at stake. They were afraid some die-hard Nazi would start shooting and end it all. They kept asking me if this might be General Patton's army. Why even his own men called him *Old Blood and Guts*, which sounded no better in German.

Carl and three more of my first squad arrived just before noon. I noticed the look on Frau Horner's face when she saw the extra mouths to feed. It was not the extra work, particularly. This return to the old days, when she ran her small restaurant at near capacity, was welcomed. But at this rate, the food we had given her was not going to last very long. Then she was introduced to the K ration. You should have seen the expression on her face when she opened her first can of Spam. And when she realized Carl had brought her a couple of months' supply of the stuff, her eyes lit up like a Christmas tree.

We started transferring the gold, after we got the

American trucks off the street and away from prying eyes. There would be no time now for anything but hard work until the job was finished. Now the neighbors might become a problem. But now the American uniforms would dissuade any and all troublemakers. However, our story would have to change accordingly. Our two trucks had engine problems and had left the column of tanks just passing through. My soldiers had just happened to see the gasthaus and had decided to stay there until they could get them fixed. It sounded plausible enough to me, even if it didn't explain away the coincidence of us already being there and in German trucks.

Ralph was in charge of the transfer, which went smoothly. He had the trucks backed up to each other, tail to tail, with planks between them. He tried a wheelbarrow first. However, that was too slow. He finally settled on passing each ingot from hand to hand from one truck to another, hours of backbreaking labor. But there was no faster way. I came around back, after talking some more with Lothar. I was in time to see the job finished and Steinmann's box being transferred from the German truck.

It was suspended from some kind of a carriage thing. It looked for all the world like a miniature sedan chair with the box suspended below in an antique metal cradle. From what I could see, it was ornately hand carved. It was too heavy for secret documents. Documents had been my first guess. But my guesses were running wild and changing at the rate of one a minute. First, as I said, I thought it might contain names, places, and secrets–things like that. Then I thought–since this Waffen SS was some kind of a cult organization–it might be loaded with books containing their secret writings, beliefs that sort of thing. But if it was, why was it so heavy? And why then was Ralph taking it so slow and being so careful not to damage the contents? And why was he so surprised to see me? Was he trying to get it out of sight before I saw it? The look on his face said he was.

I asked Lothar if it might be possible to make a sign from some of the one-by-six pine lying in a scrap pile near the trucks. He told me yes with a smile, which indicated he would be glad to undertake what I thought was a simple project.

It's customary in some parts of the country, maybe throughout Germany, as far as I know, to give your visiting friend a small present, a kind of memento, a token of your esteem or some such. I suspect he had been searching his brain for something appropriate. And certainly the sign I asked about filled the bill. When I saw his work, I was surprised. He had stayed up most of the night, carving, sanding, and varnishing one for each truck. He presented them to me now. They read in bold letters *Keep Off*. And then below it read, again in bold letters, *Graves Detail*. Hanging by a small brass chain was another smaller one that read, simply: *Morte Homme*. The look on my face was all the thanks he needed.

I couldn't believe the work that must have gone into these signs. They were obviously the work of an expert woodcarver. Then I realized it must have been Lothar who made the geranium boxes and the hand-carved and scrolled eves around the building. He told me no, it was his father. Then he told me his father wasn't coming back from the War. More than that he didn't care to discuss. But he did show me his wood carving tools, telling me his father had taught him the trade when he was a boy. Then I watched him permanently fasten one of his signs to the end gate. The other one he fastened to the front winch of our lead truck.

That night, Frau Horner ironed our newly washed khaki uniforms. After we finished with the gold transfer, we put them on and prepared to say our goodbyes. Now, of course, the gold was no longer a secret. I suspect most everyone in town was aware of what we had really been up to. But it doesn't matter. Now our two five ton trucks are cordoned off by three of my soldiers with machine guns. As we all shook hands, and I kissed and hugged Frau Horner, we promised to return again as soon as we could. It was then that I gave Lothar two of the ingots. I started to give him just one but felt magnanimous. I gave him another just to see the expression on his face. We were friends for life. It might be said we were the first American and German after the War to become friends. Gold has a way of cementing friendships like nothing else in the world

CHAPTER 22
BAVARIA, GERMANY, 4 MAY 1945

The first slowdown occurred north of Siegsdorf early the next morning. We came to a sudden stop with several Red Balls blocking our way. They were stalled near a crossroad because of a long column of LeClerc's Shermans and his trucks entering from off the autobahn.

The first inkling we had of the effectiveness of Lothar's signs was when one of the French tank commanders rendered us a salute. At first I thought it was for me. On second thought, I realized he couldn't see my rank under my field jacket. As the next tank was passing, I received another *eyes left* and another salute.

I knew they were French because their lead tank was flying a small tricolor from its whip antennae. And each of the next ten were named after French heroes and famous World War One battles, stenciled in white paint across their turrets. Passing across from me now is the *Vimey Ridge*, the name of a rabbit-warren-like fortress overlooking the Somme battlefield. It was a famous observation post defended by the French at a huge loss of life. It was taken from them by the Germans and finally recovered–not by the French, but by determined Canadians who suffered tremendous losses. There was the *Verdun*, a monster meat grinder of a battle that lasted for years and resulted in the French losing most of one generation. Then came the *Morte Homme*, another artillery observation post overlooking the reaches of the Verdun battlefield that had been fought over for most of the First War. It was a small plot of bloody ground on top of a hill, where more than seven thousand Frenchman lost their lives. Thereafter, the Americans late in the War took it from the Germans. One of the participants was none other than a young tank officer by the name of George Patton. There was the *Vaux*, a fortress at Verdun. And then the *Douaumont,* named for still another defensive fortress at Verdun, where, at the height of the War, some one thousand shells a day landed on its roof of reinforced concrete. It was taken by the Germans halfway through the War at a great loss to French national pride. American forces finally overran it as they pushed across Verdun in the Muse Argonne Offensive of 1918.

There were the General Margin, General Joffre, and other general officer heroes. And of course Foche, whose name, rank, and service to France was so well documented and remembered that there was never a need to include his rank for identification purposes. To this day, the name Foche is recognized and revered by all French schoolchildren.

It was as though we were watching a tableau of French history passing in review. Then a curious thing happened. A trio of French military motorcycle police pulled alongside of us and stopped. The sergeant in charge dismounted and saluted me. He spoke in French, telling me he had been ordered to escort us to the next crossroad and onto the autobahn. Obviously, one of their tanks had radioed back that we were being held up by traffic, and the mounted police were sent to investigate. The reason for the attention was the sign plainly visible on the front of our first truck.

The sergeant thought at first I was a Frenchman. I would be very surprised if he ever figured out where I came from. But no matter, we understood each other perfectly. And he treated me with more courtesy than usual, thinking I'm sure, that I was some kind of an undertaker.

At any rate, the empty Red Balls were asked to move off the road and make way, as was the next twenty-five vehicles in line. The tank column was stopped at the cross-road, and we were allowed to turn right on a small road leading to the autobahn. As our French escorts pulled onto the highway ahead of us, we took another right turn, and before they realized what had happened, we were a mile or so down another country road and out of their sight. We never saw them again.

I had planned to push east for about fifty miles while trying to make up my mind what to do. But we were starting to encounter elements of Simpson's First Army, moving towards Austria in brigade strength. First, there were a few scout vehicles, whose passengers looked at us curiously. They never waved but just looked at us, as if to say, *I wonder how those poor devils drew that detail?* Then we came upon the first of his tanks. It was in our best interests to look for another small road, one that would eventually take us away from Simpson's advance and away from the inevitable traffic jam.

I couldn't help but compare the names painted on our tanks to those driven by the French. Ours were high-school-frivolous, carefree; some were downright silly, and some others were given over to gallows humor. For instance: girl friends there were in profusion; others were named for a cartoon character known far and wide as *The Sad Sack*. Then there was a virtual plethora of *Kilroys*, he of the large proboscis; a much traveled, imaginary character, whose sole claim to fame was his countenance gracing the walls of men's rooms from one end of the world to the other. There were also a number of *Boot Hills*, *Tombstones*, *Dodge Cities*, *Purgatories*, and the like. You get the idea.

I'm not sure what all this means. But it set my mind to thinking once again: maybe Eisenhower was right; maybe we hadn't been taking the War as seriously as had some of the other participants. Maybe we Americans did see it as one big football game, unless, of course, you or one of your buddies just happened to be lying mutilated in some field hospital somewhere.

I suppose I had not been following the map and keeping myself properly oriented, as I should have. We had taken several turns, and I wasn't sure where we were. I wasn't even sure of the direction we were headed. The land was flat with no visible checkpoints other than the sun. And the sun was of no help, since it was almost directly overhead.

So far, we had been lucky. But I was taking a chance running around on this between-armies odyssey of ours. Eventually, we were going to encounter motorcycle *head-hunters*. They were not hunting for motorcycle heads, if I might be allowed a little frivolity of my own. They were looking for trucks like ours, which were not part of a convey and were being driven around suspiciously.

Misappropriated vehicles and soldiers on foot who had deserted occasionally inhabited the roads. Not so many now, since the War was winding down. But there had been enough to keep the hunters occupied before the Bulge. And, like a lot of things in large organizations, once implemented, they were slow to be shut down when no longer needed.

These so-called headhunter activities were taken from the pages of the German tactics book. The Wermacht had been faced with deserter problems early on and had started patrolling their roads shortly after the Invasion.

These roving teams of American military police would stop you. They would ask for identification and your unit designation, things like that. Then they would ask to see your *trip ticket*. This last was a form that had to be signed off daily by somebody in authority from a motor pool. The purpose was to ensure vehicles were receiving proper driver maintenance and to ensure accountability.

In a combat zone, this trip signoff was often delayed by necessity–sometimes for weeks. In most combat units, there were mobile maintenance crews traveling around checking on such things as proper tire pressure, radiator coolant level, oil level, and oil changes. When this inspection was accomplished, they renewed your trip ticket.

If we encountered one of these maintenance crews or head-hunters, I figured we might be hard-pressed to explain what we were doing in the middle of Simpson's sector when we were attached to General Patton's headquarters, especially with a hopelessly outdated trip ticket and a German civilian in tow. Some eager soldier might be interested enough in us to find out why. And he might well ask why we were headed in the opposite direction from the new cemetery at Luxembourg.

I recall it was close to chow time. We stopped for a K ration or two, approximately three miles from the last *gingerbreader* we passed through. One of my German speaking replacements approached me and asked where we were. I gave him a name off the top of my head, not even thinking. What difference did it make? And of what concern could it possibly be to him.

I had to say something. Ignoring squad members bent on making casual conversation could only go so far without being seen as me not knowing where we were. This translated into not caring where we were, which meant I had no plan and was confused. The worst thing that can happen to any commander is to be thought of as being confused. To satisfy his curiosity, I gave him the first name coming off the top of my head.

Now that I think about it, it must have been in my mind to do this all along. And this was an excellent location for what I had been planning since we started out.

Without thinking, I replied: *Ravensbruck.* As I said, it was spur of the moment; it was right off the cuff, pulled right out of the air, right out of my kidneys. I had no idea where or if there was such a place; it just sounded German. I knew the true identity of the last town or village, all right. I had read it on a storefront as we passed through. But I doubted anybody else had seen it, or if they had, they would have cared enough to remember. The name of the place didn't sound remotely like the one I had just given the inquiring corporal. Still, I knew he would tell everybody in the group what I had just told him, if for no other reason then to make more conversation. But I smiled, knowing this is exactly what I wanted him to do.

And I also knew the order I was about to give would have serious consequences; once spoken we could never turn back. I was about to change our lives forever. Like Julius Caesar and his Legion, we were about to embark on a journey that would take us across the proverbial *Rubicon.*

"You men, finish up; man your trenching tools. Everybody, bear a hand. I want a trench big enough to bury this load of gold. I want the trucks pulled off the road. I want any passer-by to think we are burying bodies to be later dug up by the proper authorities. And I want to be out of here shortly after dark."

They had been digging about an hour when Ralph stepped out of the trench. He came over to where I was standing, as if to say something. I thought he was going to tell me he had plans to bury Steinmann's box alongside of the gold. This might have been the case, but that's not what he wanted to talk about. He wanted to say something else and then changed his mind. But I would have to wait more than five years to find out what it was.

I stopped them about an hour later, telling them the trench was large enough. This statement was met with curious looks all around. The corporal who had asked me where we were said something to the effect that it wasn't big enough. I ignored him and walked away.

I had a new plan. I had been thinking. Why did we need all the gold? Wouldn't it be more prudent to turn half of it over to Bernstein and Patton and bury the rest? After all, they had been expecting only half the cargo we were carrying. Why not come in with the amount Intelligence had told them was at the Obersalzberg and keep the rest. That way we were all free to walk away. And it would let Patton have his day with the press.

But what about Oddlie? Why did I request the extra truck and the men? No problem. I would simply tell him I was a poor estimator. I had overestimated the amount we had taken from the Germans.

But what about Ralph and the new guys? I can't speak for Ralph, but my replacements were not going to be a problem, not as long as they were going to get a share.

I had Eric and Carl feel them out. They reported back: the replacements would not say anything if they were going to be admitted to the club. In fact, they were elated at the prospect of never having to seriously work again for the rest of their lives.

Now, here's the *kicker*, which I figure will lower the risk of them ever saying anything if we let them in. If they don't report the entire incident to Colonel Bernstein immediately upon our arrival, they'll be unable to change their minds and do it later. And if they have a change of heart and chicken out when we arrive, I'll counter by telling Bernstein that we had a legitimate reason for burying it. I couldn't make it back with the entire load, don't you know? The now-emptied truck had been acting up, you see. We thought we heard engine bearing noises, or the clutch felt as though it was slipping, or something else was haywire. We obviously couldn't be wandering around the countryside in a vehicle loaded with a fortune that was going to poop out on us at any minute. If it did, we were going to be discovered and relieved of half our cargo, which would have made General Patton very unhappy. In fact, my orders were to bury it if at any time I thought I might be in any danger of losing control.

It was not important what was actually wrong with the truck, or whether anything was, only that the four of us tells Bernstein the same story. The replacements would have gained nothing by having a twinge of conscience and telling on us. This way, they stand to gain a fortune.

Our hesitancy to include them in the first place was not because we were stingy; quite the contrary, there's plenty for all of us. In the case of gold, you don't have to give most of it to a fence in the same way you do diamonds. Then, too, another three in the split was not that big a deal. You see, we intend to get three times more for it than the set government price.

You have to understand that the value of gold worldwide is established by the United States. That is, there is a set price at which our government will buy and sell. This amount is thirty-five dollars an ounce, an arbitrary figure they've held to for the past twelve years. However, everybody knows this restriction is going to be lifted eventually. Anybody with an interest in gold is speculating that it'll rise astronomically when it happens. And then, too, many people are hoarding gold as a hedge against inflation. So far, American currency has remained fairly stable, but this could change overnight. These things make gold all the more valuable and easy to sell.

And another thing, gold can be peddled most anyplace in Europe in almost any form. It can be melted down into smaller, more manageable nuggets or made into coins or even made into objects such as bookends or knick-knacks; it can be made into almost anything, which makes it easy to hoard. So the problem is not that we don't have enough to go around; the problem is they simply can't be trusted. We're afraid if they don't get their share when they think they should, they'll start causing trouble. As I mentioned before, we agreed between the three of us to wait five years before spending any of the diamonds, and the same goes for the gold. Including the replacements in our scheme means there's just that many more people to complicate things. And this eventually is going to cause us problems. What I'm trying to say: more isn't the merrier. Now it can't be avoided. Now they are going to get a cut, whether we like it or not.

CHAPTER 23...BERCHTESGADEN, 1950

I had returned to the Horner Gashouse once or twice before. That is, before I became less than enamored of airports. Come to think of it, this aversion of mine to airports came about sometime after the burn incident. It was a long time ago.

I thought I might go over to the Obersalzberg this trip back to Siegsdorf. I had not seen Walter Reinicke since we left the night before the bombing. I thought now might be a good time to see him again and have a talk.

The gasthaus was never finished. Lothar completed the extra rooms on the second floor, but he had hardly done anything at all with the space on the ground floor. He was using it as a workshop.

The first time I came back, he told me he had plans to go into business with one of his friends in Salzburg. He said they were going to make plaster of Paris busts of Mozart. They were going to fill them with lead and coat them with bronze, to be used as bookends or doorstops. He said they planned to sell them to tourists in Salzburg in several gifts shops around the city. They also had plans to extend this line, to include some memento of the Obersalzberg. But they hadn't decided on anything appropriate and in good taste. They had considered a replica of the Berghof and then decided against it.

He was very upbeat about the whole thing, as most new entrepreneurs are. However, I thought it was a mistake. I thought he could realize more money from renting out two more *zimmers* to tourists than he could by using the space for what he had in mind. But he obviously never agreed with me. I would later find out why.

I stayed with the Horners a few days to rest up from the long flight across the ocean, and then I made the planned trip to Berchtesgaden to visit Walter.

I found him hale and hearty, if not a little older. I wanted to talk about a few things more serious than the weather. And for that I needed an interpreter.

Walter understood, and asked me in sign language to take a ride in his car. He had a new Opel, one of the first off the new assembly lines in Stuttgart.

We drove once again through the magnificent countryside, up to the old Hitler compound. I had no idea what to expect. I had heard that the devastated Berghof had been burned by the departing SS, and then later completely destroyed. And I heard that Walter's Zum Turken had also been handed back to him in ruins, but not nearly as bad.

That it was in ruins was true enough. That it had been handed back, just like that, was in error. It had not been that simple. He had to hire an attorney and fight to get it back.

It seems that when Hitler took the Turken away from him, because it was too close to his Berghof, he did so *legally*. That is, he acquired a deed sealed and recorded. It was taken under *eminent domain,* the State needing it for a public building. The designated public building meant it was to be used to house Hitler's around-the-clock SS bodyguard and several members of the Gestapo. There was a small amount of money passed to satisfy the *valuable consideration* element of the contract, but only a pittance of what it was worth.

After the War, the new German government objected to giving it back, claiming Walter had signed away any right to ownership. But Walter and his grown daughter fought them for clear title under the German version of *unjust enrichment* and won.

Walter had taken possession soon after the air raid, and immediately began rebuilding using the gold I'd given him. However, the government closed him down for a couple of years; he started again as soon as his lawsuit was settled. But I was puzzled–where did he get the money for an almost complete rebuild. The gold I gave him was more than enough to see him through a remodel, but not nearly enough for what had to be done after the bombing.

He had a concierge who spoke excellent English. He wanted to use her as an interpreter. However, we abandoned the idea when we both realized it might not be in his best interests if she were privy to what I wanted to talk about. Chitchat about his hotel was one thing. But what I was interested in was something else again.

After showing me around with her in tow, we sought a more disinterested party, one who was legally obligated to keep our affairs confidential.

Reinicke registered me in one of his best rooms, where I left my B-4 army issued bag, and then the two of us went back to town. We looked around and found another interpreter, an attorney in Berchtesgaden.

"Walter, I want you to tell me what happened to Kurt Steinmann." The attorney translating for us was young. When Walter told him our conversation must be kept confidential, he told us all conversations with him were confidential. Realizing we didn't want him for any lucrative legal work, he appeared to be quite bored, which was all right with us. The last thing we wanted was for him to take an interest in Reinicke and his old attachments to Steinmann. And we certainly didn't want him connecting either of us with any hidden Nazi gold. The lawyer may have been bored with what he thought was going to be routine conversation. But he was about to change his mind. He must have been fascinated by what he heard next:

"Steinmann told me he did not want to stay in the underground bunker being used as a hospital," Walter said. "Regardless of what the doctors were going to tell me to do, Steinmann said I was not to leave him. He was afraid of what might happen. He knew the entire SS contingent was leaving. And he knew they could not take him. And they could not leave him behind.

"He was in extreme pain. He was almost delirious by the time we arrived. He started rambling on about a box he had lost. And he seemed to be in fear of his life if they found out he had lost it.

"Then Steinmann told me something even more curious. He told me if I would get him out of there, after they finished treating him, he would give me a lot of money. Steinmann said he personally had buried part of it, nearby." And here Walter hesitated to go on. He didn't want the interpreter to be aware we were talking about SS gold.

At no time did Reinicke mention gold in front of the interpreter. He spoke of money, but not gold. That word was *verboten* for obvious reasons.

I had known about the gold Steinmann forced Ralph to hold back. He made sure I did, soon after we started talking about the total to be dumped in the lake. He wanted to make sure that Colonel Bernstein knew he had altered the tally under duress.

"Walter, I know all about the *money*. Ralph told me." That's all I had to say. We understood each other, without further piquing the curiosity of the interpreter. As far as the attorney was concerned, we were talking about old buried Nazi Reichmarks, something of absolutely no interest to him.

"The medical people gave him a thorough examination," Reinicke went on to tell me. "Then they gave him some morphine and put him in a full body cast.

"Steinmann spoke to the officer in charge about being released in my care," Reinicke said. "He told the doctor I was a relation; to make the story more plausible, I told him I would be compensated for my trouble by members of our family."

I don't know whether the physician-in-charge believed him, but under the circumstances what else could he do? But he might not have been so eager to be rid of his new patient, not if he knew what Steinmann had been doing that night, and certainly not if he knew what he had been doing when he was injured.

"I brought him back to my place, the same way I transported him there," Reinicke continued. "One of the attending physicians said he thought there was more than a good chance for almost full recovery. That is all I needed to hear.

"I remembered what you said about locating my family and immediately leaving Berchetsgaden. I did so, but I could not take Steinmann. He never cared anyway; he was full of morphine. He slept soundly all through the bombing a few hours later."

"Where did you finally keep him?" I asked.

"In my spare bedroom. My sons made a place for themselves in the garage. My family had no objections to the inconvenience, when I told them there was *money* involved. Food was no problem either. I had access to more food than did anyone else. I was well off. In fact, I stashed a lot of it in the basement of my hotel right after the bombing. The SS did not care. After the bombing, they opened the compound to the townspeople, encouraging them to take what they wanted. But not from my hotel. My sons saw to that.

"The medical people told me what to do, which was to

do nothing at all. They told me to leave his cast on for four months, at least. They cautioned me about taking him to a local doctor for any reason."

He was SS. Both Walter and I knew Steinmann had the organization's tattoo on his arm. And Walter knew I was aware that Steinmann would've been handed over to the authorities and Walter with him if they had found out. There was no need to tell me any of this through the interpreter.

"How did you explain him to your neighbors?" I asked.

"It was no problem. I had another son who was missing, recall I told you about him. We waited a few weeks and then told our friends and neighbors he was home from the War. We told them he had been wounded, and that he had been brought home one night by some of his friends. They accepted this story; no one alerted the authorities. In those days there were no nosy neighbors. Everybody kept to themselves, and they kept their mouths shut and minded their own business. We were all involved in something illegal: the black-market, buying and selling of gasoline, procuring of illegal food stamps. What was one more wounded son more or less?"

It was illegal to harbor a Wermacht veteran, but nobody cared. Now, if they had known who Steinmann really was, I mean if they had known he was SS, then things would have been different. But they didn't know. And Walter's immediate neighbors, who knew Steimann was not his son, thought he was Wermacht and kept his presence quiet.

"How long did he stay in the cast? And how was he when you took it off?"

"We kept it on for the required time. And then one of my sons sawed it off with a carpenter's saw. It was a big event in all our lives. We wanted him out of our home. We wanted him to recover, which he did. But I must say he could not walk by himself at first. He was weak and stiff and in need of a lot of rehabilitation. This took another two months. But at least he could go to the bathroom by himself. We were very tired of nursing him."

"How did your sons take to all of this?"

"Very well, indeed. Surprisingly well. Of course, there was going to be a big payoff, when he was able to travel to the Berghof. We had all been waiting for this.

"You know there was something funny," Walter went on to tell me through the interpreter. "I mean about the money he said was buried. We only found part of what he had led us to believe was there. Somebody had been there before us. According to him, that someone had helped himself. Do you find that interesting? Why did they not take it all? We chalked it up to Steinmann exaggerating about how much he really had. We figured if he had not set the amount high, then my sons were not going to be too interested in taking care of him. We supposed he worried about them doing him in or turning him over to your army.

"But he was honest with us. There was plenty left–more than we ever expected. He gave us some of it, and we were satisfied. Strange thing, though, the money Steinmann gave us was the same as that you gave me the night you left in the two German trucks, remember? And another thing, the money you gave us that night was not nearly enough to rebuild the Turken. But we were indebted to Steinmann for the rest of what we needed."

I said: "I take it then your sons got along with Steinmann. Did they really like each other, or were they just tolerating him because of the promised money?"

"No," he said, "they genuinely liked each other. They used to sit with him by the hour and talk, sometimes in hushed whispers. And sometimes in English. I suspected they did not want me to hear. I almost believed I was not supposed to know what they were talking about."

"Why didn't you ask them?"

"Because I was afraid of Steinmann. And to tell you the

truth, I was afraid of my sons. They had changed. I guess a year on the Russian front would change anybody."

"Tell me something," I asked, "did anybody come to see you after we left? I mean, did any of the group that was at your place the night you took Steinmann to the hospital, did any of them come back?"

He thought a minute: "Yes, Rolph Wahlmuller came back twice."

"Did Eric come to see your sons? Was Steinmann still there then?"

"No. I never saw Eric again. As for my sons, they left a few months after the War, just as soon as Steinmann was well. They would come back from time to time and then leave again. They would stay away for long periods without telling me where they had been."

"Did either of them appear to you to be different. By that I mean, did either of them look different to you after one of their trips home? This might have been in the fall after the War ended? Think about it, Walter. It's important."

"No need to," he said. "My youngest boy had met with some kind of an accident about that time. Neither of them would tell me what happened. I always suspected they were involved in some way with Steinmann; they had been up to no good. When I saw my son's ears, I knew I was right."

I should have been flabbergasted at what hc just told me. At least I should have been surprised. Somehow I wasn't.

"Are you going to ask me what happened to him?"

"No. I already know. But I wish I didn't." With this last remark, I stood up and reached for my wallet. I overpaid the attorney in cash. The last thing I wanted was for him to know my name by writing a check.

It was time to leave Germany. It was time to have a serious talk with Ralph Wahl back in New York.

Oh, one other thing: I never told Walter his sons had left

for the last time and were never coming home. It was a secret between me and Lucy for now. Somehow, I didn't think he would have cared very much if he had known.

CHAPTER 24… NEW YORK, 1951

We met this time at Ralph's apartment. Apartments in New York are expensive. They don't have to be very pretentious to be expensive, as if this was news to anybody. Ralph's place is not pretentious, but it is expensive; it has to be costing him a lot more than his salary will permit.

"Red, I asked you over because I have some important things to say. I know what you want to hear, and it is going to take me some time to tell you.

"I know you have been to Siegsdorf, and I know you just came back from Reinicke's. And I know you have been asking questions. But before you come to any wrong conclusions, let me be the one to set you straight. I think I can satisfy you, but I am not sure you are going to like what I have to say…."

"Ralph, what are you talking about? Have you done something with my gold!" I interrupted him, blurting it out without thinking.

Ralph was married, and his wife was in the kitchen. He had invited me out on his terrace overlooking the Hudson River. He knew what was on my mind when I came in. He knew by the look on my face, and by what his friends in Europe had told him.

I stepped back from the rail surrounding the small beam-supported patio. The rail was made of wrought iron, solid and square, set at a ninety-degree angle to the beams. The architect had taken pains to provide not only a pleasing-to-the-eye structure, but one that would withstand a heavy weight propelled against it with some force. It was sturdy. The fall to the cement below was fifteen floors, a nasty bump if the railing had ever given way.

Being afraid of heights, I moved away from it just in case, to an uncomfortable chair; one of a matched set to an art-deco, faux ice cream parlor table, the kind fashionable these days. They're small, not taking up much space, just right for a small apartment terrace.

I remembered Walter Reinicke telling me that part of the Berghof gold was missing. And I remembered Ralph saying that Steinmann had given him part of it for his son and part for himself, when Steinmann was headed for Argentina. It might account for Ralph's elevated standard of living. But I never stopped to think about this when I practically accused him of dipping into the load we had buried. Ralph anticipated me and lost no time in telling me he had taken some of the Berghof loot for Murielle but didn't take any for himself.

His wife came out with some homemade chocolate cake, but no accompanying coffee. Not even hot chocolate. She asked me if I would like a glass of milk, something I seldom drank. I accepted. I was hungry. I hadn't had a chance to eat.

We conversed a few minutes about where they met. She was from Salzburg, so I wasn't surprised to hear they had known each other during the War.

I was about to lay into him again, after she excused herself and went back to the kitchen. I really thought he had gone back to Germany and dug up our gold, mine and Lucy's. He had to account for the way he was living. He had to have gotten some additional money from somewhere.

He knew I was angry, but he paid little or no attention to me. He changed the subject. "Red, I want you to tell me what you know about the Reinicke brothers and where you think Steinmann is today."

"The Reinickes are dead," I said, raising my voice again. His wife couldn't hear me. We could only faintly hear her rustling her dishes. "My girlfriend shot them both. I'm a hundred percent certain of that." Then I told him the details of their unfortunate encounter with Lucy and her Winchester, followed by the incident at the burns. Ralph just nodded his head while I talked, and then nodded some more when I told him I had no idea where Steinmann was.

I continued: "Reinicke told me Steinmann had recovered to some extent. At least he was well enough to walk. So now I understand he took the share of the Berghof gold he promised you, the share you wouldn't take for yourself. He gave some to Reinicke and used the rest to head out for Argentina–so much the better for everybody but the Argentines."

Then I said in an exasperated voice: "Now it's your turn. Now you tell me about Ravensbruck. I know you've been back there checking to see if I've been messing about the area. That is, I think you have. And I know Carl had, and maybe some of the others have, too."

I threw this out to see what he would say. I had no idea if he had been, but I would've been willing to bet he had.

"You are right about that," he answered, not surprising me. "Carl came to see me when he could not contact you. I realize now why you kept to yourself, and why you moved around. But you see, none of us knew what you just told me. They thought you had taken the gold for yourself; that is Carl did, and so did Muller. I never saw Eric. What else were they to think after you tried to fool us all by calling the burial location Ravensbruck?"

"What did you say?...Muller?"

"Yes, Muller. I am pretty sure Muller was his name. He was with us when we buried it along with Steinmann's box."

"Does this guy, Muller...is he connected in some way to your organization?"

"No. But we know about him."

"What? Tell me what you know."

"He lives out in the west."

He didn't have to say more. It was like a light bulb going on in my head; I knew immediately who he was. This is the guy Fogerty told me about who had visited with his relatives in San Angelo. Now I remembered where I had heard the name. He had been one of my squad members. He was one of the dozens of replacements whose names I heard and then had promptly forgotten.

"Ralph, this Muller must be working with the Reinickes and Steinmann. Walter never told me Muller came to Berchtesgaden to see Reinicke's sons, but I'll bet you a dollar to a doughnut he did. Walter never said anything about Muller when I asked him if any of you ever came back. Of course, Walter never associated this guy with our gold; he wasn't there the night we came back from the lake. He joined us later at Siegsdorf. That accounts for it."

I paused for a minute, thinking: "It makes sense now. This Muller is with the Reinickes and Steinmann. They sent him to San Angelo to talk to his relatives who were there to check on Lucy." Then I took the next half-hour or so telling him about Muller and Fogerty, Worthington, and Joyce Wagner, and about how the Muller family had come to San Angelo with money enough to buy a house and a business. And of course about my suspicions.

When I finished my story, he said: "Do not be too sure somebody is still looking for you, including this Muller fellow. That is to say, they were, but not anymore.

"You came here tonight thinking you had lost a friend–me. You are thinking I dug up your gold to keep for myself. But then, you do not really believe what I said, do you? You know for a certainty that nobody has."

I was really surprised at what he just said. It made me think:

I knew no one knew where we buried it except me. But I swear before I leave tonight, I'm going to find out if it's true. And I'm going to find out what he knows about who killed my two sergeant friends. And I'm also going to find out about Steinmann's box.

I'm tired of playing games. I'm tired of the stress of everyday living, knowing I'm fair game for somebody out there who wants to dole me out some of the same treatment. There are a lot of people interested in doing so. And I'm tired of guessing who they are.

"What do you mean, you're going to tell me something not to my liking?" I asked him.

Ralph saw the perplexed look on my face and hurried on: "Yes, well, I am. First off, I want you to know I have saved your life. I have told you before about this International Tripartite Commission I work for, and how they were appointed by the United Nations to find out where all the missing Nazi gold is still hidden. That is part of their job; the other part is to distribute it to its so-called rightful owners. They are also empowered to locate and arrest anybody having anything to do with it.

"They concluded at the end of the War that more than three percent of all the gold in Germany, outside the Merkers mine, and all the diamonds inside were missing. They also knew we buried half the gold someplace between Berchetsgaden and Lintz. They knew because they knew from the Reichsbank records how much was transported to the Obersalzberg via Bavaria and the Oberbayern. And they knew how much we turned in.

"And recall, you and your men are number one suspects. Remember me telling you. Well, you still are. And, furthermore, they now know where you live.

"You were easy to find. You slipped up. I mean, they have known for some time you lived in New Orleans. It was easy for professionals, those who make a good living finding people who do not want to be found.

"The question was: What were they going to do with you?

"When they located you, they had you followed, hoping you would lead them to where it was buried. When Carl was murdered, they suspected the Reinicke brothers and Muller. But they had you down as the number one suspect for doing Eric in.

"What you just told me is the first any of us heard about Lucy killing the Reinickes and then faking her death. They thought it was you who killed Lucy. And now, from what you just told me, I realize Joyce Wagner knew the truth all the time, but she did not say anything for fear Lucy would tell Worthington's wife about Joyce and her husband. Worthington went along with it all for the same reason.

"It was at this point the Commission decided to take action against you. They had given you what they considered to be plenty of time to recant and return it. They had given up on you. When they decided you were about to dig it up and run off, they let a *contract* on you."

Ralph paused for a minute. He wiggled around in his uncomfortable chair before continuing: "This contract called for you to be kidnapped and tortured until you told them where Ravensbruck is. Then they planned to do away with you…"

"And then that's when you rescued me," I interrupted. "How did you go about saving me, because I'm obviously saved? Nobody has come near me since my set-to with the Reinicke brothers."

Ralph replied: "I saved you after the contract was out by telling them you had always intended to give it back. I told them you had a change of heart a month or so after we buried it. But the reason you did not tell them immediately was because you had forgotten where it was. That is right. I told them you had always wanted to give it back, but you could not remember where we buried it. And of course, like the others, I was not supposed to have known.

"I told the Commission the whole story; the truth as I knew it. I told them how right after we buried it, you told us all we had just passed through a village called Ravensbruck. As it turned out, it was a name that just popped into your head. The others had no idea where we were, and since Ravensbruck sounded German, they just accepted it without question. Not until they tried to find it again did they suspect you of cheating them. But I knew this was not the case; furthermore, I knew the real name of the town we had just passed through, and it was *not* Ravensbruck.

"The Commission knew Eric had been killed. They knew because Joyce told them. They concluded you did it, because you thought Eric was going to kill you. They reasoned that, since you had cheated Eric, you killed him in self-defense. To prevent your being picked up by one of the Commission's mercenary bounty hunters, tortured and maybe murdered, I told them you could not remember where you hid it. That is the truth; you had forgotten. And you can not remember now, can you?

"And if the Reinickes had found you, they would have killed you, because you would not have been able to tell them where it was. You would have been treated just like your friends. You would have been tortured to death, swearing you had forgotten; but they would not have believed you.

"I had no choice but to tell the Commission where it

was buried. And once I told them you had forgotten the name of the town and how we got there, I had to tell them I knew the route we had taken from Siegsdorf. But I told them I had no idea of the name of the town. I had no reason to believe the town was not really called Ravensbruck. I convinced them, however, that the two of us could locate it if we worked together. I waited about a month, supposedly to give us the necessary time to find it, and then I told them we had figured it out. It was either your life or the gold, and I chose your life. I hope you agree with my choice."

I was in shock, to say the least. But I was relieved at the same time. The gold had been a millstone around my neck. There was no doubt about it.

He went on to tell me more. But this time, I really became upset. This time he really shook me up.

"I made a deal with them," Ralph continued. "If I showed them where the gold was buried, they would agree to leave you alone.

"They were also to pick up Muller and to see he was either compensated for or scared away–that was part of our agreement. Of course, when Muller found out they had recovered the gold, he was no longer interested in you. But, whatever, you are not going to have any more trouble with him. And then there is Joyce: there is no longer any need to keep her in San Angelo. She will be reassigned someplace else."

I said: "This doesn't sound all that bad to me. I can live and be happy without their gold, just as long as I don't have to be looking over my shoulder constantly."

"Right," he answered, "I figured you would feel that way–but I have not told you the worst part. There is more to come. And I am afraid you are going to like it even less before I am through."

Before I could ask him what he was talking about or say anything else, he continued on: "They know you took the diamonds, as well. And the deal requires you to give them back."

Now I *was* in real shock. "Do you mind telling me how they found out? I stammered.

"Not at all. You sold two stones to the same dealer in New Orleans. The deBeers company of Amsterdam, who sets the price of diamonds through a worldwide diamond commission, monitors all large stone sales. Yours were two of the largest they had heard of in a long time. It was a simple matter to connect you with the mine incident at Merkers.

"Thoms and Veick knew there was an open sack. When they inventoried the unsealed sacks of platinum, rubies, and coins, they could not account for the diamonds. Through a simple process of elimination, they concluded you and your men took them.

"The reason you were not arrested right then by General Earnest was because Patton did not believe Thoms. He told Earnest to look elsewhere for the diamonds. He thought Thoms had them and Earnest could not prove otherwise, so he kept his mouth shut. It was later, after General Patton's automobile accident and death, that they started investigating you. If you had taken just some of the diamonds instead of all of them, you just might have gotten away with it."

"What I don't understand is how deBeers knew I sold them in New Orleans?" I stammered. I could hardly catch my breath.

"Because your dealer told them. He probably thought you had only the two stones. And I suppose he thought he was not going to get his hands on any more, so he told them. And the cartel in Amsterdam paid your dealer a healthy finders fee, to be applied against his next order-something like that. But you can rest assured it revolved around money.

"The Commission assumed you stashed them in a safe

deposit box in New Orleans," he went on. "They figured you rented it using an assumed name. It was no problem to find your deposit box after they found you. Actually they did not find you; the deBeers people told them where you were.

"You see, deBeers wants that cache of diamonds out of circulation. They want to buy them back. They want to control the market exclusively. A cache of big stones in that quantity tends to upset the market if they are ever circulated. That is why they did not want you to have them. That is the way it was explained to me, more or less.

"Getting back to the point," Ralph went on, "the Commission has put a legal *stop entry* order on your deposit box, as of yesterday, thinking you might pick them up and take off. Now here is the deal: They will leave you alone if you turn the contents of your box over to me. You have no choice. Anything else is suicide."

He was right. I had no choice. I would like to say I didn't care, but I would be lying. I care. Now Lucy and I are going to have to make other plans. I'm going to have to go back to school, and I don't want any part of it. But as Francis Bacon or somebody else once said, "There are sermons in stones, books in running brooks, and good in everything." Maybe now Lucy will marry me. Maybe things are not a total loss. Maybe she is the *good in everything* that is supposed to come out of all this.

"Ralph, tell me something: How did you know I made up the name Ravensbruck. None of the others thought twice about it. How come you knew? Since you had no idea we were going to stop where we did, how come you knew the town we had just passed through was not Ravensbruck?"

"I have a simple, a real simple answer for that," he answered. "One of my duties was to procure fresh fruits and vegetables for the SS mess halls. Before the War, farmers used to bring their produce to the compound. When food started getting scarce, I went to them to make sure they were not selling to somebody else for more money.

"I guess I had been through every town and hamlet within a radius of seventy-five miles many times. When you said *Ravensbruck*, my ears picked up on the name immediately. Ravensbruck is a city all right, but a long way away from where we were.

"I never said anything. I knew you had not inadvertently made a mistake when you told Muller the place was Ravensbruck. I knew you had some kind of plan to keep the gold. I had no intentions of questioning you or interfering in any way. I never would have if I had not been forced to. I wanted to tell you I knew you had a plan to keep the gold, and that I had no intentions of interfering, when we were in the process of burying it. But I changed my mind.

"You see, I must confess, I never objected to what I knew you had in mind. I stayed out of it, because I did not want it returned to German hands. And I knew it might be. In the meantime, if you buried it, it was not going anywhere. And later, I knew you could not find it. And neither could anybody else."

We changed the subject, which was all right with me. Now, I'm even more depressed. And I know it's going to get worse as soon as the shock wears off. But maybe it'll get better. Maybe it'll be worth it in the long run if it's been holding Lucy back. And I know it has.

Anyway, Ralph told me he was coming to New Orleans with an armed escort in a few weeks to bring back the diamonds.

I'm broke. All I have left is a few thousand dollars in currency. Lucy is going to have to give up her apartment. But again, who knows, all this might turn out for the best. But right now, I don't see her being too happy about living in a small Texas oil town when I finish school. And it has me worried.

"Ralph, does this box of Steinmann's have anything to do with the deaths of Carl and Eric?" He looked surprised I had picked up on a connection. He thought a minute. I knew what he was going to tell me would be the truth by the way he hesitated, not in a hurry, taking his time so he'd give it to me straight, not wanting to mislead me or tell me a lie. He somehow thought it did, because of his off-hand remark back at the Konigssee, when he told me it had evil powers and had been responsible for a lot of innocent deaths. I had forgotten about it soon after he said it; I had a lot on my mind at the time.

I was starting to get angry all over again, not so much at Ralph and the loss of the treasure, as I was with this whole SS nonsense. And I told him so.

He replied, curtly: "Nonsense? I guess it is nonsense if you disregard the half billion they stole, and if you can overlook the millions of deaths they caused, and the millions of atrocities they committed. If you can, I guess you can call it nonsense."

Then he paused a minute to settle down before answering my question: "You knew, when we buried the gold we buried Steinmann's box. I keep calling it his box when I really mean your box. Remember you were designated keeper by him after he was incapacitated. It did not matter that you might not have wanted the job; it was only important that it was his responsibility, and you were the only military officer available–so like it or not you became responsible to take care of it.

"Within days after the cessation of hostilities, I dug up the box and returned it to its rightful owners at the museum in Vienna. That relieved you of your keeper responsibilities, but it set you up for some bad fortune; it caused the death of your friends. And it caused a change in your life as well; it has caused you to lose your gold and your diamonds. And it is why the incident you told me about on your fishing trip occurred also. I am sure of it.

"Do not look at me so smugly," he said. "You would not, not if you knew Adolph Hitler had been the keeper before Steinmann, and you know what happened to him. Well, it happened to them both; it happened to Adolph just days after it was released from his care and keeping…."

I interrupted him: "Ralph, what are you going on about now? You haven't said one single word to me–not one word have you ever uttered about this mysterious box of yours that has made one lick of sense. Not one word. And something else. You *are* a member of the SS, and you've been beating around the bush about that, too."

I was upset with him. Still, I knew he was right in what he had done about the gold and the diamonds. But this crazy talk about that Halloween box of his was getting to me.

I continued uninterrupted with my harangue: "Now, the next thing you're going to tell me is a crazy comic-book story about UFO aliens giving this phantom box to Steinmann with a promise to help him re-conquer the world. And what about that other foolishness you were giving me about losing my soul if I insisted on getting mixed up in this mysterious box business any further than I was?"

Ralph answered again, testily, his feelings obviously hurt. He saw me as being unappreciative of what he had done for me and cavalier about a very important and serious matter to him. "Yes, well, maybe I am going to tell you about some more crazy things. Maybe even crazier then saucers or anything else you ever heard about. Maybe, even so crazy it is beyond your comprehension."

"Why don't you tell me then? Tell me what's going on and let's see. That's the third or fourth time you've told me I wouldn't understand. Understand what?"

He looked around to check on his wife. It was getting late, and she had left the kitchen and gone to bed. Even so, he closed the patio doors. There was no one to hear us now but the pigeons. If he could have spoken French he would have, he was being that secretive.

"Before I say one word, I want your promise never to tell a single soul."

"No, I won't. I mean I won't promise you. I might have twenty minutes ago, but not now. I might want to write a book someday about all this. I'm going to have to go back to square one. Maybe publishing a book about the Waffen SS treasure might be the answer to my coming money problems. You've left me with nothing. You shouldn't object. But at any rate, you needn't worry. I promise not to write anything that'll get you in trouble with the authorities."

Ralph thought for maybe a full five seconds, which is a long time to sit and stare at one another. I never wavered or blinked, and neither did he. Then he started to bite his lip; he was agitated and ill at ease. He shifted on his uncomfortable ice cream chair and began to purse his lips, touching them with his forefinger as though to consciously stifle what he was about to say. He hesitated another few seconds, as though he was about to open a can of worms and make me privy to the inside. Finally, he said: "All right."

Then I asked him if he minded if I took notes. He rolled his eyes and shrugged his shoulders before replying: "I guess you leave me no choice. If you are going to repeat it in writing, I suppose you ought to repeat it correctly.

"I want to start by agreeing with you," Ralph said. "I want you to know I *am* SS, as you have surmised. Not Waffen SS but Gestapo. And if you neglect to write it the way it all really happened, I am going to be arrested."

He saw the confused look on my face, and he hurriedly began explaining without my pushing.

"The Waffen were, and still are, the fighting divisions of the SS. The Gestapo was the state police and the Schutstaffein SS were the butchers who ran the death camps. Heinrich Himmler commanded all of them, and all of them were up to their eyeballs in atrocities–without parallel. And all of them were convicted of war crimes in absentia at Nuremberg. But I want to make this perfectly clear: It was Oddlie's idea that I make an attempt to ingratiate myself with these people. And in doing so, it naturally led to my being inducted into one of their branches.

"I could not serve in what later became known as the Waffen, because I could not complete their basic training. Most people could not, whether or not they had a bad leg; it was just too demanding. Not many of our conditioned soldiers could. Maybe our Special Forces–maybe, but few others, including our Marines. It was just too tough. But the Gestapo was something else again. And if I was to live with these people, I had to belong to something."

This much of his story I already knew, and I think I've told you about it. At any rate, I said nothing to him and he pressed on: "Now, once I became a member, I hastened to make myself indispensable. I could not risk a change in commanders, and then find myself working as a clerk at someplace other than the Obersalzberg. The thing I hit on was becoming a teacher.

"Members of the SS were continually being schooled. Advancement in *degrees* within military rank was expected of everybody. It was much like the Scottish Rite of Freemasonry, from which the system, incidentally, was derived. Not the rites, I hasten to point out, but the way it was organized. But I am getting ahead of myself. Before passing on, I want you to understand I became what might be thought of as a *master mason*. I became an authority if you will. It was a small step from there to becoming a teacher of teachers."

"Where did you learn all this?" I asked him.

"From their library," he answered. "Their underground facilities contained one of the truly large specialized libraries in the world. Before their departing units burned it, it contained volumes of history regarding the practices of ancient religions and the occult. I emphasize the *occult*, although there were some stacks containing legitimate science texts. There were others not so legitimate. They dealt mostly with biology and genetics. All the recognized authorities were there, plus those I choose to call *off-the-wall* geneticists.

"Then there was the complete works of authors who had an influence on Hitler and the other founding members of the Nazi Party. But for now, I want you to understand why I swore the required oaths and went through the required initiation rites. And I want you to understand why I made myself indispensable. They say *the only indispensable man was Adam.* But at that time, on the Obersalzburg, I might have been running a close second.

"I speak of acquiring my knowledge from the library," he went on to say, "I am afraid this is an over simplification; there was a lot more to it than that. In fact, I was sent to a special college in Berlin for training. One of the things the SS strived for was standardization. Everybody was taught the exact same thing as everybody else, regardless of where they were serving. Even in combat, the training continued unabated and unaltered. Of course, Hitler and Himmler approved this standardized program. They even collaborated in the writing of the training prospectus."

When I left Ralph, I was thoroughly exhausted. I had been talking some, but mostly listening to him for three hours without interruption, and with a focus of mind new to me. I was quite surprised to find how tiring this sort of concentration can be. And then there was my backside, temporarily waffled from the narrow metal strips cross-hatching the bottom of his dinky chairs. And my elbows were sore from leaning on the hard, set tiles of the table.

As if this was not enough, there was the disappointment at having lost everything, although I had told Lucy many times that I wished I could find a way to give it back. But deep down, I knew I wouldn't. I knew it was just talk. But never in my wildest dreams did I ever see the time I would lose it all–gold, diamonds, and self-respect.

I needed a cup of coffee. Like many people, I'm caffeine dependent, an addict. Partway up the next block was a diner. I walked in. The counterman was reading the daily tip-sheet. He barely took notice of me before discouraging me from taking a seat and interrupting his concentration.

"We're closed, buddy. The night cook's left and our day man hasn't showed yet. Best I can do is coffee. I got some day old cake." He said it with a take-it or leave-it tone in his voice I had heard many times before, acceptable in his society, but grating to a southerner like myself–especially one in my present mood.

"Don't worry about it," I retorted, with a sandpaper touch of my own. "Just coffee."

I was grateful I had the place to myself. If there was ever a time I needed to be alone with my thoughts, it was right now. And for once, I didn't want any behind-the-counter cheerful thinking he had to talk to entertain me. Friendly for a tip was not this guy, and that was all right with me. In fact, tonight I preferred him just as he was, disagreeable, sullen, morose, and un-communicating.

I sat in a well-worn booth rather than at the counter. Workmen, I presume, with screwdrivers in their belts had poked holes in the red fabric covers as they sat down. There was no way to mend them short of an expensive re-covering job. And to keep the batting from spilling out more than it had, they had patched it with some kind of tape.

The booth cushions reminded me of a yacht on the gulf, years ago. Guest fisherman had sat down in this expensive salon with needle nose hook removers in their pockets. The upholstery was a disaster.

I could see somebody nervous had fiddled with the tape on the seats like it was an itching blemish, worrying it into frayed edges. The oilcloth table covers were red and white checkered–garish, unpleasing to the eye even when new. Now they were pockmarked with brown cigarette burns, making them appear for all the world like a *Ralston Purina* something or other spawned under a rock.

Counters looked at me again with a disapproving look on his face, as though he might have an ulcer or some other form of dyspepsia. I thought he might be in the wrong line of work. I thought, perhaps, that the sight of a plate of loose scrambled eggs this time of the morning might result in his turning green. I know more than a little about his problem. He's suffering from the usual–a hangover. I've been there a few times myself. What he needs is a couple of shooters–a couple of boosters–something to settle his stomach, something to change his personality, if only temporarily, something to make him a little more customer friendly.

None of this bothers me, though, or even interests me very much, not this morning. The insular attitude of many of this city's inhabitants, some of which always rubs off on me, is of no consequence this morning. I'm too wrapped up in my own thoughts to contemplate why they always appear to be depressed. Anyway, this might be better left for religionists, sociologists, and other professional do-gooders to ponder. I'm too engrossed in my own world, thinking about things far and away more important than the mundane survival affairs of those abrasive personalities insisting on living in the squalor of New York.

What Ralph told me, in addition to his telling me he had given back my treasure, had affected me mentally. I was off balance. I entered a surreal world when he went into detail about the origins of the SS and the significance of Steinmann's box. I'm still not completely recovered, nor do

I expect to be any time soon. It's as though I entered a time warp; I'm still engrossed in things alien to respectable people: mysticism, black magic, and other forms of the occult.

After *saucering* and blowing, Cajun style, and inhaling the first cup, I began sipping the second. I'm starting to wake up. My mind, which has been numbed by the late hour and the loss of my fortune, and then Ralph's preposterous story, was recovering a certain lost clarity. Preposterous? It would have been if I had heard it from anybody but him.

I sat perusing my notes and making corrections, ignoring the occasional glare from the counterman. In addition to what I had written, Ralph had given me a copy of the training outline used by instructors in the Waffen SS. It's not an original. It's a Xerox copy. The original would be worth a fortune to a collector.

I have three hours to kill before my flight home. I can spend it here, relatively unbothered, drinking coffee, ostensibly waiting for the day cook to appear, or I can do it at the terminal, packed together sardine style with the traveling public. I choose to do it here, not because of my fear of airports, which Ralph, who is knowledgeable in such things, has convinced me is irrational. He says it's rooted in some form of psychosis, brought on by stress. But I need peace and quiet to figure out my next move, so I've elected to stay put here for an hour or so.

Speaking of my fear of airports: I had seen this Corporal Muller once in an airport. I was sure I had. I was sure it was him. He had been in one of my squads, but I couldn't remember his name; however, I did remember his face. Ralph says the fact I was running around in serious incognito, and already in some advanced state of anxiety, had led me to jump to conclusions. Muller was a figment of my imagination it seems. Oh, I saw somebody all right, somebody who looked like him. But there were just too many logistical problems, which couldn't be explained away for it to have been him. According to Ralph, while I was dodging phantoms, the real Muller was somewhere safely tucked in bed.

Adrenalin is a funny thing. According to Ralph, when you have been infused with heavy doses over time as I have, something happens to your mind. This drug builds up in your spinal cortex, and it changes the way your mind processes information. They call it psychosis. Ralph believes I was borderline psychotic. If it had continued, I might have come down with a debilitating seizure; as it was, I was just putting the wrong interpretation on what I was seeing. But thanks to him, I think I'm on the mend. At least I'm not dreading my trip back to the airport as I had been.

After Ralph told the commission people about me forgetting the whereabouts of the gold, they changed their minds. Their new theory was that Muller had been working with the Reinickes, and Steinmann was directing and financing the show from somewhere. Surprisingly, Joyce Wagner had been placed in San Angelo by the Commission to watch Muller's family and Lucy. Ralph and his organization knew this, but for their own reasons never told me. Joyce was mixed up with Worthington, but in a way that was of no interest to anybody but his wife. And I suppose no one but Ralph cared that I was chasing around the countryside scared to death of my own shadow.

He also explained to me how Reinicke's sons, under the direction of Steinmann, had tortured and killed Eric and later Carl while seeking the location of Ravensbruck. I was most gratified to hear Ralph's people had now come to the conclusion it was them and that I had never been involved with what happened to Eric and that he would see to it they understood about Lucy and would keep it confidential.

Steinmann knew Eric was in love with Françoise;

Murielle had told him so. Eric had been stationed in Nancy, France, after he left me, and Steinmann knew he was going to Paris to see her whenever he could. They kidnapped Eric and then tortured him. As I said, he never told them anything about the gold, because he never knew anything. But he did know the whereabouts of Carl.

Carl was living the life of your average American up in his home town in Minnesota, working, minding his own business, waiting for something to happen. He had traveled to Germany several times with his wife looking for the gold, but of course he couldn't find it. So he was about to give up and wait for me to contact him. Then the two of us, along with Eric, were going back with our shovels to Ravensbruck.

The Reinickes, accompanied by either Muller or possibly Steinmann, himself, beat Carl until he died. This was another thing the Commission detectives had suspected for some time, and Ralph failed to tell me. It was as though they were using me for some kind of bait to catch them; maybe they were. But Lucy's Winchester rendered moot the necessity for any further investigation of the Reinicke brothers.

It was very upsetting to have confirmed officially what I long suspected–the reason my two friends never told their tormentors anything in exchange for their lives was because they never knew anything. They never had the slightest idea where the gold was buried. I planned it that way. And Ralph knew I had. And now that I know for sure I'm directly responsible for what happened to them, I can expect some more sleepless nights.

CHAPTER 25...NEW ORLEANS, 1950

I flew over to San Antonio to see Lucy the day after I came back from New York. There was just enough time for Fogerty to contact her and let her know I was coming. I took this opportunity to thank him, and to let him know we no longer needed his assistance. He did tell me Muller had been in town for a while and then had left, and no one knew what happened to him.

When I saw Lucy, I told her what I knew about her friend Joyce, and that we were poor again and how we got that way. I also told her how Eric died and all the rest of it.

I still had the ring I had been planning to give her, and now I made the formal offer. She accepted, so I suppose Bacon had been right all along.

I was correct that it was the treasure. She never felt right about the two of us living the rest of our lives off what I had stolen.

We set the wedding date and made plans to move to Baton Rouge. Classes at LSU were starting in six weeks. I didn't want to wait until the last minute to get things organized.

We are both going to work. It's going to be a struggle, but no more so for us than it was for tens of thousands of married veterans returning from the War. I told her I thought the school still maintained married students' housing, although the big demand had come and gone. I have a small income from the G.I. Bill, but things are going to be tight with us money-wise. She knows it, but doesn't seem to be overly worried. But time will tell how she's going to take to being poor again. She has never had any money, except for the time she's known me. However, I can't help but think she's coming around to embracing my philosophy that rich is better than poor. I know I'm not going to like being poor again, but what choice do I have? If there was an alternative, I would take it in a minute.

Deep down, I'm dreading going back to school. Worse yet, I'm repulsed at the idea of going to work in the oil business. I've spent some time around wells and refineries, and among other things, I dislike the smell. I can't put it into words, but somehow the smell reminds me of the silver fox smell I told you about. I react just the way I did when I was a boy, not as bad as I did when I was around the fox, but almost. The thought of working in this environment for the rest of my life sends shivers up my spine.

I've changed. I'm not the same person I was when I joined the army; I'm more restless now. However, I have kept it to myself; Lucy is better off not knowing how I feel.

There was a popular song going around during the First World War. It was called "What Are You Going to Do with Them Down on the Farm, After They've Seen Paris?" Well, that's me. What *am* I going to do? Oil drilling for wages is a far cry from combat with Patton. And now that I've burned my bridges, the army won't take me back.

And then there's the treasure. It was a windfall that changed my life. While I had it, I always thought it was too good to be true. I always thought that, someday, it was going to be taken from me. I felt like the Chinese farmer I read about who walks through his rice field talking to his gods. He has a bumper crop and stands to make some money. The usual poverty he looks forward to each year will not be his lot this season, and it worries him. He's not used to the good life. His natural condition is poverty. He's worried the gods will take notice of his abundance and cause some major catastrophe to befall him, because after all they don't want to see him happy. So what does he do? He yells: "Bad rice, bad rice." The gods, of course, will hear him, believe him, and leave him alone. A kind of simplistic tale, but it strikes near the truth of how I always felt about things.

I'm starting to think as Ralph thinks. I'm starting to believe something or somebody doesn't want to see me happy, and they are throwing a monkey wrench into the machinery of my life.

It was at this point, I told Lucy I was writing a book. She's not exactly overjoyed. She's a realist. She knows about the problems involved in getting published if you don't have a name. And she is not expecting much income from this direction for some time to come, if ever. She was more receptive to the idea, however, when I told here I was going to finish school and get a job with an oil company somewhere. And then I would finish the book. This way it won't be my *day job*, but a hobby. And of course, all new husbands should have a hobby.

As for the oil business, she prefers it to living in a mining town out west. As I said, I'm not enthusiastic about either prospect. I just wished I had squirreled away some of the treasure money, at least enough to see me through a few lean years until I could give writing for a living a chance. But I didn't. And that's the way it goes. I expect Ralph to show any day now to pick up the diamonds, and then Lucy and I are going to leave New Orleans and be married in Baton Rouge.

I've been writing for the past couple of days, relying on my notes and what I remember Ralph telling me that night in New York. I also have the writings of Hitler and Himmler, contained in a copy of the pamphlet and the prospectus he gave me. I'm in a hurry to get the manuscript drafted. I want Ralph to read what I've written when he comes to pick up the diamonds. I don't want to hear from him later about how I should have said this or that or that I should have said it in a different way.

I want you, the reader, to understand that it's my interpretation of what he told me, plus what he gave me to read. I have paraphrased much of it and copied some of the translated writings of Hitler and Himmler. However, I should also point out that I'm not sure I believe all I've written. But Ralph will. And more importantly, so would have Hitler and Himmler. And so would the SS. But maybe I wouldn't be such a skeptic if I'd been German and had I fought in World War One on the Western Front in 1914-1918.

....

The trenches of the Western Front were arguably more hell-like than was any other place in the history of mankind. Soldiers on both sides lived in mud in the shadow of death around the clock; and it went on and on for years. There was no escape. In Flanders, and at Verdun, they literally lived with corpses that could not always be permanently buried. At Verdun, the huge trench mortars and cannon shells dug them up, shredding and re-shredding them almost as fast as they could be interred. Minute pieces of putrefying flesh of man and beast were everywhere: it was in the rain water of the shell holes from which they were forced to drink; it often found its way into their food; it was everywhere. It was much the same in the lowlands of

Flanders, to the north. There was no way to permanently bury the fallen. Many times, after being interred in *Flanders Fields*, they shifted around for a week or two in the deep muck, often to be buried again piece-meal immediately after a shelling.

This environment wrecked havoc on the minds of those who were there. Some were driven permanently insane. But all were affected in some degree for the rest of their lives.

Rumors of macabre and supernatural happenings began circulating on the front stretching from Ypres to Chateau Thierry and east to Verdun, almost with the opening salvos of the first battles of the Somme and the Marne. Many veterans of the fighting, their minds stressed to the breaking point, began reporting sightings of ghost-like creatures in the trenches and marching across no man's land.

A story was told and retold of a soldier who was standing duty on a parapet at night. He quit his post, raving madly about how he had seen his dead buddy who had been killed the day before. One such story had his dead friend appear beside him asking for a cigarette.

Columns of marching men were seen in the sky, and mud-caked specters were seen making their way outside communication trenches back to the rest areas. These ghosts were dressed in full battle gear, their rifles slung at route-step in ragged formations, spikes on the German cloth covered-helmets plainly visible in the fog and drizzle.

So many tales of the supernatural were reported by so-called reliable sources that within a few months no one paid much attention. The unreal became real, as young minds were stretched to the breaking point.

One of the tales of the supernatural, disseminated widely at home, was a phenomenon that came to be known as The Angel of Mons Incident. It was supposed to have been observed by soldiers on both sides and was written about in diaries and newspapers and after the War in books. Just who the angel was who appeared over the battlefield during the British retreat from Mons was later debated, but not the incident itself. To suggest the happening was due to mass hysteria or to question it in any way, especially if you were a civilian sitting at home reading the account from a newspaper, was to brand you a non-supporter of the troops or at worst a traitor.

It seems that during the retreat from a superior German force, a gigantic apparition appeared in the sky. Silhouetted against a bright moon, it was clad all in white on a white charger over no man's land. With raised sword, it rallied the British forces, saving them from annihilation.

Word of the incident spread like wildfire throughout both contending armies. Non-believers after the War explained it away as being the first of many Urban Legends. This, after serious investigators could not find a single soldier who had been at Mons willing to go on record as having seen the apparition. Yet, many wrote home about seeing it. However, as it turned out, most of those who did write home in the early days never survived the War.

The believers, some to this day, point to the historical fact that a lightly armed and outnumbered British regular force survived the overwhelming onslaught of a determined German advance. How they were able to do so without divine intervention was equally difficult to explain.

Soldiers entering the trenches for the first time in 1914 were mostly believers of the angel story. But those who had doubts, and who lived for more than a few months, usually became believers in varying degrees of this and other phenomena they had heard about.

As might be expected, the British and Europeans were not the same people they had been four years earlier. Death, stories of death, and supernatural occurrences at the front had been their constant companions. There was never a respite; violent death in its many forms never took a holiday.

Europe and Britain, and to a lesser degree America, saw the proliferation of spiritualists who took advantage of the situation. And for a long time thereafter, they did a land office business with their readings and séances, preying on the minds of the susceptible public who were attempting to contact their dead relatives.

But professional occultists were not the only ones afoot; there were amateurs abounding. Ouija board parties became the rage, as did parlor games involving table tapping, supposedly a method for contacting the dead. Tealeaf prognosticators, Tarot card readers, and soothsayers of every description had their followings. There were, of course, doubters. And then there were those who used church platforms to speak out against the tide of this new spiritualism. But it was said that few of them had served on the Western Front.

Adolph Hitler was one of the believers and, likewise, his lieutenants who were charter members of the Nazi party. All of them had seen action in the War that was supposed to have ended all wars. And all of them had left any traditional beliefs in Christianity in the hell of the trenches, their minds now open and fertile for the implanting of counter beliefs in the darkness of the occult.

Heinrich Himmler and Rudolph Hess saw less action than did Hermann Goering and Hitler. But they saw enough. Himmler in particular became a rabid believer in the supernatural. And under his direction, members of the Waffen SS would be later indoctrinated in the extreme to likewise believe in things not of this world–not in Judeo-Christian beliefs of a life in a hereafter, but in occult mythology, which would become a driving force in their lives.

Hitler had served as a communication runner during the War. These select groups of soldiers were considered to be the bravest of the brave. Land-line communications between trenches, and between attacking troops and supporting reserves and artillery, were crucial to the successful outcome of a battle. But it wasn't reliable. Many times telephone wires would be destroyed by rolling artillery barrages in front of advancing infantry and by enemy mortars behind. When this happened, they were forced to use runners as back-up. These men suffered the highest number of casualties; their life expectancies were shorter than were any others who occupied the trenches.

Hitler served in this capacity as long as anyone and he did so with distinction. He was decorated many times, and, being gassed, he suffered as much as did any soldier who survived the War. His valor and devotion to duty would hold him in good stead following the Armistice. When he spoke in the beer halls, and later in the stadium at Nuremberg, of hardships and a new need for discipline and sacrifice, the German population in the thirties and forties listened to this voice of experience. But above all, his new army of supermen, the Waffen SS, would be inspired by his heroics. And, like children sitting at their father's knee, they would listen and learn and adopt his beliefs as their own.

There was great dissatisfaction with life in Europe at the end of the Great War. What had been the prevailing view concerning the destiny of mankind, as taught by the church, was in question. And in many instances it was about to be replaced by secret occult societies, which taught, among other things, rebellion against rationalism and materialism.

Adolph Hitler and Heinrich Himmler were two who were dissatisfied with what they saw around them as crass materialism. Wanting a change in the established world order of the times, they, like many other Germans, sought membership in one of a dozen of these secret societies, who offered a forum for intellectuals as well as veterans who held the same views. These views contended that liberalism and materialism had long repressed the true German soul. Furthermore, they believed the Jews were the embodiment of this materialism, and somehow they must be either cast out or destroyed.

The leaders of several organizations influenced Hitler and Himmler, whose ideas were the same as their own. They collectively believed that if Germany was to emerge from the chaos resulting from the First War and again take her place as the dominant nation in Europe, and eventually the world, she must return to her ancient roots. These roots went back to the Aryans of the Indus Valley, to the Druids, to the Runics, and to the Norse warrior tribes. Here was to be found the spirit of unity so lacking in the make-up of the present day German. They saw a need for release of the ancient Berserker rage, a return to the discipline of the Spartans, and a return to the militaristic spirit and order of the Roman Legions, who were all seen as brother Aryans.

Hitler and his new friends believed these philosophies had always been part of the German psyche and that a stripping off of the thin veneer of their present civilization would release the old German eulogized in the operas of Wagner and the writings of Schiller, Goethe, Hine and others. This old-new Germany, destined to dominate the world, would then rise up and cast out the materialists.

The Swiss German Carl Jung, recognized as co-founder of analytical psychology, was a supporter of this view. He wrote in part: "We cannot possibly get beyond our present level of culture unless we receive a powerful impetus from our primitive roots....We must dig down to the primitive in us, for only out of the conflict between civilized man and the Germanic barbarian will there come what we need: a new experience."

But Hitler and Himmler were not seeking this new

experience in God. They had emerged from the War as atheists, if in fact they had ever been believers. And later, their young Waffen SS soldiers would officially abandon the God of Abraham, which had been the foundation of European society. They would replace Him with a deity of their own making–Adolph Hitler.

These two co-founders of the Nazi Party and the SS, Hitler and Himmler, eschewed the Nicene Creed, replacing it with a credo of their own. And here they took from all religions, organizations, and writings, irrespective of their origins. From the Jesuits, organization and the priesthood; from the Ancient Knights Templar, discipline; from Freemasonry, ritualistic teaching; from Christianity, certain beliefs that Jesus of Nazareth, although not the promised messiah, was in fact crucified.

The Vril Society was one of the more prominent clandestine groups of German intellectuals who met to discuss and debate such esoteric subjects as Hindu mysticism, Theosophy, and Jewish Kaballa. Their name came from a science-fiction novel, written by an Englishmen by the name of Bulwer-Lytton who lived about the turn of the nineteenth century. His book about a Utopian socialistic society that had harnessed a mysterious life force known as vril, was seen as good comic book and pulp fare in America. But it was to have an impact on the German mind, second only to Hitler's *Mein Kamph*.

Using vril, these people in the novel acquired power over themselves and others who were not privy to their secret. These lesser beings were cast out in order to purify the race of the superior Vril-ya.

The Vril-ya lived in a subterranean paradise below the lowest level of our deepest mines. The earth, as it turns out, is not composed of molten magma below the mantel. It is, according to Bulwer-Lytton, hollow and inhabited by people who have scientific knowledge, which enables them to overcome any deficiencies found in their environment.

Dr. Willey Ley, one of Germany's more brilliant rocket scientists and a member of the early Vril Society, wrote: "The Society believes they have acquired secret knowledge similar to vril, which will enable them to change the German people and make them the equal of the Vril-ya."

This vril force enabled the user to reach high degrees of concentration. At some point, fiction merged with reality as members of the Vril Society came to believe that certain others practicing spiritual exercises, such as Zen Buddhists and the Jesuits, had been taught by masters of the occult from the controversial lost city of Atlantis. They were not alone in this. Edgar Cayce, the well-known and highly respected American clairvoyant, believed the mythical inhabitants of Atlantis had not only existed, but had acquired universal truths that gave them mind power in much the same way as did vril.

Several of Hitler's mentors and early associates were also members; chief among them was a Dr. Eckhart, a noted spiritualist. Then there were Alfred Rosenberg, Aleistair Crowley, and the founder of the society, an intellectual by the name of Haushofer. This latter was a student of the Russian magician and metaphysician George Gurdjieff. There were also Himmler and Goering, and, later to become Hitler's personal physician, Dr. Morell. Morell would become best known for treating Hitler with an inordinate amount of drugs during the darkest hours of the Nazi regime.

Crowley was well known to followers of the occult in Europe, and to a lesser degree in America. He was a character known to pulp fiction as well as to serious students of the occult and black magic. He was also a *sado-masochist*, who had the deserved reputation of being the most evil man in the world up to that time.

Like Dr. Ley, other prominent German scientists and scholars were members of this Vril Society, which believed they had tapped into a higher power. They also believed their Teutonic ancestors had known this power. It was similar to vril, and if mastered, it would guide and direct them to a "brave new world." In this coming Utopia of theirs, they too would cast out the undesirables of a lesser birthright. Of course, these undesirables were Jews.

The Vril Society of intellectuals, believing in the occult and educated in the history of German origins, embraced the mostly uneducated zealot veterans who had made their own acquaintances with the supernatural during their sojourn in the trenches. Together, they formed the Thule Society that eventually evolved into the Nazi party.

Adolph Hitler was elected the leader of this new organization of Thule misfits. The intellectuals saw in him a charismatic speaker who gave voice to their political theories as well as to some of his own. With him as their leader, the nation would emulate the fictional Vril-ya. And then like them, they would rise up and dominate all lesser races and eventually rule the world.

Adolph Hitler, soon after being elected Chancellor of Germany, consulted with Himmler, whom he had grown to respect and trust. Together, they mapped out a plan for an army separate from the Wermacht. This new army would give them the needed power to overcome the political hierarchy who controlled the regular army.

This SS, later to be known as the Waffen SS, in order to distinguish them from the Gestapo and the Schutstaffel that ran the slave labor and the death camp programs, emerged from the minds of the two planners. The Waffen was to be a special army, one like no other in history. They saw it as being a brotherhood, a secular priesthood, each member being ordained in a solemn secret ritual. Himmler, who had been raised by Jesuits, and whom he admired for their organization, if not for their beliefs and precepts, would later bring to the table this special knowledge and understanding of their methods of teaching and patterns for living.

In addition, the Waffen was to be a society of Teutonic Knights who would be patterned after the fictional Vril-ya warriors. They would practice many of the same ancient occult rituals and others which were more modern.

One of the more prominent dispensers of this modern occult ritual was a Russian, Madame Helena Blavatsky. She was most famous for retranslating the New Testament, hoping to resurrect beliefs in the Gnostic Gospels and the Apocrypha. She also espoused belief in gospels of lesser credibility than the Apocrypha, such as the *Shepard of Hermes*, reported to have been written by one of the brothers of Jesus, and the *Gospel of Nicodemus*. Hers was a new-age philosophy, blending science with religion, that became known as Theosophy. She was also a spiritualist who held séances and met frequently for study with a number of occult celebrity investigators such as Sir Arthur Conan Doyle.

Many of her interpretations of the scriptures melded Christianity with Norse mythology. The result was a new religion steeped in concepts of root race theory. Central to all of this was elimination of a primitive race in order for a new race to emerge. This new race, as seen by Blavatsky, was the Aryan race from which the German nation, according to her, was descended.

Both Hitler and Himmler embraced the teachings of Blavatsky, who, although not a contemporary of theirs, lent a certain learned corroboration to Hitler's own ideas espoused in *Mein Kampf*.

These same ideas found refuge in the writings of another prominent racist, the infamous Guido von List.

Von List was an intellectual who associated with the

likes of Franz Hartmann, Commander-in-Chief of the Austro-Hungarian Army. Von List had formed his own elite occult group, similar to that of Blavatsky's, naming it after himself. He was sponsored by wealthy Austrian and German businessmen, who were also interested in his teachings.

There were many other organizations whose ideas coincided with those of Hitler. One such was the Rosicrucians, who saw a rise in their membership commensurate with Hitler's rise to prominence. They complimented each other in a sort of mutual admiration society. And while the Nazi regime lasted, they fed off each other in a kind of symbiotic relationship.

The Rosicrucians were, and still are, a society advocating control of the physical through the mind. This is not a new concept; however, the uniqueness of this society lies in the means by which it is to be accomplished. It, too, has borrowed from many sources, including Freemasonry and Gnosticism. The mainstay of its belief is that a special knowledge will enable them to rise above the degraded human condition.

The Rosicrucians doctrine, advocating rising to a higher plane through the use of mind forces, was central to the scheme of the new Nazi movement. The idea that secret power exists, and is known only to a select few, also became a paramount belief of the SS. Only the master race with its master soldiery, who possessed this secret, would triumph on the battlefield over lesser races. But there was something else besides this secret knowledge that made them invincible. This something was a box containing a talisman having occult power. This power could be used to disseminate good or evil, depending on the desires of the designated keeper of the box. The box, in turn, derived its power from the contents within.

When the children of Israel entered the Promised Land, they carried with them a special talisman, the Arc of the Covenant. God told Moses to build this Arc for transporting stone tablets He had inscribed with the Ten Commandments. The Israelites believed the Arc not only carried the Commandments, as well as other spiritual artifacts, but it was the abode of God while he sojourned among them. Special care was taken; only members of the priesthood of Aaron, the brother of Moses, were authorized, on pain of death, to handle it. When they camped, a portable temple of skins was erected. The Arc was then placed inside a center section of the temple known as the Holy of Holies.

The Arc was made of a special kind of acacia wood and lined with lead. It was made to specifications given by God to Moses, and was carried by them when they went into battle. And while they had it in their possession, Bible history tells us they were invincible.

Adolph Hitler was most familiar with these passages of the Jewish Torah. He wrote that, even at the age of twenty-one, he felt he had a destiny to fulfill, as had Joshua of old. And that he had been foreordained by some mystical power to someday lead the German nation against her inferior enemies, as did the Vril-ya of fiction, and that he would be armed with a force known to ancient Teutonic Knights, similar to vril-energy, which would help him accomplish this end.

It was at this point that he met the infamous Dr. Eckard, the dedicated Satanist and member of both the Vril and Thule Societies. Eckard saw in Hitler the means by which Wagner's opera *Parcival* would be revived and made real.

Walter Stein, another Thule member, also befriended Hitler. He would later write that Hitler at this time was deeply involved with the occult. Stein was to write that Hitler had another spiritual mentor. He was the head of the so-called Blood Lodge; he was the infamous Guido von List.

Under their early tutelage, Hitler would later write in *Mein Kamph*: "These were the most vital years of my life in which I learned all I needed to know to run the Nazi Party."

Eckard would write, on his deathbed, of his time spent with Hitler: "I have initiated him into the Secret Doctrine, opened his centers in vision, and given him the means to communicate with the powers.

"Do not mourn for me–I have influenced history more than any other German."

This Secret Doctrine he wrote of was the doctrine that would be later taught the SS. And like the armies of Joshua, they too had a special talisman that would make them invincible.

During his so-called Vienna years, Hitler spent a good deal of his time loafing around the treasury of the Hofsmuseum. He wrote that he was drawn to a display of a relic while in the company of his new friend, Dr. Stein. A docent conducting a tour showed them a spear head that he said was once mounted on a shaft and used by a Roman Centurion to pierce the side of Jesus as he hung on the cross. Hitler wrote that he didn't believe such a Christian symbol could affect him the way it did. He later told Dr. Stein, who was also very interested in the spear, that he immediately believed the docent, who said the spear was a phenomenon having legendary talismanic power. "I knew it was no legend," he said.

Stein says Hitler went on to tell him: "I knew instantly that it was all true, and that if I possessed the spear, someday I would carry it successfully into battle, just as Joshua carried the Arc."

Hitler never believed most things contained in the Bible. But the events where Longinus, the name of the

Centurion who killed Jesus, were an exception. Hitler saw the prevailing theory that the Centurion pierced His side with a spear as an act of mercy as a wrong interpretation. He believed the final scene played out that Friday afternoon on Golgotha was an act of expediency and not mercy. He pointed with finality to the fact that Longinus, later realizing what he had done, repented and joined the fledgling Christian sect.

Longinus would say that he believed the man he slew with his spear, if in fact he did, since John records that Christ had already expired, was the Son of God. Witnesses described how lymph and blood gushed forth, covering the spear and dousing the eyes of the Centurion. Longinus was said to have had bad eyes. What exactly was wrong with them, the Gospel writers never said. But the sudden darkness that came over the scene, plus the miraculous change in his eyesight, convinced Longinus he had killed the Savior of the world.

The Centurion left his Legion and embarked on a mission, whereupon he told the story of his recovery to all who would listen. Like Jesus, he too became a thorn in the side of the body politic and was later executed.

Hitler would use this event as a lesson in dedication and sacrifice. It could be said that if the SS had a patron saint, it would have been the martyred St. Longinus.

Legend had it that whoever possessed the relic literally possessed the world. It was a talisman of the caliber that fit the plans of the burgeoning monster, Adolph Hitler. He saw the relic as a uniting force for the greatest army in history. With this new army of SS behind the regular German Wermacht, Hitler saw himself as the central player in Wagner's opera to be acted out on the world stage.

Stein wrote of the scene he witnessed at the site of the relic when Hitler first heard the story of the spear: "He stood like a man in a trance, a man over whom some dreadful spell had been cast. He was swaying on his feet, as though he was caught up in some inexplicable euphoria." Stein went on to write how Hitler's "whole physiognomy and stance appeared transformed as if some mighty spirit now inhabited his very soul creating within and around him a kind of evil transformation of its own nature and power."

Stein and Hitler would spend hours discussing the spear and the role it might play in his new special army. The two of them listened to the intellectuals, and then studied legend and history in their efforts to seek the truth. They were both eager to believe what they read about the spear, i.e., that it had been in the possession of many of the world's great military leaders, and that it had been a symbol of power for hundreds of years of world history.

On still another occasion, Hitler was gazing at the spear when he went into a trance. He would write: "I slowly became aware of a mighty presence around it–the same awesome presence which I had experienced inwardly on those rare occasions in my life when I had sensed that a great destiny awaited me."

Five years after being elected Chancellor, Hitler annexed Austria and made it part of Germany. In a motorcade, the conquering hero made straight for the Hofsmuseum. With a great deal of fanfare and ceremony, which had special meaning to those of the SS attending him, he took possession of the spear and designated himself keeper.

Over the years, the shaft had been broken and worn away. But the head was intact. Now, in an act of sacrilege, he had fashioned a quarter-scale replica of Joshua's Arc in what his scholars believed was an exact detail. He placed the relic within, and, henceforth, treated it with the same reverence afforded the Ten Commandments by the ancient Israelites.

The spearhead was first carried to Nuremberg, spiritual site of the New Reich. At the outset of Operation Barbarossa, he had it placed in the care and keeping of his lead SS assault division when they crossed the Russian border. And then they carried it successfully through a blitzkrieg of monumental proportions. It was only when this unit was rotated from combat on the Eastern Front, and with them the talisman, that Hitler's fortunes changed. There was no SS and no spear at Stalingrad, and the Germans suffered a staggering defeat. Hitler had ordered it to be placed in a vault in Berlin for safekeeping. When Allied bombers began their destruction of that city, he moved it back to Nuremberg.

Finally, in the waning months of the War, when he too realized all was lost, Hitler placed it in the hands of Kurt Steinmann with instructions to safeguard it with the gold that would see the rise again of the Third Reich. It was supposed to have been taken into custody by an officer in George Patton's Third Army when they entered Nuremberg. That it was returned to the museum from whence it came was true. But not by Patton, but by Ralph Wahl. And not immediately after the War, but a month or so later.

The night I was designated keeper was the night I came into a mega-fortune in gold. It was also the night Kurt Steinmann had a paralyzing accident just before he lost the spear. And the Guardian of the spear, the SS commandant, lost his life.

It was a few nights later that the former keeper, Adolph Hitler, committed suicide in his bunker in Berlin. All of this seemed to be important to Ralph, and maybe it was when you consider what else he told me about the spear:

It seems there was a whole host of famous personages who were keepers and then for some reason lost it or it was taken from them. He rattled off names such as Herod the Great. Then there was Constantine, who owned it when he was victorious at the Milvian Bridge, where his victory had such a lasting effect on the Christian religion. The Emperor Theodosius owned it, as did Alaric the Goth who sacked Rome. Theodoric had it in his possession when he stopped Atilla the Hun and his hoards. Then there were Justinian and Charles Martel, who defeated the Moslems at the battle of Poitres, thus changing the course of history.

Each keeper owned the spear for some time. And while he held it, he was triumphant in everything he did. And when he lost it, history, according to Ralph, records the individual fell on hard times. He was then surrounded by failure, and in many cases lost his life.

Two of the modern-day keepers who stood out as conquerors but who became two abject failures after they lost the spear, were Napoleon and Kaiser Wilhelm of World War One infamy. In the case of Wilhelm, he sought out the spear before venturing into Belgium on the road to France. Whether he actually acquired the spear is a matter of conjecture. But the preponderance of evidence says he did.

....

There's no question that Ralph believed what he had told me. And what he told me gave me a glimpse inside the Waffen SS. He told me their entire ritual was patterned after the Scottish Rite of Freemasonry and the oath taking and ordination ceremonies of the Jesuits. But, he said, where Freemasonry was concerned, Hitler and Himmler had given altogether different meanings to the *Entered Apprentice*, *Fellow Craft*, and *Master Mason degrees*. And during the Jesuit-like ceremonies, unlike the Jesuits, who swore allegiance to Jesus of Nazareth, they swore an oath of fealty to Adolph Hitler.

They also had usurped the primary Masonic teaching

methods, even to the use of small books that Masons call *Monitors*. These monitors explained the meanings of important portions of Masonic rituals. The SS rituals were standardized through the use of like reference material so that wherever the soldier was serving he would have access to the words of the Fuhrer, who with the help of Himmler wrote the prospectus or monitor.

Like Masonic teaching, so the Waffen SS ritual teaching was performed behind closed doors with a guard or *Tyler* standing by. And like Masons, SS members were sworn to keep the teachings secret. They were only to be discussed in authorized *lodges* with those who were qualified. A lodge could be designated as any place three or more members were in attendance, where the surroundings were enclosed and a Tyler was present.

But here the similarity stopped. Where Masons believe their order provides an opportunity for honest, sincere men to improve themselves, the SS believed their order provided an opportunity for the uninitiated soldier to learn of his Teutonic heritage; the teachings of Madame Blavatsky; and the *blude* ritual of von List.

Now schooled and disciplined, before going into combat, the SS enlistee would became a machine capable of carrying out any order of his commander, including unspeakable atrocities, in the belief that what he was ordered to do was the desire of Adolph Hitler. And here again, he swore blood oaths in ritual settings to die for the Fuhrer and the new Germany if it became necessary.

I'm not a religious man. But as I sat there in that rundown diner, sipping coffee and reading a copy of the SS "monitor," and recalling the teachings of the learned Ralph Wahl in things relating to this infamous army of assassins, I couldn't help but conclude there is a Satan. And that Hitler had become demonized at some point. And that the SS soldier who joined the organization to fight for a greater Germany had come to believe Hitler was the Messiah spoken of in the Torah; he had attained esoteric power, transcending the power of Satan–or even the God of Abraham.

It's no wonder why SS divisions on the Eastern Front, surrounded by superior Russian forces in sub-zero temperatures, were able to reach down within themselves. They believed they had acquired vrile-like energy and had literally taken on the mantel of Teutonic warriors of old. Time and time again, the Waffen SS would stand or die in the face of overwhelming forces. It was no wonder they were the scourges of the battlefield, wherever they fought. As Joshua reminded his brethren many times, so the SS was reminded of who they were. And Hitler and Himmler had convinced them the spear protected them, as it was with Israel, who had been protected by the Arc. And regardless of how hopeless their situation, the SS would ultimately triumph. And if they died in combat, they would join their Teutonic brothers in another world surrounded by Valkyrie maidens and fellow warriors. To them, death in the service of Adolph Hitler was seen as something to be sought after, second only to victory for a greater Germany.

The organization was steeped in mysticism from its inception. Once convinced he was predestined to rule the world, the highly intelligent SS soldier was far superior to his foes. And convinced he was literally armed with vrile-like power and protected by the spear and his messiah, Adolph Hitler, he became invincible. He was capable of feats exceeding that of any soldier who fought in the War.

As I continue to write, I'm beginning to see what Ralph meant when he said if I became more involved with the spear, I might lose my soul. He believed that, rather than a Christian relic from the past, the spear was tainted with the spirit of Satan. Those who believed it had occult power, particularly if they believed it was capable of bestowing wealth and other favors on the keeper in turn for protecting it as though it was a living entity; and if they did, they were in danger of falling into a bottomless pit. He was afraid I might attribute my sudden riches to the power of this spear and not to circumstance. If I did, then there was no end to the use the spear could be put to. The gates of hell were wide open and beckoning to me. He was afraid such devil-power might drive me insane, as it had Hitler and all the others.

CHAPTER 26…NEW ORLEANS, 1951

It was Christmas vacation. I had almost two weeks. I intended to use this time studying for examinations, as the end of the semester and mid-year graduation approached. I wasn't particularly interested in excelling in any of them. I only wanted a degree and to leave graciously. I had all but abandoned any idea of going on in physics, as I once had considered.

I had been in touch with two drilling companies and one diamond drill manufacturing firm. The diamond people wanted me, I suppose, because I was a little older and more mature. They wanted me as a sales representative. I would be on the road most of the time, and when home, I would be subject to call if a well was having trouble. By trouble, I mean if they ran into granite and needed a diamond bit or a *wash-over shoe* if they had a break in a drill pipe.

Lucy was happy with the way things turned out. She found another job, which was better than her last but never paid any more. We were still struggling financially, and would be for years to come.

In due course, Ralph acquired the diamonds we took from Merkers. This made Lucy happy, but not me. As far as I was concerned, the diamonds were unjustly taken from me. I felt the loss in the same way. And it made me more depressed than ever I had been.

That's the way things were when, out of the blue, I received a call from Ralph. He said he was coming back to New Orleans and he had a surprise for me.

The three of us are heading east to one of those small cities in New Jersey named after an Indian tribe. What he wants to show us there is the surprise. He showed up with airline tickets and an offer to pay the expenses for this surprise trip of his. I was glad for an excuse not to study the full two weeks.

He asked me if I still intended to write a book about our adventure, and if I still intended to include the part about the gold and the SS. I told him I was. I got the idea he was not so much interested in my plans for a book as he was in looking for an opportunity to tell me something else about the gold.

"Red, I want the two of you to know something." He was leaning over talking to me. Lucy was in the middle seat.

"I have not been completely honest with you. I went back to the place you called Ravensbruck; I uncovered the half we kept from General Patton and Colonel Bernstein, soon after we buried it. Now, I want to tell you I took half of what was left. The remainder is what I let the Commission eventually *find* and recover. You, of course, got the credit for remembering where you buried it. And for that they agreed to leave you alone. Well, they had no idea, at the time, how much was still there. And there was so much they thought they finally had it all. But they did not. I took almost a ton and left them the rest.

"Where is it now?" I asked.

"That is part of the surprise," he replied.

I couldn't help notice the expression change on Lucy's

face. Once again she wanted nothing to do with gold. To her it meant stealing, and she couldn't reconcile it with her religious teachings. I've told you before: she believed it spelled trouble. It had already caused the death of her ex-husband and another of my friends, and had been the direct cause of her killing two men. She hadn't gotten over any part of it; she was not looking for more trouble. Ralph, on the other hand, attributed the deaths of these people to the evil of the spear. He told me if it hadn't been those killings it would have been something else. Once he had given it back to the museum and it had a new keeper, we had nothing to worry about. We could expect to have clear sailing for the rest of our lives. This was according to him, anyway. But Lucy was not buying any part of his hokum about it or the SS.

For the moment I was elated. I was in hog heaven again. My mind was going ninety miles an hour. *He was going to give me some of what he had taken; maybe he would even split it with me, unbeknownst to Lucy.*

But this euphoria was short-lived when I noticed the expression on her face. The look she gave me clearly meant it was either her or the gold, but not both. Anyway, it felt good for a moment. But the realization that it was all for naught put me further into a dark funk. I spent the hours before we landed feeling as bad as I ever had.

I was correct about Lucy and her feelings about the gold, but not Ralph; I had misjudged him. He had brought me here to show me he had not taken it for himself, and to offer again to make me rich or just well off. It was up to me. But really it was up to Lucy.

We stopped at a small warehouse and went in. There were two workmen unloading crates. They said hello to Ralph but didn't stop their work to chat. They knew him. As it turned out, he was their boss.

He took us into a back room to show us some large polished granite rocks resembling squat teakettles. I couldn't remember ever seeing anything quite like them, and neither could Lucy. He explained they were called *stones,* of all things, and they were used in the game of *curling*. He told me it was like a cross between bowling and shuffleboard. He said it's a big time winter sport in Canada, the Northeast, and in the North as far west as North Dakota.

He locked the door behind us, then took us over to one of the shelves containing dozen of these stones. He checked the top of two of them.

"Look here at this brass plate. See this one. The last digit of the serial number is even. Now watch."

He carried the forty-pound stone by the handle as though he was going to pour us a cup of tea. He set it on a bench and struck it sharply with a hammer. It was solid granite with a large hollow center or core. Inside the core was a gold ingot weighing approximately one third that of a regular gold block. I couldn't have been more surprised.

Ralph had a big smile on his face as he watched me put two and two together. But Lucy was confused.

"Stop me," I said, "if I'm wrong." Ralph nodded, still smiling. *He intended to give me some of it after all.* But Lucy saw the smile on my face, and she started to frown again at what I was thinking.

"That bottom addition to Lothar Horner's mother's place in Siegesdorf is where you're putting these things together. You're melting the large bars and recasting them into these smaller ones that are easier to smuggle. And you have these curling stones weighted to make them exactly the weight of those that are solid granite; the odd-numbered ones you are peddling to somebody else to be used in the game."

"Right, again," he said.

"You trust Lothar?"

"Completely. He is getting rich, though. He gets to keep the dust lost from the recasting process. The soft gold sheds. All the old-time gold miners knew this. Anytime you handle pure gold or change its shape or what have you, you lose a minute amount in dust. We simply set up a system to recover it. Lothar is satisfied. He is making a lot of money selling it at higher than world prices at places like Tangier, Spanish Morocco. He is happy, and so am I."

And me too, if Lucy would change her mind.

"Incidentally, we have a legitimate business on the side. We distribute the odd-numbered stones to retailers in Montreal, Winnipeg, Minneapolis, and a half-dozen other large northern cities. We also have a healthy share of the Swiss and the recovering Austrian markets.

Heretofore, the Scots had a monopoly on curling stones, since the best granite was quarried on an island off that country. But we have quarries here that are just as good, with a cheaper supply of labor. Transportation costs are about the same, so we have been able to make inroads into what has always been their sole domain. I intend cutting you in on that end of the business if you will not take any of the gold."

"What are you doing with it anyway?" I asked, surprised at what he just told me.

"Nothing yet. I collect it from our local vault periodically, and then hide it in the basement of a chalet I have in Utah. I intend giving it to Simon Wiesenthal, as soon as he has a system to return it to those who lost it, the ones who obviously survived the camps. Not an easy thing to do."

Good idea, I thought, but said nothing. I just nodded my head and watched Lucy, who had changed her expression once again to one more positive.

Then all of a sudden, out of the clear blue, something jogged my memory. I can't explain it, but there it was as plain as day. It was kind of uncanny the way it happened. One minute nothing–and then the next, the inside of my head seemed to light up–and I felt a tingle all over as a jolt of adrenalin coursed through my body. And if I was remembering things correctly, it might well be the solution to all my money problems. But regardless, this time I was keeping it to myself.

I don't like the idea of accepting money from Ralph gratuitously. But that's what he's suggesting I do with his offer to make me his partner. And I certainly don't want to work for him for wages, even though it might be a whole lot better than what I'm going to be doing. But working for the diamond-drill company at least has something going for it–we will be able to live in the South. Even if he offered me a partnership, we would be living in the frozen North. And I figure no amount of money is worth it.

But not to worry. I might just have discovered another mother lode that's been right under my nose all the time. I might be rich again, thanks to the Waffen SS and that crazy spear of theirs. Maybe if things work out, I'll be wealthier than I ever was. And my new book is going to be a best seller, too, because the first thing I'm going to do is buy a publishing house.

But then I thought about what happens when you relinquish your keeper position. *Hadn't everybody else lost everything? Why not me?* Then I kicked myself. I'm starting to go screwy. I'm starting to think as Ralph does. But if this idea of mine doesn't pan out–if I'm wrong about it, then I'm going to blame that crazy spear of Steinmann's for throwing a monkey wrench into things and sabotaging my life. And this nutty thought will plague me for the rest of my life. And then maybe I'll come to believe as the rest of them did down through the ages. I'll come to believe it has this power; then, I too might be headed down that same road to the nuthatch. For sure, I'll never be happy again. And for sure, I'll become a true believer and blame the spear for keeping me poor. Nothing I have in mind, though, is for certain; the whole thing might very well amount to nothing.

But then, if it does come a cropper, methinks another major disappointment, this one blamed on occult interference, might very well put me over the edge.

CHAPTER 27...NEW ORLEANS, 1951

I wasted no time after we landed. I gave Lucy an excuse about having to go to the school library to study, and I took off like a scalded dog. I headed to one of the el cheapo storage lockers inundating New Orleans, as I suppose they are in most other large cities. I found mine and began wading through the boxes and junk the two of us had collected. I don't suppose we have any more than any other couple; it's just that our small, on-campus apartment has absolutely no storage space.

I could hardly contain myself. I was breathing heavily, my heart pounding. I was out of shape and thought I best stop and take a breather. But I couldn't wait. Then I saw the edge of it at the bottom of the heap, in the far corner. I tossed things right and left to get at it. I didn't care what I broke. A garish lamp, a wedding present, shattered into a thousand pieces, scattering glass over the rest of the stuff. Then I saw a name stenciled on an olive drab canvas bag: *Tech Sgt Eric Schroeder, AUS,* followed by a string of serial numbers. I hurriedly removed the rest of the storage from off his duffle bag, throwing more things every which way. In my haste, I fell down. I lay panting in the bric-a-brac, which I swore was going to find itself at a garage sale soon.

I forced myself to lie there until I caught my breath, lost as much from anticipation as from exertion. I crawled across the broken glass, unsure of my footing if I stood up. Finally, I got my bleeding hands on a corner of it; heaving as hard as I could, I pulled it free.

I stood it on end, looking for an attached key to the lock that ran through the metal eyes of the overlapping flaps. There wasn't one. I rushed to my car looking for a screwdriver, knowing full well I couldn't pry the lock off if I found one. It would have to be cut or sawed off. They were built sturdy. They were designed to carry a soldier's valuable possessions, so they were almost tamper proof.

I threw the bag in the trunk and headed for home, leaving all my junk strewn about outside the locker. I didn't care if somebody stole it all. I couldn't wait to be on my way.

I found a hacksaw. And then I made sure Lucy was someplace else when I attacked the lock. I poured out the contents on the cement in front of our small apartment. One of my neighbors took note of my acting as though I was possessed. He didn't speak. He only stared. I didn't care. I was desperate. I had other things on my mind than what he might be thinking.

I found it. I really found it, and after all these years. I should have known it would be here, and that it would be loaded with a treasure worth untold millions of dollars.

I felt around the bottom seam of Eric's old field jacket. Sewn in the lining were six round objects. I could feel each one. I knew what they were. They were extremely rare uncirculated twenty-dollar double eagle gold pieces from the Merkers mine. I took the jacket inside, and using a pair of scissors, I removed the stitches. There before me, affixed to a piece of tailor's tape, was a fortune. Each coin was worth dozens of ingots, maybe a wheelbarrow full of them, maybe a dozen wheelbarrows full. They were worth only twenty dollars, but to collectors they were each worth at least a quarter of a million dollars in pre-war money.

I wrapped the tape in an elastic band and headed for the back yard. I buried them in a shallow hole and sat down, completely drained.

But gone was the depression. Gone were the memories of all those years of gloom and foreboding. Gone were all my worries. I was as wealthy as Midas. I smiled. And then I began to laugh. And then I began to laugh hysterically. I beat them. I beat them all. I even beat the demons from out of Steinmann's box. I did what no one else in history has done. I beat the spear. I was alive and well and I was rich. And above all I have the woman I want, and she loves me. And I don't have to go to work in the oil fields. What more could I ask for. What was there to wish for? What battlefields were left to conquer? I was a success beyond my wildest dreams. The world was mine. And nobody knew I had the coins. And nobody was going to find out and take them from me. Not this time.

There was another thought that came hurriedly to mind as I sat gloating on the ground in front of my cache: Ralph's story about his spear was just so much nonsense, as I always believed it was.

CHAPTER 27...DEER VALLEY, UTAH, 1952

Lucy and I had been invited to Ralph's and his wife's chalet, nestled on the side of a mountain in an upscale ski area. It resembled nothing if not the Obersalzburg, but a smaller less spectacular version.

It was Christmas again. I hadn't seen Ralph for several months. I had told Lucy we were partners in the curling stone business. I had to tell her something to justify my new income and to account for not taking the recently offered drill-bit job. So this was supposed to be a business trip, as much as it was a chance to get away for awhile.

We were happy in Louisiana, far from the cold weather of most of the nation. It was all right with me if we never left. But she saw it as a chance to see a new part of the country. And I needed to talk to Ralph. My new book was almost finished, and I wanted to talk over some things with him.

He picked us up at the Salt Lake airport, and we headed for the mountain country east of where his parents lived. It struck me immediately how glaciers had whittled away at the canyons, just as they had on the Obersalzburg. It was as though Mother Nature had been practicing here, before she went to work in earnest in Austria.

His so-called chalet was custom built. I couldn't help but notice how much it resembled the old Berghof, complete with the bay window and view. What this means if anything, I can't say. I had observed, though, that spending years so close to the SS had affected him more than he let on. This might be one of those subliminal indicators.

We were sitting in his living room in front of an imported Austrian ceramic stove, looking out the window at the local panorama. I started the conversation by asking him a question. There was something on my mind that I had been wondering about.

"Ralph, was the SS involved in some kind of a ceremony the night we were hiding among the boxes in the back room of the Zum Turken?"

"Yes, they were," he replied, without hesitation. "It preceded the party and lasted about an hour. The spear was there, too; the box was being used as a dais or altar."

What went on at this ceremony?"

"At one point, Steinmann was formerly inducted as keeper. There were also a dozen or so high-ranking officers who were being raised in the order. And there were ordinations performed on a few who had not had the chance to attend one of these secret blood rites before."

"What went on, exactly?" I asked him. But he was reluctant to tell me more, even after this long a period. I pressed him to answer:

"I am not too proud of my participation," he said. "In fact, I am sorry I ever had anything to do with it. I now believe it was Satan inspired. I will tell you this, in addition to what I have already told you, it was a kind of court of honor with religious overtones resembling a mass and a Freemason ceremony. Alistair Crowley and Doctor Eckhard had contrived it before he died. Of course it had Hitler and Himmler's input as well.

"This was not the first one I participated in. I have

thought a lot about it since, and I realize I went too far. I should have avoided attending the first one at all costs; but being German, I was caught up early in the nationalism of the thing and I couldn't let go. I know this is no excuse, but I could not help myself. I began losing sight of my fundamental Christian beliefs soon after I arrived. And I started to look upon Hitler as someone who had been designated by God to change the world. Now, I think of both Hitler and the spear as being demon possessed."

"Ralph." I said his name and then stared into his eyes for the longest time. He knew something was wrong. He knew I was going to ask him something he had been holding back since we first met. I knew it. I could tell by the almost embarrassed look on his face. And I was right.

"You're a commissioned officer in the SS, aren't you?" He waited before he answered.

"I was, yes."

"You mean you are. It's for life. You took a blood oath for life."

"I did. But that is another thing I am not proud of. And I prefer not to talk about it"

"I didn't mean to imply you were. But I have to know. And I also want you to tell me if you were when you worked for Oddlie and the OSS." He could see I was most serious, and I suppose he thought for a moment that if he didn't tell me he might be in trouble. He needn't have worried on that score. I wasn't going to say anything to the authorities; but he had no way of knowing, so he answered me. Now, the more I think about it the more I feel he wanted to tell somebody he trusted. And he may have wanted to do so for a long time.

"By the SS you mean the Waffen. You knew I was Gestapo, which was a branch of the SS; I told you that early on. I told you, when my leg was still mending, I was forced to join something if I intended working on the

Obersalzburg. But I was not part of the Waffen, the elite of the corps. But to answer your question: I was given a commission in the Waffen during that last ceremony."

"Was it because you wanted it. It certainly wasn't necessary at that late date because of your job–or was it?"

"Both. It would have looked suspicious if I had rejected the offer after I had voiced my desire many times over the years. But then, I also wanted to join. It was my own idea. It was, however, more of an honorary thing; it was bestowed on me as a kind of payoff for services rendered. You see the Waffen SS looked down their noses at the Gestapo. The Commandant, who was a friend of mine, did not want me going to Argentina with them unless I was a full-blooded member. So he tendered me a commission.

"Why is this so important to you now?" Ralph asked me. I was hesitant to answer him. I avoided his question by changing the subject.

"Did you ever give the gold to Weisenthal?"

He stood up and asked me to follow him. We went down a staircase into what is best described as a wine cellar. I knew Ralph didn't drink, so I figured the casks were fake or held something else besides wine. They weren't empty. The first row held some kind of liquid. He poured me a small glass. It tasted something like cider, the kind we used to drink around Halloween. Then he removed the back of one of the casks stacked on the second tier. It was full of miniature gold ingots, the kind they had smuggled from Siegsdorf to the United States.

"So," I said, "you didn't give it all to Weisenthal then?"

"I have not given any of it to him," he replied.

"You know I have always considered it to be the property of the United States. But I have also been leery of it ever finding its way into our Treasury. I have never believed the Commission had a legal right to any of it. And certainly, I never believed Germany was the rightful owner.

"But to answer your question: I have been afraid to give it to Wiesenthal for fear he would tell the Commission, which is still stumbling along trying to make up their minds what to do with what they have. If Wiesenthal ever did tell the Commission, then it is jail for me. And worse yet, if the Jews ever find out I am SS. I could never discover if my name, Rolph Wahlmuller, was officially added to the membership list. But I think it was. Wiesenthal has the complete list, and he would turn me in if he found out, no matter how much gold I gave him. I just do not know, so I have hesitated. I just have never made a move to do anything with it.

"By the way, does your wife know we are not partners in the curling stone business? Now tell me: How do you manage to live so well without my help? I am satisfied you were not able to keep any of the diamonds, and you have not published your book. So how are you getting along?"

I don't know exactly why I didn't tell him about the coins and how I had one of them appraised by a bank in Switzerland. They estimated it would auction for at least three-quarters of a million. And maybe half again as much in a few years. They kept the coin and gave me a letter of credit for half of what they figured it was worth, against a ten-percent interest when I decided to sell.

I guess the reason I kept the coins to myself was because I had lost a fortune twice and I was gun-shy. I didn't feel secure even telling Ralph. There was nothing to gain, and there might be everything to lose if I did.

But I had to tell him something, so I said: "I had quite a bit of cash from the sale of the second diamond. But I'm running low. Lucy thinks you've been giving me money, for what she doesn't know. She's getting suspicious. I don't do anything for *our* company, and she suspects I never have."

"That is what I thought," he said. "I want you to start on the payroll like the rest of us and so does Lother. If it had not been for you, I would never have met Lothar Horner.

And without the two of you, none of this would have been possible. And something else: if it had not been for you, the Reinicke brothers, Muller, and Steinmann would have finally gotten around to me. And another thing: if you had not helped me get away, I might have ended up in Argentina or the Konigssee. So, if I offer you part of the money we are earning legitimately, do not feel as though it is some kind of gift.

"Mike, I have something to tell you, a confession really. But do not give me credit for telling you, because you would have figured it out eventually. Maybe you have already. Maybe that is why you have been quizzing me about my membership in the Waffen. I find it hard to believe all you are interested in is information for your book.

"You have to wonder why Steinmann made you the keeper of the spear. You have to know the story I told you about your being the only commissioned officer present was a lie. You have to know I was not telling you the truth. Because I have just now told you I had been tendered a commission at the ceremony. True, it was unearned and honorary, but a commission none the less. Commissions and warrants down through history have been granted and bestowed on millions of people by kings and potentates of all descriptions. The only thing necessary to make it legal is whether the giver has the authority. The authority is the thing. As I told you, the Commandant had the authority bestowed on him by Adolph Hitler. So whether or not I was a combat soldier does not matter. I was made an officer and given all the rights and privileges of a commission."

"Are you trying to tell me that Steinmann never made me the keeper?" I asked him, surprised at what he had just said.

"Right, that is what I am saying. He gave me and not you the responsibility for the spear. I know you do not believe any part of the history of the thing, but I have to tell you anyway. My conscience has been bothering me for a long time about it and my participation in the Hitler worshipping I was part of for so long. It would not have been so bad if I had been standing on the outside looking in. But I was a teacher…."

"Were you a Tyler?"

"I was more than that. I was the grand master of the lodge, even the *Blue Lodge* if you want to couch it in Freemasonry terms. At the time, I was Gestapo and the most important official at many of the ceremonies held on the Obersalzburg over the years. By the way, I should point out that military rank did not count for advancement in the order.

"I could not help myself. I was a believer. I know you are not, but I was. I believed it all. I believed that Adolph Hitler had been sent by the Lord to straighten out a sick world. I changed my mind after I realized he was responsible for millions of needless deaths and untold suffering. But by then it was too late.

"I know you think it is all nonsense, this talk about Hitler being the Messiah instead of Jesus Christ. And the talk of Satan and Norse myths and vrile-energy and all the rest. But let me tell you it is not. There is a Satan, and Hitler was his disciple. Even before he invaded Russia, even before he was Chancellor, friends of his described him as being demon possessed. 'And by their works ye' shall know them,' the Bible says. And anybody who willfully takes the lives of millions of innocent people and who raises up an army the likes of the SS, who committed such atrocities as they did, has to be in league with Satan. I know it now but did not realize it at the time. And though I did not participate in any of it personally, my egregious sin was in my contribution. And if I had been put to the test–if I had been placed in a position of choosing sides–I might at one time have chosen Germany over America. In a manner of speaking, I did; most of the intelligence I passed to Oddlie was either watered down or not important. But he thought I was doing a good job. For instance, I never made an attempt to tell him when Hitler visited the Obersalzburg. Hitler would have been in a vulnerable position many times had I reported this information to the OSS. They might have made an attempt on his life or to take him captive if I had. The Allies might even have bombed the place while he was there. But I just could not do it. And for that I am truly sorry; the War might have ended years earlier with the attendant savings in lives if I had."

Ralph was certain I was an atheist or an agnostic, a non-believer of some sort. But if I started out to be an agnostic, I later changed my mind. His story was true. And the more I learned about the spear, the more certain I was that it was capable of influencing world events and the lives of those who possessed it. True, my fear of the unknowns who had killed Carl and Eric was the root cause of my depression, I won't argue with that. But my believing that a tool of Satan had been controlling my life from the time I heard about the spear had certainly been a contributor.

I went back to the museum in Vienna once after the War and listened to another docent talking about the spear. I suspect his revised story now is much more detailed than the one Hitler was privy to. I would like to tell you that what I heard him say didn't bother me, but it did. I would like to tell you about how I thought it was just another Urban Legend of the occult like the Angel of Mons or some of the other stories extant, but I can't.

And as I stood there gazing at the spearhead, listening to the guide's speech, I had a funny feeling come over me. Nothing like the trance reported by Hitler, but a feeling just the same. And I wondered how it really had affected my life. Was it really responsible for the loss of my first two fortunes and the death of my two friends? Was I once the keeper, and did this keeper thing have anything to do with acquiring riches or the death of Eric and Carl. Did Ralph tell me the SS story about him being commissioned just to make me feel better? He knew I was suffering from guilt and fear of the spear, and had been for years. Did he tell me he, Ralph, really was the keeper just to make me believe I had never been in the picture? Maybe so. But I'll tell you this: Ralph Wahl was really a straight shooter and a compassionate man. It would've been just like him to tell me a cock-and-bull story about him really being the keeper just to allay my fear of what was going to eventually happen to me. And it goes without saying: I have a hard time reconciling him being an SS officer in either branch of the SS with the man I knew he really was.

I know many of you reading this believe it's all made up–a book of fiction. None of this ever happened. If you're one of those who believes there's no such person as Satan, I ask you to ponder how millions of supposedly honest and moral young men–as the SS started out to be–were changed into monsters by the influence of one man. And consider, if you will, how all this could have come about if there were no Satan. And if you're still a non-believer, and if you think I made up this story from whole cloth, if you think there is no such thing as a spear of Longinus, go over to Vienna and see for yourself. Stand by the spear, as Hitler did, and think about the dozens of men who have been keepers. And while standing next to it, go ahead and gaze on it and contemplate what happened to them. And while you're there, attempt to rationally explain the *holocaust* to yourself without dwelling on Satan.

And one more thing: the holocaust descended on the world twice in the recent past, once in 1914 and again in 1933. And if Satan and this spear had anything to do with it, why couldn't it happen again? But I warn you in advance, just as Ralph warned me: don't look too closely into the history of Longinus and the spear, lest occult forces inhabit your mind, as they did with Hitler and his minions. And you may come to believe there are vrile-like forces in the universe that predestines your superiority, just as Hitler and his SS did. And you should be aware of concluding that some humans are superior to others, and that they are entitled to privileges in this world society of ours because of some birthright. There lies the real sin. There lurks Satan and his minions–among those who are believers in racial, religious, or intellectual superiority, and among those who believe the rest of us owe them some kind of allegiance.

AFTERWARD

Ralph finally moved permanently to his home on the ski slopes of Utah. But he never lived to a ripe old age. He died young, very young, of one of the bad diseases. He suffered for a long time. When I arrived, just before he passed away, he told me it was because of the spear. He said he never spent a nickel of the gold, and because he had been one of the keepers and had taken the spear back to the museum, he was paying the price.

I have a hard time agreeing with his thinking. But there you are: the facts speak for themselves. But then you might argue that there was too much of a time lapse betwcen the end of the War and his death many years later to be anything but coincidence. You might. But thc way I see it, the misfortunes of the others who lost it, for whatever reason, were sometimes immediate and sometimes years in coming. But it always happened; and it was always superceded by a good deal of unpleasantness. It happened to every one of them in just this way down through history. If Ralph did make up that part of the story about him being the keeper, while it really was my job all along, then his death for certain was a coincidence. But if not, then my fate awaits. Not a pleasant prospect, if you ask me.

His wife wanted to sell their home and return to Austria. I made her an offer way above the market price. It wasn't enough to make her suspicious of anything, yet it was enough to see her living comfortably for a long time. And with her income from Ralph's business with Lothar, she was in good shape financially for the rest of her life.

Yes, the gold was still in the casks. And as the experts predicted, the price ceiling was removed a few years later. The last I checked, it was selling above three-hundred dollars a troy ounce. I have no idea how much the total is worth now, but it has to be in the hundreds of millions of dollars.

Why haven't I given it to Wiesenthal? Well, probably for the same reason Ralph didn't. Ralph was afraid in the end such a large sum would be traced back to him, and then to me if he did. I always liked to think this was his reason–and not that he was waiting for the price to go up. Incidentally, you might well ask why I don't give it to a Swiss bank for certificates or cash and then give that to Wiesenthal. If you read the papers, you know the Swiss bankers are embroiled in some kind of controversy over Nazi gold, real or perceived. Being pushed by Israel, the United Nations wants all Swiss gold tied to Jewish sources turned over to the Jews. Not much to the liking of the Swiss.

Where's the gold now, you ask? I removed it from Ralph's home, of course, and then buried it. What better way to hide gold than to bury it? But where? I'll tell you this much; I didn't tote it too far away. Too much trouble and too easy to get yourself discovered carrying around a lot of gold. I figure we were all very lucky we got away with it as often as we did. No need to tempt fate–or if you are now a believer–no need to tempt the spear. So, the gold hoard, the last of the Waffen SS' ill-gotten gains, is buried someplace in Utah. Not up north in the mountains, because

I don't like the cold. But down south in a more remote part of the state.

And what about the rest of it, the Merkers hoard that we soldiers considered to be mostly ours. Strangely, it's still being hassled over by that same commission of debaters. Germany over the years has been pushing more strongly for them to give it back. But Russia and Israel are just as determined as ever to keep it from them, while we Americans sit on the sidelines and say nothing. And so it goes, year after year. You see, if we had given all of what I called the Ravensbruck gold back to Patton, it would all have ended up in the same pot. And of this writing, none of it would have found its way back to the heirs of the rightful owners.

Well, my story has ended. I set about explaining the death of my two good friends, and I believe I have. And to tell you a strange tale, which I believe you'll agree was pretty strange. What I haven't told you is what I intend to do with the gold I buried. Whatever I decide, Lucy mustn't find out. She'll conclude I've been selling it off in small batches. But what really worries me is the spear itself. If Ralph was here to consult, I'm sure he would agree the spear has had a say in most everything that's happened to us both, from near the close of the War to the present time. And I'm afraid it might continue on as long as I have the gold. To be absolutely honest with you, I don't know what I do believe. But I'm leaning toward the idea that Ralph was never a commissioned officer in the SS. He might have been a member in some capacity, but he was never commissioned. His story about him being the keeper was just too slick to be believable. And if he wasn't, then I truly was the keeper of the spear. If this is true, then this isn't the end of the story for me. And my fate awaits me in the same way it did all the others who lost it. And I can't get it out of my mind. And I'm starting to run scared all over again.

AUTHOR'S NOTE

Five years after he became Chancellor, Hitler invaded Austria and immediately confiscated the Spear of Longinus from the Hofsmuseum in Vienna. His associations with the spear are quoted from what is believed to be reliable historical sources. The general history of the spear is a matter of public record, which is only partially discussed in this book.

Third Army began crossing the Rhine River near the Remagen bridge on 22 March, 1945. Patton's objective was the cities of Gotha and Leipzig, where he was to turn, in due course, to Lintz, Austria.

Shortly thereafter, two French women, one of them *expecting*, were driven by American soldiers to a field hospital a few miles to the east of Merkers, Germany. The other one showed the Americans where the Kaiseroda Potassium Mine, containing a hoard of Reichsbank and Waffen SS gold, believed to have been looted from banks and from Jews throughout Europe, was located.

In April, Generals Eisenhower, Bradley, Patton, and Weyland, accompanied by Colonel Bernard D. Bernstein, American interpreters, and German guides descended to the two-thousand foot level of the mine to inspect the reported cache of treasure.

The room where the treasure was stored was one-hundred feet deep, seventy-six feet wide and twelve feet high. There were rows of over seven thousand sacks containing 8,198 bars of gold, laid out in twenty rows some three feet high. There were also fifty boxes of gold bullion and hundreds of bags of other gold items. In addition, there were over 1,300 bags of gold Reichsmarks, British gold pounds, and French gold francs. At the back of the room were eighteen bags and 189 suitcases of jewelry. The bags contained rare American twenty-dollar gold pieces, and precious stones marked Melmer. Masterpieces worth millions were found in a nearby addit to the main tunnel. No separate diamonds were mentioned on the final inventory.

The total value of the Merkers gold bullion alone amounted to 520 million dollars in 1945 money. The gold, appraised at the then fixed rate of thirty-five dollars per troy ounce, was turned over to an International Tripartite Commission. Gold was removed from price control in 1963, making all Nazi gold at this writing hundreds of times more valuable than it was in 1945.

A small contingent of Army gold hunters was formed at the request of Colonel Bernstein. Additional Waffen SS gold believed to be in the amount of eleven million dollars (1945) was recovered and turned over to the Commission.

In 1997, all claimant countries agreed to relinquish their share of the gold that was being held. The Commission had been trying with limited success to solve the distribution problem for decades. These countries agreed to donate the gold to a Nazi Persecution Relief Fund to help survivors of the Holocaust.

Early in September 1998, eight years before this writing, at a ceremony held in Paris, the gold commission announced that its task was finished and that it was going out of business.

Generals Eisenhower, Bradley, and Patton entered the town of Ordruf, gateway to the notorious Buchanwald death camp just days following their visit to the Merkers mine. They were accompanied by photographers and noted journalists, among them was Edward R. Murrow.

On 25, April, 1945, squadrons of the RAF, escorted by fighters from the American Tactical Air Command, bombed the Obersalzburg. Hitler committed suicide in his bunker in Berlin five days later. On 5 May, tanks and infantry from the Third Division of the Seventh Army entered Berchesgaden. Hermann Goering had left just days before for the Kitzbhuel, where other soldiers of Seventh Army captured him. He committed suicide by cyanide poisoning during the subsequent Nuremberg War Crimes trial.

Three percent of all German gold reserves of record was never recovered.